SC

SUGAR MAMA

SUGAR MAMA

JOHN NICHOLSON
Artie Taylor Series No.2

HEAD
PUBLISHING

The author tends to get all the credit for writing a book, but no novel ever comes together without the help of a team of people.

So, thanks to my trusty triumvirate of tremendous talent;
Robert for his advice, editorial wisdom and knowledge about the squiggly lines and dots.
Proof reader, Janet, for her unerring ability to spot mistakes and her quiet, guiding hand.
Dawn for love, ideas and artwork.

CHAPTER 1

'Oh, god, Artie, not a vegan, wholefood store, you know these places give me the creeps,' said Kaz, as Artie pulled up in the parking lot of a Mother Earth store in the forever hippie Topanga Canyon, set in the Santa Monica Mountains, west of Los Angeles County. They got out of the black Ford pickup. It was noon on a hot late May day, already in the high 80s. He put his sunglasses on, looked around at the chaparral of California oak, sagebrush and ragweed strewn over the hills and put an arm around Kaz's shoulder, patting her briefly, as though to comfort her. 'And they don't even sell cheese, Artie. No cheese! A life without cheese is no life at all.'

'Don't worry, we won't be in there long enough for you to get infected by their veganism, I just have to pick up some of that 90 per cent cocoa organic chocolate that Colleen likes. This is the only place that sells it.'

'Good, if I spend too long around textured vegetable protein, I start to break out in a nervous rash. And don't get me started on people in hemp trousers and the whole hippie dreadlocks thing. I don't get hippie dreadlocks. Never have, never will.' She hitched up her old blue jeans; an embroidered rainbow on a back right pocket was fraying. She wafted her loose black Springsteen t-shirt, rubbed at her spiked blonde hair and wiped some sweat from her brow, looking up at the sparkling diamond white-blue sky. 'Wow, it's only noon, it's really going to be a hot one today.'

The large, ramshackle wood-built store was set back on a bend in the road and looked like a rustic cabin, but with the front-facing wall comprised mostly of glass. A nut-brown, tanned hippie woman in her early 20s, with long blonde hair, in which she had put a red rose, worked on the door as a greeter. She was wearing a cropped white t-shirt, cut-off denim shorts and a smile so beatific and wide that she looked hypnotised, or stoned, or both. She greeted them at the door with such joy that it was as though they were long-lost friends, or possibly the reincarnation of Jesus and Mary, or, given this was Southern California, Jim and Janis.

'Hey, there! Great to see you guys. How are *you* today?' She put the emphasis on *you* like she really cared.

'We're good, thanks,' said Artie, nodding, long since acclimatized to the shallow Californian way of life. She was absolutely stunning. You could go blind in California ogling the beautiful blonde 20-something women. They seemed to be made out in the Valley, possibly in some sort of hadron collider. At one end you threw in some blonde hair, blue eyes, and a slightly annoying accent along with a bag of tanned skin, and at the other end it spat out another one.

'I'm not good,' said Kaz, wilfully grumpy, stopping to confront the woman. 'I've got a terrible case of the farts.'

'Aisle three for mint tea to aid digestion. Uh huh. Beautiful. You are *so* welcome,' said the greeter, without missing a beat. Artie laughed out loud and put his thumb up at the woman. Maybe she was smarter than she appeared. Or maybe not.

'Stop winding up the locals, you arsey sod,' said Artie, as he went in search of the chocolate. 'I'm the skinny, grumpy heterosexual one, remember, you're the chunky, positive lezbo. You know fine well you don't hate vegans and veggies. You're just having a big moan up. Anyway, these places are a magnet for your mob, aren't they? Your typical lady liker around here loves a low-fat vegan meal, followed by stroking a cat called Sunflower and reading astrological charts.'

Kaz groaned. 'Sadly, you're all too often right. I could never get with the New Age default setting that seems to come with being female and gay. But then, I'm from Leeds, which is about the least New Age place on Earth. Mind you, the screeching and howling noises from the council flats near where I grew up could have been mistaken for whale music.' She stopped and pulled at a plastic packet hanging from a hook at the end of an aisle. 'Oh, look, just what I always wanted - meatless, vegan, hickory-smoked soy jerky! What is it with soya and these people? They make this stuff in massive factories, y'know. I was reading about it in a magazine. It's a huge industry. I refuse to believe it's food. And why can't they call it *soya* over here? Soy, my arse. Give me something dead and bloody, something that used to be alive. We're the dominant species, it's only right we get to kill and eat the tasty beasts. That's how nature works and all these hippies love to think they're in tune with nature. There aren't any other animals sitting around stroking other animals. "The big 'un eats the little 'un". That's how it goes. Deal with it, hippie.'

Artie grinned at her. 'You're very philosophical and unusually sarcastic this morning. Remember, if it wasn't for hippies, both of us would have had a lot less sex. You love a hippie chick as much as I do. What have you been hoovering up your beak to give you the hump?'

'Nowt, sadly.' She dragged her feet behind him like a sulky child. 'I just hate it when we come off the road. It gives me the bends, being in one place and not endlessly moving on. I like moving on. If you're always moving, no-one can catch you.'

'Yeah, I know what you mean, especially after a fantastic three-month haul around North and South America with Springsteen.'

Artie found a shelf full of organic chocolate bars flavoured with everything from goji berries to ginger and macadamia nuts. It was ridiculous, there had to be 18 different brands of posh chocolate.

'More choice just makes life harder,' said Artie, looking for the one Colleen liked. 'Why aren't there just two - a cheap one and an expensive one?'

'You've misunderstood the whole point of Capitalism, Artie,' said Kaz, her arms folded across her chest.

'Aye, well, it wouldn't be the first time. My old dad used to say shopping made you soft in the head. Mind, he wasn't exactly an adventurous man. He never went outside Yorkshire, except to fight in the war. All the same, he was onto something, I reckon. Ah, there it is.' He picked up three bars. 'Right, we're outta here, baby.'

'Not a moment too soon. It's air-conned to buggery in here. I'm freezing.'

Artie looked at her. 'Aye, I can see, your nipples are out on stalks, lass. You're poking Bruce's eye with one. Ha ha. I've got some gaffer tape in the truck if you want to clamp them down.' He raised an eyebrow and gave her another amused look.

She looked down at herself. 'Bloody hell, you could hang a mug off the end of them. I look like I'm ready to be milked.'

'They do probably sell breast milk in here somewhere. Seriously. They might milk you, if you ask nicely.'

'As long as someone doesn't want to suckle me - not unless she's an especially good-looking woman, anyway.' They stood in line at the checkout. 'They won't go down, Artie,' said Kaz, looking at herself again and now giggling a bit. 'I'm permanently erect. I've not even taken any Viagra.'

He put his long arm on her shoulder as they stood in line at the checkout. 'They're impressive nipples. I've always thought that. Big and sticky-out. They've got a real rubber-teat quality to them.'

She pushed at him. 'Don't say it like it's a compliment, as though it shows how clever I am. It's not like I had a choice, is it? It's not like I qualified, through my wit and intelligence, to have lovely big, hard sensitive nipples, is it? It's like blokes with big cocks who think they're God's

3

gift, it's just the luck of the genetic draw, it's not like they've done something great to deserve them.'

'More homespun philosophy. Are you sure you're not hyped up on goofballs?'

'Why do you always say "hyped up on goofballs"? What does that even mean?'

He grinned again. 'I have no idea, but I just like the idea of goofballs.'

The checkout guy had dreadlocks.

'This is great stuff, man. It's my favourite brand,' he said, admiring the chocolate bar, like it was some sort of elixir of life. Americans seemed programmed to worship a product and took brands as part of their own identity. How else to explain the popularity of Twinkies?

'Why is it so cold in here?' said Kaz, to the checkout guy, arms folded across her chest, to hide the bullet-like protrusions.

The dude didn't seem used to having to answer questions. He looked concerned, as though she'd said she felt really ill. 'I'm sorry, ma'am. I really don't know what our policy on in-store temperature is. Do you want me to ask my manager? I can do that for you. It's no problem. It can get kinda chilly, I know, but it's a hot day today.'

What a weird response. It was as though he wasn't used to regular human chit-chat. Maybe he was told to be worried someone might leave a negative comment on social media.

'Nah, it's all cool, thanks,' said Artie, pushing Kaz in front of him, before she began being sarky with the lad. 'C'mon, lady, let's get back out into the heat of a Southern California summer and see if we can't make your nipples go soft.'

The greeter waved at them as they left, 'Thanks for comin', guys. Great to see you today.'

Artie smiled at her. That Rainbow song, 'All Night Long', came to his mind: 'Don't know about your brain, but you look alright'. They had only just walked out into the oven-like blast of heat, when there was a terrible scream behind them. Artie turned around to see a man fall to the ground holding his throat. He was just behind them and in his hand was a strip of something in a packet.

Artie strode up to the stricken man. 'Are you OK?' he said. The man stared at him with fierce eyes.

'I'm f-f-f-fine. Thank you. I don't need any help.' He struggled to get the words out and he obviously wasn't OK and obviously did need help.

Artie knew right away what was wrong. He'd seen it before. The man was going into anaphylactic shock and he was swelling up visibly.

'Kaz! Get the...' but she was already running to the pickup to get her black bag of tricks.

'Take it easy fella, relax, don't struggle, take little breaths, we'll get you fixed, don't worry,' said Artie, patting the man, as a crowd gathered warily around him, seemingly fearful of anyone who wasn't happy and smiling and, whilst not wanting to get involved, quite fascinated as to what might happen.

The store manager came over. Artie looked up at her. 'He's having a reactive shock to something he's eaten. Probably that.' He pointed to the open packet that he'd now dropped. The man then let out a horrible choking noise, a manic stare in his eyes now, as he struggled to get breath. His neck and face were puffy and had red blotches on them. It was an intense, fast reaction but he just stared at Artie with a fixed expression, his eyes hard and unwavering.

Kaz came running back at speed, holding an adrenaline pen, kneeling down beside the man. She held it up at him. 'I've got to stick this in your leg. It'll hurt, but only a bit.'

She took off the cap and swiftly jabbed it into the man's thigh through his cotton pants. He flinched at the needle hit his skin, now staring at her with his strange manic look. It had to be a terrifying thing to happen to you. As she sank the adrenaline into him he was really gasping for breath.

Artie looked at him. He was young, probably in his early 20s. He looked scared, but he also looked angry, or maybe indignant, or possibly just embarrassed. Public illness was the thing Artie's parents had always feared most. Being 'any trouble' was to be avoided at all costs. But then, that was in Yorkshire, not California, the home of the emotionally incontinent and immediately confessional.

'I've called paramedics,' said the store manager, a gaunt woman who looked like she needed a good meal or 20.

'What's your name, mate?' said Artie, squatting beside the man.

The man stared back at him and seemed to already be finding breathing easier. 'I'm Ben Goldman.'

'What are you allergic to?' said Kaz.

Ben Goldman swallowed hard and took a deep breath. The adrenalin had worked quickly, almost like magic. 'Peanuts,' he said. 'Must be peanuts in that...' he nodded towards the packet he'd dropped.

Kaz picked up the wrapper and held it up to Artie, with a withering look in her eyes. It was the hickory-smoked soy jerky she'd been pointing at earlier. On the front, it said in bold lettering, 'Dairy and peanut free'.

'Anything else, apart from that?' said Kaz.

Ben Goldman panted and licked his dry lips. 'No. Just peanuts, but I have it bad, even a small amount messes me up, man.' He panted, looked up at her and said, 'You stopped me dying.' He didn't seem overly grateful, but then, he was under severe stress.

'Ah, you're welcome. It's all in day's work when you're on the road with lunatic rock stars,' said Kaz. 'I always carry a little black bag of tricks with me full of plasters, pills, vitamins and painkillers. Everyone is allergic to something these days, so I always have an adrenaline pen loaded and ready to rock.' She smiled at him nicely and patted his bare arm. 'You'll be alright now, kid.'

'Are you in a band?' He squinted at them.

'No, more traditionally, we're *with* the band,' said Artie. 'Well, if you're feeling OK, we'll get off. The paramedics will give you a once over and doubtless you'll be charged heavily for the pleasure.' He smiled and handed the manager one of his contact cards. 'If they need to ask us anything, we're here.'

'Thank you so much,' she said, taking the card. 'You were great. Wonderful in a crisis. I wouldn't have known what to do.'

Kaz nodded. 'You're welcome. Trust me, nothing much fazes you when you've been on tour with Mötley Crüe. I once had to pull a g-string out of a girl's throat to stop her choking on her own underwear. Don't ask why. It's unhygienic, immoral and possibly even illegal.' She gave her big, cheesy grin, bouncing on her toes as she did so.

The woman looked shocked at this information and was happy to wave them off. The good people of the world were always freaked out by what was just the same old, same old, in the land of rock 'n' roll.

CHAPTER 2

They walked back to the car.

'We did a good thing there, Kaz,' said Artie, as he started the pickup.

'Yeah. We're angels in the City of Angels.' She looked back at the store. 'That place is going to get a big lawsuit for poisoning its customers, and whoever makes that soy jerky is in big trouble. Peanuts in a peanut-free product is a bit of a no no.'

'Poor fella, though. I feel lucky not to be allergic to anything, except Perrier, responsibility and daylight.'

She squinted at him and flicked him the Vs. 'Oh, don't go quoting bloody Marillion at me, you skinny wassock. You know what? Part of me thinks that all these allergies are psychosomatic or just affectations. Not that fella. Obviously. But out here everyone has got an intolerance, haven't they? Everything makes them feel a bit bloated, or do a runny shit. I mean, fucking hell, I grew up drinking Guinness and that made me shit like a good 'un. I didn't call it an intolerance. Intolerance all too often is a lifestyle accessory, these days. People want to be intolerant. "Feel my pain" is such a big hit single in 2014. Well, I'm intolerance intolerant. Ha ha. Yeah, that'd fuck these people up.'

Artie drove down Topanga Canyon Road, his arm resting on the open window, relentless hot sun on his skin. The thermometer in the car said it was 88 degrees. Man, that was hot for late May. He put a classic rock radio station on. It was playing the Blues Project's 'Flute Thing'. Lovely.

'You know what, Kaz?'

'No. But I'm sure you're going to tell me.'

He paused and looked over at her. 'What is up with you? You're so arsey today. It's most unlike you. Going off on one about hippies and that; you're always the chirpy one. I don't like the pressure of having to make jokes and cheer us both up. That's always been your job. '

She shook her head. 'Sorry, Artie. I've got a proper nark on. Just ignore me.'

He gripped her thigh and gave it a shake. 'Come on, beautiful, cheer up. We're driving to Malibu, to a beachside house, on a hot early summer day in Southern California. If you'd been offered that when you were growing up in Leeds, you'd have taken it, wouldn't you?'

She put her clammy hand on top of his. 'Of course I bloody would. But you know what I'm scared of?'

'You? You're not scared of anything. I never knew anyone so fearless. You're the lass who told a knife-wielding roadie on an Aerosmith tour that he was a wanker and to "come and have a go if you think you're hard enough"...err...let's get this exactly right..."you soft, fucking prick". Magnificent Leeds-ing, that.'

She laughed a bit. 'Using *Leeds* as a verb. I like it. Well, he was a toss pot.'

'So what *are* you scared of?'

She didn't reply for a while and then let out a sigh. 'Artie, I'm just turned 47. I've no family, mam and dad are dead, I've no brothers or sisters, I've not got a partner and I don't have any kids. I just feel a bit...I don't know...a bit alone in the world. It bothers me, sometimes.'

'Nah, c'mon. You've got me and Coll and all your mates. You've got loads of mates in LA, far more than I do.'

'Yeah, but I'm just...I'm in the way in Malibu, aren't I? I don't know, I'm just waffling on. Ignore me. It's just sometimes I wish I did have kids...or something. I don't want to grow old alone.'

'What's brought this on? That's not something that normally bothers you.'

'It doesn't. Not usually.'

'You don't want me to inseminate you, do you?' He said it as a joke, then immediately worried she might take him seriously.

'No, thank you. Mixing our genes would create a weird creature with long thin legs and a big arse and huge nipples. Albeit one which could set up and take a good photo. Anyway, one sex session with you in Las Vegas was plenty enough, thank you *very* much.'

'How about the old turkey baster?'

She looked at him, pushed a hand through her punky, spiked blonde hair and pulled a face, her cheeks pink from the hot sun. 'I'm not saying I want to have a kid. I never have before now, but then I've been on the road with you for 15 years, so there's hardly been time. But it does feel weird. I mean, everyone has kids and it'd be nice to have someone to look after. Someone who isn't a stroppy photographer, anyway.'

'That's not true. Not everyone has kids. Especially out here.'

She looked over at him. 'Don't you want kids?'

Artie wobbled his head. 'Well, it's not possible. Coll's gone through the menopause and I'm probably too selfish to be a dad. And anyway, it looks like a lot of stress and hard work. People with kids are less happy than people without kids. It's been proven in psychological tests.'

'Has it? Ha. That's funny. That makes me feel a bit better. And it must be weird having an animal growing inside of you. That's what puts me off it - that and having to push it out of your fanny. Jesus. I'm sure mine's not big enough to do that. Why haven't we evolved an easier way to reproduce? Growing them in some sort of amniotic rucksack would make more sense.'

'I totally know what you mean. When Colleen had Fay she was in labour for about three days. She was nearly 11 pounds when she finally dropped her.'

Kaz looked at him in astonishment. 'Bloody hell, Artie, the skinny bitch hasn't put much weight on since then, has she!'

Artie laughed and pointed at her. 'Now that's more like my Kaz.'

'Hey, lady,' said Artie, walking out onto the deck of Colleen's house right on Malibu beach. 'We did a good deed up at the store.' He put the chocolate on the table.

Colleen was lying on a lounger wearing a white vest and cut-off denim shorts, her tan deep chestnut brown. She looked over the top of her shades at him. 'Oooh, choccy. Thanks. Oh, yeah? What was that?'

Kaz sat down opposite her on a canvas seat and explained what had happened.

'Wow, you did good, man,' said Colleen. 'What did you say he was called?'

'Ben Goldman,' said Artie, pouring some iced water from a jug into two glasses and handing Kaz one. In the distance, the ocean washed in over the silvery gold beach, with a low rumble and hiss.

Colleen took a sip of a water. 'Huh. What did he look like?'

'About early 20s. He had a mop of curly brown hair - like it was permed, but it was natural,' said Kaz. 'He was good-looking, a pretty sort of bloke, but with a slightly weird look in his eyes - but then, he was choking to death and that will give you a weird look.'

'Yeah, he was just scared and embarrassed, understandably enough,' said Artie.

Colleen took off her Ray-Bans and looked at them with her liquid caramel eyes. 'I think I know who that is.'

'Really? Who is he?' said Artie, sitting down opposite her and rubbing her feet.

'He's Ralph and Babs Goldman's kid. They're famous music industry lawyers. Ruthless people, by reputation. Famously, they send people out to places like copy shops or printers and ask them to print a t-shirt with a trademarked logo on, then when they do, they sue the shit out of them for producing unauthorized merchandise. They had teams of people doing that. Probably still do, though they must be retired now.'

'Is that actually legal? Surely that's the intellectual copyright equivalent of a honey trap,' said Artie.

'Well, I'm not sure anyone ever tested it in court. A judge might think it was bad practice and throw it out but they just bully these little mom-and-pop stores with legal letters and screw a few thousand dollars out of them to stop it going any further. People in this town are scared of lawyers, so they back down and cough up,' said Coll.

'The rotten bastards. How can anyone live with themselves by doing that for a living?' said Kaz.

'However, they do it, honey, they do it in some style. They have a huge pile in Pacific Palisades overlooking the ocean. The sort of place that makes my little three-million dollar place look like a rabbit hutch.'

'How do you know them, then?' said Artie.

'Oh, a few years ago, I dated a guy for a while who mixed in those circles. He ran a merchandise operation. They used to throw regular parties at the house. I went along a few times. Loads of famous people used to go - rock stars, movie folk. I even met Gore Vidal there once. The paparazzi used to hang around outside, but it has a narrow private road into the back of the house, so we'd scoot in that way to avoid everyone. It was quite exciting for a while. Anyway, Ben is their only son and is following his parents into the legal business, I heard.'

'Ha, well, in that case, he probably poisoned himself on purpose in order to sue the store,' said Kaz. 'It's a sort of family tradition, by the sounds of it.'

'It'd be a bit dangerous to do that. He got lucky that we were there, with your doctor's bag,' said Artie.

'Nah, he probably had his own pen. He'd have used it, had we not been there,' said Kaz, rubbing at her face, a little.

'That is top-quality conspiracy paranoia, lady,' said Colleen, 'and it wouldn't surprise me in the slightest if you were right.'

Kaz got up. 'Right, well, I'm going over to Wanda Bailey's. She's taking me to that new place on Third Street, the English Way, for fish and chips. Remind me what our next gig is, Artie.'

'Tomorrow night. We're shooting Benny Ace at the Scene Club in Tarzana. We're in at 6pm to do some portraits and then some live shots, though all he does is sit on a stool and strum an acoustic guitar so it'll hardly be very exciting.'

'Oh, yeah, he's one of this new breed of sensitive folkies, isn't he? I bet *he's* a bloody vegan.' She sneered at him.

Colleen laughed. 'Everyone in this town under the age of 25 is a vegan. None, and I mean literally none, of Fay's friends eat meat.'

'I bet they eat bloody soy jerky,' said Artie.

'I wouldn't be at all surprised. She tells me she lives off veggie burgers, sausages and veggie bacon and she still thinks she's living this wholesome, green life, when really, she's just living off processed food. She won't be told, though.'

After Kaz had left, Artie made coffee.

'Coll, Kaz was talking about not having kids earlier and not having any family, except for me and you. It seemed to be bothering her.'

She gave him a concerned look. 'Not having kids? How old is she, again?'

'Forty-seven. So she's no chance, has she?'

'Not a zero chance, but not a good chance, no. Huh, funny, I don't figure her for that type of gal. She just ain't a mommy, is she? That's not a criticism, by the way.' She smiled at him.

'I don't think she is. I think she's just feeling a bit philosophical about it all,' said Artie.

'Well, I didn't think I'd be a mom. Fay was, as you well know, an accident born out of my lifestyle at the time, and the grief that girl has given me over the years would test the patience of a saint. I'd be lying if I said there weren't a few moments when I cursed the day I gave birth to her. And I'm still damn well worried about her, even now. This crowd of kids she hangs out with, they all think they're so aloof and cool by dressing in black and not eating meat.'

'Coll, Fay just messes with your head for her own entertainment. You know that. I never understood why wearing black is a radical thing here. Everyone in Britain wears black, it doesn't make us anarchists.'

'Oh, they think it's deeeeep maaaaan, when the reality is they're bourgeois beyond belief. But she's so easily led astray. How do you stop a headstrong girl who thinks she always knows best from messing up her life?'

'That's above my pay grade. I haven't a clue. I've spent all my working life in a business which is stuffed full of young women who are messed up and looking for love in all the wrong places and with the wrong people - usually with guitarists and singers. But you can't tell some people. I mean, over the years, I've tried to steer groupies away from blokes I know are bad men, but they get it in their head that the bad boys are rock 'n' roll.'

'We've all done it. But it is dumb. There ain't nothin' good about bad. It'd be called good, if there was.'

'Bad would be called good, if it was good, that sounds like a country song.' He smiled at her. 'But, really, I wouldn't worry about Fay. She's wiser than it sometimes appears.'

He went up to his studio - a converted bedroom with a panoramic view of the beach with floor-to-ceiling windows - and began work on his portfolio of photos from the Springsteen tour which he was turning into a photo-journal book to be called *The Boss on the Road*, which had been commissioned through a San Francisco publishing company called Now Books. They'd approached him with the idea and were even paying him a decent $20,000 advance. It was the first book of this sort that he'd done and the first book he'd ever had total artistic control over, so he was enjoying the work. It also had a chance of selling a few copies because Bruce was so popular and he looked absolutely great in almost every single photo he'd taken - the very essence of the older rock guy. He oozed grit and integrity and, just as crucially, plain good old fun, even if he did charge up to $45 for a t-shirt.

He was just filing shots into Yes, No and Maybe folders when his phone buzzed. It was Ronnie Saunders, an old friend and ex-pat who ran a guitar shop on Santa Monica Boulevard. His wife, Gracie, had died a couple of years ago after a long battle with cancer, leaving him to bring up their only kid, Carly, on his own.

'Hey, Ronnie. How goes it?'

'Alright, Artie,' he said, in a South Yorkshire voice, unaffected by 20 years living in Los Angeles. 'When did you get back from Bruce's haul?'

'Just two days ago. Still got road fever. Feels like I should be packing a bag and moving on.'

'Aye, I bet it does. Did you do the tour with your Colleen?'

'Yeah, she joined me and Kaz for the last few weeks. She loved it.'

'Cool. And how's little Kaz?'

'She's her usual punky self. All grit 'n' gristle, as per normal. So what can I do for you?'

'Do you want to come down to the shop? There's something I need to pick your and Colleen's brains about. I'm really worried about my Carly. I just don't know what the hell to do, Artie.'

He blew out air in a tight, tense exhalation. He was obviously very stressed out.

'Carly? Is she in trouble?'

'Yeah. Sort of. She's not well, Artie. It's this bloody diet she's on. I've been trying to get her to change from being a vegan for months but she won't listen and now she's not well.'

'Sorry to hear that, man. How can we help her?'

'She's friends with Colleen's Fay, isn't she?'

'Oh, yeah, that's right, we were just talking about them - how none of them eat meat and they all dress in dark clothes. You're not bothered about that, are you?'

'Well, yeah, I am. Not the black clothes. That's just kids being kids. Only weirdo Yanks worry about black-wearing. They get hysterical over that sort of shit. Look how crazy they were over Marilyn Manson. We just laugh at that sort of schlock rock, but they take it seriously over here. Wankers. Doesn't mean anything. No, it's this vegan diet. It's bloody doin' my head in. I keep telling her it's making her sick, but she won't listen!' He shouted into the phone, making it distort.

'Alright, man. Take it easy, eh,' said Artie.

'Sorry...sorry...it's just Carly is really unwell. She's fainted a few times. She looks just plain ill. But she won't go to a doctor and she's 21, so I can't really make her. She's underweight. I know she's not eating properly, but...I dunno, man, I need some help with her. I'm out of ideas and I thought maybe Coll could get Fay to help me make her see how ill she is.'

Artie looked at his watch, it was quarter to two. 'OK man, we'll swing by the store now. Be with you in half an hour.' The poor guy was obviously hurting. He had no-one to turn to after Gracie's death. Maybe he just needed a shoulder to cry on.

CHAPTER 3

Fifteen minutes later, Artie drove into the city. Colleen picked a crust from the corner of her eye, looking in the vanity mirror.

'We could have taken the Porsche, babe.'

'I suppose so.'

What he didn't want to say, but which was certainly true, was that since moving into Colleen's Malibu house after they'd married the previous year, he had been growing tired of luxury and wealth. Mad as it would seem to anyone on the outside, it didn't sit well with him. It felt like you were living outside of society, cut off from the vast majority by your money. Not that he wanted to live in squalor, but your quality of life is lived in your head and not in a multi-million dollar home by the beach and not in a top-of-the-range $250,000 Porsche, even though it was a fantastic car - exciting and sleek and he loved driving it. But you couldn't get into the city any quicker than in his nine-year-old Ford pickup. He didn't know what to say about it, though. Colleen had access to millions of dollars. Money just kept rolling in. What was she supposed to do, give it away? Well, maybe. But she was totally used to money and what it could do. She'd grown up with it her whole life. Her mother, a big hit author, had made millions and Coll had inherited it all on her death. It wasn't a big deal to her. She had no real perspective. But Artie did. And increasingly, he hated it. Bukowski had it right, money really is piss. It's just an expulsion of waste, about which you feel nothing. Beyond the ability to pay your bills and buy your food and live somewhere safe, it was...well...nothing. And also, when you were 53 and could put most of your possessions into a couple of suitcases, developing a shopping habit didn't seem at all likely. Your worth is not judged by what you can buy. That had always seemed like the philosophy to live by, inculcated into him by his Yorkshire parents, both of whom had come from mining stock.

As they sat in traffic he chewed on his lip. It had got to the point where the money actually disturbed him. All his coping mechanisms in life had been forged in relative poverty and born out of that brilliant feeling when you got through another week through the sweat of your own brow and still had a few dollars in the bank for a drink. That was 1-0 to the good guys. That specific Friday-night feeling wasn't something people who always had money and were always comfortable, could ever understand or appreciate.

He'd briefly had money in the 90s, when he'd been the go-to man for album covers and such, and with a bank account that at one point had peaked at an unspectacular but satisfying £89,427. But not any more. Those were fleeting days. You couldn't earn big money in his game any more. But it didn't matter. It was the art, not the money, that was the important thing. That had been his starting position way back in 1984 and that was how he felt now. He knew Kaz felt exactly the same way.

Since they'd been married, he and Colleen had had a good a time together, especially on the road, and never a cross word, so far. But at the end of the inevitably sun-kissed day, a life of money and luxury just wasn't his gig, nor was it Kaz's. How they would sort it out, he had no idea, but he knew, at some point, it needed to be resolved. How did you get poor, when you were so rich? And that was before even thinking about other emotional issues between the three of them.

Ronnie Saunders's store was a substantial place on Santa Monica Boulevard. A hub for a lot of LA's rock and blues fraternity, it was commonplace to find famous musicians trying out guitars in the sound-proofed booths. Ronnie did PA rental too, so there was always a buzz about the place as one band or another humped gear in and out. The walls were lined with hundreds of guitars on racks and even more were on stands. It was staffed almost exclusively by long-haired men with tattoos. Ronnie was no different himself, looking like a cross between a Hell's Angel and Jesus; a substantial presence in any room. He greeted Artie and Colleen at the front counter and led them through to the back-room office, away from the sound of men trying to impress each other with their ability to play really, really fast, seemingly unaware that very few people are impressed by people who can play really, really fast, apart from other guitarists who want to play really, really fast.

'Good t'see you both. Take a seat.' He pointed at two leather armchairs and sat down on a tall stool.

Artie sat and took a look at Ronnie. He'd known him for the most of the 20 or more years he'd worked out on the coast. Like most men in his position, Ronnie had had his wild days, but had put all that behind him years ago. His face looked drawn and his skin, though tanned from the Californian sun, looked dry and cracked. Normally, he was the picture of rude health; a solid, muscular man, thick of arm and broad of beam. His muscles had been built in a career lifting heavy amplifiers in and out of trucks, first as a roadie and then as a guitar tech. He was bursting out of a close-fitting V-necked t-shirt and wore a copper pendant on which 'Blues

Is A Healer' was engraved. His long white hair was tied back in a ponytail and his goatee beard was now turning white, as well.

'So, how sick is Carly?' said Colleen. 'I've not seen her for a few months. Fay keeps me at arm's length from her friends, if she can.'

'She says she's fine, but she looks anything but fine. She's always going on at me for eating meat and butter and that. You know she's a strict vegan, don't you, Coll? I mean, she's crazy about it. Says eating animals is cruel and unhealthy. She's proper mad about it. Animal rights, and that. I mean, alright, she's 21 and we all go off on one when we're that age. I understand it and I wouldn't mind but she's lost weight, she's that skinny you could see through her.'

'Is she anorexic?' said Artie.

'Well, I don't know. She eats when she's at home but all she'll have is salad and brown rice and that. She won't eat any fat at all, says it'll give her a heart attack. If you ask me, she's been brainwashed by the health police. It's mad. I eat steak and butter and fatty curries and I'm built like a brick shit house and as fit as fiddle. She just doesn't want to know. I've tried to stop her, but she's got it into her head she's right and there's no changing her mind, even though she keeps fainting and going dizzy!' As he spoke the volume of his voice rose with his passion and anger. Artie leaned forward and gave him a few reassuring taps on the top of his arm.

'OK, buddy, take it easy, eh.'

'Yeah, yeah, sorry. I just want her to eat normally. I don't see why she won't. She used to take notice of Gracie but she just ignores me.' He was clearly very stressed out, with real worry in his eyes. 'If only Gracie was alive.'

Ronnie hadn't for a moment thought to replace her with anyone else, though he could easily have done so. But Gracie was his big love.

Colleen laid a hand on Ronnie's arm. 'Do you want me to ask Fay if she thinks Carly is OK?'

'Yeah, if you could. I can't get her to go to a doctor's and you're the only people I know whose kids she mixes with.'

'The low-fat vegan lifestyle is very LA, isn't it?' said Artie. 'Everyone is always on some sort of health kick and to be fair, you do see people who are vegan who look good on it, including, it has to be said, Fay. She's got a nice glow to her and isn't super skinny or anything.'

'I know, but it just doesn't suit Carly. It's hard to describe, but when you see her, you'll know what I mean.'

Artie turned to Colleen. 'It might be better if I talk to Fay about this. You know how defensive she is with you, if she thinks you're poking your nose into her life.'

'Sure. You and Kaz get on with her. I'd like to, but...huh...what can you do? They'll probably move on to another fad soon enough, Ronnie. They've all been on this no-animal protein trip for about what, four or five months? It won't last much longer. Fay has dabbled with vegetarianism on and off for years. For what it's worth, I think she likes the idea of it more than the food.'

'I don't know, it's a big thing to Carly. She's really serious, man. I've been getting the "my body is a temple" lectures from her. They all go to that fucking Mother fucking Earth store in Topanga and sit in the restaurant feeling holier than thou about themselves. I fucking hate that place. Fucking hippies can fuck off.' He was getting really angry again.

'Take a chill pill, daddy-O,' said Artie, trying to lighten the mood, wishing he'd brought Kaz along. She was ridiculously good at smoothing people out with her mixture of light-hearted chatter and flattery. It was one of the reasons she was so good at her job. 'I was just in that store this morning, actually,' said Artie. 'Kaz was saying how ridiculously processed all the soya foods are.'

'Oh, she eats all that shite.' He blew out air. 'Wanna beer?' He was about to reach into a Budweiser-branded fridge when the door opened from the parking lot and in walked a young woman in black leggings, canvas baseball boots and a long, loose, plain black t-shirt.

Ronnie turned around. 'Hey, honey. How are you feeling?'

Artie was shocked to see Carly. He'd not seen her for maybe seven or eight months, but she'd changed so much from being a soft-looking, bright-eyed young woman with a heart-shaped face, to being a thin, drawn, pale imitation of that girl. It made her look 10 years older, too. She looked really ill. There was no doubt about that. At the very least she was anaemic. Her skin looked sallow and had a greyish hue to it. Everything about her lacked vitality and spark. Fay, though slim, was still pink of cheek and full of energy and zest for life, albeit often a zest for confrontation and argument with her mother, or anyone else who got in her way. Carly, by contrast looked like she wouldn't have the energy to even have a row. As Aerosmith once put it, her get up and go had got up and went.

'Artie and Colleen dropped by,' said Robbie.

She smiled nicely at them in turn, gave them a small wave of her hand and bent at the knees a little. 'Hi, there. How's Kaz, Artie?'

'She's good, thanks for asking. We've just been on tour with Bruce Springsteen.'

'Oh, right. Daddy had Nils Lofgren sitting right where you are the other day, didn't you, daddy?'

'Yeah, Nils is often here.'

Carly turned to Colleen. 'I actually just came from Fay's apartment, Miss Holmes. She's a great girl.' She gave her a genuine, if energyless and watery, smile.

'I'm glad someone thinks highly of her,' said Colleen, returning the smile.

'She's a kind person and I know she's a bit worried about me, I think. But I'm fine. Please reassure her of that when you see her.'

'It's nice to hear she has a kind side,' said Colleen, ruefully.

Carly was a specific kind of American polite to her elders, a kind of polite which the British just don't do. Respectful and deferential, almost. Certainly well brought up. 'Oh, she's just got a little bit of attitude about her, Miss Holmes. That's her thing. That's Fay. That's why we all like her. But she says nice things about you, about both of you.' She smiled, but again looked so weak, if the smile had slid from her face onto the floor because she didn't have the strength to sustain it, you wouldn't have been surprised.

She spoke pure unadulterated Southern Californian. Raised in the Southlands, she had never even been to her father's home town of Sheffield and was very much a citizen of the Golden State. Artie watched as she went to the sink and filled a glass with water, stood for a moment and drank it down. As she turned from the sink, her legs buckled from under her and she passed out in a dead faint, falling like a felled tree, or at least, like a sapling. She narrowly missed hitting her head on a Mesa Boogie amplifier, which would certainly have been a very rock 'n' roll way to kill yourself.

They all leapt up as one to try and catch her as she went down. She wasn't out for long, maybe seven seconds at most. As she swam back up to consciousness, her dad kneeled beside her, cradling her head in his large hands.

'Carly, honey we can't go on like this. You're not well, luv. You've got to change your lifestyle. Change what you're eating. That's what's doing this.'

She sat up, resting on her hands. 'I'm fine. I've just got low blood pressure and it's such a hot day. I got a bit overheated. Don't fret daddy. Please.'

There was no point in trying to bully the girl into seeking help, she'd only dig her heels in more. There had to be a way to help her, though. They got her onto a chair and Colleen gave her another glass of water and stroked the back of her head.

'Just take it easy for a bit, Carly. Have you eaten recently, honey?' she asked. 'Sometimes, I feel light-headed when my blood sugar drops low.'

'Maybe that's it. I should have a couple of rice cakes.' Ronnie was clearly exasperated by that. His face was set in a frozen, tense grimace. His jaw working as he ground his teeth together.

'You need something more substantial than that. How about a sandwich?'

'I don't eat wheat anymore. It's bad for you. Gluten destroys your stomach flora. I'll have one of those soy jerky bars.' She pointed to a box of packets on the table. Artie reached over and handed one to her and then took one to look at. It was the same Green on Green brand that Ben Goldman had eaten, though this was bacon flavoured. He put it in his top pocket.

Ronnie was still angry but tried to not show it.

Artie could see where she was in all of this. Controlling your food and exerting a discipline to live by, was often a way to try and get some power in your life. If you feel helpless or at the mercy of the vicissitudes of everyday existence, at least you can control what you put into yourself. And also, when you don't eat much, you never really get hungry. It becomes self-perpetuating and your appetite just goes away. He should know because even now he still had to force himself to eat regularly. Years on the road going 16 or 20 hours without eating because it just wasn't convenient, or he was speeding or drinking or was coked up, had been a way of life for him. As a result he'd been thin since he was in his early 20s. In the last year he'd put on a few pounds for the first time in years, but his relationship with eating, if not with food, still wasn't especially healthy. There were times when the thought of putting food into his mouth actually made him feel a bit queasy. That had to be the thin end of the anorexia wedge.

When she spoke, her breath smelt bad - a sort of metallic, nail polish smell. He felt really sorry for her. The relationship between food and mental health is so intertwined, not least because what you put inside of yourself gears how everything works, up to and including your brain. When it all starts to go wrong, it can be hard to put it all back together again. And he knew a little bit about losing your mind, too.

The way to get under her guard here was to be on her side and buy into her worldview to have a chance of getting near to her.

'I think you might be suffering from some sort of intolerance,' said Artie. 'I know a bit about this sort of thing. Can you stick your tongue out, Carly?'

She did as she was asked. It was yellow and coated.

'Do you feel dizzy when you stand up quickly?' he said.

'Yeah, I do. I keep walking into things as well. Why? Is that a sign of something?' she said. It was the only bit of eagerness or energy she'd shown so far.

'Could be.' He tried to invent something on the spot, but was beaten to it by Colleen. Of course he was, she was the best liar and spinner of stories he'd ever met.

'Yeah, it's lack of calcium y'see. Calcium is the most important mineral in the body. It's not just for building bones, it maintains your arteries and veins and your equilibrium. You know statins that they give people to reduce their cholesterol? That's a sort of calcium as well. You're a vegan so you won't be eating much calcium. Do you take a supplement?'

She shook her head. 'I eat sesame seeds. They're supposed to be high in calcium.'

'Yeah, but you can't eat enough of them, y'see, babe.' Colleen went on. 'I was a vegan in the 80s and I used to faint all the time. You need to take a supplement - make sure it's vegetable derived, of course.'

'OK. I will. Fay didn't say you used to be a vegan.'

'It was well before she was born. Couldn't bear the idea of animals being killed to feed us when there are so many things we can eat which don't harm any living thing.'

It was impressive to see her deploy her outright fiction creation on the hoof, like this. Colleen had always loved meat - many would have said especially if it was attached to a rock musician.

'We should get a holistic physician to look at you, as well. Not a regular doctor. Get them to run a load of allergy tests, then an intolerance analysis. You can't be too careful.'

Ronnie spoke up. 'Do you know someone like that, Colleen?'

'Yeah, a good friend of mine, Kath Yaltz. She has offices on La Brea. She'll analyse what you're eating and what's working for you and what isn't. She might tailor a diet specifically for you. What do you say, Carly? She's very cool. Very...y'know...clued up. She's not mainstream, but she is good. I'll get you an appointment, yeah?'

Carly seemed to like the sound of this. 'OK, if you think it's for the best, Miss Holmes. The human body wasn't meant to live in this artificial version of the world that we've created with roads and cars and chemicals. It wouldn't be surprising if some people got sick because their bodies can't cope with the pollution.'

'Right on, sister,' said Colleen, and held her hand up to hi-five her, but Carly clearly didn't hi-five, it was probably either an older person's thing, or a jock thing to her and thus to be dismissed if you were an alt.kid. She looked a bit embarrassed.

'Thanks, Colleen,' said Ronnie.

'No problem. Give me your email address, Carly, I'll contact you when I've fixed up an appointment for you.'

She did so and then Ronnie saw them back out to the truck.

'I can't thank you enough for that,' he said, blowing out his cheeks as they got to the car. 'Will this Kath Yaltz get her off the vegan trip? Tell me she will. Please. I'm desperate.'

'She'll make a good case for a better diet, I'm sure,' said Colleen. 'She's good on eating disorders and the psychology behind them.'

'You've got to be really on her side to get any traction with her, I think,' said Artie. 'Life for kids is, in a lot of ways, so much harder than it was for our generation. Also, this food thing - we never had issues about food, except we sometimes didn't have enough - I reckon it's a neurosis encouraged by the health food industry. Marketing is being passed off as science, if you ask me, and it's fucking kids like her up.'

'Life was a lot more simple for us when we were 21, wasn't it? Beer, birds and rock 'n' roll. That was all we needed.'

'It's all some of us still need, Ronnie,' said Artie with a smile. 'We'll go out for a drink sometime soon, right?'

Ronnie put his thumb up and waved them off, as Artie drove the pickup away down Santa Monica Boulevard.

Colleen turned to him. 'Isn't Carly sweet?'

'She is. A really nice lass. Awful to see her looking so ill.' He sucked his teeth. 'It's a hard gig being a kid in 2014.'

'Totally. I often wonder if Fay is like that - a really nice person to other people's parents and only a bastard to me. It sounds like she is, which is a little galling, I must say.' She flicked a strand of dark hair off her eyes and chewed her cheek a little.

Artie moved out into the middle lane and accelerated past an old Dodge which was coughing out exhaust fumes. 'From what I can tell, Fay is a strident leader of her group of friends, including Carly. She's that sort of personality. Kids probably look up to her. She's quite worldly wise these days, especially since her little episode with that creep in the desert last year. She's done a lot of growing up in the last year, I reckon.'

Colleen nodded. 'Yeah, that is true. Though I think Carly has got her own little thing going on. Like a lot of quiet girls, she's a determined young woman, even if that determination is to eat herself into an early grave.'

'Aye, it is worrying. Ronnie's obviously at the end of his tether about it all. I've never seen him looking so stressed out. So, who's this Kath woman? Does she actually exist?'

'Yeah, of course, she's a friend of mine from way back. She's a doctor, but one who specializes in eating disorders and I think Carly has some flavour of eating disorder. But the last thing you want to be told is you've got an eating disorder, when you've got an eating disorder. It might make things worse. Especially when someone like Carly has convinced herself that she's the holy one and is on the side of the angels for not being co-opted into the slaughter of sentient creatures whilst, at the same time, eating herself into low-fat heaven. It's a win-win, from her perspective. She doesn't look in the mirror and see someone ill and underweight.'

He looked at her and smiled. 'You know what? You're alright, you are.'

'You figure?' She smiled and winked at him.

'Yeah. That was nice work. I hope she gets some help. I hate to see a nice kid like her go through some sort of hell.' He took the soy jerky bar out of his shirt pocket and tapped the steering wheel with it. 'Kaz is right about these things. They're the most unnatural shit you could eat, dressed up as a health food. Green on Green's logo is a plant growing around a tree, like this stuff is as natural as that, but it's full of flavourings and god knows how it's made.'

His phone rang.

'Artie Taylor.'

'Oh, hello, sir. This is Georgina Rodgers. I'm the manager of the Mother Earth store in Topanga Canyon.'

'Oh, hello again. Is Ben Goldman OK?'

'Yes, yes, he recovered. Thank you.' Her voice was the sort of American voice that Artie's generation had grown up with; polite, oak tree-solid and without a hint of hip-speak or Valley Girlisms. 'I wonder if I could trouble you to drop by the store at your convenience in the near future?'

'Sure. Do you need a statement or something?'

She paused and seemed unsure what to say. 'I found something that is a little puzzling. Could we talk? I won't take a lot of your time.'

Artie looked at his cheap watch. It had been such a busy day but was still only half-past three. 'Of course. Is four OK?'

'Lovely. Thank you.'

'We're taking a detour to Mother Earth,' said Artie.

He drove down to the coast, went north on the Pacific Coast Highway, then took the 27 up Topanga Canyon Road.

'Way back, Mother Earth was one of the first hippie wholefood stores in the 60s,' said Coll. 'Legendarily, LA's rock community used to meet up there to hang out and eat wheatgrass smoothies...y'know...or whatever,' said Colleen. 'It was owned and run by a guy called Honest Joe Halford until a couple of years ago. He sold out to someone. A big company, I think. They expanded all over the state.'

'I guess a lot of rock people lived within a couple of miles. There was a whole community of musicians living in Topanga Canyon in the late 60s and early 70s. It still seems like that, except now it's really monied and not down home, like it once was.'

'Yeah, it's like Laguna Beach. Man, that was a beautiful artist colony until about 1980 and now it's a place for millionaires to buy a second or third home,' said Colleen.

Yeah, millionaires like you, if you wanted, he thought, but didn't voice. See, that was the problem, right there. He was swallowing down his antipathy to her wealth. It was dishonest and it was going to come between them sooner or later. And he didn't have that issue with Kaz. And that was another issue.

He pulled into the parking lot. It was now edging into the low 90s as they walked to the characterful, patched-up wooden store. It looked held together with string and sellotape. Lord knows how it had survived the Northridge quake in 93. The same blonde greeter girl as earlier was still on the door - or was it a different 20-something blonde girl? It was impossible to tell. Maybe they were all replicants.

'Hey. I'm Artie Taylor. Your manager, Georgina Rodgers, asked me to drop by,' he said to an entirely hairless man on the customer services desk, his head as smooth and round and brown as a hazelnut.

He made a call and the tall, thin woman soon arrived, extending her hand out to him.

'Thank you for coming by so soon, Mister Taylor.'

'No problem. This is my wife, Colleen.'

She nodded and gave a stiff smile. 'Shall we step into my office?' she said and led them out the back of the shop and into a room divided from the store by a half-windowed wall. It was mostly filled with a desk and a large, wide computer screen. She closed the door behind them and pulled out three seats from along one wall and arranged them so they all faced each other. 'Right, good. Can I get you anything? An iced tea? It's such a hot afternoon.'

'We're fine, thanks,' said Colleen.

She patted her thighs and seemed to compose herself. 'Good. Well, firstly, let me thank you again for your prompt reaction to Mister Goldman's allergic attack.'

'Artie is good in a crisis,' said Colleen. 'Being a photographer in the music business prepares you for most eventualities. Isn't that right, honey?'

'Well, there's not much I've not seen happen, that much is true,' said Artie, crossing his left leg over his right and fiddling with the zip on his leather boots, noticing that Georgina Rodgers was tense and that she was grinding her teeth together as he spoke, just as Ronnie had been, earlier.

'OK, well, here's my question. When your friend stuck that adrenalin pen into Mister Goldman, did she by any chance leave another one behind?'

Artie frowned. 'No. Kaz only brought one.'

'Are you sure?'

'Certain. Why?'

'Because another one was found beside the door. It was tucked in the well in which the large doormat is set. It seemed an odd coincidence to me.'

Artie paused and thought for a moment. 'Have you checked your CCTV footage to see if Ben Goldman dropped it or placed it there, at an earlier time?' said Artie, remembering what Kaz had said about him setting up his own allergy attack.

24

'No.' She knitted her eyebrows together. 'Should I? Why would he do that?'

'Yes, you should. He didn't know we would be there and be able to help as we did. He might have discovered that the soy jerky strips had nuts in them by accident, and gone in there to poison himself, to bring a lawsuit not just against Green on Green, who make them, but also against you for selling them. He'd double his money. But he'd need a pen on him, to counteract the allergy.' Artie explained about the Goldman family's reputation. 'If you get a letter from his lawyer in the next few days, you'll know what his game was.'

She shook her head and looked quite shocked. 'What a strange world we live in. That hadn't even occurred to me. Perhaps I'm too trusting or naïve.'

'Or just a nice person,' said Colleen.

Artie folded his arms across his chest and looked at her. She did seem shocked by what he'd told her. 'Might be worth getting the Mother Earth legal department onto it, just so you know where you stand. Is the store liable for the integrity of everything it stocks or is it buyer beware?' he said.

'I'm not sure, is the honest answer. I'll have to call the head office.'

'How many stores are in the Mother Earth chain now?' asked Artie.

'Oh, there are over 20, up and down the west coast from San Diego to Seattle. We're hugely successful. I know there are plans to expand to the east coast and parts of the midwest.'

'Wow, so it'll be the go-to place for vegans like my daughter,' said Colleen. 'She's a customer of yours, here. You must be expanding quickly.'

'Indeed. It was only two years ago that Honest Joe sold this place. The expansion has been super quick.'

'He's an LA legend. I used to know him, actually. A little bit, anyway. He was fêted like a guru,' said Colleen, rolling a silver bangle around her wrist.

'When he sold out to Long Run, a capital investment company, I was worried things would become very faceless once big money people got involved, but I'm pleased to say it's gone from strength to strength and they've given us all a wonderful 50 per cent staff discount, which is worth a ton of money each month to every employee.'

'So you all buy your shopping here. You'd be crazy not to when it's half price,' said Artie.

25

'Indeed, they really look after us all from top to bottom. It's been hugely encouraging.'

'Are you vegan?' said Colleen.

'I am.' She nodded with that quiet pride people who have a made a big lifestyle choice often have.

'Do they insist that everyone who works here is?' said Artie.

'No, I'm not sure that would be legal to discriminate in that fashion. However, a high proportion of us are because we just naturally tend to attract people with a similar outlook on life.'

Artie rested his chin on his upturned hand. She was a nice woman; though a little underweight, she didn't look ill like Carly.

'Can I ask what you eat as a vegan?' he said. 'I imagine it's all veggie burgers and such.'

'It's much easier today than when I became vegan in 2004 because there are so many convenience foods. We stock hundreds and hundreds of different things and they're delicious. We get a lot of people shopping with us who are meat eaters who just want to pick up something low fat and healthy for a change.'

Funny how she, just like Carly, was obsessed with meat and fat being unhealthy and vegan eating being super healthy. It was a religion that they really wanted to believe in. It was who they were, both to themselves and to everyone else. It offered a complete identity, as well as a lifestyle. But just like Carly, the fact she really didn't look in rude health at all seemed totally at odds with what they thought they were doing to themselves. Couldn't they see it? No, they couldn't, or at least they didn't want to admit it to themselves, or anyone else and understandably so, when it was such an integral part of their self-identity. They shut out or disbelieved the counter-evidence, then sought out and embraced only the views that proved them right. But regardless, she was obviously a good, well-meaning, caring woman.

'Well, if I you want me to make a statement about Goldman and what we did for him, I'm happy to do so, Georgina. I just hope you don't get any legal crap from them.'

She shrugged. 'Well, I appreciate your insight into the situation. If the worst happens, at least I shall be prepared. I shall get the CCTV checked, though, to be honest, I'm not even sure how to do that. We've never had to do it before.'

'Isn't it just recording to a hard drive in here?' said Artie.

'No. It's contracted out to a specialist security firm. All stores feed the same data centre, as far as I know.'

As they got back into Artie's truck, he turned to Colleen. 'What do you make of her?'

'Nice person, but maybe not a 100 per cent well person. There's a theme developing here. I liked her, though. She's just doing something that doesn't work for her, man. This vegan gig, I dunno man, this city messes with people's brains in so many ways, but the food thing has always been its speciality. I remember back in about 2004, everyone was low carb. Low-carb beer, low-carb bread, low-carb pizza, low-carb oral damn sex. It was fucking crazy. Then, I don't remember why, but low carb was discredited and it fell off all the menus overnight. Now I hear it's back again for an encore via the whole Paleo diet thing.'

He took off down the road towards Malibu.

'Paleo? What's Paleo? I tell you what, Carly and Georgina there were both "pale-y, oh" - ha. Sorry.'

'Oh, man, that's pun-hell. Paleo is when you eat meat, butter and such and not many carbs, like a caveman-type gig. It's another obsession for people to build a life around. But y'know, Fat America is messed up on food, one way or another. This is the land of the lard ass. Sometimes it feels like being fat is considered patriotic now. Love America? Here, have a soda, have a Twinkie, have a 72oz steak and three pounds of fries. I really hate that culture.'

'Yeah, when you see the old film of Woodstock or anything from that era, you never see anyone overweight. I mean, it's remarkable how much it's changed. Something went wrong, somewhere.'

She leaned over to him and jabbed her finger in the air. 'I tell you this - Fat America is a joke the world over and most of Fat America doesn't even know it. These rubes who never leave their own state, let alone go abroad, they don't realise that the world is laughing at them. The Land of the Free? How free are you when you can't even break into a brisk walk because you're 22 stone?'

Artie laughed loudly. 'Ha ha, excellent ranting, Coll.'

But she was genuinely annoyed. 'Well it's bullshit, man. America used to be so cool. Like you say, those old films show a different country. Now it has to take its dead out of an apartment with a crane...I dunno man, it's not heading to a good ending, if you ask me. Not for any of us.' She shook her head, her face set in a scowl.

'That's unusually bitter for you, Coll.' He rubbed her leg, just as he'd rubbed Kaz's earlier.

'Well, this isn't the country I first came to with mom in the late 70s. Weight issues aside, it's so divided. Liberal versus Conservative. We're two separate armies fighting for the soul of the country, each pointing a gun to the head of the other, daring the other to shoot. It's a kind of Mexican standoff.'

'It's the inequality of wealth that's the problem. When you've got a lot with not much, and a few with a lot, one side feels pissed off and the other feels defensive and scared. Then both sides call on their own troops to fight their cause for them.'

'You're right.' She turned to look at him. 'You know, I've got to do something about this. I'm on the wrong side of this whole thing.'

He frowned at her. 'What do you mean?'

'I mean, I'm a rich bitch. And I never did anything for it. I fell ass backwards into money. I've never had to do a day's work in my life and that's almost certainly stopped me from achieving anything of note. I spent decades just partying and the occasional bit of charity work or whatever. You've got an amazing portfolio of work as your legacy, I've got nothing and it's time I did.' She stopped for a moment, biting her bottom lip. 'I've had thoughts about this for a while. But it's clear to me now. I should find a way to give the money away, or set up something that can go on after I'm gone. Why haven't I done that before now? Sorry.'

Artie felt shocked and astonished in equal measure to hear that. Where had it come from? Had she picked up on his own thoughts, somehow? She'd made no indication of thinking such a thing in the past. Was it just a fleeting notion that she wouldn't ultimately act on? She could be very flakey at times.

'Why don't you just stick the money into something which will pay out, say 100 thousand dollars a year - that's plenty to live off when you own your own house. Let anything over that go to feed the poor or whatever other cause you want to support. It's not as if I'm not earning anything. I can pay my way. There's only so much money you need, I reckon.'

'Yeah, man, and I don't want to be your sugar mama. I totally dig that ain't cool for you.'

Sometimes the fact that she could read him, really caught him by surprise. But that's why she'd always been such a great liar and spinner of fantasies. She understood people. She understood him. She'd understood him well enough to all but suggest that he and Kaz sleep together before their wedding, to test how they felt about each other, knowing there was a deep bond between them. Oh god, yeah. And maybe they should never have done it, because how much it had helped clarify things for either of them was open to question. Artie would have been lying to himself if he didn't admit to regularly thinking about them doing it again and, if he knew Kaz at all, and he did, she was exactly the same. And that was bit of a problem, because there was never any shortage of opportunity if the mood took them both at the same time, and all in all, it felt like sooner or later, there would be a time when that would be the case. And, because Colleen knew them both so well, he also couldn't escape the feeling that she knew that, too. It was all very confusing.

'Would Fay mind if you didn't leave a huge inheritance for her? Not that a house by the beach in Malibu wouldn't be a huge inheritance.'

'Well, it's all set to go to her, right now, whether she likes it or not. She'd say she wouldn't - because she likes to think she's above filthy lucre - but whether that'd be true or not is a little hard to tell with that girl. And like you say, that house isn't going to go down in value.'

They gripped hands together and grinned at each other, as they turned onto PCH. The forever sun in their hair, the smell of sage wood and gasoline, that was the essence of Southern California, woven into the hot late afternoon air. She looked at him with her beautiful caramel eyes and he remembered again exactly why he fell in love with Colleen Holmes. The truth was, it was hard being in love with two women at the same time, but also very rock 'n' roll and, though confusing, it was also some shade of wonderful.

.

.

CHAPTER 4

The Scene Club in Tarzana marketed itself as an 'intimate venue', which just meant it was small and basic, with a bar, some tables, a wooden floor and a small raised platform in a corner. However, it did have a great reputation for giving a start to people who went on to do well as solo singer-songwriters and Benny Ace looked set to be exactly that.

'It'll be rammed in here tonight,' said Kaz as they parked up and walked to the club entrance, armed with camera bags, lighting, tripods and make-up gear. 'He had that bloody horrible hit, "Our Love Hurts", which was like being spoon fed treacle by a weeping puppy. I hate songs consciously written to be romantic. You can't do romance like that. Romance is where you find it - you can't be led by the nose to it.'

'You won't find me arguing with you. I get embarrassed by that weepy shit. What's wrong with swallowing down your emotions like any decent Yorkshire man?'

'Or Yorkshire woman, for that matter. I always feel vaguely disappointed in the public when a song that makes me want to puke is a big hit.'

'Well, you say big hit, and it was, in that it went top 5, but I looked it up this morning, how many copies do you think it sold in the week it hit its peak chart position?'

'Top 5? Gotta be 250,000.'

'21,000.'

She stopped and looked at him aghast. 'Is that all? That's ridiculous. In a country of 350 million?'

'Yup. It was a quiet week.'

'That's so poor. I could sell more than 21,000 copies of a recording of my fanny farting.'

He didn't even blink. 'Yeah, I remember that sound from the Mandalay Bay.'

She hit him playfully on the head with a tripod. 'And you can wipe that from your synapses, you dirty bugger. It never happened. And my fanny farts *especially* never happened.'

He put a hand on her shoulder and then her warm neck and kissed the top of her head. She looked up at him and smiled a sly admonishment.

Pulling open the heavy door, they strode out of a hot LA afternoon into the cool, air-conned club. Inside it smelled of cinnamon, vanilla, coffee and pot pourri, which was just very Californian folkie. Not for them a bar smelling of stale beer, mixed with the whiff of vomit, oh no.

Benny Ace arrived soon after looking artfully and expensively dishevelled.

'It must take a lot of money to look that cheap,' said Kaz, sitting on a bar stool. 'That's all designer gear he's wearing. It comes ripped, torn and stained and branded. And I hate that.'

'Call me old fashioned but wearing designer clothes which ape being a tramp is somehow dishonest and the very definition of phoney,' said Artie.

Kaz made a disparaging *pffft* noise in agreement and slipped off her stool and went over to Benny, who was setting down an acoustic guitar, slipping by second nature into her work schmooze mode.

'Hey, Benny. I'm Kaz Clarke. That streak of piss over there is Artie Taylor, he's here to photograph you and I'm here to make you look even better than your normal gorgeous self.' She held up her make-up bag and gave him a big smile.

'Cool. That won't take you long, then,' said Benny. He'd have eaten himself with a spoon if it was possible. He looked at her with milk chocolate eyes that plainly expected women to find him irresistible, which they probably did, far too often. Kaz was good at playing to that sort of ego, largely because she'd had years of working with people who were full of themselves.

Artie groaned inwardly. He'd seen guys like this many, many times before; wrapped up in their own brilliance. Kaz was his defence against them. She kept them happy and occupied them with chitter-chatter, so he didn't have to say much. She was great at faking interest and an expert in flattery. In the old days he'd have lit a cigarette and watched it all unfold with a cynical squint. These days he had to make do with just a big drink.

Doing portraits was a piece of piss. With the aid of Photoshop, you only had to get it 75 percent right and then fix it in the mix. The crucial thing was to get your focus, lighting and context right. It was hard to fix an image which didn't have the right balance of angle, shadow and light. He sucked down a large vodka on the rocks as Kaz set up the lighting, using the stage as their set. She knew her job inside and out, upside and down. All he had to do was point the lens. When it came to live work, you needed to use your experience and art a lot more, but this shit was

31

easy. It was why, since their earliest days working together, he'd shared the fees he got 50/50 with her. He had the name and the reputation, albeit a faded name and faded reputation, but she knew a good photo from a bad one and knew how to give him a chance to make a good one happen. Splitting the money was only fair.

Kaz came over after setting up two lights and a reflective screen, rolling her eyes and mouthing the words 'what a fucking prick' at him. Artie laughed a little and handed her a gin and tonic.

'Here, take a hit on that. You're doing a good job.'

She drank half of the glass and pulled an ecstatic face and let out small sigh.

'That is bloody lovely. This is like a play. You take on your role and play it out, not engaging the real you. Weirdly, I really enjoy that. It's liberating. But he's still a wank chops.'

'Are we ready for some red-hot shutter action, then?'

She spoke quietly. 'Yeah, with a twat like this we just feed him his own self-image, don't we? So we should really be photographing him sucking his own dick, which, by the way, I think he could do - but he'd probably pass it off as some spiritual yoga shit. He's that sort of self-absorbed egotist. He's good, but he's got an ego bigger than his talent, by a factor of about 100.'

Artie finished his drink and went over to Benny, who was chatting with his manager, a woman with a short dark haircut who appeared to worship her iPhone, so religiously did she pay attention to it. They were all like this, these days. Gone were the days of fat twat with muscle in tow. She stepped in front of her act, as though screening him from the grubby public. Artie, as he always did in these circumstances, totally ignored her and did a body swerve, holding out his long, bony arm.

'Now then, Benny. Artie Taylor. All we're going to do here is concentrate on you. What I'm going for is articulate and sensitive. OK?' He said it in a quick, off-hand way, on purpose, as though it was a given. Then he glanced up at Benny. He was beaming. It was amazing how choosing to say words that people wanted to hear made them trust you a lot more than they really should.

His manager looked at her phone again, as though to find approval for this. Oh, do fuck right off.

'Beautiful. Yeah, man. Thanks Artie. I loved how you photographed Jewel Kilcher for *Rolling Stone*. That's why I asked for you.'

'Oh, cool. She was quite something, huh?' said Artie. Yeah, whatever. He didn't care. It had been 15 minutes in 1995 and was just another job. And if you couldn't take a good photo of Jewel you were in the wrong game. There'd probably never been a bad shot of her. She was just one of those people who probably looked paused in a moment of still beauty even when she was taking a shit or vomiting. He set up his tripod and camera.

'OK. Let's just get one of you exactly as you are on stage,' said Artie. 'Can you do his hair, Kaz, it's all flat on the side?'

She skipped up onto the small stage with a comb and some hair wax. She cooed around him, chirping and chattering at him as she did so, flicking at his long hair and then holding a mirror up to him for his approval of her work.

Artie yawned. Someone tapped him on the shoulder. He turned around to see a familiar face.

'Hey, ya old cunt.'

'Jack Silver, bloody hell.' He held out his hand and had it gripped by a huge, strong, leathery paw.

The old man breathed whisky into his face.

'What are you doing here, Jack?'

'I own this place. Didn't you know?'

'Get outta here. This has been owned by Rodney for years.'

'Yeah, I bought him out last year. I'm the head cheese now, man.'

He had a face carved out of oak and stained with nicotine from a million cigarettes. Jack Silver was a legend of the west coast music scene. One of the first festival promoters, he'd spent the 60s and 70s fighting the authorities for the right to put on festivals in places where the locals didn't want them to be held, fearing their little town would be flooded with naked freaks and whacked-out druggies, which, of course, they usually were, albeit they were mostly peace lovin' naked druggie freaks. He moved into more regular music promotion in the 80s and 90s, and then opened the Rock Ballroom in Burbank. Artie had met him on his first trip to the west coast while photographing Winger and Extreme. He was a wily old operator, now in his late 60s, with an anti-establishment streak running through him like lettering through a stick of rock and the sunburnt, weathered skin of a polar explorer.

'So what do you make of the latest feel-my-pain artisan?' said Jack, with the sort of tired, wry look that only a man who had seen it all before could muster.

Artie pushed his greying hair back behind his ears. 'It's not my sort of thing, Jack. I'm too emotionally repressed to enjoy some kid with a wobbly voice coming on like he's going to cry by the time he hits the chorus. It all feels...I dunno...self-indulgent, I suppose.'

'It's treacle music. Yeah. He ain't no Tim Hardin, that's for sure. Look, I'll let you guys do your job. I'll be at the bar if you need me.'

Artie spent half an hour shooting portraits just to make it look like he was doing something and was worth the fee, but the truth was, he probably got the shots he needed in the first five minutes. He'd been doing this all of his adult life and he knew when he had taken a good shot, almost by instinct.

He loaded the photo card into his laptop and pulled the shots into Photoshop to make sure he was right. He was. Kaz stood looking over his shoulder, drinking. She pointed her short stubby index finger at the screen.

'That's the essence of him in those two shots and in that third one. All soulful, fuck-me eyes and yet with a hint of overbearing self-regard. Ha!' The ice in her drink clinked in his ear. He nodded.

'Yeah, agreed. OK, let's get some angles for live shots sorted before they let his fans in.'

When the doors opened at 7.30pm and Benny Ace's fans came in, it was remarkable how similar they all were. Between 18 and 25, white, girls with long hair, black leggings, long black t-shirts, boys with some semblance of facial hair and expensively, artfully dishevelled clothes from Abercrombie and Fitch. Artie and Kaz sat at the bar as the audience took seats around tables. Some were too young to even drink.

'This is going to be the least rock 'n' roll gig we do all year,' said Kaz, sipping at her gin. 'Slightly different from touring with Bruce.'

'True, but it'll be useful for me to have my name associated with this kid.'

'Yeah, you just know he's going to be massive within a year. He even knows it and that doesn't make him exactly lovable.'

'Jack reckons that there's 200 in here and 400 outside. Never harms to work for the Next Big Thing.'

'How long have you known Jack for?'

'25 years or more. He ran the Rock Ballroom in Burbank and all the up-and-coming rock bands played there. I photographed Winger there just before they got big.'

'Kip Winger? Oh, dear me. Chest and vest rock.'

'That place was crawling with groupies. Famously so. It was my first exposure to it over here. It was quite wild backstage. Jack used to walk amongst it all dressed like a pirate, long before Johnny Depp. If he liked you, he'd let you snort speed off his big sword. I didn't know he'd bought this place from Rodney Drinkwater. Never was a man more inaccurately named.'

As he talked he saw a familiar face enter the club, laughing, with a long-haired lad in his early 20s. Artie tapped Kaz on the arm.

'Look who just came in.'

Kaz turned to look. 'Oh, why am I not surprised Fay Holmes is here? This is her demographic down to a tee. The vegan folk singer. Oh, fucking hell, Artie, can't we go and photograph some rock people, pleeeeeze! I can't bear these self-conscious, sensitive types.'

He patted her on the leg. 'Don't worry, lady. I'll get us something with more tight pants soon.'

'Good. I feel more at home with a bloke whose wedding tackle is stuffed down one leg, or a woman with leather pants up her vulva. Christ, that sounded·more pervy than I meant it to.'

'Ha, well I'd better go and say hello to her ladyship.'

'Good bloody luck.'

Artie slipped off his stool and walked up to the bar where Fay was standing, her long legs in black leggings which she'd put with a long black shirt and black leather boots. Though she had an almost gothic, otherworldliness aspect to her, and though never one to try and show off her figure or project sexuality, she was a really attractive young woman; the sort of person who radiates something indefinable which pulls people into her orbit. If you didn't know her, you'd want to know her, even though she was hard to get to know. It had to be something in the Holmes DNA, because her mother had it, too. Artie had long wondered what that indefinable thing was and the nearest he could get to it was quiet passion. Her mother had it, Fay had it; Kaz had it too, for that matter, though she wasn't so quiet.

'Hey, Fay.'

She looked up at him, very much her mother's daughter, but with added haughty disdain, which she used as a kind of cultural Kevlar to keep the world at bay.

'Oh, it's you,' she said, expressionless. God forbid she should ever show any emotion except perhaps disgust or faux outrage. 'What are you doing here?'

'Working with Kaz on the old snappy snappy,' he said, holding an imaginary camera to his eye.

Fay hadn't shown him or Kaz much in the way of warm friendship since he'd married Colleen in Las Vegas. But neither had she been especially hostile. Her gig was to give off an air of indifference and weary tolerance at best. But it's hard being just 21 in the 21st century, you're bombarded with so many different types of pressure. Fay was a spoilt kid, in that she'd grown up knowing money was never going to be a problem, but at the same time, that fact had robbed her of an impetus to do anything with her life, just as it had for her mother. She was still searching for herself, but had no real direction, nor any imperative to shape her existence in one direction. She lived in a very nice flat in Santa Monica overlooking Ocean Way, which her mother paid for, didn't have a job, didn't seem to have a romantic relationship with anyone and she was always flitting from one idea and fad to another. Underneath all of the pouting, disdain and shrugging she was, just as Carly had confirmed, a good kid. She showed no signs of obviously liking him, but the ornery rocker in him quite liked that, too. I mean, old people, what the fuck did they know about being 21? Kids who really got on with their parents, or parents' friends, always seemed a bit weird to him. There should be a generation gap - a place where generational grit can make a new pearl.

'Oh, yeah, of course.' Kaz waved at her, but she didn't respond other than to raise her dark eyebrows.

'You did well to get tickets for this, Fay. Are you a big fan?'

That was stupid question, really. Even if she was, she'd not admit to it because it would look too 'dweeby'.

'He's OK. My friends like him. They should be here, actually. Oh, they've just come in.'

He glanced over to the door to see three girls, dressed very like Fay, one of whom was Carly, who still looked sickly, even in the lowlights of the club.

'I'd better get to work. Catch you later.' He turned to go and then, quite shockingly, felt her cold hand on his arm.

'Can I just say something, Artie?'

He looked down at her slim, pale, long fingers, surprised to feel them on him. 'Yeah?' He looked into the liquid caramel eyes she'd inherited from her mother. They looked back at him fearlessly.

'Thanks for helping Carly. She told me you and mom are getting her an appointment at a holistic doctor...that was really good of you. Of both of you. I've been really worried about her, too.'

That was about as open and honest as she'd ever been with him. She couldn't crack a smile but the fact she'd actually touched him - again something she never, ever did, had to mean something. These sorts of gestures have so much power when they're so out of the ordinary.

'That's OK. Her dad is scared she's really quite unwell. You all go up to Mother Earth in Topanga Canyon, don't you?'

'Yeah. To their restaurant. It's all...y'know...kinda pure vegan food...' She glanced over her shoulder at her friends as they made their way over. 'It's OK...but Carly is a little too crazy about it.' She lightly squeezed his arm, gave him what from anyone else would have been a watery smile, but from the always-frosty Fay seemed like her warmest expression. 'I'd better go.'

That was the conversation over. Artie made his move back over to Kaz, just as the lights went down and Benny Ace came out holding a lovely blue acoustic guitar, perched on a stool and adjusted the microphone whilst the cheering and applause died down. The room was lit up with kids holding their phones up to film the moment, seemingly more concerned with documenting their lives than living them.

Photographing people in a live setting was almost a sixth sense for Artie, after so many years. He'd spent so long in the pit with other photographers in aggressive, inhospitable conditions, often under pressure from arsey twats in the band's management who would only allow you to shoot for one song. By contrast, this was a soft, easy gig.

He got plenty of shots of Benny, eyes closed, singing something self-pityingly lachrymose and unconvincingly world weary, especially coming out the mouth of a 23-year-old. Nevertheless, the response to his music was almost hysterical. At the end of every song, they'd all stand and applaud, never stopping filming him on their phone, of course. Some of them were in tears. At least the ones not busy on social media telling people who were not there, that they *were* there and it was great, at least it was last time they took their eyes off their phone. Good god. Did not eating meat - and most of the 250 in there had the holy air of the young non-meat eater - make you more prone to cry? Judging by this crowd, it did. When he performed a song and dedicated it to 'all the animals killed to feed greedy humans' some openly wept, indulging themselves in a collective orgy of empathy. The more they cried, the less convincing the whole thing was. It was more akin to a religious rally, with Benny Ace as a kind of preacher or guru.

Kaz leaned over and spoke into his ear. 'If you ask me this lot are collectively menstruating - even the men. I can't cope with it. Makes me feel nauseous. It's all fake, isn't it? No-one is really upset, they just want to present themselves as upset. It's all part of the "I'm so sensitive" trip, isn't it?'

'Aye. That's how it looks to me - but we're old and cynical...and from Leeds. These kids aren't.'

'Or wise and perceptive and from Leeds. Take your pick. Shall we go? We've got plenty of shots and he's just rhymed "slaughterhouse" with "without a doubt". That's a red-card offence.' She scowled in the direction of the stage and began to zip up bags.

Artie found Jack Silver at the bar, shook his hand, gave him his phone number and agreed to meet up for a drink soon. As they slipped out of the back door of the venue, Artie took one last look in the room. They were still in some state of rapture, or at least, they were doing a good job of pretending to themselves and to each other that they were, even while still experiencing the gig through the screen of their iPhone. Shit. It made you feel very old.

'Fancy a drink, Kaz?' he said, as he drove away. 'I don't feel like going home yet.'

'Do I ever turn a drink down? I'd have to hand in my Yorkshire passport if I did. We've already had a couple, though, so we'd better go somewhere close to home so there's less chance of you getting pulled over on a DUI charge. How about Mike's Diner?'

Artie hit PCH and went north towards Malibu, pulling into the old 1950s diner that was set back from the roadside, just as you left the city. Red, white and chrome, it was everything you wanted a place that sold burgers, fries and cold beer to be like in California.

They got a red naugahyde booth, ordered a plate of cheeseburger sliders and two bottles of Pabst.

'So how come you don't want to go home yet? You've not had a row with Colleen, have you?' she said, picking at her fries.

'Nah. We never argue, you know that. We're too old.'

'So what is it?'

He clinked his bottle against hers and sank half of it in two big gulps, grateful for the cold fizz on his dry throat. 'Well, don't tell Coll this, right, but I don't like that house.'

'You don't like a 1960s beachfront house in Malibu? Are you bloody mad, lad?' she said biting into the mini burger. 'It's a primo house, Artie.'

'I didn't say it wasn't. I just don't like it. I mean...oh, I don't know...it's just not my style, is what I mean.' He knew he still wasn't really saying it right.

'Style? What style? You haven't got a style. Not unless cheap motel room is your style.'

He finished his beer and gestured to the waitress for another two.

'Do you like the house?' he said. 'You've got that lovely big suite on the top floor. It looks like an 80s porno set.'

'It does a bit, doesn't it? Aye, well, I've got my own bog and everything. Views over the beach. I can lie in bed and watch the sun sink into the sea.' She looked out to the highway as traffic rolled past ceaselessly.

'But you haven't said if you like it.'

'Like I said yesterday, it feels weird being back. I've got road wanderlust. I just feels odd being in one place. So I'm not really settled back in yet. I'm not sure it's ideal, really, on...well, on many levels. But we'd be mad not to like living there, though, wouldn't we?'

'Yeah, we would. Maybe that's what it is with me. Just being home is weird. Can't say I'm looking forward to settling into domestic life.'

She shrugged and gave him a wry smile, which was also part grimace.

'We're road rats, you and me. We weren't made for home life, Artie. We both know it and we both know that we're pretending to ourselves that we can do it, when we both know we can't. The problem is...' she paused and drank beer.

Artie ate some food. '...is what?'

'Well, it's Colleen and her money, isn't it? If you'd fallen in love with a poor woman, everything would be different. We'd be in our usual survival mode and we know where we are with that. We'd have to keep working to survive but now we don't, not if we don't want to and I don't know what to do with that sort of freedom and neither do you.'

It was typical of her to be so blunt and it was just as typical for her to be right. He finished off the sliders and beer.

'One more for the road, eh?' he said, gesturing to the waitresses for two more beers. 'It might surprise you to know that I've already sort of raised this with Coll and she's interested in downsizing.'

'Eh? What does that mean?'

'Getting rid of a load of money, basically. You invest in something which will pay you 100 grand a year and the rest you give to good causes.'

She raised her fair eyebrows and rubbed at a blue eye. 'Bloody hell. Really?'

'Yeah. Not that she'd give the house away. So it's still hardly poverty. But it'd make me feel a lot more comfortable, I reckon. I don't want to be sucking on the tit of a sugar mama for the rest of my days.'

She raised her beer at him. 'Nice one Artie, you're alright, you are. You're fucked up, but you're alright.'

He picked at the bottle's label. 'So if I read you right, you'd rather have your own place.'

'You read me right. I know it seems ungrateful...'

He interrupted her. '...nah, it doesn't. I'll put my fees up and see if we can't generate enough money to pay you enough dough to rent your own place - if that's what you'd like.'

'That's exactly what I'd like, aye. I need to be able to bring dirty women home and I can't when you and Coll are in the house. It feels like you're my parents. That's not your fault, but it's how it feels, all the same. And...I can't be...' she stopped mid-sentence and bit her tongue.

'Can't be what?' he said.

'Oh, just...being there. Like I say, it's like you're my parents.' She looked out the window and clearly hadn't said what she really wanted to say.

'So where do you fancy living?'

She didn't miss a beat. 'A basic one-bed place near Third Street Promenade in Santa Monica would be perfect.'

Artie laughed. 'You said that so quickly that I can only assume you've been thinking about it.'

'Yeah well, it'd mean I'd be within 10 minutes' walk of a lot of mates and you can just walk out to a bar or for something to eat. I love it around there. I don't want to have to drive all the time, not least because I don't have a car of my own, but also because I like drinking.'

'How much would that rent be? Two thousand a month?'

She laughed and drained her bottle. 'You're so out of touch, man. It'd be $3,000 - at least - maybe more if it's not going to be too evil.'

'Wow. OK, well I only need one good shoot a month to cover that and the publishers will stump up the second third of my advance for the book when I submit it next month. That's six grand - so that'll sort you out for a few months. We'll make it work, one way or another. Might be a bit tight sometimes...'

'I don't care if it is. We'll busk it somehow.' She looked around her beer bottle at him. 'I love how you're not even mentioning leaning on Colleen's money. I like that a lot.'

He rubbed his neck and sat back, arms crossed. 'Yeah, well, as mad as it sounds, her money is making me unhappy. Funny how life works, eh? Right, come on, let's go back to the multi-million dollar house by the sea and sit in misery.'

They walked out to the car, the hiss and swish of the high tide washing up the sand made a white noise soundtrack, punctuated by traffic roar. The sun was almost down now, leaving a few yellow and blushed peach stains on the horizon of the otherwise navy blue night sky. Artie sucked in the warm, dusty, petrol-fumed air, looked around and instinctively reached out to put his arm on Kaz's shoulder. 'Yeah, we must be fucking mad, lady.'

'Yeah, well, whatever gets you through the night, is alright,' she said, resting her weight on one hip, hands in her jeans pockets.

It was just a short drive to the house. Artie pulled into the garage beside Colleen's Porsche. 'Don't mention what we've been talking about to Coll. Not yet. It sounds...'

'...like I said, bloody ungrateful. I know. I'll leave it to you to handle, big fella.' She squeezed the top of his thigh and looked in his eyes again, almost said something, but didn't.

Artie's phone chirped into life as a text arrived, just as they walked into the big kitchen from the garage.

He stopped and read the words. But he couldn't really believe them. He stopped and stared at the screen. 'Bloody hell. Shit.'

'What is it?' said Kaz, filling a kettle with water for tea.

Hearing them, Colleen came in from the living room.

'Hi, guys. Good gig?'

Kaz made a puking gesture. 'Heinous. We saw Fay there with Carly and some friends.'

'Oh, really. I'm sure she was pretending not to be that interested...'
Artie interrupted her. 'Carly is dead.

CHAPTER 5

He felt cold and sick. 'Fay just texted me.'

'What?!' exclaimed Colleen. 'How is she dead? How...how has she died? Was she shot or something? Is Fay alright?!'

'Yeah, Fay's fine.' Artie read from the screen. ' "OMG Carly passed out after the gig. I thought she'd fainted but she just never woke up. Paramedics say she's died. They've taken her away to UCLA Medical Center on 16th Street. I called her dad and told him what happened. He's gone to the hospital." '

She was a fearless kid, was Fay. Calling a friend's father to tell them their daughter had died wasn't a job most 21-year-olds would put their hand up to do.

'I...I...I don't know what to say,' said Artie, looking from Colleen to Kaz.

'You said she looked ill,' said Kaz, 'well...she did look ill when you pointed her out. Sickly and pale. Poor kid. Poor Robbie. God, that's just terrible. A young lass like that.'

'I'm going to go over to the hospital,' Artie said. 'He's an old mate of mine from way back. I can't let him deal with this on his own. It's not like he's got a wife or partner, is it?'

He drove off into the night, heading back into Santa Monica, driving east on Wilshire Boulevard until he reached 16th Street. The hospital looked like a palm-fringed, upscale hotel. Built in the 1920s in brown and cream brick, it stood out as an old building.

Where would he be? Where would Carly be? In the morgue. God, poor lass. She'd seemed such a gentle soul. Alright, she was a vegan, but she was only doing that because she meant well and didn't want any harm to come to animals. However misplaced or naïve you might think that was, it came from a good place. God knows the world needs more gentle, peaceful people, not one less. She must have had some sort of underlying, undiagnosed medical condition, though. No-one dies from being a vegan, do they?

He walked down a long corridor to a reception desk, the hardwood heels on his leather boots clicking on the floor and echoing off the plaster walls.

'Hi. My friend's daughter Carly Saunders was brought here. She...err...well apparently she passed away tonight. Her father will be here somewhere. I've come to comfort him. Where would he be?'

The middle-aged woman on the desk gave him nice, sympathetic smile. 'I'm sorry for your loss. He'll likely be in the ER. Straight down and first left.'

Hospitals always felt weird. Like you had entered an alternative reality. Everything looked different. Normal life was suspended. American hospitals had the added weirdness of being places you could pretty much only use if you had money or insurance, as though they were indeed up-market hotels. If you couldn't pay, you pretty much couldn't stay. Medicare only did so much for you.

In Britain, the A&E department of any hospital looks like a war zone most of the time, especially on a weekend, when it's full of people so drunk that they've walked through a window or headbutted a car. This was much less the case here. It was relatively quiet and not even the faintest whiff of vomit. No-one raging off their head on vodka, at least not yet.

Robbie was sitting on a row of seats, his head in his hands. As Artie approached, he looked up at the sound of his footsteps. He'd obviously been crying. His girl had been taken away from him just like that. He'd looked after her, from being a baby to being a young woman. He had every right to expect her to be in his life until his final breath but no, she had gone, with a click of death's cold, arthritic fingers.

'Artie. What are you doing here?' he said, standing up.

'I heard about Carly, man. Fay told me.' He gave him a tight hug. 'Do they know what happened?'

He couldn't even bring himself to say anything about it for a minute, just shook his head and looked at the ground. 'Thanks for coming, Artie. I've really let Carly down. I was supposed to look after her and I didn't. I did the opposite. But all I wanted for her was the best. Everything I did I thought I was doing for the best.'

'Of course it was. It's not your fault, Robbie. So what's happening now?'

Robbie was shaking a little. 'It's a sudden d-d-d-death...so...there has to be a post mortem, at some point and the police get involved. I'm waiting for a doctor and the police.'

'Has anyone even speculated what caused this?'

'Nobody knows. The girls said she was fine, or at least, you know...not sick...or no sicker than she has been...they got outside of the club after the Benny Ace gig and she just collapsed.'

'Fay said she thought she'd fainted at first but then they couldn't revive her.'

'That's what the ambulance people that brought her in said to me, when I got here.'

It was hard to know what to say. The instinct is to try and be comforting but there is no comforting to be done in a situation like this. No words can be spoken to improve the situation.

'It sounds like the lights just went out,' said Robbie. 'I never thought that'd happen.'

'Well, if so, at least she didn't suffer, Robbie. It sounds like she was here one minute and gone the next.'

'I knew she wasn't well. You saw that yourself, didn't you? You and Colleen.'

'Yeah, she didn't look well. She obviously had something going wrong with her for a while.'

'That bloody vegan diet.'

Artie shook his head in disbelief, as a man in a white coat came through some swing doors and made his way over to them. 'Here's your doctor.'

'Mr Saunders?'

Robbie nodded.

'Firstly, I'm sorry for your loss, sir. This must have been a terrible shock for you. Let me assure you that we will get the bottom of the cause of your daughter's sudden death, sir. And when we do, I think you may find some closure, or at least people have told me so in the past. At the moment it seems inexplicable but there will be a reason.'

'So how long will that take?' said Robbie.

'In a case like this, it will be prioritised in case there are drug implications.'

'Drug implications? What do you mean?' asked Artie.

'Carly didn't take drugs,' said Robbie. 'I know parents always say that - I'm not naïve. I've been in the music business my whole life - but she didn't. She hated putting anything into her which wasn't natural.'

'Of course. I was thinking more about her drink being spiked. If someone did that, this could even be a murder investigation.'

'Murder? You think she was murdered?' said Robbie, his face strained taut with stress. 'Maybe she was. Yeah.'

'It can't be ruled out, is all I'm saying. It does happen.'

Artie put a hand on Robbie's shoulder. 'Take it easy, man.'

'If you feel up to it, the police will want to speak to you about this asap.'

Robbie let out a shuddering breath, his eyes red. He nodded.

'Are you sure you want to do this now, Robbie?' said Artie, whose long and occasionally painful experience with Los Angeles cops told him they'd be anything but sympathetic. They seemed to employ some of the hardest, coldest humans on the planet. Unsurprisingly, perhaps, considering what they had to do.

'Might as well. It's not like I'm going to suddenly not feel utterly fucking sick to my soul, is it? This is my life now. A life without the love of my life. Without my Carly. I don't know if I want to live without her. She was my everything. So yeah, let's fucking do it.'

The doctor nodded and disappeared, returning in a few minutes with two LAPD officers and took them all into a side room. Both policemen were crammed into high polyester-content clothing that looked two sizes too small. Both had big bellies and what Artie always called Meat Hands, big flabby paws that hung heavy, like dead flesh on a butcher's hook, off the end of their arms. You only saw Meat Hands in America, for some reason. It was a specific physical consequence of a specific type of upper body obesity. Maybe it was growth promoters in the meat.

As he'd assumed, they were pretty expressionless and while not actually hostile, the feeling that this was all just getting in the way of an easier life for them hung in the air. They asked if she was a drug user. Was she in a gang? Did she have a boyfriend? Did she have a girlfriend? His answer to every question was a flat no. They took a statement from him. Was that legal? Shouldn't he have a lawyer present? But Robbie didn't care about anything in this frame of mind. His world was torn apart; all the seams unpicked and ripped asunder. He saw no future.

After half an hour, they left. The doctor said the post mortem would take place in the morning and reassured Robbie that it would, almost certainly, reveal the cause of death. But that was no reassurance of anything to her dad, other than reassurance that she was no longer alive and that was the one thing he didn't need to be reminded of.

'Come on back to Malibu and stay at our house. You can't spend tonight on your own, man,' said Artie. There was no reason to stay in the hospital any longer.

'I just want to be with my Carly. I let her down.' He stared at the floor, shaking his head slowly. 'This never should have happened. It all went too far and I should've been able to stop it.'

45

Robbie nodded firmly to himself and stood up, as though coming to a conclusion about something. 'I'll just go the bathroom.'

Artie sat down to wait. He was usually pretty good in a crisis. Like many Yorkshiremen, he wasn't prone to drowning in emotion and had the ability to keep his head when everyone else was losing theirs. But also like many Yorkshiremen, comforting the bereaved wasn't an art form he'd shown any aptitude for. Grumpy he could do effortlessly; cynical he had down as an art form, and passive aggressive indignation is in the Yorkshire DNA. But none of these were of any use right now.

He felt like a smoke, but didn't have any cigarettes and the chances of buying them in a hospital were not good. You'd probably lay your hands on some heroin more easily. He had given up, anyway. Well, mostly.

How had Carly died? She had looked anaemic and listless and fainty, but you would never have thought she was on the verge of death. Not for a moment. So what can kill a young woman like her, just like that? Maybe someone *had* spiked her drink at the club and she'd had an allergic reaction? You heard about rohypnol being used by rapists to render their victims helpless. Maybe it had been something like that. Or maybe she had some undiagnosed heart issue. Maybe maybe maybe, nothing but maybes. Oh, god. What a terrible bloody thing to happen. She was such a nice young lass. He kept thinking back to the look in her eyes when Colleen had said she could get her an appointment with a holistic doctor. She'd looked relieved and happy. Trusting, even. She clearly hadn't any faith in conventional doctors, but Colleen, with her open and hip demeanour, must have given her faith that hers was the direction to go in. But now that intervention was too late.

He looked at his watch. 11.20pm. He waited another five minutes.

Where was Robbie? He'd had nearly 20 minutes to use the toilet. Artie went to look for him.

He pushed open the bathroom door and walked in. It was, like so many American public toilets, absolutely immaculate. For some reason, British toilets seem to attract people whose bowels require them to splatter every surface whilst performing a handstand, and it made life unbearably insanitary, but in America, this was not the case.

'Robbie!' he called out.

There was no-one in the toilet. It was silent. There were six stalls to the left and six to the right.

He turned right and walked to the end. No-one was there.

He walked back.

'Robbie!'

Maybe he'd gone to another toilet.

He stood there and listened. Silent. No-one was there.

That's when he noticed the thin, dark trickle.

Artie narrowed his eyes and walked to the fifth stall on the left and squatted down. It was blood.

Oh, no.

No!

He pushed at the toilet door. It was locked.

Leaning back he began kicked at it with the flat of his foot. It gave way on the third kick, but didn't open. It didn't open because the body of Robbie Saunders blocked the door. He'd sat down on the toilet and shot himself in the head with a small pistol and slumped forward, bleeding from an instantly fatal head wound.

Even before kicking the door open, Artie knew. He'd gone to meet Carly. Oh, Robbie. Oh, god.

Artie walked out of the toilet to go and report another death. This was so very wrong and he had to make it right. Right for Robbie and right for Carly.

CHAPTER 6

Death by gun is an everyday event in Los Angeles, so freakin' normal, so typical, that someone shooting themselves in the head with a concealed weapon that he carried illegally barely even registered on the news Richter scale for more than a couple of bulletins. You have to try really hard to make the news for longer, or just be famous. Dying when you're not famous is just a downer, man. And here's Bob with the weather.

So by the following day, Robbie's and Carly's deaths were each just another statistic. Another report for the police to file away. There'd be another one along in a minute.

Artie kept going over his last two meetings with Robbie. In the shop he'd been very tense, very stressed about Carly. He had obviously been worried sick about her, then to hear she'd died must have just pushed him over the top. The trouble is, when you think of someone losing their mind, you think of them acting like a crazy person in a movie. Robbie had been deeply upset but you couldn't have guessed he was suicidal. Maybe he only briefly had been, but it only takes a split second to squeeze a trigger. We all have moments, sometimes only fleeting moments, when things look so dark that maybe we'd pull that trigger, when the balance of our minds is upset by grief or worry or fear. It's such an instant and profound painkiller that anyone who has ever felt really desperate would be tempted by it as a solution.

'Don't blame yourself, Artie,' said Kaz as they ate breakfast in Mike's Diner two days later. 'There's nothing you could have done. There's no way you could have guessed that's what he'd do. I didn't know him like you knew him, but he seemed like a regular guy. A typical rock guitar store guy. Life is full of tragic shit like this every day.'

'Hmm. Maybe if I could have found the right words to say to him about Carly, but it was hard. Hard for me, anyway. I mean, his whole world was instantly shattered by her death. You can't just pat him on the head and say there there, everything will be alright. There are no words you can say to make the situation better. There is no silver lining, no way to get a positive out of it.'

She shook her head. 'How come he even had a gun on him? I mean, that's proper weird, that is. He must've left the house or wherever he was, when he got the call from Fay, seen his gun, put it in his pocket and thought, I might need this in the hospital. But no-one in their right mind would think that. It's illegal, for a start. You'd likely be talking to the police and you're in a hospital, which are not places you traditionally need guns. Makes no sense. Shows how crazy in the head he was, I reckon. He did keep getting angry, you said. Anger and guns is a bad mix.'

'Maybe he carried a gun on him at all times.'

'Maybe, aye. The store isn't in a rough part of town, though.'

Artie didn't say anything for a while and picked at some bacon and eggs. 'Coll had a good idea in bed this morning.'

Trying to lighten the mood, Kaz put her fingers in her ears and closed her eyes. 'La la la la...don't want to hear this if it involves you two sexing each other.'

He kicked her under the table. 'I wouldn't tell you about that now, would I? When do I ever tell you anything like that?'

She chewed a cheek. 'Alright, thankfully, you never do. Though sometimes I hear funny noises in the house, which is another reason for me to move out.'

Artie wasn't in the mood to joke around. 'She said that given Carly had an extreme diet, that was the first thing to look into. Had she eaten something which she'd been allergic to, or which had somehow poisoned her?'

Kaz nodded. 'Makes sense to start there. Will the hospital release details of Carly's post mortem?'

'Yeah, I think so. Things like that are a matter of public record, I think. Unless the police want it kept quiet, if they think a crime has been committed. If it just turns out she had a weak heart, or something, then I'm sure they'll make it public. They told me at the hospital it'd be done this morning. It was going to be yesterday but with him shooting himself, things got put back.'

He took out his phone and called the hospital.

'Hi. A post mortem is being done on my friend today. Carly Saunders. Will it be possible to get the results of that?'

The woman on the phone made an agreement noise. 'Uh huh. I'm aware of this. Two pm in the media room.'

'You've got a media room?'

'Uh huh.' She seemed surprised that he was surprised. But then this was LA and illness and death was all part of the entertainment business.

Kaz finished off a Danish pastry and drained her coffee cup. 'You know what I was thinking about? Carly and Fay and her friends all eat and shop at Mother Earth in Topanga. That bloke, Ben Goldman had an allergy attack there after eating that soy jerky. Taking Coll's idea that it must be something to do with her diet, is it possible that she's been eating something in there that has made her ill?'

'I suppose if we speak to Fay and find out exactly what Carly ate, see if there was something she loved which they don't eat, then maybe there's something in that. I wonder how Fay is taking this?'

Kaz did an exaggerated shrug and affected Fay's Southern Californian accent. 'Oh my god it's, like, such total bummer. Gross. Like, totally.'

He smiled a little. 'You do her a disservice. She's much more emotionally distant than that these days. Which was why what she said to me at the gig the other night was such a surprise. I always think that she's trying to give as little away about herself as possible.'

'Yeah, she is pathologically defensive.'

'After everything she went through in Las Vegas with that creepy guy, I think it's made her even more wary of people. To my knowledge she's not had a boyfriend since then.'

'If she did, she'd have kept it quiet. Even so, this is a really upsetting thing to happen to anyone. The fact she'll bottle it up and try to be cool doesn't mean she won't be really upset. She reminds me of myself at that age.'

'Getaway, two people have never been so different as you and her.'

'I was just like her, though. Full of myself. Thought I was more grown up than I was. No-one could tell me anything and every time anything bad happened I'd make out I wasn't bothered. I swallowed a lot of hurt down for a lot years. Bloody unhealthy way to live. I like Fay a lot and I see so much of me in her - only with added money, smaller breasts and a lot less fatty thighs.'

'Hmm, I like her as well. I'm not keen on kids who get on with their parents or parents' friends. It always feels weird to me. There should be a generation gap and if there isn't, the kids should create one. You need to cut your own place in life. I don't mind that she's arsey. She sodding should be. And, though I do say so myself, I think under it all, she likes us both and, on the quiet, thinks we're cool.'

'Well, we are. But if I read her right, she really doesn't like her mother. Not just as a daughter-mother thing. I mean she doesn't like her as a person. She's totally cold with her.'

'Yeah, it really bothers Coll. They're just very disconnected. But the whole mother-daughter thing is a long relationship. There's plenty of time for them to kiss and make up.'

'I didn't get on with my mother, did I? She brought me up fine and everything but I just never took to her. She annoyed me. She was a Yorkshire snob. Common as you like, but snooty. Voted Tory. Same as dad. She actually said to me once that she voted the way dad voted because men knew more about politics. I was 17 and it made me so livid. On every level she was wrong and so, like, you can't choose your parents, but you can choose not to have anything to do with them and that's what I did.'

'Now they're dead don't you feel regret about that?'

'Nah. It was hopeless, man. You can't feel what you don't feel. My parents were OK. They didn't beat me or anything, but I had no affection for them. Sorry. I don't know why I'm saying sorry, because I'm genuinely unapologetic about it.'

Artie groaned and rubbed his face, sticking a fingernail into one of the deep lines on his forehead.

'Well let's see if we can get hold of Fay. We could go to her apartment but probably better to do it on neutral territory.' He sent her a text.

Hey, Fay. Fancy a drink this lunchtime? Me and Kaz will be in Chick's Bar on Montana at noon. Would love to see you. Also need to talk about Carly.'

He read it out to Kaz.

'Haven't been in Chick's for ages,' she said. 'He makes the best bloody Long Island Iced Teas this side of Huddersfield. So are we dealing with all of this stress by persistent drinking, broken up only by consumption of fried meat? I bloody hope so.'

'Aye, why break the habit of a lifetime now? We've no work in the diary for a few days. I've got to compile the book, but I don't feel like sitting in the house to do it.'

'Well, bugger it, let's just have a couple of days off. It'll give me a chance to find a flat, if nothing else.'

'I'd like to get to the bottom of Carly's death. I feel like I owe it to Robbie.'

She shook her head. 'You don't owe him, Artie. I'm not saying don't do anything, but don't go feeling like you owe him. He lost his mind and did something terrible. You were only there because you wanted to help him in some way.'

'Yeah. Maybe. Come on, let's go over to Chick's now. Get an early shot of something in our bloodstream.'

She looked at her watch. '10.45am. Shit me, Artie. That's impressive ambition. When I first started working with you in 1999, we often started the day with a Bloody Mary, remember? We'd be shit-faced by noon, coked-up sober by tea time, ready to go out on the lash.' She let out a deep sigh. 'Oh, those were glory days.' She ruffled her hair and yawned. 'Exhausting, mind. Not sure I could do it now. I'd need a good nap at some point.'

'So you'll be on the mineral water at Chick's, will you?'

She looked righteously indignant in the way only someone from West Yorkshire can. 'Will I bollocks.'

He drove back into the city, hanging a left on the palm tree-lined, up-scale Montana Avenue. This was the sort of area of LA where you could buy a diamond collar for your cat for $100,000, a wooden carving of a vagina, or have colonic irrigation performed with snake piss, done by a Native American man dressed as Cher. Basically, any service or product you could imagine was somewhere behind the expensive doorways of Montana Avenue.

'I once went back to a woman's house down here - there, that one on the left...' she pointed to a big stucco house which had to be worth several million '...she was really weird.'

'In a good way, or a bad way?'

'The latter. She wanted to push vegetables into me and then make soup with them afterwards. Seriously, she did.'

Artie laughed. 'When you say "into you"...I take it you mean your lady cave.'

'Front door or back door - she wasn't fussy. I was very high at the time and I'd have been OK with it if it wasn't for the soup thing. Seemed un-hygienic. When I declined and asked if we couldn't just have normal les-bian sex, she went crazy and threatened to cut me up and put me in the trash can. Harsh, that, I thought.'

'Maybe she was just very hungry. Low blood sugar can drive you into a murderous rage. She just needed your special flavour of vegetable soup very badly. I tell you what, though, it's the same the world over. Behind the posh doors, they're all so bored of themselves and their lives that they have to invent new perversions to occupy themselves through another day of wealth and luxury. The rest of us are too busy working to push an aubergine up our arses...'

'...or put a marrow in our fanny, as the case may be. God, that'd make your eyes water.'

'At least it wasn't in the Edgewater Inn, rock 'n' roll tradition of being a red snapper.'

'Red snapper? I'm blonde, not ginger, aren't I?' She punched him playfully on the shoulder and pointed at a space to park in. Artie threw the pickup into it, looking at his watch as he did so; 11.10am. 'The sun is definitely over the yard arm,' he said, pointing at the azure blue sky and the burning heat which would push the temperatures into the 80s again, probably into the 90s in the Valley.

Chick's bar was a bit of an anomaly for the locale. It had been there in one form or another since 1962. Chick, or Chris Chiquito to give him his proper name, had owned it since 1982. Now in his mid 60s, he looked a bit like a Mexican bandit from a 60s spaghetti western, but with a huge belly. With long silver hair and goatee beard, he was one of those guys who ran a business which paid his bills and let him save a bit, but was never an empire builder. Never wanted to have a chain. Never wanted to do anything except make a living from one bar. And that's what he did and he loved it. Lack of ambition isn't always the bad thing it's painted to be by wealth-obsessed capitalism.

It had a regular rocker clientele for one reason and one reason only: the jukebox. And it was still a proper jukebox full of 120 vinyl singles which Chick took great care and pleasure in changing every month himself, stocking it from his own collection. It was almost certainly the only place in the city and indeed, in the whole of America where you could listen to the Peanut Butter Conspiracy's 1966 debut single, 'It's a Happening Thing'.

Kaz pushed open the door and walked into the cool air-conditioned bar. The smell of beer and hot lard from the kitchen was wonderful. Artie sucked it in as he followed her. Jefferson Starship's 'Jane' was playing. A nice bit of AOR in the morning. Yeah, this was the sort of place he could get his head around. This was where he'd lived his life - in places like this, doing this, to music like this. If anything was his natural environment, this was it. Excited, he grabbed Kaz around the waist and kissed her neck, happy to be here with her.

Sensing his mood, she laughed, turned and pecked him on the cheek, affectionately. 'Yeah, this is who we are, eh. What are you drinking?' said Kaz, taking out a roll of notes and hopping up onto a bar stool.

'Tequila and ice, Kaz. Cheers.'

She whistled. 'Old school, man. I'll join you. Here he is...hey, Chick...' She leaned over the bar and held out her hand. He beamed at her.

'Well, if it ain't Chick's favourite Chick-a-dee.' He kissed her hand.
'And Artie Taylor, too - we are blessed with rock royalty. Ha ha.'

Artie shook his hand in a firm grip. 'Seems ages since we've been in.'

'Where you been then, man?'

'We were on the road with Springsteen: official tour photographer. I'm doing a book about it.'

'Oh, man, I love Bruce, such a cool guy. You so big time, buddy. I love it.' He beamed at Artie.

'I have never lit a more good-looking dude in his 60s, than Bruce,' said Kaz. 'Chick, man, he was just awesome. Funny and in great shape, too. All muscle.'

'He's so cool. So what can I get for you two this fine morning?'

'Tequila man, on the rocks,' said Kaz.

'Two cactus juice coming up, baby. Yeah. Believe it!'

He grabbed a bottle of Cuervo Gold and poured two big drinks, throwing in a handful of ice. He didn't do measures, he just poured the bottle. Kaz gave him a 20 dollar bill. He took it, kissed it and gave it back to her. 'On the house, my beautiful baby girl.' He said it with a smile and a wave and went to the other end of the bar to serve someone.

'Cheers, gorgeous,' said Kaz, grinning at him.

'It's busy for this time of day,' said Artie, looking around the bar.

'Any time is the right time for tequila,' said Kaz and handed him the glass. 'Here's to Robbie and Carly, eh?'

Artie raised the glass up into the air and looked to the skies. 'Cheers, guitar man.'

'And here's to us, as well,' said Kaz.

He clinked glasses again. 'Yeah, here's to us.'

Chick returned and wiped the bar with a towel.

'Did you hear about Robbie Saunders, man?' said Artie. 'You knew him, right? Runs the Robbie S guitar shop in Santa Monica.'

'Oh, yeah, he come in here, sometime. I ain't heard nuthin'.'

Artie explained what had happened. Chick stood there, mouth open.

'No way, man. He was a good guy. Fuckin' guns, man. Ain't nuthin' good about guns. I hate 'em. You get a crazy idea and boom, you're gone, man.' He shook his head sorrowfully. 'And I remember little Carly, too, man. This sort of shit makes me think the world ain't no good, man. How come she died?'

'We don't know yet. Hoping to find out this afternoon at the hospital. They're doing a post mortem.'

Chick walked away with a shake of the head.

The tequila tasted good and the buzz it put into Artie was even better, but it didn't take away the sight of Robbie slumped on that toilet with a bloody hole in his head. That'd haunt him for a long time and he knew he couldn't just drink it off his mind; only making it right for Robbie would have a chance of wiping it away.

As he sipped at the icy spirit his phone rang. He didn't recognise the number.

'Hello?'

'Is that Artie Taylor?' said a male voice.

'Yup.'

'Artie, it's Ben Goldman. You helped me the other day, when I had an allergic reaction.'

Kaz looked at him with her watery blue eyes and asked him who it was. He mimed Ben Goldman's name. She looked surprised.

'Hello, Ben. You don't need us to come and rescue you again, do you?'

'Thankfully, no. I'll tell you why I'm calling. I just heard about the death of a girl called Carly Saunders who was a friend of your wife's daughter, Fay.'

Artie sat upright and squinted into the middle distance. 'Yeah?'

'It's just that I knew Carly. We dated for a while. We used to eat together at Mother Earth. We fell out because I told her that her diet was making her ill. Anyway, I think it's weird that she died.'

'When did you tell her that?'

'Only a few weeks ago. She said it was over between us and...well...it was because she was getting sick from being vegan and that I'd been pointing this out to her. She didn't want to change. But that store is evil, Artie. It poisoned me and it poisoned Carly.'

Artie listened to him, but for some reason, wasn't sure if he believed him.

'And why call me about it, Ben?' he said, with suspicion in his voice. Also, he must have looked him up to know that Fay's mother was his wife. Maybe nothing unusual in that. He looked people up all the time.

Ben didn't reply immediately, suggesting that there was something he was unwilling or unable to say. Instead, he went quiet.

'Ben? Are you there?'

'Sorry.' He made a noise in his throat. It sounded a bit like he'd been crying. There was a phlegmy tone to his voice. 'Could we meet up, Artie? I want your help to investigate Mother Earth. I'm sure something bad has been going on there. Carly ate there all the time. Can we meet up there so I can go over what I'd like to do? It won't take long.'

Artie weighed up what to do. 'OK, Ben. I'd like to know what happened to Carly, too.'

'Are you free now?'

'I can be.'

'So, see you there in about 30 minutes?'

'OK, Ben.'

He hung up and looked up at Kaz. 'Now, there's some weird shit. Drink up, we're off.'

'What about meeting Fay?'

'She's not texted back yet, so I'll just tell her where we're going,' he said, tapping at his phone. 'Right, let's go and deal with Goldman. I've got the feeling he's some shade of weird.'

CHAPTER 7

Pulling into Mother Earth's parking lot, he took the same space as last time. They walked to the restaurant, which was set to one side of the main part of the store. Typical for a wholefood, vegan place, it was all wooden tables, benches and chalkboards and staffed by slim young people dressed in ecru t-shirts and jeans.

'What do you think the nicest thing to eat here would be?' said Artie, as they walked in.

'The tables,' said Kaz, spotting Ben Goldman in the corner. He stood up and gave them a little gesture of acknowledgement.

He was a good looking young man, with soft hazel eyes, long eyelashes, delicate features and shapely pink lips. His soft, curly, light-brown mop of hair fell just over his ears in a retro fashion, making him look a bit like a late-60s pop star.

Artie shook his hand, then Kaz. He had a surprisingly strong grip.

'Thanks for meeting me so quickly,' he said. 'Can I get you anything?'

'They don't sell tequila here, do they? Joke. No, we're OK, thanks,' said Artie.

Ben gave them a non-smiling polite smile. 'OK, well, I won't take up much of your time, I promise. There's no reason why you should know this but my family are...'

'...music industry lawyers. My wife recognised your name - she mixes in those circles, or used to, anyway.'

'She's right. It's not something I admit to normally because of their awful reputation.' He looked away and down at the floor, eyes narrowing. 'I just can't bear them. They're bullies. What they do – it's abusive. They've always been like that. But I am cut from different cloth, I assure you. I don't want that sort of life. I never have and never will.'

'Colleen said that you were following them into the business,' said Artie.

'In a way I am, but I'm not interested in who does or doesn't own a licence to print a logo on a t-shirt and other merchandise - that's all ephemeral bullshit, verging on immoral. I'm interested in environmental and ethical issues.' He paused to look around, a little conspiratorially. Did he think he was being listened to? 'You see, that soy jerky is made by a company called Green on Green, based in San Francisco. They make all sorts of vegan products, mostly from soy. Mother Earth sells the whole Green on Green range. Now, Carly was a big fan of that brand.' He picked up the menu and pointed to the list of entrees, all of which were vegan versions of meat dishes - meat loaf, 'beef' burgers, sausages, something called Tofurky. 'See this tuna gluten-free pasta melt, that was one of her favourites. She ate it here all the time and she bought frozen packs of it to microwave at home. It's all made by Green on Green.'

'This might be a bit controversial, but isn't tuna made out of fish,' said Artie, 'and thus, not vegetarian?'

'It's a Green on Green vegan product, made from TVP - textured vegetable protein and flavoured to make it taste like tuna with mayo through it. It's...well...an acquired taste.'

'That's shocking, that is,' said Kaz, looking at the menu with a downturned mouth. 'This is all factory-made garbage. It's not real food. It's totally contrived. It says "All Natural" in their tag line here. But that's not true. It's not natural if you have to make it in a factory and then flavour it. A steak cut from a cow that stood in a field eating grass, that's natural.'

Ben nervously tapped at his lips with the tips of his fingers, his eyes flicked from side to side, as though being distracted by something. 'Well, yes, you're right in the most commonsensical way. But then, *natural* is a slippery word. What does it really mean? What are the legal obligations to comply with the term "natural"? It's a very grey area and the soy industry loves to exploit that, in fact, all food processing does. It's marketed as super healthy, of course.'

'But you eat it,' said Kaz. 'You ate that jerky garbage.'

That seemed to embarrass, or possibly annoy him. He flushed a little.

'Hmm. Well, I have, yes. But not like Carly did.' He produced a Chromebook from his bag and opened it up. 'As I said, I'm interested in ethical and environmental issues and I've invented a role for myself in the company, looking into various fraudulent and...err...what you Brits call, dodgy, activities. Foremost in this is veggie foods - the claims they make and the practices used in production.' He swung the laptop around so they could see a pdf of various Venn diagrams.

'Before we look at this, Ben, can you tell me why you're showing it to me? I mean, OK, we saved your life here and I'm pleased we could. But, speaking frankly, the politics of the vegetarian processed-food industry means the square root of fuck all to both of us. We're rock 'n' roll people and whatever your fight is, it's not our fight,' said Artie.

'I understand that. But as I said on the phone, I also know that Carly was a friend of your wife's daughter, Fay. And once I knew that it felt like a bit of kismet that you'd saved my life.'

'Don't take this the wrong way, Ben. But I don't like people knowing who we are, what we do or who we're related to,' said Kaz, jabbing her finger at him. 'It's very bloody intrusive and you've no fuckin' right to...'

'...haven't I? What do you mean? A quick Google search revealed who you both were, who Artie is married to. He's a world-famous photographer and you're famous as his make-up and lighting person. It's public knowledge. All it took was research.' His tone was a little indignant and defensive and the anxious, manic look that had been in his eyes when he collapsed, reappeared. It was a little disconcerting. Artie held the flat of his hand up to both of them.

'OK, kids, let's not fall out.'

'I know you might feel weird because I'm a Goldman, but really, I'm one of the good guys. I'm not my father and mother's son,' said Ben Goldman.

'OK. I believe you. But so what? Why are you telling us this?'

'It's my belief that Green on Green is selling contaminated foods. I think their production methods are lax, hence why I ate peanut in their soy jerky. I came here specifically to test the efficacy of what they were selling. There were reports of allergy attacks involving their products in the LA *Times*. I'd bought a few things and was going to have them checked out. I made the mistake, because I was hungry, of eating the strip of soy jerky as I was checking out.'

He spoke in a machine-gun style, rattling words out with the precision of a lawyer deconstructing the defence's case. Was he some flavour of autistic? He was certainly intense, especially when challenged. He'd countered Kaz's words instantly and with a rapier-like attack.

Artie narrowed his eyes. 'So you deliberately ate something you knew could kill you?'

'Well, no I didn't. I mean, I always have my adrenalin pen ready if I have a reaction but I didn't know I would react to the jerky. But I'm so sensitive to peanuts that it hit me really quickly, I couldn't get my breath, I panicked, freaked out and dropped my pen and that was when you arrived. I mean, I was really terrified. I'd never experienced a reaction so extreme and so fast, like that. It went totally nuclear on me.'

'The store manager found your pen later,' said Artie.

'Did she? Where was it?'

'By the door. She called me about it.'

He smiled on hearing that. In fact, he just gave off a very odd vibe altogether. 'Oh, right. But we can't allow people to get sick because of sloppy business practices. Green on Green and this place needs taking on. They killed Carly and nearly killed me.' He jabbed his right index finger into the table to make his point.

'And her dad, Robbie shot himself in the head as a result,' said Artie.

Ben clearly knew this already, as he just nodded. But he didn't seem concerned about that at all.

Artie ran an index finger up and down the bridge of his nose and then pushed some strands of hair behind his ears. For some reason, he thought it best not to tell Ben about the post mortem results coming out. In fact he felt, by gut instinct, that he didn't want to tell him much about almost anything.

'So you think that Carly was ill because of what she ate here?' said Kaz.

'Yes.'

'With all due respect, Ben, that *has* to be bollocks,' said Kaz, folding her arms across her chest like a Yorkshire matriarch. 'If there was some sort of contamination in their food, all these people here would be ill as well, and looking at them, they don't look that ill. Fay's been eating here for a few months and she's in great health. You can't selectively poison someone with food that is sold to whoever picks it off the shelf. It's everyone who buys it or no-one.'

Ben just ignored her, like she'd not even spoken. 'I'm going to get some products tested and we shall see what we shall see.'

Artie's phone vibrated with a text. It was from Fay. '*Will be with you in 5 minutes.*'

'Have you reported the fact that the soy jerky was contaminated by peanuts to the city health board?' said Artie.

Goldman shook his head. 'Not yet. I will though, as part of my overall case.'

There was something not right about Ben Goldman, but Artie couldn't quite put his finger on what it was. He was pretending to be transparent but somehow felt evasive and he had an odd air about him. He stared at him with an intensity that you sometimes saw in people who were speeding, a look so powerful that it could burn holes in paper. But Ben wasn't speeding. He could tell that much. Maybe he was hyped up on something else, maybe one of the huge amount of legal highs that you could now get.

'Are you actually a lawyer, Ben?' said Artie.

'Yeah. UCLA. Graduated last year.'

'And so what's the outcome that you want to get from this investigation?'

'To bring this place down and the industry that supplies it. When I heard of Carly's death...'

There were footsteps behind Artie and Kaz.

'Err...like, what's this weirdo jerk doing here?' said a familiar voice.

They turned to see Fay in long black t-shirt, leggings and baseball boots, her long, dark hair tied back, hands on hips, doing her best look of stroppy indignation.

'Hi, Fay. You got here quick. Do you two know each other?' said Artie, pointing from one to the other.

Ben got to his feet immediately. 'I'd better be going. Thanks for your help, Artie. I'll be in touch.'

'I haven't been any help. I still don't really know why you asked us here. Ben...why are you going now?'

He gave them a terse smile, glanced at Fay and made his exit. 'I'll be in touch when I have more info. Thanks again.'

And with that he strode away, Fay's sharp eyes and haughty expression burning into the back of his head.

Kaz looked at Artie, he looked back at her, then at Fay, and made an open hands gesture to get her to explain. She pulled out a chair with an exaggerated huffy sigh and sat down.

'He's Ben Goldman. Carly used to date him. He's like, a totally creepy weirdo. She broke up with him a few weeks ago and he couldn't accept it and got all stalky. Just wouldn't leave her alone. Always calling and texting and waiting for her outside her apartment. Why was he here? How do you even know him?'

Artie explained about the allergy attack.

'Are you *sure* he didn't just fake it?' She threw the typical Southern Californian emphasis on the word *sure* and left her mouth open a little to express her cynicism.

'Not unless, at will, he can break out in red blotches while he puffs up and can't breathe. I've seen allergy attacks before and he definitely had one,' said Artie.

Fay was unimpressed. 'What*ever*.' She said it in the typical SoCal way with the emphasis on the second syllable. A waitress came over and Fay ordered some mint tea for them. She leaned on the table with her elbows. 'He's the kind of guy who might just want to meet people who knew Carly, almost like he's talking to her by proxy. Seriously. He might be right about this place, though. It wouldn't surprise me if it was corrupt from top to bottom. You can sell vegans anything as long as you put a picture of a cat on it, or some flowers. Sappy assholes.'

'Yeah, but you and your friends eat here a lot. So how come you didn't get ill?' said Kaz.

Fay looked from side to side, and let her eyelids fall in a slow, heavy blink. 'You can't tell anyone what I'm about to tell you. OK? But...' she let out her 'I'm so weary with the world' sigh '...I'm such a phoney, OK?'

'I don't get you,' said Artie.

But Kaz understood right away. 'She's been faking being a vegan, haven't you, luv?'

'Uh huh. And don't call me luv. I *hate* that particular British affectation...'

'...it's not a British thing, it's a Northern thing,' protested Kaz.

'Yeah, what*ever*. Just, like, don't,' said Fay, dismissively, pushing the flat of her hand away from herself, as though to expunge the word from the air. Artie laughed a little. She was, what his old mother would have called, 'a proper little madam' and he couldn't help but like it.

'I mean, I didn't start out to be, y'know, fake...but good grief, have you ever tried to be vegan? It is barfo profundo, man.' She made a vomiting noise. 'All you do is eat carbs. Oh, my god, my belly was out to here with gas and I put on weight and it was gross. I mean, man, I like a nut or two, but I don't wanna live off the freakin' things. And beans? Jeez, I nearly gassed myself. Gross.'

They both laughed at that and even Fay managed to make a small smile at her own joke.

'So you didn't eat here much, then?'

'I did the sensible thing and I ate cake and coffee. I tried one of those tuna melts - it was liked eating tangy wet cardboard. I don't how Carly kept it down. Urgh. Gag me with a spoon.'

Artie laughed at her expression again and said, 'So then you'd go home and make yourself roast chicken?'

'Uh huh. And I wasn't the only one. OK, I'm a total phoney. But Carly and Helen were serious. They were soy everything and Helen isn't well and Carly isn't alive. It can't be a coincidence. It just can't.'

'Well, that's what Ben wants to find out about,' said Artie. 'That's not that weird, even if it is motivated by his crush on Carly.'

Fay was able to make incredibly cynical expressions just by reshaping her mouth a little, or pulling her chin in. 'Is it? Or is he doing something else and using that as a cover? I told you guys, he's creepy and his parents, like, they put the evil in devil, according to mom.'

'How ill is this girl, Helen?' asked Kaz.

'Not as bad as Carly was. She's gone to the doctor today for tests. Carly just collapsing like that scared the crap out of her.'

'If you don't mind me saying so, you don't seem very upset that Carly is dead, Fay,' said Kaz. 'I mean, you've handled it all very coolly, even calling up Robbie when she collapsed.'

She threw a shocked expression at them. 'What? You're kidding me. I'm devastated - but I almost, almost, almost expected it. She went downhill fast and I told her time and again to give up being vegan as it didn't suit her, but she wouldn't. She said she'd rather be dead than have animals killed to keep her alive. Well, she got her wish, the silly girl.' She scowled contemptuously and sipped at her tea.

She was a hard-faced young woman, determined to keep her emotions private, but there was sorrow in her voice, all the same.

'You were old friends with her dad, weren't you?' she said, after a pause.

'Yeah, I'd known him over 20 years, on and off. He was a good guy.'

'Can I ask you what happened when he shot himself?'

Artie told her everything. She sat and listened, her face emotionally neutral.

'I only met him in the store, but he seemed just a solid kinda guy. Very, uh...alpha male...the sort of typical older rock guy, that mom knows sooo many of.' She raised her eyebrows in a vaguely disapproving expression.

'Yeah, well, that's a good description of him,' said Kaz.

Fay closed her eyes for moment and then slowly opened them again. 'So what happens now?'

Artie looked at his watch. 'The results of Carly's post mortem will be known soon. We're going up to the hospital to get hold of them. We can't make a decision on anything until we have that. It may turn out she had, I don't know, liver cancer or something and that the food was nothing to do with it.'

'Cool. Can I come with you?'

'Yeah, of course.'

Fay finished her tea.

'She was a nice girl, Carly. I knew her right through school. I can't bear that she's gone. And if someone is responsible for making her sick then I want them fucking dealt with.' She said it with quiet determination.

'Well, she said how much she liked you, when we last met her. She said you were a great girl,' said Artie.

That almost cracked Fay's permafrost. Her bottom lip quivered and she bit down hard on it, but still couldn't stop a thin veneer of tears varnishing her eyes.

'Come on, kid. Let's get out of this Nazi health club,' said Kaz, getting up.

There are moments in our lives when we touch souls with people. When we transcend the work-a-day nature of existence and commune on a higher level. It's innate and instinctual and you can't stop it happening, even if you wanted to. It's usually fleeting and manifests itself with a unique feeling of warmth and a special swirl of connected emotion. We can't grasp it, in the same way we can't grasp steam, but it is no less real. It comes and it goes. Too intense and emotionally overwhelming for us to endure for long, it's one of those special aspects of our peculiar existence. And as Fay got to her feet, Artie felt it, an overwhelming empathy for her, so he took her in his arms and hugged her to him. She didn't resist, and for a kid defined by her cold independence, that was perhaps extraordinary. She buried her face into his neck and seemed to treat his embrace as though it was fuel. He could feel her warm breath on his neck, still maintaining some degree of self-control, she let out a single dry sob. Sometimes a young person needs an older person to cling to. This was one of those moments.

It was soon over. Fay cleared her throat, coming back to herself, just quietly saying, 'Thank you.'

In a state which specialises in producing overly confessional, overly emotional, but shallow people, Fay had perhaps an English quality to her character; a reserved, dignified aspect. Not for the first time, Artie found himself admiring her.

CHAPTER 8

They stood in a small room in the hospital with a press man, and waited.

'Did you know the deceased? I'm Danny Blind from the LA *Times*. It's spelled Blind but pronounced Blint. It's Dutch.' He smiled.

'Hey, man, I'm Artie Taylor, it's spelt Taylor and pronounced Taylor,' he said holding out his hand to the journalist, who was a tall man with swept-back blonde hair and skin the colour of a caramel-dipped peach. 'Yeah, I knew her dad well and I knew Carly since she was little.'

'She was a good friend of mine, too,' said Fay.

'I heard that she just collapsed. Is that right?'

Fay nodded. 'We thought she'd fainted. But it was worse than that, obviously.'

As she spoke, a man in a white coat came into the room holding some paper. Did they have to wear white coats? Was it a required uniform or just a culturally expected thing? All you had to do to get taken for a doctor in a hospital, was to wear a white coat. The white coat was a free pass.

Artie looked around, expecting more people to be in the press room, a room where they often did live news broadcasts when there was a celebrity being treated or if a high-profile murder victim had been brought in. Amazing that in LA, as though imitating the movies, hospitals had media rooms. No need for it today, though. Carly wasn't famous. She was just a nice girl. A dead nice girl.

The man sat down behind a desk and looked across at the four of them standing there and then read from the paper. It was all very formal. Initially, it was all dates and times and who had done the post mortem, before he got onto the results. Trouble was, it was all done in medical and biological terminology, reading out various blood test results and analysis of bodily fluids.

Artie put his hand up, like he was in class. 'Excuse me, doc. This isn't any good to us. I failed my CSE biology in 1977, you might as well be talking in Latin. Can you just sum up what Carly died of, so we can understand? I'm sure Danny here would appreciate that, as well.' The journalist put his thumb up at Artie and nodded.

The doctor, a man in his 60s, with thin white hair, raised his eyebrows. 'I shall release the full results to you by email if you need them.' He drummed his fingers on the desk and cleared his throat. 'In essence, it was renal failure which finally killed this young woman, though, frankly, she was very unwell and could have been...taken...as it were...by any number of fatal conditions. Her lungs were not functioning properly and she likely had high blood pressure for some time.'

'Her kidneys failed?' said Kaz.

'Yes. Can you tell me if she had poor co-ordination in recent weeks?'

'She was clumsy, if that's what you mean,' said Fay. 'She would like, walk into a door frame, like she missed the door. Stuff like that. She fainted a few times and was weak, in general.'

The doctor made a note, nodding as he did so. 'Did she find lights too bright?'

'Well she often wore sunglasses,' said Artie, 'didn't she, Fay?'

'Yeah, but I never thought anything of that. I thought she was just trying to be cool.'

'So what caused her to be like this?' said Artie. 'Was it kidney disease?'

The doctor put a pen back in his top pocket and looked at him squarely. 'Mercury poisoning caused it. For that reason, I will have refer this to the public health people and to the police.'

'What? How do you get poisoned by mercury, exactly?' said Danny Blind.

'Good question. Did she eat a lot of fish?' said the doctor.

'She was a vegan. She didn't eat any fish and no, she wasn't eating it secretly. She was deadly serious about her diet choice,' said Fay.

'Mercury poisoning from fish isn't unknown, though is still quite rare in this degree. From any other source it is, outside of some industrial processes, unheard of.'

'Did it happen quickly, or over long time?' said Danny Blind.

'Oh, this has been a slow but steady process, ingesting tiny amounts of mercury, probably most days, until the toxicity finally began to break down the workings of her internal organs. Her kidneys went first. Poor young lady.'

'She had been obviously ill for about six months,' said Fay.

'And when did she become a vegan?'

'About 18 months ago, she turned all of our group of friends on to it. Well...sort of. She ate a lot of vegan meals...soy protein, soy milk, all that sort of thing, along with veggies. She got a lot of stuff from the Mother Earth store. If her food poisoned her, then she will have bought most of it there.'

The doctor stood up. 'OK, well, the relevant authorities will investigate and make a judgment. I'm just a humble doctor.'

He left the room. Artie turned to Danny Blind. 'Have you heard of any other cases like this recently?'

'I've not heard of mercury poisoning before, no.'

'But there are tens of thousands of vegetarians and vegans in this city and millions in California, there'd have been a lot of deaths similar to Carly's if there was widespread contamination of foods in places like Mother Earth,' said Kaz. 'Fay, you said your other friend Helen was unwell. Does she have similar symptoms?'

'She's nowhere near as bad or extreme. She just looks like she has the flu. But she and Carly stopped eating meat at the same time. I'm going to text her and tell her what killed Carly. Surely heavy metal poisoning will show up in her blood tests.'

'Good idea,' said Artie.

Danny Blind gave Artie his card. 'Call me if you find out anything else. We can't have kids dying like this. It's a damn outrage. Someone will have to pay for this. I'm interested in diet and food, anyway. I'll do some digging into the vegan processed food industry, the people behind Mother Earth and Green on Green, the makers of this soy jerky crap.'

'Sure. If you hear anything, let me know.' He gave Danny one of his own cards in return.

'I will. Nice to have met you all.' He made his exit.

'We've got to go back to Mother Earth and get hold of some more of the soy foods they sell and get it tested for mercury,' said Fay. 'I'll pay.' She jutted out her jaw and jabbed a finger in midair. 'I tell you this - if they've been selling dirty shit, I'll burn that fucking place down for what they've done to Carly. They come on like they're so holy. Like those TV evangelists going on about people being immoral and then they get found with a hooker. The ones who shout loudest are always the most corrupt. You just see.'

They went back to the store in Topanga, picked up a selection of nine vegan products, all made by Green on Green. The soy jerky had been removed from sale. As Fay paid for them, Artie looked up a testing lab. There was one just off Wilshire, so they headed there. After filling out a lot of forms, he handed over the bag of nine items, and then, finding the soy jerky packet he'd picked up at Robbie's office still in his top pocket, added that in, too. 'Can you make sure you test everything that says "peanut free" for peanuts, please?' said Artie, tapping it. Fay handed over her unlimited-credit black Amex for the tests. Afterwards the three of them stood in the parking lot in the warm late afternoon.

'Do you guys want to come back to my apartment for a cup of tea or something?' said Fay, rolling a fine silver bangle around her bony wrist, in just the same way as her mother did. She had never asked them to do that before. It was far too friendly. Because of that, it would have seemed wrong to refuse, even though Artie really wanted strong drink and not just tea.

Her apartment on Ocean Way in Santa Monica looked across the beach and out to sea. It was more like an upmarket hotel than a block of flats, with its own coffee shop and gym. As Fay unlocked the door to the one-bedroomed apartment and pushed open the door, the scent of fresh apples and lemon greeted them. Artie stood and looked around. Christ, when he was her age, he had a crummy, damp student flat. This was really well to do. The living room faced out across the road, to the blue ocean in the distance. A large TV hung on the wall and opposite was a long cream-coloured chenille sofa. Moody impressionist pictures hung on the walls. It was modern but not fashionably so and it was neat and tidy, the way a hotel room is when you first check in.

'Did you decorate this yourself, Fay?' said Artie. 'It's very smart.'

'Err...no. It came like this. I'm not interested in buying shit to put on a table or hang on the wall. Sorry, but it just doesn't interest me. The view is more beautiful than anything I could buy.' She went through to a small kitchen.

'Have you any booze?' said Kaz, following her in.

Fay turned around. 'Alcohol? No. Sorry, I don't drink here. In fact, I don't really drink anymore. Makes me feel dizzy. I've got some grass somewhere, if you want a smoke. I haven't used that for a while. Sorry, I'm not my mother's daughter, these days. No booze, no sex or drugs, and only occasional rock 'n' roll. We're a boring generation, the millennials. I know mom thinks I'm going off the rails - but that's just because I feed her misinformation, just to mess with her head. I make out that I'm party-ing all the time and I'm doing this and that. But I'm not. Mostly, I'm sit-ting here reading.'

'Are you typical, though?' said Kaz, doubtfully.

'Probably not. I have a lot of, let's say, unusual friends. They're all the children of rich people, or famous people, or both. Fuckups with a whole team of step-parents and half-siblings. It's quite sick.' She made the "k" in *sick* really click in the back of her throat.

She boiled the kettle and plucked some green tea bags from a box. Artie's heart sank. Colleen drank green tea, but he couldn't get with it, at all. It was just too weak and felt sort of healthy, which he was traditionally against.

'Carly wasn't like that, though. She was a regular person, wasn't she?' he said.

Fay sighed. 'Yeah, she was. Well, she only had her dad. She was close to him. But she was quite grounded - except for her vegan thing, anyway. So sad.' She sighed again. 'Say that some of those things we just bought turn out to have traces of mercury in them. What do we do then? Do we go to the police?'

'We'd have to,' said Kaz. 'It means one of two things: either the production was contaminated by accident, or someone is doing it on purpose. Either way, it's got to be stopped. Can we agree on something, though?'

'What's that, Kaz?' said Fay.

'That we say nothing about this to Ben Goldman. As far as he's concerned we know nothing about nothing. I just didn't like the vibe he gave off.'

Artie nodded in agreement.

'Like, totally,' said Fay, drawing an imaginary zip across her lips. 'A pity, really, 'cos that guy is cute. He's a pretty boy. But he gives off that...' she shuddered '...weird vibe. What is that, Kaz?'

'Oh, I think it's your subconscious telling you something. We've all got that inner alarm that some men trigger. Trouble is, some women find the guys that set off those alarms exciting. Silly cows.'

They took the tea back into the living room. It was such a stunning view of the yellow beach and blue ocean. Colleen's house, being right on the beach, had a less panoramic aspect to it. This was like looking at a wide-screen TV.

'It must be great living here, you know,' said Kaz. 'I'm going to get a flat in Santa Monica soon. I like being down here.'

'Oh. Where?' said Fay, with a surprised look.

'Near Third Street Prom is what I'm aiming for.'

'Cool. Maybe we could go out sometimes, when you get somewhere? You can teach me how to drink.'

'Ha ha...that could get messy but yeah, OK, I'd like that,' said Kaz, with a flick of her eyes to Artie. Fay was being nice, open and approachable. In short, the opposite of normal.

'It is nice here. Well, obviously. But I can only live here because of mom's money and I can't go on living off that for ever. It's not right. She's my sugar daddy...or mommy, as the case maybe and I've realised that is what's wrong with my life. I'm just drifting on the sea of her money, I've got to get a job and find my own way in life.'

Artie grinned at Kaz. 'She's a sugar mama to all of us,' he said.

'Yeah, I definitely have to get a job,' said Fay, feet up on the low wooden table.

'What would you like to do?' said Artie.

Fay did her big shrug. 'I'm still working that out. Maybe I should go to college. I finished high school and couldn't wait to get out, even though I had all the grades I needed to go to a university, but you can't achieve much without a degree.'

'I don't actually know what you're interested in, Fay,' said Kaz, in her typically bluff Leeds way.

'No, well, you and me both,' she said, almost under her breath. 'Carly dying makes me realise that life can just end, like that. I don't want drift any more, no more hanging out at the Rainbow with the kids of rock stars and film people. It's just so shallow. I'm not an LA airhead and it's time I started trying to achieve something.'

'I think that's great,' said Artie, but Fay shook her head, dismissively.

'Don't say that. It's just a normal thing to do - everywhere except among LA's rich kids, anyway. I don't want congratulating for doing something that should be a normal thing to do.'

Kaz and Artie raised their eyebrows at each other.

'Aye, you're right,' said Kaz. 'There's nowt worse in this town than the rich kids who think they're getting all down with the working class, just because they donate designer clothes to charity stores or serve soup to the homeless once a year at Christmas.'

Fay paused and sipped at her tea from a white china mug. 'Do you get used to people dying, as you get older?'

Artie scratched at his stubble. 'You start to expect it more, but you don't get used to it. When it happens it's still shocking, unless someone is 87 or something. You just draw on your experience to deal with it. I'm upset by Robbie's suicide...'

'...me, too. He was a nice man. He loved Carly...'

'...and seeing him there, well, it wasn't nice. But life's taught me that you can dwell all you like on stuff, but it doesn't change the reality. It's shit, but it's still how it is. You've got one choice and one choice only and that's to just keep going. Bad shit has always happened and it always will.'

'Also life is about having a good time and having a laugh,' said Kaz. 'That's how I see it. So letting things depress you, even tragic, terrible things, just wastes valuable potential good times. Doesn't mean you don't care, but you can't get weighed down it by it all. Like you say, it could all end at any moment with a bullet in your head, especially in this city.' She pointed two fingers at her head, as though discharging a pistol.

Fay didn't say anything, but nodded.

Artie finished the piss-weak green tea. How long did they stay with her for? Did she need their support? Would she just sit here on her own? Didn't she need company?

'Do you want to come to your mother's house tonight? Rather than being on your own,' said Artie.

'No. I'm fine.' She sat upright. 'I'm going to look into applying for some jobs and then I'm going to bed early.'

'Why don't you get some mates around to keep you company?' said Kaz.

'No, I can't handle being around people, right now. I'm OK on my own.' She stood up, gave Kaz a short hug, then Artie. 'I'll let you know as soon as I get those test results. OK? Then we'll decide what to do.'

CHAPTER 9

Artie and Kaz adjourned back to Mike's Diner. It was after 7pm. Time for more beer. They seemed to have spent all day just hanging around, first in the hospital and then in the testing lab and there's nothing likely to drive you to drink more than just hanging around while the clock ticks.

They ordered some chargrilled chicken wings, coleslaw, fries and hot sauce, with a pitcher of beer. Kaz poured beer into glasses. 'Here's to Fay. That's some chick, Artie.'

He clinked her glass and they knocked back the cold fizzy beer quickly, grateful for the drink, then poured the rest of the pitcher.

'Yeah, she's growing up before our eyes. She's...I dunno...from where we're from, she's really an exotic creature, don't you think?' He took a toothpick from its wrapper and snapped it.

'Oh, god, yeah. I think she's got a unworldly quality about her and I love her attitude, I suppose that's what it is. If I was 21, I'd fancy the arse off her.'

'Would you?' he said, finishing the beer at speed and belching.

'Yeah, she's got this...I don't know what it is, exactly...it's an air of mystery about her. You end up wanting her to like you. Wanting her to laugh at your joke or give you a smile. But it's not a power trip with her. It's just who she is. She's like a much more intelligent, sexy, attractive version of her mother.'

As soon as she said it, she slapped her hand over her mouth and looked embarrassed in a way that she never did.

'I'm so sorry, Artie. That was out well of order. Engaged mouth before brain. Sorry.'

She wouldn't look at him for a minute and finished her beer in a few gulps.

'Oh, man, stop it. I know it's an issue, right?'

She gave him an innocent, eyebrows raised and totally artificial look. 'What?'

'You know.'

'I don't know anything, other than the fact we need another pitcher of beer.' She gestured to the waitress.

Artie cleared his throat. 'Alright, I'm parking this. But we both know it needs sorting out, one way or another. Me and you and Coll, it needs dealing with.'

'OK. Yeah. You're right.' The waitress came with the jug of beer and their food. 'That was all a bit weird, in her flat, I thought,' said Kaz, ripping meat off the bone, hungrily. 'It was almost like not being with Fay. She was really lovely.'

Artie dipped a wing into the hot sauce and thought for a bit. 'You're a woman of the world, Kaz.'

'What's that supposed to mean?'

'I don't know, do I? It's something people say.'

'Which people?'

'You know what I mean. Shut up. I was going to ask you something serious about Fay.'

'Sorry, go on then.'

'Well you know all of that business out in the desert last year. We found her in that mobile home with that creepy guy who she thought was KK May...'

'...yeah, that was sick. Poor kid.'

'Well, since then, I think she's really gone into her shell. I know her mother offered to pay for therapy for her, but she wouldn't go. She just wanted to forget it. But you can't forget something like that at her age, can you?'

'Of course not. But...I dunno...I think she did right. Everyone is obsessed with therapy, out here. There's a lot to be said for just getting on with life, knocking the bad thoughts back with a few drinks, gritting your teeth and forgetting about yesterday and concentrating on tomorrow. How would talking about it for $200 an hour help?'

'Yeah, but that's a very Leeds way of going on.'

'Sensible, you mean?'

'It might have disturbed her badly, though. You can't just tough some things out.'

'It probably did disturb her. Men have been disturbing women since the dawn of time, in case you haven't noticed. She's resilient, though. You can see that. Women generally are. We have to be because it's still a man's world and we still get the shitty end of the stick. OK, she's not had a boyfriend since, but that's not the be all and end all of a young woman's life. The whole thing probably taught her to mistrust blokes a lot more, and that's a good thing. You should mistrust blokes. There's a lot of evil sods around. We see that all the time in our line of work.'

He nodded and took a big drink of beer. 'Yeah, I guess you're right. I just find myself worrying about her. She's so young...'

'...not that young, and this city makes you grow up quickly.' She pushed the plate of bones away from her and took a napkin to wipe her mouth. 'But you're right, Artie. We should keep an eye on her. Nothing too heavy. Hard as it is to imagine, we're the grown-ups compared to her, and since she and Coll just don't seem to be able to get along...'

'...I don't know why that is, y'know. Fay genuinely seems to dislike her and because of that Coll seems to reciprocate. She says she loves her, but doesn't *like* her.'

Kaz took a toothpick out of its paper sleeve and began hacking at some meat stuck between her back teeth. 'Oh, if you ask me, they're very similar. Fay's just trying *not* to be like her mother, because she fears underneath, she's *just* like her.'

Artie wiped grease off his fingers just as his phone buzzed.

'Yeah?'

'Oh, hello Artie. It's Danny Blind.'

'Hey, Danny.'

'Can you tell me which Mother Earth store it was that Carly used to buy food from? They are all over the Southlands and Fay didn't say earlier.'

Artie told him and said which lab they'd gone to with the samples.

'Cool. Can I get an exclusive on those results?'

'I don't see why not. You were the only member of the media who bothered to turn up. We need some exposure for this. The shit has to really bloody well hit the fan at some point. An innocent girl has died and driven her father to suicide. If someone is to blame for that, we'll need your help.'

'See, I just found out something interesting. Both Mother Earth and Green on Green are owned by Long Run.'

'Yeah, the manager told me that herself.'

'It's an investment company based in San Francisco. And I spent the last couple of hours researching them. There are five investors in that group and all of them have huge money in the soy industry.'

'Well, I guess that makes sense, that's all these places sell in terms of processed food,' said Artie. 'Green on Green alone must use millions of tons of soya products.'

'It would do, if they didn't also have major investment in the beef industry as well. From a brief look, it seems like their investment in intensive beef farming is substantial. They have some huge feedlots in the midwest.'

74

Artie bit his thumbnail and chewed on it.

'Oh, right. Well, they're just some multi-million dollar investment group, they won't have any morals, will they? Whatever turns the big bucks, they'll stick money into, even if it's ethically contradictory. They won't care if, on one hand, they're investing in vegan food and on the other in intensive animal farming. They're all about the money, and pretty much nothing else.'

'Hmmm. I guess that'd be right. I'm interested in this sort of thing, about food production and diet and such. I'll keep digging. I agree with you but then, I think it's odd that a legend of the alternative scene like Honest Joe Halford would sell to a group like them. He's the opposite of that kind of capitalist. He's an idealist, a visionary, a facilitator. There's just no way he'd sell out to a bunch of money men, like that. He's not interested in that kind of money and has lived in opposition to the culture of venture capitalism for 40 years.'

'Well, he did it. Do you know him?' said Artie.

'Only by reputation. Do you?'

'Not personally, but I know someone who probably does. You want me to go and have a word with him and see why he sold out?'

'It'd be interesting to know. If those product tests come back positive, we've got a 24-carat scandal on our hands and you know...there's big bucks in a 24-carat scandal.'

'I get you. But I'm not interested in money. I'm only interested in making Carly's and Robbie's deaths right.'

'Making them right?'

Artie rubbed his eyes. 'I mean, finding out how and why and who is responsible and fucking taking those fuckers down!' He lifted himself out of his seat and slammed his fist into the table. His emotion and anger caught his more rational brain by surprise. It rose up out of him, from the sea of stress and empathy that he felt for Fay, for Carly, for Robbie. The bastards. Who the fuck had done this? Tears were suddenly in his eyes and he had no control over it. Kaz reached across the table and gripped his arm in reassurance.

'Steady, big boy,' she said, cooing it at him in a calm-it-down tone.

He wiped at his eyes with his right thumb and sat back down.

'Yeah, well, let's try and do that,' said Danny Blind.

Artie cleared his throat, agreed and rang off.

'You OK, honey?' said their regular waitress, stopping by their booth with a jug of coffee.

'Yeah, it's fine, thanks, Gina,' said Kaz, knowing that actually, no, it wasn't.

Suddenly, it felt like things had gotten serious.

CHAPTER 10

The following morning, Artie and Colleen took her Porsche north up the Pacific Coast Highway to Big Sur while Kaz went to look for an apartment in Santa Monica.

'Honest Joe Halford was always at the Esalen Institute back in the day, along with all the hippies and freaks. I first met him at a party around there in maybe the early 80s. I was about 20, he was probably only in his mid 30s but he seemed really old to me at the time. Didn't stop me screwing him, obviously.' Colleen grinned at him. 'The only thing I remember about it is that he had the biggest balls. He was like a freaky spacehopper. Ha ha. I'm not sure I ever saw bigger balls than those on HJH, but his cock was regulation standard. Weird.'

Artie made a snorting laugh. 'I reckon if you'd been blessed with big balls, but not a big cock, you'd feel like nature was really taking the piss, because big balls are no good to anyone. Nobody gets any more pleasure from big balls, in fact, they probably just get in the way. Close, but no cigar. Even size queens don't care about big bollocks. I'm glad I don't have big balls, you'd just wear the crotch of your pants out more quickly.'

She laughed. 'You are so right. In fact, they looked kinda stupid. Joe's are probably swinging around his knees now that he's 70.'

'But you do know him, apart from a one-night stand 35 years ago and for bollock dimension reasons?'

'Yeah, mostly because I once helped curate an exhibition of his festival memorabilia at a gallery in Venice. That was about 2005. He said he remembered me from back in the day, but he obviously didn't.'

'I dunno man, you're pretty memorable, Coll,' said Artie. 'Your nakedness is burned into my synapses, so maybe Joe is the same. The 20-year-old Colleen must have been a red-hot chick.'

She laughed. 'Maybe. I *was* a damn good lay back then, back when everything was perky and firm. He was a good guy, though. I mean, by LA standards, anyway. And he remembered me from Venice when I emailed him. You know, he ran that store for years, must have opened it in '68 when he was in his 20s and he was always the go-to guy for every hippie activist to raise money for one thing or another. So, yeah, it is surprising that he sold out to some money guys. They probably just offered him more money than he could refuse.'

'But he must have done well out of it after so many years. Did he need the money?'

'He was never into it for the money, as far as I knew. If he had been, he could have sold it years ago. So, yeah, it is weird.'

She turned off the road and took a small winding track up into some woods. Occasionally, other tracks led off into the distance to properties entirely hidden from view by trees. Slowing down to a crawl, she leaned forward, looking for the signpost to Honest Joe's place.

'There it is,' she said, stamping on the brakes and pulling up alongside a Grateful Dead 'Skullfuck' symbol in blue, red and white, about the size of an apple and nailed to the base of a black oak.

It was a dirt track, hardly suited to being negotiated by a high-end sports car. They made slow progress, but after about half a mile, the track opened out onto a substantial clearing where a large single-story ranch had been built.

'Wow, what a place to live,' said Artie, getting out of the cold air-conditioned car into the hot air.

A man with long, white hair, wearing a stars and stripes top hat, a Leon Russell t-shirt and a pair of brightly coloured tie-dyed pants emerged from the house. He looked like he belonged on the Merry Prankster's 'Furthur' bus in 66, or was Wavy Gravy's brother. This sort of man didn't exist in Britain, except perhaps in Glastonbury and if he did exist, he certainly wasn't a multimillionaire businessman. That was a great thing about America. A freak could still score big.

'Hello hello!' he yelled, as though it was a greeting to the sky, hands in supplication to nature, looking up at the blue blue sky. 'Colleen Holmes! You always were an angel sent down to save us from ourselves with your beauty and shapely hips!'

'Hey, Joe. Man, you're a sight for sore eyes,' said Colleen, hugging him like he was an old friend, as opposed to someone she hadn't met for the best part of 10 years.

'How's life on earth treating you?' she said.

'Oh, you know how it goes - one breath in, one breath out. It's one of existence's great traditions, man.' He cackled a laugh - the sort of woody, resonant laugh you'd imagine a redwood tree might make.

Sometimes, Artie, as an Englishman, and especially as a Yorkshireman, felt very outside the groovy California love-in thing, even after all these years and even despite the fact that he was no fan of how things were back home. But he could never really be part of the SoCal hippiefest, not least because an irreducible part of his soul hated the dopey way they went on with each other, even though, at the same time, he sort of admired its openness.

Joe came towards him - what was he going to do? Hug? Fist bump? Hi-five? Handshake? And if the latter, what sort? One of the upwards rock grips or a good old-fashioned shake? What was wrong with that? It was simple and easily understood, nowadays greetings came in so many different shapes and styles that you had no idea where to start.

'Joe. I'm Artie Taylor,' he said, putting out his hand straight out, so as to circumvent any other greeting possibility.

Joe's hand felt like it was made of leather. His grip was strong, even though he looked old enough to be God's brother.

'Ah, an Englishman. Where you from, brother?' He grinned at Artie with big ivory teeth and open eyes.

'Leeds.'

'Ah, yeah. In Yorkshire, right? God's own country, ain't that what they call it?'

'Yeah. How did you know that?'

'Courtesy of Mr Graham Nash. He's from the other side of the Pennines though, ain't he?'

'Yeah, he's the enemy - a Lancastrian.'

'Oh, yeah, the Wars of the Roses and all of that. You guys invented hating your own countrymen long before we got to the Conservative versus Liberal divide.' He grinned at Artie with bright eyes.

That was nice. Meeting a Californian who had any knowledge of American history was rare enough, one who knew something about the history of anywhere else, was in an even more exclusive club. This *was* a different dude.

'Your email dropped outta the clear blue sky, Colleen, and I thought to myself, hmmm, now, there's a chick I ain't seen for far too long.' He looked her up and down. 'Man, you're groovin' it strong in those old jeans. What are you up to these days and how come you wanna come see this old freaky deaky?'

She obviously liked his way of going on, but every fourth word made Artie's teeth hurt. 'Oh, this and that, more this than that. Me and Artie got married last year and we were on tour with Springsteen for a while. The man here was official tour photographer.'

'Whoa, major dude alert!' He took off his stars and stripes top hat and gave him a dramatic bow. 'Well, come into my abode, said the spider to the fly, which is actually crazy if you think about it because it requires that spiders and flies might speak the same language and that seems pretty unlikely to me. Ha ha...yeah, man.'

He led them towards the large, sprawling ranch-style house. Two black labradors with psychedelic neckerchiefs on came out to greet them. Artie squatted down and gave each of them a good ruffle of the ears. Dogs were cool and, had he not been on the road so much over the years, he'd always have had one as a companion. Their non-judgemental affection was a near to pure love as you could get in this world.

'This is Flo and Eddie,' said Joe, 'because they're Happy Together. Ho ho...I'm such a wit, huh?' He led them out of the hot sun into the air-conditioned house.

'Joe, this is a very cool place,' said Colleen looking round. 'Do you live here on your own?'

'No, man, I hooked up with Chynna Wyndham. You remember her, Coll?'

Artie had heard of her. 'The astrologer to the stars?' he said.

'Uh huh. That's the lady. She's up in Santa Barbara for a few days with a certain famous lead guitarist who shall be nameless but who relies on the alignment of the planets to make all his decisions.'

Artie's instinct was to take the piss and take it royally. What a crock of shit he thought astrology was. But he bit his tongue. His mother had brought him up to always be polite to someone in their own house and it had stayed with him.

'Of course, it's all a con...but you give people succour where you can and for as much money as possible,' said Joe, with a twinkle in his mottled brown and blue eyes. Ah, well, maybe he was alright, after all. 'Take a seat. Can I get you folks some drinks?'

'I'll take a beer, if you've got one,' said Artie.

'I don't. But I do have some fine single malt, which by anyone's standards is surely an upgrade on beer. One for you too, Coll?'

'A small one with lots of ice. My days of driving whilst heavily fucked up are behind me. Or at least I like to think they are.'

'OK, Lady Holmes. Follow me into the laboratory.'

It was just the kitchen. Just call it the bloody kitchen. All the groovy guy, hippie clown schtick kept rubbing him up the wrong way. Then again, he was a grumpy Yorkshire sod, who admired Geoff Boycott, and Boycs would've hated HJH.

He found himself wishing he had Kaz with him for support. She'd have given him a little narrow-eyed glance which said "what an arsehole" without the need for ever saying a word, and in that way, she was on his side in a way that Coll could never be. And that was just another problem in his life.

Joe poured them a shot of a Scottish single malt and threw a couple of ice cubes in.

'Ah, so why are you here?' he said, wandering into a large living space and ushering them onto a long, wide, dark purple sofa that looked like it could be a blue whale's liver.

'Like I said in my email, we're interested in how you came to sell Mother Earth to Long Run,' said Colleen.

'Uh huh. And why does that you interest you, exactly?'

Colleen looked over to Artie and gestured for him to explain.

'There's a possibility that some of their stock is contaminated and making people ill. A girl who ate there all the time and bought a lot of their vegan processed food, has died,' said Artie, swilling the ice on his drink around as he spoke. 'We're having some of the products from the store tested now.'

'My god. What did she die of?'

'Mercury poisoning,' said Colleen.

'Wow. Man, oh man...that's terrible. That's very heavy. I'm sorry to hear that.'

'Her dad was so distraught that he killed himself. He shot himself in the head,' said Artie. 'He was my friend.'

HJH turned away in sorrow.

'Oh, my god. Damn! This country and guns.' He took off the hat and laid it to one side, pushing his thinning long hair behind his ears.

Artie leaned forward. 'Yeah, it's shit beyond belief. So look, Joe, Georgina Roberts told me you sold to a company called Long Run. What are they like? What are they all about?'

'Ah, bless Georgie. She's such a lovely woman. Yeah, well, Long Run are Bread Heads. They offered me a lot of money right when I wanted to retire.'

'But money wasn't your trip, man,' said Colleen. 'You could've cashed in years ago.'

'Yeah, that's true. But I didn't. Then I got to the age of 65, then 66, then 67 and then 68 and they came along. It was the right time.'

'What do you know about them?' said Artie.

'They're an investment group who buy up successful companies, largely leave them alone and take a small percentage of every sale. I

knew exactly what they'd do once they acquired the store. They wanted
to turn it into a big vegan brand and that's what they've done and they've
done it very quickly. They threw a ton of money at it and opened 15
stores in 15 months, probably more now. This is the time for vegan living.'

'Didn't you think it was weird that they wanted to invest in a vegan retailer when they've also got money in intensive beef farming?' said Artie.

Joe looked at him square in the eyes. 'I ain't a boy, Artie. It's a bad-ass,
mean world out there.' He sighed. 'I spent 45 years fighting The Man and
I was through. Let some other fucked-up hippie do it. So no, it didn't surprise me what they had money in - and believe me, I looked into it all -
because they're dirty capitalist pigs with their snouts in as many troughs
as possible to maximise revenue. You do know they bought up Green on
Green, too, don't you?'

'Yeah, it's Green on Green's stuff we're having tested. So they own the
stores and most of what they retail, too. That's gotta be some sweet
meat...or sweet soy, anyway.'

Joe smiled and nodded. 'Just to give you a bit of history, Green on
Green was set up in a small hippie commune back in '69 up in Marin
County, using some money donated from the Sky River festival people.
They used to make soy milk yoghurt and drive it down to the southlands
in a truck which had a refrigerator running off the battery in the back.
They supplied me for years. That's their roots. But also like me, they
tired of just getting by. So they sold to them six months before I did.
Once they had a company making vegan burgers and the like, they were
obviously going to want to buy into places to retail them. Retailing what
you're making is where the sweetest dollars are. Cuts out the middle man.
I knew they'd come for me, so when they did, I made up a stupid number
and they said yes. Whatchagonnado?'

Artie drank his whisky. It was smooth and delicious. The cubes of ice
clinked together in his glass.

'Are *you* a vegan Joe?'

'Me? No. Never have been. I was macrobiotic for about half an hour in
'69. Ate nothing but brown rice and umeboshi plums. Can't quite recall
why now. Ha ha...doubtless trying to get onto a higher spiritual plane.'
He shrugged a little. 'Hey, it ain't such a terrible ambition, I guess.'

'Well whatever you're eating now, you look good on it,' said Colleen.

'Thanks, Queen H. I put it down to eating a lot of fish and grass-fed
steak and drinking fine whisky.' He poured a little more into each of their

glasses. 'See, my gig was always as a facilitator. The store was a cultural thing, as much as a retail thing. It allowed people to explore being different and I liked that. I loved the creative spirit that came with it. But that didn't mean it was my lifestyle, any more than owning a baseball stadium means you've got to be good at playing baseball. I was happy to just let it be part of people's lives. It became what it became, not because of me, but because of the people who orbited around it.'

'And it ended up making you rich. That's the American Dream,' said Artie.

Joe nodded. 'Capitalism's greatest quality is being able to turn everything, even anti-capitalist ideas, into an enticing profit margin. It buys into its enemies, in order to co-opt them into its mindset. It's like a wasp that lays its eggs in a host body. You know what I think? I think making profit is a natural human instinct at this point in our short period on earth as the dominant species. But it's how much you make and then what you do with it, that is where America is going wrong. Just my opinion, of course.'

'I'm inclined to agree,' said Colleen. 'See, I'm worried, Joe. Worried about the country and where it's headed. It seems so divided between those without and those with. One side is angry and feels hopeless and the other side is scared and defensive about keeping what it's got. No-one believes in anything any more, apart from those who love their God and guns and that seems a pretty lethal mix, to me. All that beautiful altruism and ambition for a life not defined by what you can buy, that was still a part of the culture here when I first arrived with mom in the late 70s, that's all gone now. It's like America got rich, took a look around and wasn't sure why it had bothered, because it was still unhappy. So then it got fat, trying to eat its way to happiness, but that still didn't work, so it's turned inward and started beating the crap out of itself, in a righteous fit of self-loathing and paranoia. Sometimes I wonder if it won't be truly happy until it's killed itself.'

Joe clapped a little. 'Well, that was quite a speech, Colleen. And I agree. Throw in a big dose of guns, religious fervor and xenophobia, stir in a cup of corrupt media and you've got a new revolution stewing, man.' He half laughed, half groaned. 'Yeah, where did the 60s spirit go, sister? I thought my team was taking over, but you know what? Capitalism ate us up, while telling us it was giving us a great blow job.'

Artie's Yorkshire twattishness couldn't let that go. He was a northern rock music guy and had never had a moment of hippie in his bloody life.

He found himself lapsing into a broader version of his normal Yorkshire voice.

'Aye, well that's one way of looking at it. Another way is to realise that the late 60s dream was largely just middle-class rebellion. Understandable and worthy, but very few were in it for the long run. Plenty couldn't wait to get back to the suburbs and get on with making some money from a good career. I tell you what, I did a tour with Carlos Santana about 15 years ago and he said for him it was all real, the hippie dream, the love and peace and flowers. But back then, the rest of the band just wanted to get high and get laid. They didn't give a shit about the rest of it. Carlos was very disillusioned for a while, I think. A small percentage took it seriously and the rest were weekend hippies, who just wanted to get laid, make money and buy shit. That's probably how I'd have handled it, if truth be told.'

'Yeah, I think you might be right about some of that. Not that we shouldn't try to keep the dream alive. The Grateful Dead turned into a multi-million dollar enterprise. That tells you how it is. Ain't no-one could've told you that was gonna happen back here in '69. But I tell ya, man, capitalism is an ugly demon dressed up as a beautiful rainbow-hued chameleon and will do what it needs to do to win. It doesn't hate you or me, it feels nothing and it has no morals, no principles to adhere to, other than the long-term goal of turning a dollar.'

'With all due respect though, Joe, left-field hippie store sells out to Big Dollar, is your story. It must have pissed off a lot of people. People who saw you as delivering something beautiful into the devil's hands.'

'Uh huh. I hear you, brother and you're right on both counts.' Honest Joe drank his whisky and slowly unscrewed the cap from the bottle. 'But here's the thing, man. If we're getting serious here. I'll tell ya something that ain't public knowledge. I kept $250,000 from the sale and then gave every other cent away.' He shrugged and held his arms out wide. 'I've got this place paid for, so I figure I need 35k a year to live the life I wanna live. The interest on the capital will mean I'm cool until I'm about 90 and if I ain't dead by 90, then fuck it, I'll blow my brains out 'cos I don't want no limp-dick existence, man. The one who lives longest doesn't win, the one who lives best wins. After that, it all goes to charities.'

That made Artie prickle with appreciation. He hated it when he agreed with people who annoyed him. Maybe Joe wasn't a hippie fuck-wit after all.

Colleen leaned forward and took the bottle, poured herself another, and squinting at him said, 'You gave all the money away? Jesus, brother. Can I ask you how much that was?'

'An indecent amount. They paid well over the odds, because it would give them a billion-dollar brand within five years. They were not just buying a profitable store, they were really buying a brand established over 45 years. I'm talking 15 million. I've given away, or am in the process of giving away, 14 million, 750 thousand dollars.'

Colleen stood up, leaned over and hi-fived him.

'Right on, man! Fuck. They paid 15 mill?! Good work. I'll lay my shit on the line for you. Mom's estate, book royalties, syndication rights from TV movies, interest from capital and shit that I couldn't even tell you what it was from when I see it on statements, well, all of that crapola, man, it's about 15-20 million a year, year in, year out. It's stacking up like peanut butter in Elvis's colon. Me and Artie were talking about this shit. There's no way we can ever spend this level of money, so what do we do? I want rid of it, man. I'm on the wrong side of history, here. I ended up, by luck, on the side of the 1 per cent. I ended up with the corporate cock-suckers and greedy fools. I want to go back to being the barefoot hippie chick, who doesn't care about what money can buy you. All this money is useless to me, I see that now, but I want to help people with it. It's sick, the whole system is sick. Being part of the problem, and not part of the solution, is a bad fucking vibe, man. I'm just getting with this, really. Marrying Artie slowly opened my eyes to it because this dude is one of the least materialistic people I've met and that's really shone a light into my life.'

Artie squeezed her leg in appreciation of that comment.

HJH smiled widely, revealing huge white teeth. 'The weird thing is, if you're giving it away, you kind of owe it to those who will benefit from it, to play the Big Money game and invest it so it gives a good return and thereby generates more money. Sounds crazy, but giving money away is a kind of business in itself.'

'Yeah, I can see that. It'll take planning but something's got to be done,' said Colleen.

Artie's phone chirped into life as a text came in. It was from Fay. She'd sent it to Kaz as well. He read it out loud.

'All products clean except soy jerky. No peanuts but contains traces of mercury. Carly ate it all the time. That must be what killed her.'

CHAPTER 11

'Jesus Christ,' said Joe, half under his breath. 'This is a scandal that could destroy Green on Green.'

'It's not good news for Mother Earth, either,' said Colleen.

Joe shook his head. 'The store can market its way out of this, it's just one product, but the manufacturer will get sued by the city for dirty practices, by the dead girl's family and probably by other members of the public, too. Long Run will have to spend a lot of money to make this right.'

Artie's phone buzzed.

'Hey, Kaz.'

'Did you read Fay's text?'

'Yeah.'

'Explains about Carly. It's fucking outrageous, Artie. Someone has done that on purpose. Poor lass. They must have! It's like a form of bloody terrorism, man. Whoever did it murdered Carly. We've got to go to the police with this, Artie.'

'Alright, calm down, lady. We will. We've got to do this right, because further down the line, there'll be a court case, so we've got to take the right steps now to make sure whoever did this gets banged up. First we need to tell Georgina Rodgers to make sure they don't sell any more, though there wasn't any on the shelf yesterday. Then we need a lawyer...'

He was interrupted by Colleen, tapping him on the arm. 'We'll go and see Mo Casson...'

'...is that Coll's high-powered lawyer? The one in Laguna Beach?' said Kaz, hearing her voice.

'Yeah.'

'What's the Honest Joe bloke like?'

'Hard to say,' said Artie, looking at his leather boot. 'Take the pickup and we'll meet you at the store in Topanga in an hour.'

'OK. One thing I don't understand, though.'

'What?'

'Why didn't the soy jerky have peanuts in?'

'Oh, yeah. I hadn't thought of that.'

'Strange if it was just in the one that Ben ate,' she said. 'I don't bloody trust Goldman. I still think I was right. He poisoned himself.'

'Nah, he's alright. He's just another rich kid looking for a route through life.'

'Alright.' She blew air into the phone. 'Artie, I'm really upset about this. She was such a nice girl. I'm not having it...I'm not having her being killed like this. It's terrible. I want to get the fuckers that did it and kick the shit out of them!' She wasn't shouting, but, full of emotion, she was very unusually on the verge of tears.

His instinct was to calm her, speaking in a soft, calming, emollient tone. 'Sssh. I know. Don't worry. We'll make it right. One way or another.'

She groaned. 'Alright. I'll see you in a bit. Will you be with Coll?' She said it in a short, aggressive manner.

He paused, having to frame his words right. 'Is that what you want?'

'Not really.' She made a noise. 'Sorry, Artie. She's your missus. Do what you want, I'll see you later.' She rang off.

Artie picked up his glass, drained it and weighed up what to do. He knew Kaz so well, knew her emotions so well, knew where her head was at so well, and he wanted, more than anything, to keep her happy.

'Come on, Coll. Let's head back into the city.' He stood up and held his hand out to Honest Joe. 'Thanks for the superb whisky.'

'Hey, any time.' Then Joe leaned into him and patted him on the shoulder. 'Take it easy, brother. Work your way through this. But don't give too much to it, or it might eat you up.' He hugged Colleen, said some more hippie bollocks to her which Artie closed his ears to, and soon they were back in the Porsche.

He rubbed his eyes. 'This is all so fucked up. So wrong. How can a lovely kid like Carly and, by extension, a decent man like Robbie, end up being the victims of some shit like this?'

Colleen took the Porsche back down to the freeway and headed south, back to Malibu.

'Right, we've got to be very proactive, here,' she said, cranking up the a/c. 'I'm gonna call Mo and plan out a course of legal action. We've gotta break this shit wide open. And whatever it costs, I'll pay it.'

'Well, Mo Casson doesn't come cheap. Isn't she the highest-paid female lawyer in California?'

'In America, I believe. And with good reason. She's lost just one case in 15 years and the only one she lost was later overturned and went to retrial because the judge had been bribed. She won the retrial. If Mo takes your case on, she will win it for you. She's rigorous beyond belief and has a huge dedicated evidence-gathering team. She covers every angle to the point where it's been said that she is Orange County's alternative police force.'

'How do you know her?'

'Oh, honey, You don't wanna know.' She pulled a duck face at him.

'No I do.'

She crossed her eyes. 'Really?'

'Really.'

'OK. Well, I was a kind of Journey groupie in 1982. Mom's big hit book, *The Death of Gigi Blonde*, had just been turned into a huge movie starring Barbara Streisand. I was 21, full of the first tranche of my inheritance, stinking rich and out of control. She was fresh out of law school on some sort of secondment to their legal people.

'She was out of the her depth but really nice, so we hung out at their shows and somehow we stayed in touch ever since. Then I had a stalker in the late 90s.'

'Really? Fuckin' hell, Coll. You never said.'

She waved it off. 'It was just a jerk guy who I met once and got crazy on me...he was messed up...but out here, the mentally ill live amongst us. There's no money in crazy poor people, so they're left to their own devices. By then she had started her own gig so I got Mo on it and the guy melted away.'

'So the crazy fella, despite being crazy, took notice of the lawyer's letters?'

'Yeah, though later, I heard, he walked in front of truck on PCH in Dana Point which made jam of him. It was nothing to do with me, in truth. He was just unwell and I got in the way.'

'Oh, shit.'

'Yeah, poor guy. She's been my legal gal ever since. We're good friends now. I was maid of honour at her wedding to Danni.'

'Ah, right. She's rockin' the lesbianism, as well. She sounds like a great friend to have. Some lawyers in California are like rock stars. OK, so call Mo, get a plan of action together. Kaz is at Mother Earth. We'll talk to the manager, Georgina. Drop me off up there, and then head back to Malibu.'

She burned up Topanga Canyon Road and dropped him off in the parking lot, next to the black Ford pickup, in the back of which was sitting Kaz, taking the sun, Ray-Bans on. Coll tooted the horn and drove away. Artie peered over the side of the truck.

'Now then, lady. Been here long?'

'Not really.' She hopped out. 'Has Coll gone back to the house?'

'Yeah, she's calling her lawyer. We'll probably go down to Laguna later. Any news on a new flat?'

'Nothing yet. There's a good place on Arizona, but it's too pricey.'

They walked towards the store. It was desert hot again, maybe over 90 degrees in the shade, probably 110 in the sun. Artie put his arm around Kaz's shoulder as they walked. 'You OK? You were well pissed off on the phone.'

'I owe you an apology...'

'...no you don't...'

'...yes, I do. I was rude about Coll.'

'You just spoke from the heart.'

'Even so. I mean, you love her...'

'...you don't have to say any more. I'm cool with what you said.'

'Are you sure?'

'Yeah. You do know that I love you, right?'

She stopped and looked at him, a stern look in her eyes. 'Why are you saying that now?'

'Because it feels like you need to know.'

'Do I?'

'Yeah...'

'...just shut it, man. Don't say any more. I don't want to hear it.'

'Why not?'

'Because of Coll. You love her. And I'm not having you deny that. It's true.'

'You're right. I love both of you, but in different ways. And I...'

But she wouldn't let him speak, waving a hand in his face. 'Just shut up before you start to upset me. Now come on, let's see Georgina Roberts and bring her up to speed with this mercury poisoning business.' She marched off ahead of him.

They were greeted at the door by another blonde woman, almost shouting at them this time. 'Hey! How are you today?!' They ignored her. It was bloody ridiculous to ask people to do that for a living. Georgina Rodgers was in her office at the back of the store, visible through one of its three windows. Artie knocked on the door and put his head around and then walked in.

'Georgina. Sorry to disturb you...'

She looked up from a laptop screen, shocked to see him. 'Hello, Mr Taylor...'

'...you remember Kaz?' he said. She bent her knees a little and did her usual exaggerated arc of a wave.

'Yes, of course. Come in and sit down. Has something happened?'

They went in. 'Yes, we had some Green on Green products tested and the soy jerky is dirty. It has mercury in it. It literally killed a girl called Carly and the distress from that led her father to shoot himself in the head. They were our friends. You've been selling deadly food,' said Kaz, bluntly.

Artie glanced at Kaz. Her jaw was grinding away on her back teeth, and she had a look of hard defiance in her eyes, emotion not far from the surface.

'Oh, my god. Are you kidding me?' Georgina Roberts got to her feet and clutched at her throat with her right hand. What colour there was to her face, which wasn't much, drained away.

'First things first. Have you got any soy jerky left on the shelves?' said Artie.

She shook her head firmly. 'No. None. I had it all removed an hour after the Ben Goldman incident. And I sent an email to G on G central to alert them to possible pollution of the product. So how did someone die from eating it?'

She was astonished and upset in equal measure as he explained.

'Oh, my god...the poor girl...oh, god...' She put her head in her hands, tears in her eyes. 'We've betrayed that girl, terribly. She came to us, trusted us and we let her down.'

He looked at Kaz and shrugged, not in the mood to deal with weepy people. Kaz slumped her shoulders and made an Elvis curl with her top lip.

'Don't expect me to be the touchy-feely woman,' she said, thrusting her hands into her jeans pockets and half turning away.

'I'm sorry,' said Georgina, wiping her tears from her eyes with her fingers. 'We're all about peace here. It's about not killing.'

'Good point,' said Kaz. 'Surely that's why someone has done this. They're taking the piss out of people who think killing is wrong.'

'What? What does "taking the piss" mean?'

'Taking the mickey,' said Kaz.

'Oh, but why would anyone do that?' said Georgina.

'The world is full of fucked-up people, that's why,' said Artie. 'But let's get this straight. The jerky was where the mercury was. We took 10 products from here and had them all tested and that was the only one which came back as polluted.'

'I don't understand. Why pick on that? All those soy Green on Green products are made in the same factory in San Francisco. I've been there. Why just that product?'

'We don't have to answer that, do we?' said Kaz, leaning on her desk. 'We only need to know who did it and get them banged to rights.'

'This is just awful. I'm scared to sell anything from there now. It might all be contaminated.'

'Like I said, the jerky was the only product with mercury in,' said Artie. 'The good news is that there were no peanuts in it.'

She frowned. 'Well, that's odd, considering Mr Goldman's allergic response. Even so, I'm clearing the shelves of all G on G soy products.'

She stood up, walked past Artie and Kaz and had reached the door from her office, which led out onto the shop floor, when there was some shouting, a scream, then another scream and a man's voice shouting one word: 'No!'

One second, two seconds, three seconds elapsed. Georgina turned to look at Artie with a puzzled look, said, 'What was that?' and had just turned back to the door when there was an explosion. Big and full of gut-wrenching bass, rising to an ear-piercing cracking noise, it was sonically overwhelming and blew all three of them to the ground. Glass from the office windows rained on them in a billion tiny shards, followed by a gust of air as the explosion pushed everything outwards from it. The sound of falling masonry washed through the air like a dry waterfall.

And then there was a brief silence, followed by humans making noises, noises of pain and of death.

Artie raised his head from under his arms, stood up from the crouch he'd instinctively adopted, and looked around. Kaz did likewise alongside him. Georgina was lying sprawled on her back by the door.

Was that it?

No.

Another explosion, louder and much more powerful than the previous one, and the entire, old, ramshackle building was ripped apart. All Artie could do was drop to the floor and adopt the feotal position and pray something big and heavy and fatal didn't fall on them.

This was no way to die. He had always thought he'd go out on the road, driving drunk off a cliff, from a drug overdose, or being shot by a crazy roadie. But not like this; the victim of an act of terrorism.

But then something fell on him. A sheet of roofing maybe, or a beam. It hurt like fuck. The noise was unbearable, tearing at his ears like a jagged blade inside his head, as the wood and plaster building came down on top of them. The bomb had demolished the building; torn it apart.

Christ, this was it. They'd had it. No way out. The Mother Earth store was burying them alive.

CHAPTER 12

Folded up on himself, Artie was both scared shitless and furious that some twat dare do this to him and to Kaz. His mouth filled with clouds of plaster and drywall as the building collapsed. The air was no longer breathable in this thick soup of destruction. He tried to push upwards against the weight of crap that was on him but it was immovable. He could hardly get a breath, but could just move his arms, so he tugged at his t-shirt collar, pulling it up over his mouth to try and create a filter.

The roar of destruction abated after maybe 30 seconds. He took small gasps, getting the idea in his head that if there was only so much breathable air around him, he'd use it up slower that way. Whether it was the fear-induced adrenaline acting as a painkiller, or maybe just the fact that when push came to shove, Artie was Yorkshire hard, but as it went quiet, he felt in reasonable nick. The pain across his shoulders wasn't too bad. He tried opening his eyes, which he'd clamped tight shut by instinct. Everything was dark. No light at all. Shit, he must be under a lot of vegan store.

'Kaz!!! Kaz!!! Can you hear me?! Are you alright?' He yelled at her as loud as he could through his t-shirt.

There was no reply. Fear was in Artie's heart like never before. She had only been a few feet from him when the second bomb had gone off. Maybe she'd been knocked unconscious. Maybe she was...

'Kaz! Kaz!'

Still nothing. Oh, god. He felt so claustrophobic...so trapped...so desperate now. He pushed upwards again but it was pointless. He was trapped in a kind of improvised bunker. It felt like there was a sheet of something smooth on top of him - it had to be some roofing material - but it was jammed on something else - a beam possibly, and that was taking most of the weight, creating a rat's nest for him to survive in.

'Kaz! Are you OK? Make a noise if you can.'

He prayed to God.

Please let her be OK. I give myself to you in this moment, please. Not like this. Not after so long. I love her and I want her to live. Love rules. That's right, isn't it? Love conquers all. Please. I beg of you. Don't take her like this. She's a good person. Take me instead. I give myself to you instead of her. I don't want to live without her, so take my life and bring her back. She spreads joy and good vibes, I don't. No-one will miss me. A lot of people will miss her. Please God. I've asked nothing of you my whole life and you know I could have. I always saved it up for when I was out of lives, when there was no other option. That's when you need God, right? Well, God, I need you now. Take me. Let her come back. Please. Amen.

Tears fell down his cheeks, creating streaks in the dust mask that covered his face, as he spoke in his head to a deity he had never believed existed. But maybe there is more joy in heaven at the repentance of one sinner and the Lord surely knew that Artie Taylor had been a sinner.

'Kaz!! Can you hear me! C'mon, Just give me noise, lady.'

Still nothing. There was no human noise at all. Was everyone dead? Where were the alarms and sirens? Was he just insulated from them?

The pain in his heart to think of Kaz not being alive was too much to bear. He just didn't want to live without her. It was pointless to shout again, but he did it anyway.

'Kaz! Are you alright?!'

'Fucking shut up shouting, Artie. My head is fucking splitting! I got knocked out, I think.'

Her Leeds accent vibrated the air and caressed his ears. She still wasn't more than six or seven feet away.

Thank you, Lord. And he meant it. You make a deal with God, you'd better stick to it.

'Are you alright?' he shouted.

'I don't know. Could use a drink, mind,' she said.

'Yeah, me, too. A pint of Sam Smiths from the Tadcaster brewery would go down nice. Can't hardly breathe for this dust. Are you hurt?'

'I don't know. Something fell on me. I feel like shit.'

'You'll be alright. Tough Yorkshire lass like you. This'd be a good night out in Leeds.'

'Aye. Being crushed under a blown-up building? Bloody luxury.' The Northern instinct to turn everything into black humour never leaves you, not even when you're close to death.

Georgina. In his panic about Kaz he'd forgotten her. He called her name.

'Georgina! Can you hear me?'

There was no reply.

'Artie,' said Kaz. 'I don't think she made it.'

'Why? How?'

'She was nearer the first explosion by the open door. She took it full on.'

Now there was some noise. Voices. In the distance, sirens.

A male voice. 'If anyone is in here, give me a shout, so I know where you are.'

'Here!' said Artie.

'Fuckin' here!' said Kaz.

Other voices shouted somewhere in the store. But not many. The bomb must have killed a lot of people. The store had been busy and well staffed. The first explosion was bad enough, but the second was devastating.

Kaz's voice came again, shaking this time. 'Artie! Artie, I'm scared.' She never said that.

'It's alright, darlin'. We'll get out of this. I promise you.'

'I feel weird. Fainty. This isn't good. My head is swimming. I feel terrible.'

'You just took a whack off something. It's OK, don't worry. Just relax.'

'Oh, god...I don't know what's going on. Oh, god, Artie. I...I...I can't really breathe.' He heard her panting and spitting. 'Artie...listen...' He heard her cough, choking on the thick clouds of dust. He tried to get a breath himself, but struggled to do so. It was like inhaling dry soup, so you had to stop breathing in but then that meant you were holding your breath and you can't do that for long. '...I don't think we're getting out of this. I want you to know something...' she gasped a little and spat again.

'...what is it?...'

'...that I love you and I'm so lucky that I knew you, even though you're a grumpy shite. We were a perfect fit. We both know it. We should've been a couple all along. We're...we're the same soul.' She coughed again, struggling for breath. 'I really love you...'

But he didn't hear what she said next because suddenly, profoundly, he knew he was losing consciousness through lack of oxygen. Everything went woolly around the edges as he drowned in the thick air and then, as profoundly as someone flicking off a light switch, it all went black. But in the microsecond of consciousness he had left in his brain, he grabbed her deathbed confession to his heart and took that silver pearl of love to his own grave.

CHAPTER 13

Silence. Sleep. Smell.

Artie was half aware of a lot of things as, like a drowning man, he kept coming back up to the surface, only to sink back down again. There was no life-flashed-before-his eyes moment, he was far more passive than that. Not fighting. No. Merely experiencing. That's all he had. And yet he knew, somewhere in the base of his existence, that he was just hanging onto life and only by a fine strand of cotton. Our knowledge of the nature of aliveness is deep and beyond our normal experience, but when it's in danger of being snuffed out, it is a hard bastard. The life force, though common, will do anything it needs to do to keep on keepin' on. It's a tenacious beast; like a Yorkshireman opening the batting at Headingley on a cold late May afternoon with a swing in the air, it is determined not to be dismissed. As Artie lay fighting for his life, it felt like it was all beyond him, that the elemental forces of alive and dead were fighting to claim him. And it all happened somewhere beyond his own dreamscape. Was it within his control, or was it a struggle being conducted outside of his consciousness?

Sometimes he knew people were there. He half heard voices and sound shapes, which in another reality were certainly words, but they made no sense and were gone as soon as he'd heard them. He kept focusing on Kaz's voice, on the last words he'd heard her say. Gripped tightly to them, like they were a life bouy. 'I really love you.' If any words were going to keep you afloat, it was those four.

Unconsciousness is a profound blankness: a state of nothingness and yet one in which you still manage to breathe and just keep going, somehow. The human body is incredibly resilient. Given even a small chance of survival, it'll take it.

And that's exactly what Artie's body did.

When full consciousness finally washed back into his synapses, it came with a pain in his back and shoulders and a soreness to his throat and lungs, so vicious it felt like he'd had his throat cut. There was grit in his mouth, a coating of gunk on his tongue. He was lying in a bed.

'Hey, baby.'

He turned his head to the left, sending a shooting pain across his shoulders. He groaned. Colleen came into focus. She was smiling and gave him a little wave with her fingers.

'Welcome back, honey,' she said. 'You've been out for 40 hours.'

He had only one thought.

'Is Kaz alive?'

'Yeah. She is. Thankfully. She's a bit poorly, but she's alive. She's just down the corridor in her own room.'

He shut his eyes. Well, that was a relief. 'Where am I?'

'UCLA Medical Center in Santa Monica.'

'Where Robbie...?'

'That's right. Just relax. They say you'll be fine.'

'My ears are ringing like I've been stood in front of Lemmy's bass bin.'

'Do you remember anything?'

He lay still and thought. 'I just couldn't breathe. The air was thick with dust from the explosion.'

'Yeah, you sucked a lot of it in.'

'Who did it?'

'The bombs? No-one has owned up to it yet. The LAPD are under pressure to get a result. People are saying it was a Muslim terror attack, but there's no proof of that. Why would they blow up a vegan store and kill so many people?'

'How many died?'

'Fifteen. You and Kaz and Georgina and...'

'...Georgina made it? She was by the open door.'

'She survived, but...' she was clearly pulling back from saying anything too upsetting.

'No-one else?'

'Two guys who had left the store to help a customer with her bags. That's it. I've been up there, the place is devastated. It was a huge blast. It took the roof off and blew out two walls. I don't know how you got out alive. It's not much more than a heap of rubble.'

'Just lucky. Sort of.' Artie lay still and thought for a minute. 'There were two explosions.'

'Yeah, they know that. They'll send someone to interview you soon, I should think.'

'The second was the big one. Before the first one went off someone shouted, "No!" Georgina was leaving the office and heard the shout, and then the explosion happened. It knocked us over and blew out the glass, but then there was about a few seconds' gap until the big one went off.'

'Some have said it was a suicide bomber, but I don't see that being the case.'

'Killing yourself to kill people who don't want things to be killed, just doesn't make sense.' He coughed and once he started coughing it seemed to dislodge dust in his lungs, making him cough even more. She handed him some water. 'I could do with this being a beer,' said Artie, sipping at the glass.

She smiled sympathetically. 'I'll sneak some in for you later, if you're feeling OK.'

He lay still and composed himself. 'I actually think I'm alright. I just hurt, basically. Feels like some roadies took me outside and knocked the crap out of me. And it feels like I've been smoking asbestos, which we probably did in the 70s anyway. Yeah, but apart from that, I'm alright.'

She stood up and straightened out her loose sweater. 'Now, you take it easy. I've got to meet Mo Casson. She's taking on the case.'

'The case?'

'Yeah, the mercury poisoning and now she's gonna bat for you in this explosion. The two things must be related. The poisoning and the bomb.'

Artie frowned. 'What do you mean, exactly?'

'You don't need to worry about it just now, honey. Just get well.'

After Colleen had left and a pretty male nurse with long eyelashes and soft brown skin had taken his blood pressure and temperature, Artie got out of bed. He was as stiff as if he'd run a marathon. He tried stretching to loosen up a bit but was fairly sure a big JD and Coke would loosen him up more than any amount of exercise. Inspecting his shoulders in a long mirror, he saw he was covered in bruises, from where the roofing material had hit him. But he was at least clean. Someone must have washed him from head to foot while he was spark out, which was a weird thought. He threw on a pale blue lightweight gown over the hospital issue pyjamas they'd dressed him in. This was like waking up after an almighty bender, and your life before and during the bender now all seemed like a half-remembered dream or a myth that you'd only vaguely heard about. He felt almost disconnected from his own life as he stared at his weather-beaten face, lined heavily around the eyes, tanned like brown leather.

He took a right down the corridor checking names on doors, stopping at the one that had 'Kaz Clarke' written in neat black pen on a small whiteboard, and pushed it open.

What confronted him made his heart hurt.

Kaz was lying flat on her back, hooked up to a machine with a large digital display, presumably measuring her vital functions, which was even beeping intermittently, in the traditional movie style. There were tubes going into her from bags of clear liquids that hung on what looked like some kind of optic. The white sheets and white pillow contrasted with her pink face, tanned from the hot early summer sun. Her normally spiked blonde hair had been washed and combed back. It made her look older than she usually did.

'Hey, lady,' he said closing the door quietly and walking up to the bed. She was unconscious. He'd seen her asleep thousands of times, over the years. This wasn't that. Expressionless, she just lay there, breathing almost imperceptibly. Why was she unconscious? Was she ill? Or was she just sleeping?

He found a chair and placed it by the bed, sat down and took her small, warm, hand, put it to his lips and kissed her. Life throws you curve balls. This was a hell of a pitch. He could barely cohere his own thoughts about what had happened. That explosion had ripped apart everyday life, everyday thoughts and mental patterns. It'd take time to stitch regular life back to together.

He began chatting to her, as much to comfort himself as her. 'You know what, Kaz? This reminds me of that time we were working in New York in the fall of 2004, remember? We were backstage at the Garden doing portraits of Tony Bennett, of all people. He was so nice and looked so great in every photo that we were done in 20 minutes. So we went to that bar off Times Square we love, the Blue Monkey, remember? Someone spiked our drinks, remember? Just for the hell of it, probably. I remember it coming on and it was like being hit by a train. You grabbed hold of me and said something like, "I'm about to explode with insanity". Next thing I can remember is we were clinging to each other in a hotel and we thought we'd died. Remember? We thought we'd crossed over together and were now in the Universal Mind. Turns out we hadn't, it was just the drugs.'

As he spoke, he continued to hold her hand.

'We've got ourselves into some right scrapes, me and you. Trouble has always just found us. Only me and you could've been blown up in a vegan store by...well...who the fuck knows who? Coll's got Mo Casson onto it, already. She'll have her alternative police force out collecting statements and evidence. Yeah, probably cost her five grand a day, maybe seven. Not that it makes a difference. Coll must be paying for us in here as well. Shit. She really is our sugar mama. Imagine if we were poor - well, we are poor - but getting blown up when you're poor is bad shit, in America. We lucked out with Coll, you know. Not just the money but, in a way, she forced us to confront the fact that we love each other. Why couldn't we just admit that to each other for all these years? Well, I know we weren't denying it, we just didn't realise, did we? I don't know why we couldn't see it. It's so obvious. Well, you saw it before me. I should've pulled out of the wedding. I'm sorry.' He kissed the back of her hand again, half expecting her to just start talking the way she had in the store when he'd thought she was dead.

But not now. This was more serious. Much more serious.

The door opened and a man in a white coat came in and recoiled slightly at seeing Artie.

'Oh, I'm sorry. Do you need some time?' he said.

'No, it's fine.' He stood up as quickly as his sore, aching bones would allow and held out his hand. 'I'm Artie Taylor. Kaz is my...my...my love, err...friend. We got blown up...'

'...I'm aware of the situation, Mr Taylor. My name is Brad Phillips. I treated you for your injuries when you were admitted, sir.'

'Oh. Thanks, man.'

'How do you feel now?'

'Like I've been beaten up by the Hells Angels at Altamont.'

'Where?'

'Forget it. I'll be fine. I'm tough. I'm from Leeds.'

'Where's that?'

'Somewhere you never wanna go, but which breeds tough-assed muthafuckers like me and Kaz, here.'

Brad Phillips plugged an instrument into the bleeping machine and considered the info.

'Is she OK?' Artie said.

Phillips cleared his throat a little. 'I'm sure you wouldn't like me to sugar-coat this for you, Artie. You rock people are tough, as you say, I'm sure. Kaz isn't well, at all. We put her into a drug-induced coma...'

'...a coma?! She's in a coma?'

'It sounds serious, I know. But it's for her own welfare, while we assess her situation. It reduces the stress on the body and takes away the need to load her up on painkillers. She'd likely be hurting badly if she was conscious.'

'I don't understand, doc. She looks fine.' He kept stroking her hand.

'She took a heavy blow to the base of the back of her head - probably from a wooden beam falling from the roof, swinging down and hitting her. As a result, her brain is swollen.'

Oh, shit. Artie put his free hand to his mouth and glanced at her. She looked at peace, bless her.

'The last time I spoke to her she said her head was splitting, then she started feeling dizzy and weird.'

Brad Phillips nodded, sombre and downbeat. 'X-Rays have shown the base of her skull has a small crack in it. That in itself isn't that much of a problem. It'll heal. It's the swelling we need to control.'

His lovely little Kaz, damaged so profoundly. Life was such a crap shoot. You survive a massive explosion only to get randomly whacked by a wooden beam.

'Will she be OK - eventually?'

Phillips cleared his throat again. 'I wouldn't want to give you any firm assurance, at this time.'

'Well, what's the problem?'

'If she responds well to the anti-inflammatory drugs, there is absolutely no problem. In fact, she could make a very quick recovery.'

'And if she doesn't?'

He let out a sigh.

'Let's cross that bridge when we come to it.'

'When we come to it? You said "when"; you mean "if".

'Yes, if we come to it.'

But the implication was clear, he thought it would be a case of when.

'How long will it be before we know if she's responding well?'

'Soon. In the next 24 hours. She's stable, right now. She hasn't got any worse since she was admitted, but brain swellings are hard to predict. We need to make sure she keeps her oxygen levels up to prevent brain damage. She's hooked up to the IV to keep her blood pressure up for the same reason. Ventriculostomy is an option if she gets a buildup of pressure.'

'What's that?'

'We cut a small hole into the skull to drain fluid off.'

Artie rubbed his face. 'Bloody hell.' It was hard to believe she was in such a bad way. She just looked asleep. There wasn't a mark on her, not so much as a graze. They'd cleaned her up nicely.

'So there's nothing I can do, except wait?'

'Nothing. If it's any comfort, this sort of injury is quite commonplace. Blows to the head happen to a lot of people from construction-site workers to linebackers, so we totally know what we're doing. It's all well-established procedure and she'll get the best of attention. If she remains stable we'll bring her out of the coma and give her a 30,000-mile service and I'm sure she'll be fine. I suggest you go back to your room and get some rest. We'll assess you tomorrow for PTSD.'

'PTSD? Post Traumatic Stress Disorder?'

Brad Phillips nodded. 'You've been through a lot. But physically, bruises aside, you're fine. Not even a broken finger bone. You really lucked out. It was carnage in there.'

'I don't have PTSD. I can't get it because I'm from Yorkshire and we're genetically programmed to resist it. We grow up expecting trauma, stress and disorder. In fact, life without any of those three things would be too bloody easy for us. What happened to Georgina Roberts, the manager? Coll said she'd survived.'

Brad Phillips raised his dark eyebrows. 'She's alive but lost a lot of blood. She took the blast full in the face. She's pretty messed up. Likely blind. She's tough lady, though. She pulled through when it looked touch and go for a few hours.'

'God, the poor woman. So somehow, I was the only one in the building who got out unhurt?'

'Not unhurt but relatively unscathed, yes. I must go.' He checked the display on the machine Kaz was hooked up to and then nodded. 'She's in a good shape. Everything as it should be. Now, go and get some rest.'

Artie did as he was told, went to bed and slept, waking at just before 7am feeling a lot more like his normal self.

It was really more like staying in a themed hotel than a hospital. He was given a choice of breakfasts, opting for eggs, smoked salmon, spinach and an English muffin. This was what money could buy you in the American healthcare system. They still couldn't make a decent cup of tea, though, that seemed to be completely outside of any American's ability, no matter how much you paid them. Quite why, remained a mystery to every Brit that ever went to America. How hard was it to pour boiling water onto some leaves? And was it possible to have it in a cup that wasn't an inch thick? They invented rock 'n' roll, though, so he was prepared to forgive them for the tea thing.

He asked a nurse if Kaz was awake, but there was no change. There was a text on his phone from Colleen.

'Hope you're feeling better, babe. If you're OK, Mo will visit you this morning 10.30am with her team. Things are moving fast. Will drop in on you later today. Am tied up all day sorting out my legacy thing.'

And if one of the top lawyers in the country says she's going to come at 10.30am, you can be pretty sure she will. Right on time, there was a knock at the door and in came Mo Casson. She was 55 and dressed in a plain and yet incredibly fashionable and expensive style, that you really only saw in high-powered Southern Californian circles. She wore a beautifully tailored two-piece suit of ecru linen, a collarless white silk shirt and a fine silver and turquoise necklace. Her hair, coloured yellow-blonde to look like it probably had always looked, was swept back. A pair of round, fine, silver-rimmed glasses sat on top of her small nose. She oozed class and money, despite wearing absolutely nothing ostentatious at all, unless you could call a small desert rose embroidered in gold and blue onto the collar of the shirt, ostentatious. Like a lot of women in their 50s that Colleen knew, she was a bit rock 'n' roll, a bit business, and a bit older fashion model.

She came with two young men in their 20s in tow, one bearded and shortish, one tall and willowy, who looked like he'd walked out of a Calvin Klein ad. Both carried iPads.

'Hey, Artie. Mo Casson. Did Coll tell you I was coming?' she said.

He nodded. She spoke in what would pass for a well-to-do accent in LA: clipped and without affectation.

'This is Joe Reed,' she pointed to the bearded man. 'And this is Stefan Larsson. They're part of my evidence-gathering team. Now, how this is gonna work is we're going to get you to recollect everything you remember about the explosion.' She spoke as if time was short. There was no chit chat or small talk or condolences. Artie liked that. He'd grown up with a spade being called a spade and any other way seemed a waste of everyone's time. It had been a good quality to have in rock 'n' roll, as it turned out, where a bit of blunt honesty was often at a premium.

Mo walked up and down slowly, pacing to and fro at the end of his bed, asking him a lot of questions while Stefan filmed his response and Joe Reed took notes.

'This feels weird. It's like you're making a TV show,' he said, looking at the iPad filming him.

'I know, but it's so much easier for our purposes to have you talking about this while it's fresh in your mind. We can see what you're sure about and not so sure.'

'I wish Kaz was here to do my make-up,' he said, half under his breath.

It was a rigorous, detailed interview. Mo left no stone unturned as they went back to the Ben Goldman incident and their subsequent meetings with Georgina and Honest Joe. Colleen had obviously briefed her about that, too.

'Before the first explosion, there was a commotion on the shop floor,' Artie said.

'What sort of commotion?' asked Mo.

'Voices raised. Shouting.'

'Arguing?'

'No. Protesting or maybe warning. Then someone shouted "No!" really loudly.'

'Male or female?'

He thought about it. 'Male.'

'Then what happened?'

'The first explosion.'

'How long did that happen after you heard someone say "No"?'

'It was pretty instant. Georgina walked to the door and then turned to look at me and Kaz with a frown. She turned back, and Bang!'

'So she was surprised to hear a raised voice?'

'Yes, very much so.'

'Did she know whose voice it was?' she asked.

'No, she didn't seem to.'

'OK, then what happened?'

He described the first explosion and how they'd reacted.

'How long before the next explosion?'

Artie tried to recall. 'It wasn't long, just a few seconds. After it had gone off, there was almost no noise apart from some screams and moans.'

'Tell me about the big explosion.'

He paused to think about that hideous moment.

'I just covered my head and dropped to the floor at the same time. Just out of instinct.'

'But you had stood up.'

'Yes, I'd just got back to my feet after the first bang.'

'Now think carefully. When you stood up did you see anything through the shattered glass, looking out into the store?'

'My only thought was for Kaz.'

'Of course. But think. Did you see anything at all?'

He didn't respond for maybe as much as half a minute, as his memory led him back through the series of events, trying to let what was surely in his brain somewhere come to the fore.

'The glass windows were all broken, but the plasterboard divide was intact...so it must have gone off on the far side of the store. I just couldn't believe it. Shelf units had fallen over and there was a lot of dust in the air...'

'...and at that point, there was a huge explosion?'

'Yes...hold on...no...that was...' He counted five seconds on his fingers. '...a few seconds later. I stood up, looked around and...' it came back to him '...there was movement - someone running.'

'Running? Where?'

'There were steps going away from me. Then in a split second came the explosion.'

'Were those two things related?'

'I have no way of knowing. Do you know if the bombs were planted or thrown in, or was it a suicide bomb?'

'The first was by the door, which is why you felt less impact and the second was far bigger and more powerful, at the end of an aisle. That's all we do know. LAPD forensics are working on it, not to mention the CIA.'

'CIA?'

'Terrorist implications,' she said. 'Now, Colleen has given me all the details about the mercury poisoning. At some point, we will put together a team to go up to San Francisco to nail Green on Green down about that and to see the people at Long Run. Unless we're well prepared and time this right, they aren't going to do much, except place their lawyers in front of us and say no comment for a while, then feign concern, then say it's a rogue issue and that there's no proof Carly was killed by the soy jerky - and in that, they're kinda right - because it's purely a circumstantial thing, right now, albeit a weird coincidence. That would normally allow them to kick it all into the long grass. That's how these things work, so to head that off, we're planning a media strategy right now to break the story nationwide. That'll flush them out and force them to take it seriously more quickly, if only for PR reasons. We'll also eventually issue lawsuits against Long Run for Carly's manslaughter, on behalf of her estate.'

'Her estate? She was a kid, she didn't have an estate. She doesn't have any surviving family.'

'Not true. Robbie's deceased wife has a sister in England.'

'Wow, I didn't know that.'

'We're onto that, too. We'll also be suing on your behalf for distress in relation to the matter, including Robbie's suicide. So we'll be going at it from several angles.'

'On my behalf? I don't want you to do that.'

Mo Casson looked over her fine silver wire-rimmed glasses at him. 'You have good cause. And you will win once we prove culpability. And we will prove culpability because, self-evidently, someone is culpable.'

'I get that, but I don't want to profit from this human misery.'

But she wasn't fazed by that. 'Understandable. Creditable. Two things. One. You can give the money away to someone who really needs it, thus turning a bad thing into a good thing. Two. It will help pay for Colleen's legal costs which, as I have already told her, will be extensive...and extensive is the word we use in the legal profession to mean, what I think the world of rock 'n' roll might call, an absolute fuck-ton of money.'

The fact that she swore caught Artie by surprise. She was so well-spoken and intelligent, dropping the f-bomb had a much bigger impact out of her mouth.

'A fuck-ton is a lot,' he said.

'Oh, yeah. We're going balls to the wall on this...and I have no idea what that even means.' She pulled a cross-eyed face and made her mouth crooked. It was the first time she'd cracked the thick ice mask face of legal efficiency and it was good to see, because he was beginning to think she was a robot.

'Whatever it costs, Coll can cover it.'

'Even so. Innocent people have been hurt by the malice or negligence of parties unknown. We need to get them brought to justice and, if I know the LAPD, we should not rely on them to do so with any haste or accuracy.'

'Do you think the bomb is related to the poisoning?'

She gave him a briefly disparaging look as if that was a given. 'Of course, Artie...of course, it is. Ask yourself, why wouldn't it be? Two out-of-the-ordinary events revolving around the same place - we have to assume a connection.'

'Any theories as to why?'

She made a throat-cutting gesture to indicate to stop filming. Joe and Stefan put their iPads down.

'I actually think it's quite obvious, what's going on. It's a concerted attempt to put Green on Green and Mother Earth out of business. First you poison the customers, then you destroy a store, and you've made everyone too scared to buy its food or shop at any in the chain. So, as they're both owned by Long Run, I suggest they are the target.'

Artie took a drink of water. 'That doesn't make sense.'

'Why not?'

'The poisoning has only affected Carly, and Ben Goldman as well, in relation to peanuts. But no peanut was found in our tests, which I find odd. So as far as we know, the mercury was in the soy jerky alone, and in no other product we had tested. It takes ages to have an effect when administered in small doses, so what good was that in terms of destroying the business? Carly had been eating it for months, so they were prepared to be very bloody patient if it *was* purposefully done.'

Mo nodded, her lips pursed together. 'This is good stuff. Give me more,' she said brusquely.

'Think about it, Mo, whoever was doing it could simply have tipped off the FDA, had some soy jerky tested and exposed the contamination that way. There was no need for Carly, or anyone else to die, if all they wanted to achieve was to close the stores down, or at the very least, undermine confidence in them. By contrast, the bombing is an instant terrorist act which kills loads of people. Why deploy both ways? They wouldn't, is your answer. What you've got is two different individuals or groups of people, committing two different crimes and if you ask me, probably for two different reasons.'

Joe and Stefan kept making notes as he spoke.

Mo kept looking at him impassively, as though processing what he had said. 'Interesting. But would you agree that it is highly unlikely that the same store was targeted for *two* different reasons?'

'That does seem unlikely, but not impossible.' He thought for a moment. 'Or maybe it was attacked by two different people, but for the same reason.'

'Wow, are they pumping the good medicine into you, Artie?' She gave him what was probably her warmest smile. 'OK, we'll leave you now.' She gestured to the two men. 'I've got your cellphone, so I can text you, if I need you to be in touch. This will all take some time, so get well and we'll reconvene soon. Give my good wishes to Kaz. We'll get to the bottom of this and we'll make the guilty pay.'

'So will the LAPD, I hope.'

She raised her eyebrows at that. 'Well, that'd be nice, but in this city, I would not put any bets on them doing that and even if they made an arrest, I would not rely on it being the right arrest for the right reasons.'

'You mean they're corrupt?'

'Not all of them. But it is endemic to one degree or another and you know, Long Run is Big Money. And where Big Money goes, a river of shit tends to follow. Have the LAPD talked to you yet?'

'No.'

'Well, there you are, then. That tells you a lot.'

He watched her go, a bit in awe of her. Maybe it was the drugs they'd given him, but she was like Steely Dan's music made flesh. Complex, smooth and classy, studied and intellectual, she made you feel a bit better than you had beforehand. She was super professional; a big star in the legal world, but not one of those Gloria Allred-type lawyers, who did celebrity trials, who was a perverse sort of TV star, playing up for the cameras, defending the indefensible. No. Mo was old school. Hard working, unremitting, totally scrupulous and forensic and she commanded a huge fee because of all those things. And because she was at the top of her profession - and it was a bloody hard profession to be at the top of in LA, let alone across the whole of the States - she could pick and choose the cases she took on. If she lost a case it would damage her reputation and fees, but if she just took easy cases, that would do likewise. So she needed tough assignments, but ones she felt strongly she could win. Based in Laguna Beach, her operation was spread across three floors of a modern building, oceanside on the Pacific Coast Highway. Part modern art gallery, part interior design magazine shoot, it was all very cool, very hip and very, very serious. She had assembled a team of lawyers and investigators who could and did rip the great, the good and the evil apart. The gutting and filleting of a defence case was a speciality; her summing-up for juries, an act of irresistibly edited logic. Recently, she had taken on a major car manufacturer and won in a case over misreported CO_2 emissions. She had sued the city of Beverly Hills for not protecting its citizens against the effects of cigarette smoke by allowing smoking on the streets, and she had won. And the law was changed to outlaw public smoking as a result. Mo Casson made things happen. She was feared from city hall to the county line; and rightly so. If Mo Casson was coming after you, it was because she was sure she could take you down.

And, beyond all of that, she had a nice arse. Well, you couldn't be a photographer and not notice such a thing. He was good at shape and form. Men or women. Always had been. Not that she was his sort of woman. Too neat and tidy and intellectual. No stink of rock 'n' roll about her. People like her intimidated him because he had no idea where their minds were at. His life had been lived so far away from the careerist mentality that when you met someone who had relentlessly dedicated themselves to theirs, it felt like meeting an alien life form. But even so, for 55, she definitely had a great arse.

He lay back and took a nap, feeling stressed about everything. Life had fallen apart.

CHAPTER 14

When he woke up, he felt disorientated, having to regrasp where he was and what had happened. It wasn't good. But if there was one thing being born a Northerner gave you, it was an iron will and a determination to get the fuck through whatever travails life threw at you. All of his family had been the same - never more at home than when fighting adversity. You gritted your teeth, got your shit together and kicked back.

So he got up, put on the dressing gown and went in search of a toilet. After a piss, he went to see Kaz again, looking tentatively around her door. She was still just silently lying there. Breathing. Still in the induced coma. He walked up to the bed quietly and looked at her, then spoke to her like she was awake. Talking like they always talked with each other.

'Hey, lady. Just met this legal bint of Coll's. Very impressive. A touch of the wire-rimmed glasses war-movie SS officer Nazi about her. Ruthless. You'd like her arse. Shapely. She's loaded. She came with two mincers, not gay, just...you know...modern blokes, they're all puffs, aren't they? Those skinny jeans - every man under 30 looks gay to me now. All that hugging and touching. Urgh. Not like men when we were kids. I miss that. I miss blokes being blokes. It's like movie stars - you'd never get a Charles Bronson or Robert Mitchum type being a star now. You've got to look gay to get anywhere these days. That's why my stock has fallen. I'm just not gay enough. And I won't grow a hipster beard, either.'

He rambled on and on and on, just saying stuff randomly, as he held her hand, one long, slow, tear falling down his cheek after another.

'They've put you in a coma. I mean if I'd known they wanted to do that, I'd have at least given you a good bottle of tequila. We could have gone to Palm Springs to that Mexican place we like and got fucked up on tequila sunrises. Remember Manny? That dude knows how to make a drink. I had to carry you out of there, down the road to that place we were given while we covered the Sundance Film Festival. Nearly broke my back. You didn't wake up for 16 hours. Yeah, that was a good trip.'

He leaned over her so that his face was directly in front of hers, just so he could feel her breath on his face. The little soft exhalations that said she was still alive. The machine she was hooked up to kept its steady beeping.

As she lay there, impassive but lovely, he placed his lips on hers. They were bone dry and could easily split, so, on impulse, he licked them with the tip of his tongue, and then kissed her on the lips. It was such a bizarre

110

experience, being so close and intimate with someone you knew so well, but they were unable to respond in any way whatsoever.

Or perhaps not.

As he put his lips to hers, the bleeping on the machine became a little more rapid. Her heart rate increased on the machine from 60 to 75, only for perhaps five seconds. He watched the green number go up a few beats and then sink back down; maybe it was going to do that regardless but he smiled to himself. Somewhere in there, wherever *there* was, Kaz still existed. Briefly, he thought of lifting the sheets, putting his hand inside her hospital gown and rubbing one of her big nipples, to see what happened - but maybe that bordered on some sort of abuse. Ha ha...she'd think it funny, though.

As he returned to his room, he realised he felt a lot better. His lungs were sore. It put him in mind of his days as a chain smoker when he'd go through 60 fags a day and wake up feeling like he had a bonfire burning in his chest. Actually, it wasn't as bad as that. Similarly, the aches and pains were not especially worse than the ones that came with being 53 years old.

He found his phone in his locker and plugged it in to charge it up, then sat in the armchair and twiddled his thumbs, feeling like taking a big hit of tequila. How did you discharge yourself from hospital, anyway? In the movies they just walk out - but that seemed disrespectful. These people had looked after him while he'd been sparko. They'd made sure he wasn't in danger of dying and that was A Big Thing. You couldn't just walk out on that.

So he put the TV on, but he hated TV. He'd not watched more than a few hours of TV, apart from football games in sports bars, in the last 10 years. Why would you? It was a dumb drug. It had never been his thing. Life drained away fast enough without passively letting it leak through a TV set. And mainstream American television had always seemed highly tuned into the dumbest common denominator, and worked on the basis that you were an idiot. He put a news channel on. The woman reading the autocue had one of those American voices without any bass in it. Dry and croaking and yet somehow also very piercing, it was the sonic newsreader equivalent of a hot needle in your ear. And worse yet, she had hair that looked like it had been sprayed out of a can and moulded into a helmet. Yeah, really, where the fuck was that tequila when you needed it?

Then came the old man, who always sat alongside the painted 29-year-old woman. He looked like he was made out of polyester and cheese.

They both spoke words like they weren't words at all, but rather some sort of weird ancient tongue; as though they couldn't really comprehend what the noise emanating out of their mouths might mean. They didn't listen to themselves. They were automatons programmed to deliver garbage. It was dehumanizing to hear a story about a shooting at a school and a specially created shampoo for poodles, both delivered with the same degree of faux gravitas. Yeah man, Henley had it right 30 years ago. We all know that crap is king.

"More news now on the bombing of the Mother Earth store in Topanga Canyon. LAPD assistant director Chad Blondell said today that quote, good progress is being made in our investigations, we expect to be making arrests in the near future. More on that story from our reporter Channing Fish.'

It cut to the improbably named reporter, standing in front of the devastated store. She repeated the exact same words that the newsreader had said as her introduction. Artie sat forward, looking over the reporter's shoulder at the destroyed store.

His heart beat harder in his chest when he saw the remains of the store. Bloody hell, how had they taken him, Kaz and Georgina out of there alive? It was little more than rubble. Only one small section of the roof remained intact, the rest had collapsed into the building, and the whole of the front of the store was gone, replaced by big shards of plate glass and heaps of plaster, brick and dust. The fire crews and paramedics had done a great job. How could you just black it all out and lie there like a piece of meat? Suddenly, he felt weak and exhausted. Shit. What was he thinking? You couldn't just get over something like this, like it was a hangover. He'd been unconscious for nearly two days. No-one had said he'd come near to death but surely he must have been able to see it from wherever he was.

So he turned the TV off and got back into bed with a groan, picked up his phone as it was charging and flicked through the screen. As he did so, the door to his room opened a little way and a man slid into the room as though trying to be as quiet and surreptitious as possible. Dressed in black jeans, canvas baseball boots and black t-shirt, he was middle-aged and olive skinned. Italian or Greek, maybe.

Artie propped himself up a little. 'Who are you?' he said, his bad-dude radar twitching.

The man turned to him, only briefly catching his eye. 'You don't know me.' He took the bedside chair and jammed it under the door handle.

What the hell was he doing? Artie cast a look to his right to locate where his glass of water was. That glass was his only weapon here. This bloke meant business. He had a mean look about him. His adrenaline levels went ballistic. This was serious. This man had come for him. Shit. He took the glass, drank the water and held it in his hand, ready to jam it in the fucker's face.

'Here, take this,' the man said, thrusting an envelope towards him, that he'd taken from his back pocket.

Artie looked at it but didn't take it. 'What's this about? Tell me who you are.'

Be strong. Be brave. Don't let him know you're scared. Above all, don't go down without a fight: the Yorkshire mantra.

'Who I am doesn't matter. Take it.' He tossed the envelope on the bed. 'When you leave here, you'll be in a lot of danger. The information in there will help you.'

Artie affected a cynical sneer. 'In danger? In danger of what, and from who?'

'Long Run and Green on Green. They've nearly killed you once, they won't stop now.'

'Long Run was behind the bomb?'

The man looked at his watch. 'Listen to me.' He had yellowing teeth, which was unusual for America, the home of bright white and even smiles. 'You and your friend in there, you got lucky. These people are evil bastards. You've got in their way, they don't like it and they will try to kill you again and they won't stop trying until they've succeeded. The only chance you've got is to bust the whole thing wide open.'

Artie just sat there in bed. Some sixth sense, a sixth sense born out of dealing with bullshit promo people, arsehole promoters, twattish managers and bastard lead singers, told him this man wasn't bad ass, at all. He was faking it. He didn't look right. No. He was a phoney.

'Are you taking the piss, mate?' said Artie. You met crazy people like this quite regularly in California. People who would sidle up to you at a bar and start to unload some weird paranoid conspiracy theory. Rock 'n' roll was a planet that pulled those people into its orbit all too easily.

'Take it seriously, my friend. Read the document in the envelope. They won't come for you in here, but as soon as you leave, watch your back. I'm telling you, look into Long Run and Green on Green. Get the word out that they're bad people involved in a bad industry. That way, you might be able to scare them off.'

Artie, picked up the envelope. 'Alright, mate, but what's this to you?'

The man didn't say anything more. Instead he picked Artie's phone up, took his own phone, skimmed the screen and then put the two together and pressed something on his own iPhone. 'You've now got a quick code on your phone. It'll take you to a password-protected message board. Your login is on the form in the envelope.' He glanced up at Artie, seeing the doubt in his eyes. 'Take me seriously Mr Taylor, if you want to stay alive.'

Artie crossed his arms across his chest and deployed some proper Northern arseyness. 'Why do you care, either way, mate?'

The man went to the door and took the chair away. 'Good luck. You're really going to need it. Read that immediately.' He pointed at the envelope again, pulled open the door, looked from side to side and then left.

Feeling cynical, Artie opened it and took out a sheet of paper. On it was a Venn diagram and at the bottom, two lines of jumbled letters, which was his password and login. He turned over the sheet. It was just a couple of names and addresses.

He let it drop on the bed, feeling too exhausted to look at it just now. Was the guy a random crazy? Probably not. Mo had said it was all related, the mercury and the bombs. He'd better get this stuff to her, so he took pictures of both sides of the sheet of paper and emailed them to her along with the quick code. Within 90 seconds he got an email back from Joe, acknowledging receipt. They were some machine to have on your side, and god knows, it felt like he was going to really need them.

He was tired but couldn't sleep and yet he felt physically knackered, so he tried the TV again and found a couple of reruns of *Seinfeld*, which, despite never watching much TV, he had loved since day one. He'd done some portraits of Jerry to advertise his Las Vegas shows in 2008 and had really liked him. All comedians have a touch of rock 'n' roll about them, even super-straight guys like Jerry.

Before the end of the second episode, Colleen arrived, standing in the doorway with a smile on her face, looking, as usual, like she'd just walked off the set of *Charlie's Angels* in 1977.

'Hey, there, Mister Taylor. How are you feeling?'

'I'm already a bit bored of being here. Good to see you, though.'

'Any news about Kaz?'

He shook his head. 'They're just hoping she responds to the drugs they've given her to reduce the swelling in her brain. I'm trying not to think about the worst outcome.'

Colleen shook her head ruefully.

'Well, we've just got to pray for her and I don't know any other way to do that than by toasting her with a drink. She'd dig that, right?' She produced a bottle of Jack Daniels. 'All we need is two glasses, some ice and some Coke...oh, what's this? Look what I found.' She took out two tumblers, a can of Coke and a small flask of ice cubes and gave him her pearly smile. She was some rock 'n' roll woman.

It tasted sweeter than an angel's piss. Intoxicating and strong, he sank it all down in one, relishing the taste of every swallow.

'Can I have another please, mother,' he said, holding out the glass to her. As she made the drink, he began telling her about the visit from the man in black. She looked up at him with her hypnotic caramel eyes.

'That's weird. Very weird. You think he was a crazy person?'

'I don't know. I sent it all to Mo.' He took the sheet of paper from the bedside table. 'This is what he left for me.'

She took it from him and looked at it, sipping at her drink. 'I'm not sure I understand this diagram. It's just names. Have you looked at the website?'

'No, I'm too tired to make sense of anything, right now. He said I'd be in danger when I leave here but not in here, so I'll deal with it when I'm feeling a bit brighter.'

'Was he for real?'

He puffed his cheeks out and blew out air. 'What does "for real" even mean? If he's nutter, he's done some work on creating his fantasy world. Whatever he's on about, he definitely thought it was the truth. Whether it is the truth, is another matter altogether.'

'So when he said you had to blow it all open, what did he mean?'

'Seemed to think I should expose Long Run and Green on Green. Obviously, he doesn't know we've got the Mo Casson team on the payroll to do that.'

'Too right, baby. She'll get to the core of it all. But I'm worried that this guy is right and someone wants to harm you and, I assume, Kaz as well.'

'Well, I don't know what I can do about it, if they do. I'm not going to get a bodyguard.'

'Huh, we could get you a bodyguard. I mean, LA is home of the bodyguard. There are more bodyguards per square foot here than the rest of America put together.'

'Yeah, but if someone puts a sniper on a grassy knoll, no bodyguard is going to be able to keep you alive. It's bang bang, thank you and goodnight LA.'

'OK, I'll see what Mo thinks is the best course of action when she's seen what you sent over.'

'She was saying about suing on my behalf, for distress or whatever the fuck, so that I'd get payout to put against your legal costs which are set to be officially a "fuck-ton".'

She waved his comment away. 'Oh, screw that. I don't care. I only want to see Carly and Robbie and you and Kaz get justice.'

'What exactly is a fuck-ton in this case?'

'10 mill.' She said it without emotion or expression.

'What? 10 million dollars? That's about six million quid, in real money. What the fuck do you get for that?'

'You've seen her. You get, effectively, your own private investigation and evidence-collection team. You get to win. I want to win. Who cares how much it costs?'

'But all the same, it's so much money...'

She took out her phone and tapped at it and then held it up to him. 'This is the main deposit account at Wells Fargo. Tell me the number.'

He took it off her. The account balance was...fucking hell. He had to count the noughts. '95 million, four hundred and 27 thousand dollars and five cents.' He looked at her. 'It's the five cents that I'm most impressed with.'

'And that's just what I can access pretty much immediately. On top of that there's all the stock and there's the property. That account generates four million a year in interest alone. If Mo came back with a 50 million bill, it makes literally no difference to me. When you're super rich, you just can't spend it before you've earned a heap more. Mom's royalty cheque will be in at the end of July. That'll be another five to 10 million dollars onto the 95.'

Rich is a concept we're all familiar with. We hear the numbers and what they can buy but until you've got it right there in front of you, until you know someone who is seriously rich, it doesn't really impress itself on you exactly what it means. Artie just looked at the huge number and realised that actually, with a three-million dollar Malibu home, Coll was living frugally for someone with this sort of wealth. She could buy a huge Brentwood estate and have enough change for a pizza made of diamonds.

He handed her the phone back. 'You've never hidden your money from me, but I think I'm only just realising how much it actually is. It's insane, Coll. I mean, the people who keep this hospital clean will earn $25,000 a year, if they're lucky. You'll earn more than that in interest, in a couple of days.'

She nodded and did a little lip curl. 'Like I said at Honest Joe's, I'm on the wrong side of history. I'm the living embodiment of the sickness of the American Dream, where the rich get richer and the rest fight for the crumbs from our table. I'm disgusted at myself for taking so long to fully realise this. For years I just stuck money into charities to assuage the guilt. Now I see I have to do something far more profound. I've got more of Mo's team working on the legals of that for me, as well as overseeing drawing up a new will.'

'Yeah? You're working out a way to get rid of money?'

'Uh huh. I've given her notes about where it's all going to go. She'll set up the trust funds and such. I'll tell you about it in detail when you're better. Need another hit?'

'Yeah, just straight with ice please. A fucking big one.'

She slung some crushed ice from the flask into his glass and poured in four fingers of Jack. He drank it down like kissing an old friend. This was the best sodding medicine.

'There you go, a big hit of rock 'n' roll. I brought your iPod, laptop and some books, as well. How long do you think you're gonna be in here, have they said?'

'I'm alright. They'll check me out tomorrow. My lungs hurt but the rest is just bruises. Nothing that drinking and Advil won't make better. But Kaz is a different matter.'

'She'll get the best attention here.'

'I know, but I don't want her to wake up on her own. Assuming she does wake up.'

'Of course she will.'

'She's got a fractured skull, Coll. Her brain is swollen. People die from shit like that...or worse, they get turned into vegetables.'

'She'll be fine. She's tough girl.'

But it was just words. Tough was nothing to do with it. It was all down to the medical care. Had they treated her in time? Was the blow to her head just too powerful for her to survive it?

After Colleen had left, he fell into a half-pissed sleep. A nurse looked in on him just before midnight, waking him up in doing so. She came in, cooing at him, squeezing his hand and brushing hair off his forehead. She sat with him as he dropped off again. Just a voice and a shape in the dark, a lovely energy in the room. Like your mother when you're little. By 6am he gave up on trying to stay asleep and went for a piss. On the way back he looked in on Kaz. She was still lying there expressionless and asleep.

How do you deal with shit like this? It was so quiet and warm that he nodded off in the bedside chair, feeling oddly comforted by just being beside Kaz. They'd shared a room and often a bed, so many times over the years, especially in the last five or six, when the money had dried up, that being with her felt much more natural than being on his own or with Colleen.

Just after 7am, a nurse came in.

'Oh, hello again, Artie.' She was the same nurse that had checked him in the night. 'How is her ladyship?' She was English, a chubby five foot eight, maybe in her mid 40s, with a short, mid-60s Mia Farrow-style haircut and pale blue eyes, dressed in the regulation green hospital pyjama-type uniform.

He yawned and rubbed sleep from his eyes. 'Still the same.'

She checked the readings from the bleepy machine. 'Well, she's had a good night by the look of it. I think they'll bring her out of the coma this morning, if the x-ray shows the swelling has gone down.'

'Really? Wow. Can I be here for that? I don't want her to come round and not have a friendly face in the room.'

'I'm sure that'd be no problem. I'll keep you up to date with everything.' She smiled and put her hand over his. 'You look so tired, Artie. Why not go to your room and sleep a bit more?'

'I want to be here...we're old friends.'

She spoke gently and kindly. 'I know. I know all about it. I looked after you when they brought you in from that bomb site. You were in a right state, kidda.'

'I don't remember any of that.'

'You were unconscious for a day and a half. Not so much as a flicker, not even when I gave you a proper bed bath to get all the muck off you. And that took forever because you were covered in plaster dust.' She smiled again.

'Huh, well, it's not often you talk to someone who's seen you naked whilst you've been unconscious. Not since I did a tour in 1991 with Guns n' Roses, anyway.' He smiled and reached out for her hand. This was emotional stuff.

118

She chuckled as her warm, soft hand gripped his. 'Don't worry, I didn't abuse you, darlin'. Ha ha. Now, come on, let's get you into bed. I'll call in on you when anything happens with Kaz. You've been through a major trauma, you can't just brush it off. I know you Yorkshire lads think you're hard, but you need to rest.'

'Yeah, we do. Mostly because we are. Where are you from in England? Somewhere in the northeast?'

'A place called Redcar. I've been here for 15 years now, though. I've got my green card and everything. I love LA, it knocks Redcar into a cocked hat, whatever a cocked hat is, like.' She chuckled again.

'Ah, that's Teesside, isn't it? You've not lost your accent. Me and Kaz have worked at Middlesbrough Town Hall many times. We did that Teesside Blues festival in 2009. That was fun.'

She gave him a nice smile and continued to coo at him. 'I know. I looked you up, didn't I? You're famous. My album collection has got your photos all over it. Cover photo by Artie Taylor.' She traced the words in midair with her index finger.

'I used to be famous. Well, as famous as a photographer gets, and that's not very famous.'

She bent over him and said, in a motherly sort of way. 'Come on, back to bed with you.'

Considering he was 53, he fell into being led like he was a small boy, very easily. Maybe we never really grow up. At 53, being a little kid didn't seem that long ago, less long ago than it did when he was 30. Yeah, time is some weird shit.

Back in his room, she pulled his sheets down and brushed at them to straighten them out. 'Come on then, let's be having you,' she said, taking off his dressing gown and patting him on the backside.

'Can I do anything for you?' she said, with a bright look in her eyes.

'What did you have in mind?' he said. She stood between him and the bed.

'Oh, I don't know. *Anything* you want.' She had a look in her washed-out blue eyes.

Artie had spent his life backstage. He knew a groupie when he saw one and this was some sort of groupie. Not that he minded.

He smiled, put his hands on her hips and ran his fingertips over the elastic seam of her underwear underneath the cotton hospital pants.

'Thank you.'

She smiled at him in an unaffected way. 'Why?'

He drew her into him and kissed her on the lips once, feeling the curve of her buttocks as he did so.

'Because anything that is an expression of the nice part of the human soul, is exactly what I need right now. Though my wife wouldn't approve of us getting down and dirty, obviously.'

She raised an eyebrow. 'But she's not here. And that door locks. If you just need to feel the loving hand of a woman, I could be that woman.'

'I know but now has to be lived with forever. Know what I mean?'

She nodded. 'Alright, then. I bet you're a nice man, you, Artie Taylor.'

'I do my best but I wouldn't put any money on it.'

She kissed her fingers and put them onto his cheek. 'Sorry if I was inappropriate.'

'No, you were very appropriate. And if I desperately need a hand job, I'll just press my buzzer.'

She laughed. 'Well, I'm a professional. I've got Kleenex and everything...' she pulled a wad of tissues from her pocket '...and I know you're nice and clean, don't I? I'll see you later, eh, mister. I'll let you know about Kaz.'

He put his arms around her and gave her a tight hug, feeling emotionally mixed up. Life had taught him that you accepted love or affection, or whatever the hell it was, wherever you found it and whenever you needed it. And he needed it now.

She radiated warmth and a familiar northern womanliness, with lovely big breasts, soft, fatty hips and a doughy belly. It was hard to break away from her without rolling her onto the bed, taking off her pants and going hell for leather on her bones. But he was 53. And he was tired. And probably had PTSD. But a woman who wants to have some sort of sex with you, no matter how inappropriate the location, or how weird or unlikely, is never not a wonderful thing, even for a grizzled old cynic like him.

'My shift is over. But I'll be back later this afternoon,' she said, patting him on the backside.

Sometimes not having sex is better than doing it. The anticipation and imagination are almost everything, the doing, not so much. Then again, as he watched her leave the room, he reckoned that, like so many northern British women, she'd be fantastically passionate in bed.

What a weird thing to happen. He snorted a laugh to himself. Rock 'n' roll.

CHAPTER 15

He slept for a couple of hours, then someone brought him some eggs and toast. After eating he felt a lot brighter and picked up the letter that the man in black had left. There were four elongated circles in four colours - red, blue, pink, yellow. Where they all intersected was jade green and titled Mother Earth. The red circle was labeled Long Run, the blue Green on Green, pink was titled Keith Perez, the yellow, Honest Joe. All these elements were related to Mother Earth but in addition there were arrows laid out clockwise, linking one circle to another, as though to suggest that not only were they all brought together by Mother Earth, but also had a relationship to each other. He shook his head, trying to work it out. Why not just write this shit out, rather than make a diagram? It made it look like a school project.

Picking up his now fully charged phone he went online and via the quick code the man in black had put on his phone, arrived at a blank page with a login and password box. He entered the string of letters and numbers and clicked enter. It loaded a screen which said, *Hello Artie. We hope you're feeling better. We'll do what we can to help you. We are the Paleo Patriots. We're dedicated to changing America's health by promoting a grass-fed paleo diet as the norm, to end the mass consumption of carbohydrate and processed food and the industrialized intensive farming of animals.*

Oh, Christ, they were more nutters. And food nutters, next to gun nutters, are the biggest nutters of all. He read on.

We have been investigating the Long Run Investment Group for some time. They own Green on Green and the Mother Earth chain of vegan stores. They have a lot of money in the soy industry. It's our belief that they are trying to corrupt their own products in order to undermine their own business, to scare away trade from the stores and their brands, to put people off being vegans and back to meat eating. They are huge investors in feedlots. You exposed their plans when the soy jerky tested positive for mercury and as a result they have tried to kill you and accelerated their campaign to undermine their own company. They won't stop now. The names on the document are Green on Green executives past and present who we think might be sympathetic to our cause. Go and talk to them. We will help you gather evidence against Long Run. We will put updated info here. Be careful at all times and trust no-one.

Artie read it through again and let out a groan. This was garbage, surely. It read like something from a cheap movie. It had to be some sort of sick joke or just the work of weirdo conspiracy theorists. They'd gone to a lot of effort, though. How had they found out about the mercury poisoning? That man couldn't have known Carly, could he? Maybe the hospital had put out a press release. He looked at the names on the sheet of paper. Why have this sheet of paper as well as the password-protected website? No reason. They were just trying to be clever. Patricia Gunn. Artie looked her up and found someone of the same name working at Long Run in San Francisco as an accountant. Keith Perez. He was honorary president of Green on Green and seemed to be the man who started the company in Haight Ashbury in the late 60s.

There was a tap at the door and a doctor walked in.

'Mister Taylor. I'm Doctor Piper. I thought you'd like to know that we will be bringing Kaz out of the induced coma this afternoon. Nurse Armstrong left a note saying you'd like to be present.'

'Yeah. I would. Thanks. Doc, am I good to go home at some point today?'

'We'll check you over and then make a decision. You passed out through lack of oxygen and were unconscious for a relatively long while. The fire department got to you only just in time. We always worry about brain damage when someone suffers a prolonged lack of oxygen. There's no value in hurrying these things. How do you feel?'

'Tired and beat up, but I've felt like that for most of the last 15 years. My lungs feel like I've smoked a joint made out of nuclear waste.'

'You took in a lot of dust. It is very abrasive. We'll see how you are later. I'll give you a heads up when we're ready for Kaz.'

'What will that entail?'

'We just reduce her intake of the drug that's kept her in a coma and she'll come out of it naturally. We've not given her anything today so she should start to come back to the surface soon. As soon as she shows signs of waking up, I'll have you called into the room.'

'So, this is a good sign, is it? The swelling in her brain has gone down?'

'Yes. We've just scanned her and she's responded very well to the drugs. She'll be fine, I'm fairly confident.'

'So she's going to be OK? Thank god.'

'One step at a time, Artie. The brain is a complex thing and there are any number of side effects that a blow to the head can induce, from slurred speech to blackouts. But it may be that she doesn't suffer any adverse effects. We just can't tell right now.'

'But she's not brain damaged?'

He shook his head. 'Not obviously.'

The obfuscating language the doctor used was frustrating, but he understood exactly why he was hedging his bets.

The door opened and in walked Colleen. She looked at Artie and then the doctor.

'Is everything alright?' she said, concerned.

'Fine. I'll see you later this afternoon, Artie,' said the doctor.

He left them alone.

'They're bringing Kaz out of the coma.'

'Will she be OK?'

He groaned. 'Well, let's hope so.'

'She will be. I'm sure she will be. Did you get any sleep?'

'Oh, bits here and there. I've been looking into this...' he held up the sheet of paper. 'I think it's all a load of rubbish.' He outlined what it had said. She pulled a face of disbelief.

'Maybe they're fantasists. I've never heard of the Paleo Patriots,' said Colleen.

'I tried to find them online but there was no group called that.'

She sat on the edge of the bed and took out two DVDs from her shoulder bag. 'I just came from meeting Mo in the Mondrian. She gave me these. They're copies, both Mo's team and the LAPD are on them right now, looking for the bomber, but I thought you might want to take a look, just to keep you busy.'

She put his laptop onto the bed.

'What are they?'

'CCTV recordings from Mother Earth.' She picked up a DVD marked with the number 1. 'This is from the camera which covers the main door, the day you helped Ben Goldman, and also on the day of the explosion. Mo thinks we need to focus on him. She's suspicious of him and his motives.'

'Fay doesn't like him. Said he's a creepy, stalky guy.'

'Fay says that about a lot of people. The second disc is from the store's other camera, from an hour before the explosions, right up until they go off. That might be a bit harrowing for you, man. Don't feel like you have to watch them. Quite how much it'll reveal, I'm not sure, but since you've got time on your hands...'

123

'I'll take a look. We have to nail the bastards that did this and I've not forgotten about Carly and Robbie, either. We need to make this right for them, Coll. Has there been anything released about the bombs? Did someone just lob them in, or had they been planted hours or days ago?'

'Nothing yet, forensics are still all over the site. Mo has people inside LAPD who will keep her right up to date. Look, baby, I can't stay. I've got yet another long legal meeting about mom's estate. I want to get it sorted. Will you be alright?'

I'll be fine.'

'Text me when there's news about Kaz.'

After she'd gone, a wave of tiredness crashed over him again and he took a nap for half an hour. He woke up when someone brought coffee in for him. As he sipped at it, he loaded the first DVD into the laptop.

This was top-notch CCTV. Gone were the days of grainy black and white footage. This was HD, and each disc ~~and~~ was taken from one of two ~~two~~ wide-angle cameras, one at the top back corner of the store, focusing on the entrance and left side of the store, the other in the opposite corner and covering the right side. It was just as well the footage ~~it~~ was stored remotely, because there was no way it'd have survived the blast.

Watching footage of ordinary life happening is a strange experience. Quite interesting really, much more interesting than most television programmes. The greeter by the door, the airhead blonde woman who had said hello to him and Kaz, smiled and waved and nodded at every single shopper, each time with the same degree of enthusiasm. Remarkable, really. It was like she was an automaton.

He kept an eye open for Ben Goldman. A clock running in the bottom right corner of the recording displayed the real time it had been shot in. Artie thought back to that day. What time was it when they'd gone in there? Noon. Yeah, he'd turned off the radio as the news on the hour was starting. So by the time they'd walked from the car to the door, it had to be 12.02-ish. He pressed fast forward and took the clock to 11.59am and waited. It was quite exciting waiting to see yourself on film.

And there they were. 12.01.43pm.

He stopped the playback as he and Kaz came into view. He had his arm around her shoulder. It was funny seeing them in the third person like this. He was so much taller than her, she much more stocky than he. They were an odd couple. Very distinctive. One of those funny electric tingles fired up his spinal column and spread across his back and neck. It was no wonder people knew them as a team. You could create a logo based on the outline of them and it'd be completely distinctive. Artie and Kaz. They were almost a brand.

And that just made him pause a little longer and shed a few silent tears. They rolled down his cheek and splashed onto the computer. He wasn't crying. Not heaving sobs. It was just tears, tears for the woman that lay in the other room, fighting to recover. Tears for what had happened to them. Tears for the life they'd lived with each other. Tears for her last words to him. Tears for the fact that for so long, they had both looked for love with people other than each other, when there had never been any reason to. They had loved each other but somehow had been blind to it and even when she had finally realised and had told him, he'd gone and married another woman, regardless. Maybe the wrong woman.

He played the recording again, wiping his tears away. Watched as they stopped to talk to the greeter and Kaz said about having wind and the woman had pointed to the aisle for mint tea. Then they walked into the store. He paused it again. As they walked away from the greeter, she had, not demonstratively, but very definitely, given Kaz the finger behind their backs. Ha ha...go on, girl. He'd wondered at the time if she was some flavour of stupid or actually very knowing. Now he knew which of those it was. Bless her. Hopefully, she'd not been working the day the bomb had gone off. The thought that that kid might now be a corpse was too much to bear.

He rolled it forward and then hit the pause button again.

Ben Goldman was walking into the store. He walked towards the display of soy jerky and then out of view of that camera.

He spun it forward until he and Kaz were leaving. He smiled to himself. It really was cold in there and her nipples were sticking through her t-shirt, rather dramatically. The HD video documented that very well.

They walked to the door and into the shot came Ben Goldman. Artie stopped the video. He'd already eaten about a third of the soy jerky. He hadn't bought anything else.

When he grabbed his throat, just as he was leaving the store, even at this distance, it was a shocking thing to witness. He was totally overcome with the effects of the peanuts in the jerky, which he must have only eaten a minute or two previously, possibly while he was waiting to check out, the way some hungry people often do. It seemed to come upon him in a rush, the way speed does. One minute you're your normal self, the next you're in a different place altogether.

Artie looked closely at Goldman as he hit the deck, holding his throat. Freezing the image. There was no faking the fear in his eyes. And that was what Artie remembered most powerfully from that moment. Goldman lay half on the entrance mat, the pocket of his pants over the well which the mat was set into. That had to be when his own adrenaline pen had dropped out, even though he couldn't spot it doing so. Artie reversed the recording and watched again as Goldman walked away from the checkout holding the jerky in one hand and chewing. Even if the attack had come on super-quick, there was still time for him to inject himself. He must have felt it coming on as he checked out, all it'd have taken would be to reach inside his pants pocket. But at no time in the sequence of events did he try and do that. It wasn't as if he tried and in his panicked condition dropped it. He'd not even made an attempt.

He rolled it forward, watching as he and Kaz attended Goldman, then Kaz ran to the truck and returned with the pen, jabbing it into Goldman's leg.

When you're involved in something like that, you just do what you've got to do and if you've got some experience of it, you have half an idea of what needs doing. So it was here. Experience of life on the road had educated both he and Kaz how to react and behave in a scary situation like this. Goldman was within minutes of dying, but they hadn't panicked. At a distance, it did look impressive. Other shoppers stood around, looking on, fearfully. But he and Kaz were in charge. They totally bossed it.

This was why, to the straight world, rock 'n' roll people were so cool. Not the people in the bands, necessarily, but everyone else, from the road crew, to the drum techs, to the journalists and photographers. When you live the rock life, an edgy situation is pretty much normal life going on as normal. You live around the wild, the willing and the innocent. You live a life which is based on the very notion that the next minute might not be the same as the last minute and that's what you love about it. It's addictive. It's why you get the post-road blues. That's what your life is and it is the very opposite of the regular world, where predictability is everything, where routine gives structure and confers understanding and even status. Rock 'n' roll was the opposite of that. The more structured and tight you were, the less you were the real deal.

He laughed in silent amusement at Kaz's face as she held the pen up to Goldman. Stern and with authority, she looked like a rock 'n' roll nurse. Then, bam, she'd jabbed it in his leg and grinned at him as she did so, clearly in control and clearly enjoying the moment. Yeah, that's what they did - they enjoyed the moment. The more it had one foot over the edge, heading towards oblivion, the more they understood it. You couldn't say it wasn't impressive, and it had saved Ben Goldman's life.

He put the dressing gown on and went out into the hospital. The smell of antiseptic was everywhere. At the end of his corridor was a reception desk. A black woman looked up at him as he leaned on the counter. He saluted her.

'Hey. I'm Artie Taylor.'

She smiled. 'I know, sir.'

'Ah, cool. Do you know if Georgina Rodgers was brought here after the...y'know...the big bang?'

'Yes. She's on Ward 254 but I'm not sure she's available for visiting. They'll let you know.'

Artie put his thumb up and walked up to the elevator. 254 was on the second floor. The reception desk was unattended. It was funny how lax security was in a hospital. You could pretty much wander where you wanted, and especially if you looked like a patient. It was laid out just as the floor below, so he walked down the corridor until he came to a room with Georgina's name on it. He put his head around the door.

She was hooked up to a lot of machinery, her head entirely covered in some sort of modern type of bandage. She'd taken the explosion in the face in that doorway. Poor woman. He was about to close the door when she spoke.

'Who's there?'

'Hello, Georgina, it's Artie Taylor.' He walked back into the room and closed the door, standing at the end of her bed, the machinery beeping and making little clicking noises. 'How are you?'

'Oh, Artie. How are you doing? They told me you'd made it out with Kaz.' Her speech was a little slurred, probably from heavy painkilling medication. Having your face blown off was bound to sting a bit.

'I'm fine, really. Bruises and sore lungs. How are you, though?'

She swallowed, her lips dry. 'Not really very good at all. I can't see...'

'...oh, god. I'm so sorry.'

'It was that big flash as the first explosion happened. I got all sorts of crap in my eyes.'

'Can they do anything?'

'They don't know yet.' She let out a sigh. 'I accept it, though. Acceptance is everything. What has happened cannot unhappen.'

'That's brave of you. I have to say, I feel bloody furious...really angry at what whoever did this. I want to find them and make them pay for it.'

'Justice must be done, of course. But anger will hurt you more than anyone else.'

'Well, to be fair, if I get hold of whoever did it, my anger will hurt the fuck out of them as well, especially when I kick them in the balls.'

She held the palms of her bandaged hands up to him. 'No. Anger will cloud your brain. Don't be a slave to anger. All pain stems from attachment. Just let it go and let justice take its course.'

In a way, he admired the Buddhist thinking she was giving him and it made sense, at least in theory, but the Yorkshireman in him couldn't accept it - not kicking back, not fighting, not using your anger as a driving force was an abdication of duty and was basically giving in to the bad guys. And he didn't do that.

'Georgina, can I ask you something?'

'What's that?'

'You remember you told me that you'd found that adrenaline pen by the door?'

'Oh. Yes. Right.'

'Well, Ben Goldman told me he'd dropped it there when he was taken ill.'

'Did he?' Her couldn't quite work out her tone. Was it surprised or defensive?

'But I've been looking at the CCTV footage of him being taken ill...'

'...oh, how did you get that?'

'My lawyer obtained it. The point is, he didn't drop anything. He didn't even try and pull it out of a pocket. Where did you find it again?'

'I can't talk about it.'

'Can't talk about it? I don't understand. Why not?'

'I just can't. I'm sorry.'

He was puzzled by her response but she was badly hurt and surely also suffering from PTSD, too. 'The thing is, Georgina, the cops will ask you this as well as Mo Casson - she's my lawyer...'

'Mo Casson? Isn't she the woman who sued the city of Beverly Hills?'

'Successfully sued them, yeah. She's one of the best lawyers in the country.'

'Oh, god...' she let out a bitter bark of a laugh '...I am so screwed.' Desperation was in her tone now.

He couldn't not be sympathetic to her, lying in her own private darkness.

'It's no big deal. It's just that they're going to want to know everything. Fifteen people have been murdered.' She let out a little howl of pain at those words. 'Hadn't you been told?'

'Fifteen! Oh, my good god. Oh, lord...15...so many colleagues...' Clearly, the answer to that was no.

'I'm sorry. The whole place was ripped apart. It was two big blasts; the second one, especially. I saw the store on the news. It's rubble. We were the only ones inside the building to survive. As mad as it sounds, we got lucky.'

She was crying now. 'So many of my co-workers must have died. Oh, god...oh, god.'

He took hold of her hand, wanting to do something to stop her weeping. He hated weeping, hated emotional incontinence in himself, as much in others. But he had no idea what to say as she wept. Still, at least she couldn't see his awkwardness. And having a head wrapped in bandages at least meant the tears would be soaked up. Then Artie felt guilty about even thinking that.

After a few minutes, she settled down and stopped crying.

'Artie. I have to tell you something.'

'OK. I'm here for you, Georgina.'

'Ben Goldman paid me 50,000 dollars to say I found that adrenaline pen.'

CHAPTER 16

'He what?'

'After he'd recovered from his attack, he left. He didn't go with the paramedics. Then an hour later he returned with a packet of cash. If anyone asked, I was to say I found that pen by the entrance to the store.'

'Did he say why?'

'No. But then he mentioned you quite specifically. He told me to call you and tell you I'd found it.'

'Did you ask him why he was paying you to lie to me?'

'Of course I did. But he wouldn't tell me and I really needed the money. My mother isn't well, she has terminal pancreatic cancer, she needs help with medical bills. Fifty thousand is the difference between a painful death and a good death.'

Artie pulled his fingers across his mouth. Jesus Christ. Sometimes, it really was still the Wild West out here. You paid 50 grand for your mother to die in less pain? That was wrong. Making big money out of death was wrong. This was sometimes such a brutal country.

'It didn't seem like much of a thing to do. I thought it must be something to do with an insurance claim, that perhaps his insurance was invalid if he went out without his medication. You know what these companies are like - they look for any reason not to pay out.'

That was as good a guess as any and maybe it was the right one. But why tell her to ring him specifically? Just to firm the story up, probably. Insurance companies can be ruthless if you're making a big payout claim.

'Did you know who he was? That his family are a famous law firm?'

'Not until you told me later, but even if I'd known, I'm not sure I'd have turned the money down. Will I get into trouble?' she said.

'I'm sure you won't. You've not even broken any laws. Lying to me isn't against the law. If it was, the jails would be full of rock stars and their managers.'

She sighed. 'I suppose not.'

'You've got bigger things to worry about, Georgina, if you don't mind me saying so. You need to get well. They'll give you the best treatment in here.'

'They will until my insurance runs out. I mean, I just don't know how much I'm covered for or how far it'll go. I'll get workers' compensation from Mother Earth, I think...but I don't really know how far it extends or...or anything. I could never understand the forms, anyway. It's all so worrying. The meter is running all the time.'

Christ, this was desperate.

'Look, don't worry about that. My wife is Colleen Holmes, she can pick up any bill you're not covered for. She's...well...very rich. So don't go fretting about that.' It seemed vulgar to say so, but then Americans were far less shy about money than the British.

Georgina, on hearing this, started to cry a little again. Artie patted her on the arm, hoping such a gesture might help. 'Are you sure? That's so kind.'

'Yeah, well, kindness seems to be all too lacking these days. So don't worry. Just get well. I'll visit you again tomorrow.' He got up to go. 'Just one more thing. Did you see anyone before the explosion? Do you remember? I'd stood up after the first one...then someone shouted "No!"...do you recall?'

She swallowed. 'Yes. Well. All I've been able to do is go over and over those moments. So much so that I'm not sure what really did happen, but I'm certain as I stood in the doorway before the bomb went off, there was someone running away from aisle 14 and down aisle 13, that was the aisle closest to my office. They were the person who shouted "No!". But I couldn't see anything after the first blast blew everything in my face.'

'So you didn't get a good look at them? I was further over and I just saw a blur, really.'

'Well, this is what I've been dwelling on. You see, in my mind's eye, the figure running away looked very like...' she stopped as though not wanting to say the words for fear of being laughed at.

'Go on. I won't hold you to it.'

'Well, it looked like...like...Ben Goldman. But I'm probably getting confused because he's on my mind.'

'Goldman?! Really?'

Bloody hell. Surely, she wasn't right. Had he been there? Maybe he was and maybe he was now dead.

'Yes. Brown jacket and stone-coloured pants, but it was his hair. He has that distinctive mop of curly hair and that's what I remember seeing an albeit blurred glimpse of. But I'm really not at all sure it was him. He's just in the forefront of my mind. But whoever it was must surely have been killed in the blast. I mean, look what it did to me and I was further from it than that person must have been.'

Artie chewed his lip. He'd have to brace himself to watch that CCTV. 'What was stocked on aisle 14?'

'Aisle 14 is...was...the catering section.'

'What does that mean?'

'We sell catering-sized cans of tomatoes, chickpeas, black-eyed peas and such. We get restaurant trade coming in to buy basics in bulk.'

'I see, so if it was him, he'd have no real reason to be down that aisle?'

'I guess not, unless he runs a restaurant. Like I say, Artie. It probably wasn't him.'

'Well, I've got CCTV footage of the bombs going off. Maybe they'll reveal who it was.'

'Oh, my word. I do not envy you having to look at that.'

He promised to look in on her the next day, leaned over the bed and kissed her on the cheek, feeling so powerlessly sorry for her.

As he returned to his room and loaded ~~one of~~ the second DVD, which recorded the inside of the store from the front corner.~~s~~. Nurse Armstrong walked in. He turned and smiled at her.

'Hello again. You don't get a lot of time between shifts, do you?'

'Six hours. Just enough time to eat and sleep a bit. That's about all. I get three days off for every four on, though. How are you feeling? You've got a bit more colour to you.'

'I always do when I'm around attractive women.'

'You must be hallucinating, then. Now don't go overdoing it. Get yourself into bed. I'll go and check on Kaz and give you an update.'

She left and he began to play the DVD again, starting it on the day of the explosion. Knowing what was about to happen on it, made it the worst kind of horror movie. You wanted to reach out and stop it, but it was all inevitable. Here were people who, in a few minutes, would be dead. In the wrong place at the wrong time, they wandered around in blissful ignorance picking up packets and cans, weighing fruit and vegetables.

Crucially, there was no sign of Ben Goldman, no-one he recognised at all until he and Kaz arrived again and went through to Georgina's office at the back of the store. He sat and waited. Waited. Waited. Then without warning, the first explosion happened. There was nothing to indicate that anything was going to happen. One second everything was normal and then the device went off. It had been left in a recycle bin for coffee cups just inside the door and that was why it seemed more distant to them in the office at the back. The whole ramshackle store - a big space in itself and with 14 or 15 aisles of foodstuffs between the office and the bomb - had insulated them to a degree. While the blast had sent debris through the open door of the office and into Georgina's face, and had blown out the office windows, it hadn't destroyed anything on that side of the store at all. The glass windows at the front however, just shattered and fell like a disintegrating curtain. He saw one man blown off his feet backwards towards the checkouts just before the camera stopped working, as the blast hit it.

He stopped the playback and rewound it by 20 seconds. It wasn't a really massive explosion. The damage it caused was largely breaking all the glass front of the store, along with some displays of fruit and vegetables and blowing plaster from the roof. The camera shuddered and shook, the lens cracked and then the camera went black. He rewound it again, freezing the frame just as the bomb went off. Then came the cracking of the lens. Then blackness. He rewound it again.

Something just wasn't right.

Why hadn't the lens cracked when the bomb went off? It had taken up to five seconds. He counted them off on his fingers. Boom, shudder, shake, crack, black. It could only have broken because of the noise. No flying particles of debris could have reached it from where it was, or not at enough speed and power. But it had broken too late for it to be the noise. Also, why would it crack, and only then stop working?

He rewound it once more and held it at the moment that the lens cracked.

Oh, shit.

He grabbed the image, edited it and made it larger. The lens was broken, but the camera was still working for a few seconds, and you could actually still see through the cracks a semi-shattered image of the storefront. And in the top left corner, there was a blurred image of someone. They were not there before the explosion and only appeared a couple of seconds after it had gone off. And they had a gun. A handgun. They'd aimed at the camera, cracked the lens with one bullet and then probably destroyed the camera with a second. Who the hell was that? There was only one reason to shoot out this camera and that was so it would not record someone coming into the store after the first explosion. It meant the second bomb wasn't planted, it was brought in by someone after the first explosion, which had been pre-planted. The figure was blurred, so had fired while on the move. They looked like a shadow, so had to be dressed in black or dark navy, were probably male and had dark hair, but it was impossible to know for sure.

Artie blew out air and loaded the other~~second~~ DVD, which had the footage from the ~~second~~ camera. ~~It was quickly obvious that it was~~ mounted on the back wall, above Georgina's office ~~and i.~~ It effectively showed the half of the store that you couldn't see from the other ~~other~~ camera. When the first bomb went off, the camera only shuddered a little, and a backdraft of smoke and dust poured down the store towards the camera like fog rolling into San Francisco bay. What it did show was the panic and fear in people's reactions. Everyone knew what it was. But they couldn't run to the exit, because that's where the bomb was and so where did they go? To the back of the store, of course. That had to be intentional. The first bomb by the door drove people to the back where the bigger, more devastating bomb was to be placed. Artie gripped this mouth in contemplation, watching the horror unfold.

The bomb that wrecked the place went off in aisle 14. The last aisle, nearest the rear camera. There was a vivid, white flash and that was it. All over. ~~In contrast to~~ The camera was knocked out immediately, because the huge explosion was so ~~huge~~close. It was a blessing really, as it meant there was no death and destruction to witness. Artie rewound it to seconds before the moment it exploded and, conscious of Georgina's idea that Ben Goldman was the man running away from where the explosion occurred, he leaned into the screen. As the first bomb went off customers and staff naturally moved away from it, coming towards the camera, their faces set in horror and panic. But there was one exception.

There was someone running away from the camera up aisle 13, and they did have curly hair, but were only in view for a couple of frames, before they took a left and headed towards the exit. They must have known what was about to happen, so they had to have planted the bomb because there was no way anyone would run towards where an explosion had happened, unless they knew it was safe to do so.

He rewound the ~~film~~ disc to well before the first explosion to try and identify the person. Watching a full five minutes worth of ~~film~~ footage before the first bang, revealed nobody with curly hair. Then the explosion happened and the plume of dust and smoke was pushed at down the store towards the camera. The camera shuddered as the sound wave hit it. There were a few seconds when the debris from the bomb obscured the clarity of the images, the way swirling mist makes seeing the road ahead difficult and it had to be in that moment that Curly Hair had run down to

134

aisle 14, probably planted the bomb and then ran back out up 13, only to be briefly captured as the images cleared.

Artie froze the best frame, cropped it out and blew it up. Whoever it was certainly had curly brown hair, just as Georgina had said, in thinking it was Ben Goldman. But it was impossible to say for sure that it was him. All you could see very briefly in the image was a bit of shoulder, neck and some back of head. The rest was obscured by the big catering-sized packs and tins. Was it Goldman? It couldn't be ruled out or confirmed. Whoever it was had taken a hell of a risk of getting blown up. Maybe he just didn't care about that.

It was a blessing that the camera hadn't recorded any blood and viscera before breaking. It had been a huge explosion. But was it one that no-one could have survived? On aisle 14 just before the bomb went off, there were...he counted them...seven people. None of them could have survived. The big bang would have just eviscerated them. As he looked at aisle 14, he remembered what Georgina had said - that it was where the catering-sized tins were kept. And there they were, stacked up on either side to a height of about seven feet. That was a great barrier to protect yourself behind.

He rewound and watched it again. Yeah, if the runner down aisle 13 had placed the bomb, they maybe could have made it out before the whole place collapsed and have been semi-protected from the main blast by those big tins and packs. Alternatively it could have projected them into the back of their head.

'Hey, Artie.' It was nurse Armstrong, pushing the door open. 'Kaz is coming back to us a little. You might want to make your way to her room.' She smiled and held out her hand.

He put the computer to one side and got out of bed.

'You know, I don't even know your first name,' he said, as he pulled on a dressing gown.

'Jackie.'

He walked to the door and put his hand on her hip. 'OK, Jackie. Listen, thanks for being a lovely lass. You've already made being here a much better thing than it might otherwise have been.'

She put her hand to his cheek and grinned at him with a natural warmth. 'You're welcome, kidda. We're all a long way from home, eh.'

'Yeah, you're so right.' He put his hand on hers.

Jesus, northern women were so sexy. He'd worked all over the world, but women from the north of Britain, just had something special about them. It was the blend of bluntness, bosoms and bloody loveliness. What someone had once described to him as the three Vs - Voluptuous Viking Vaginas. Yeah.

He followed her to Kaz's room.

Inside the doctor turned to look at him and nodded.

'Hi, Artie. She's OK. Her numbers are all good. So don't worry. Take a seat and I'll let you know.'

He did as he was told, feeling like now would be a very good time for a shot of Jack. He could tell she was in a different state because her face looked less neutral, a slight frown on her face now. Also her eyelids occasionally twitched and she'd turned on her left side a little.

Then she made a random noise, the way we all do in our sleep, and licked her lips.

The bleeping machine began to bleep a bit faster, then, all of a sudden, went crazy...like it was doing double time.

Kaz began to twitch and gibber and make big snorting noises, thick saliva coming out of her mouth as she lay on her back.

Artie reacted almost before it had started. 'She's having a fit!' Before they could stop him, he got on the bed and pushed Kaz onto her left side. She was having a full tonic-clonic seizure. He leaned into her as her body convulsed, in and out...tense, loose, tense, loose, all the while snorting and blowing out air.

'You must let us treat her, Artie,' said the doctor, standing by the bed, but Artie wasn't about to let go of her.

'It's alright, lady. It's alright. Everything is gonna be alright.' He cooed at her, as though to calm her, even though she couldn't hear him. He held her until the seizure abated after about 30 seconds, with one last long tense of her whole body and her heart-rate began to slow down again.

She fell into a sleep with a rattling snore.

Artie got off the bed.

'You shouldn't have done that. It's our job to look after our patients,' admonished Doctor Piper.

'I've dealt with it before. What would you have done differently?'

'Nothing, I guess.'

'Well, then. What's your problem?'

The doctor looked awkward. 'OK, but if it happens again, please let us deal with it. Has she had a fit before, do you know?'

'Yeah, a couple of times when really shit-faced drunk and drugged. I've seen it a few times over the years. A doctor who worked at Woodstock once told me what to do. All I worry about is them choking on their own puke, because so many people have booze-induced fits, or choking on their own tongue. So you roll them on their side.'

'You dealt with it well. It scares a lot of people.'

'Yeah well, as I seem to keep saying these days, a life in rock 'n' roll prepares you for most eventualities.' He patted her as she fell into a more regular sleep.

'Her brain will be a bit shredded for half an hour while everything gets reconnected. Best to let her sleep it off now,' the doctor said.

The bleeping had subsided and gone back to its normal, regular beat. The doctor left, promising to come back in half an hour.

As he sat alone with her, he chatted about the DVDs, just for the sake of saying something. It would have been nice if she'd just sat up and become conscious, but real life isn't like the movies. She just lay there asleep.

But slowly, she did wake up, at first just blinking a lot and opening her eyes, and then falling asleep again, but then she finally came awake properly.

He sat on the edge of the bed and waved at her.

'Hello, you,' he said, as she looked at him with more conscious eyes.

Her stare betrayed someone trying to get a grip on the waking world.

'I think I've wet meself,' she said. 'Was I ratted?'

'No, man. You had a bad case of the epileptic gibbers. You probably pissed yourself during that.'

'Oh...sorry. I didn't know. Are we on tour with Aerosmith, again?'

'No, lady. Sadly, we're not. It doesn't matter. They'll clean you up.'

'Where am I?'

'A hospital in Santa Monica.'

She was silent for perhaps a minute, her face set in a puzzled frown.

'Has something really shit happened?'

'Yeah, you've been in a coma, but you'll be OK. Just take it easy. I'm here for you.'

She lay still for two or three minutes, coming back to herself.

'I can't remember anything. Last thing I recall is...me and you fucking in Las Vegas. Tell me you didn't fuck me into a coma, Artie.'

He laughed, pushing tears from his eyes as he did so. This was too much to cope with.

'Yeah, that's exactly what happened.'

'I've told you often enough, I'm allergic to cock.'

The doctor came back in with Jackie Armstrong.

'Ah, you're back with us. Excellent,' he said. 'I'm Nate Piper.'

'I've wet your expensive bed. Sorry,' she said.

'We'll get you cleaned up. Don't worry about that,' said Jackie.

'No hurry. I quite like it,' she joked.

'How do you feel?' said the doctor.

'Like I drank two bottles of whisky and then started the serious drinking.'

'Does your head hurt?'

'Yeah, like I drank two bottles of whisky and then started the serious drinking. What happened to me?'

'You took a serious blow to the head,' said the doctor.

'So I'm the victim of a heavy-duty blow job?' she said. It was such a Kaz thing to say and, as such, felt like she was properly back in the room.

'Actually, you've got a fractured skull. But I think you'll make a good recovery. You might struggle to remember things for a while, but it'll all fade back in.'

She rubbed her nose.

'There was a bomb, wasn't there? We got buried under the roof of the store.'

'Yup. That's exactly right. A roof beam hit you on the head.'

'Fuck. Do I not like that? Who did it?'

'We don't know yet.'

'I'd like to volunteer to kick them in the balls.'

'It might be a woman,' said Artie.

'It might...but it won't be. It'll be an arsehole bloke. Almost all the shit in the world is caused by arsehole blokes. How long have I been here?'

'It's over four days since the bomb. I was out for 36 hours myself.'

'Shit, that explains why I'm so bloody hungry.'

The doctor explained. 'We put you into a drug-induced coma, while we assessed how badly hurt you were. We've got you on a course of anti-inflammatory drugs and painkillers. We'll need to monitor you for a few days.'

'Oh. Right. I actually feel quite good.' She yawned. 'Head hurts a bit.'

'We'll keep an eye on you for the rest of the day. Your scans all look good. You've made good progress,' said the doctor.

In the early evening, after she'd had something to eat and settled down for a nap, Artie went back to his room and began to write a note to Mo

Casson about his observations of the video and to update her about Kaz. He did the same for Colleen.

Jackie Armstrong looked in on him, just as she was going off duty. She came in smiling, now dressed in a loose blue shirt and black leggings and blue trainers. 'You OK, honey?'

He gestured for her to come in. 'Are you in a hurry?' he said.

'Not really.'

'Fancy a drink?'

She looked puzzled and pushed at her cropped brown hair. 'I don't get you, Artie.'

'Look in the bedside cupboard.'

She did so and took out the half-full bottle of Jack Daniels that Colleen had left, and another full one.

'Eee, you're a cheeky so-and-so you. Are you allowed alcohol?'

'Probably not, but I'm still alive. If you've not got a hot date, will you stay with me for a bit?'

She tilted her head a little then shrugged. 'OK. Why not? I'll just go and get some Coke from the machine to go with this.'

She returned with a chilled can and two glasses and poured them both a big glass, then sat cross-legged on the bed, facing him. 'Cheers, Artie. To your good health.'

'Cheers, Jackie. Thanks for being so nice. It's made being here easier.'

She smiled her sly, attractive smile. 'It's funny, I propositioned you and got turned down and yet I don't feel embarrassed or awkward about it. Why is that?'

'Because you're cool.'

'Nah, I'm not cool. It's because *you're* cool. Probably all those years in the rock business mean you're not easily...whatever.' She smiled again.

'Can I just state for the record, I very much wanted and in fact still want, to have wild sex with you.'

She howled a laugh. 'Eee, is that why you've got us in here? You didn't have to get me drunk, lad. Shall I lock the door?'

He held his hand up. 'It's just that, being an old sod, I know how these things can mess up your life - at least when you've got a wife at home. We said we'd be faithful and my old dad told me to be a man of my word. I've tried to stick by it, most of the time, anyway. Not long ago, I'd have been all over you like white on rice.'

She grinned. 'And I'd have liked that. I thought that's what you'd be like, being in the rock business. Sex and drugs and rock 'n' roll, and all that. I didn't know you were married.' She grinned at him, mischievously. 'Chatting up patients isn't something I do on a regular basis. In fact, I've never done it in my 25-year career. I don't know why I chose you to have a go on. Admittedly, I have already washed your cock and balls. Maybe it was that sight that drove me crazy.'

'I find that hard to believe, unless you think not much is a lot. Ah, man, who knows why we get taken with such notions?' He clinked glasses with her again. 'So tell me more about yourself.'

'Oh, there's not much to tell. I came over here with a boyfriend 15 years ago, split up with him, got work, got a visa, eventually got my Green Card. I live in an apartment in West LA with Boro, my cat. Named after Middlesbrough FC. I love living out here. It's just brill. Meeting people is harder than at home, though. Everyone lives in their car and no-one bloody drinks. I'm sure the place would be healthier if they just ate less and drank more.'

He laughed. 'I've long thought they got the food and drink relationship the wrong way round in America. So there's no Mister Jackie Armstrong?'

'I wouldn't be trying to get in your pants if there was, would I?'

'Ha ha, I suppose not, no...well, you never know.'

'I go on dates, but at my age, I just don't think I even want to settle down with someone. I'm set in my ways.'

'I totally know what you mean. I thought that was my gig, too. Me and Coll only got married last year.'

'I didn't see her when she visited. Is she very rock 'n' roll?'

He got his phone and showed her a photo he'd taken of her in Malibu in a classic Coll pose - all old jeans, cowboy boots, embroidered waistcoat over a white capped-sleeve t-shirt, hair streaming in the breeze and reflective shades.

'Bloody hell. She looks like a movie star or a member of Fleetwood Mac, or something.'

'I know.' He looked at it ruefully and bit his lip.

'Do you know Chick's bar on Melrose? We go in there quite a bit when we're in town. You should get down there, they do good food and they'll call you a cab to take you home when you're rat-arsed.'

'You and Colleen go there?'

'Err, no. Me and Kaz, more usually. We've gone in there for 15 years. She loves it. Great jukebox with actual vinyl singles. Call me sometime and we'll go down there all of us together.'

'OK, I will. I'm so pleased she came out of the coma OK. She's a funny little thing, isn't she? Always making jokes. The things she was coming out with when I changed her sheets and got her cleaned up. It was very funny.'

'Yeah, that's Kaz through and through.'

'How long have you worked together?'

'Fifteen years now. But it's not like a normal working relationship...it's...it's complicated.' He sank his drink and poured another, topping up hers, too.

'No, well, I could tell that. You're not just friends, are you?'

'No. It goes way beyond being friends.'

She took a long drink and rested her elbows on her knees, looking at him all the while.

'Forgive me if I'm talking out of line here, but the way you go on with each other, it's like you're an old couple who know each other's ways and what'll make each other laugh. You're obviously...well...close, like.'

He took another drink, not quite able to look at her. 'Yeah, we are.'

She frowned and shook her head a little. 'Have you got yourself into a bit of a mess with Colleen and Kaz?'

He snorted a little. 'Oh, god, you don't know the half of it.'

'OK, so let me guess. I'm an old bird, me. I've been around. Had my heart broken and broken a couple of hearts meself, like.'

He looked up at her friendly, soft face. 'Go on, then.'

She looked into her drink and swilled it around a little. 'You and Kaz fell in love, but didn't realise it because you spent all your time together. You thought she was just your best friend. You both saw other people but the only consistent relationship in your life was each other and you only realised this after you'd got married.'

He laughed and copied her glass-swirling movement. 'You bloody Teessiders, you're smart, aren't you?'

'Never underestimate a Redcar lass.'

'It's more complicated than you know. Kaz is gay and is very committed to being gay. By which I mean, she has shown no interest in, or sexual attraction towards men...'

'...except you?'

'Yeah. Well, sort of...we had sex once, the night before I married Coll.'

She let out a small whoop. 'Just to see what both of you thought of it? Very rock 'n' roll.'

'Exactly.'

She gave her sly grin again. 'Well? What was it like?'

'Like we'd actually done it for years.'

'But you still got married, anyway?'

'Yeah. I love Coll. She's great. She pulled me out of a terrible mid-life crisis, or depression, or something. I really respect her. I do love her, but...but...but not like I love Kaz. I just don't know how to resolve it without hurting at least one of them.'

'How does Kaz feel?'

'Messed up. It's even harder for her because she's gay. Usually.'

They didn't speak for maybe a minute. Artie cleared his throat.

'Do you think I should tell Coll the situation?'

'No. I think you need to sort it out with Kaz first, then decide what to do for the best. You need to sort it out soon, though. It'll make you all unhappy if you don't.'

Artie nodded. 'Thanks, Jackie.'

'No bother. Now I see why you didn't want to get jiggy with me. Would have complicated things even more.'

'I'm an old rock dude, getting jiggy isn't my giggy. That's the weird thing, actually. It's not really about the sex, though it is in the mix, it's about that feeling in your heart. I love Kaz in one way and I love Coll in another.'

'Well, I've realised that I never really fell in love. I've thought I did, but on reflection, I never really did.'

'Aw...come here, you.' He held his arms out towards her. She scrambled towards him and fell into his arms. They hugged each other and then kissed briefly, but a little too passionately.

She pulled back and resumed her cross-legged position. 'Well, that was interesting.'

'Yeah, have you still got that wad of Kleenex?'

They both laughed.

'You are messed up, Artie.'

'Well getting blown up does that to you.'

She laughed again, her lush lips parted a big smile, revealing very English teeth, a bit wonky and yellow, her eyes bright and amused.

The door to the room opened.

With every second that passes, you simply can't be always on your guard for something weird or violent happening. We trust that things are going to be alright, even in the face of the knowledge bad shit happens on a regular basis. Life lived in permanent fear is no life at all.

It was all over in two seconds.

Artie leaned to one side to see around Jackie, and look at the person who had come in. Except no-one came in. The door opened, a tanned left arm, wearing a black t-shirt, came around the door. In the arm's hand was a pistol, fitted with a silencer. The index finger squeezed twice in quick succession and then withdrew.

The two bullets hit Jackie in the back of the head. The last expression on her face was her lovely laughing smile. It was her last moment of life as the first bullet removed the back of her skull and the second blew off the top of her head, sending a fine spume of pink blood and viscera exploding into the air.

CHAPTER 17

True shock is another universe from mere surprise. Artie's brain wouldn't compute the situation. There was no time to dive out of the way or try to hide. He just sat there and watched as Jackie's lovely alive body was murdered. As the bullets hit her, she just ever so gently slumped forward a little as the life force left her in an instant. Her eyes were still open, the shape of the smile still on her lips but the light in her eyes, the look of amusement that was a living thing, that was a mainline to her humanness and not a mere physical response, was gone in the same instant. She had died as quickly as it was possible to die.

The door closed. Artie was frozen in fear and stunned to the point of paralysis, eyes double-glazed with shock. He reached forward to touch her, putting his hands around her neck. She felt warm. Not dead. But the blood now pouring from the cranial explosion told a different story.

In the same way ice melts as you pour hot water on it, the reality of the situation poured onto his frozen synapses. He leapt out of bed barefoot, pulled open the door, looked up and down the corridor for the shooter. No-one was around. He sprinted down the long straight passage, took a right and arrived at the reception desk. Leaving the building was a man with tanned arms, wearing a black shirt.

Artie sprinted after him. 'Stop him! Stop him in the t-shirt!' he yelled at nobody in particular. 'He's just shot someone on the head!' The black woman on the reception desk stood up and shouted something but the blood was pulsing in Artie's ears and he couldn't hear her. All he could think to do was run. He went past the desk and headed to the automatic doors, which parted. Outside it was a warm early LA evening, all herby petrol softness. He stood and looked for the t-shirt man, heart pounding. There. On the sidewalk. He sprinted as fast as he could, his bare feet on the warm pavement.

The man was quite a long way ahead of him, now sprinting hard. There was no way Artie could keep up with him. He was so far ahead, it was a lost cause. His lungs hurt and his feet burned, he had to slow down and stop.

The man got into a black car. Artie halted, hands on his hips, gasping for breath. The car was away and gone. Get the plate. He squinted, his brain racing and tried to focus. CMT 83 or was it 38 or maybe 80. His eyesight wasn't good enough in the dark to tell, as it accelerated away and took a left out of view.

He made the walk back to the hospital, his brain spinning at the last five minutes of reality. Instinctively he wanted to hide from the shooting, not wanting his brain to touch it, as though it was a hot piece of psychic molten metal. His emotions were all over the place. The sight of Jackie, dead, burned into his synapses.

A police siren came howling down Santa Monica Boulevard, not just one or two, but six cars. As he got back into the hospital, the whole place was in uproar with people shouting and running. Artie couldn't bear it. He felt numb, as though his body was anaesthetising him from the pain of this brutal slaughter. He walked down the corridor and went into Kaz's room. She was sitting up in bed.

'Ah, there you are. What the hell is going on out there? It's been all shouty shouty for the last 10 minutes...it woke me up -' she stopped mid-sentence, seeing the look on his face. 'What's wrong, Artie? What's happened?'

He tried to focus, licking his dry lips and spreading his hands out in front of him as a physical way to calm himself. 'Jackie Armstrong, the nurse who looked after both us, was shot in the head while she was sitting on my bed. They were trying to shoot me but they hit her. I chased after them...'

But Kaz had stopped listening to him. 'You what? You what?!! Jackie...No!! No!! That's not right...' she was in tears. 'She was shot!?'

He nodded. 'In the head. It just burst, Kaz. Just went everywhere...'

Now the tears came, all the blind, visceral emotion. He sank to his knees, and buried his head in his hands, overcome. Not just for Jackie but Robbie and Carly too; it was all too much. It felt like he was both insane and drunk and out of his head.

'Artie...get up, lad. Sit on the bed.' Kaz's voice came to him from somewhere else. He did as he was told.

He dragged himself to the bed and sat down. She had been crying, too. She took his hand and finally they looked at each other.

'What's all this about, Artie? I'm scared shitless.'

He snorted up his crying snot and swallowed it. 'I don't know, but we're going to find out. And you know what?'

'What?'

'I'm going to find the people responsible and fucking put a bullet in their head. My dad always said take and eye for an eye and a tooth for tooth. And I've two murders and one suicide to make right.' He wiped his nose. 'Are you with me?'

She gripped his hand. '100 per cent. Until justice is done.'

And they really bloody well meant it.

'How does your head feel?' he said, holding her hand.

'Good, all things considered.' She ruffled her hair and gave him a watery smile.

'Can you walk OK?'

She got out of bed and walked around the room.

'Yeah, I'm fine. A bit stiff and I need some more food, but it takes more than a crack on the head to stop a Leeds lass. Back home, being hit with a piece of timber is called lovemaking.'

'Yeah, hence the expression, "getting a woody".' Why was he making jokes at a time like this? Because it was the only thing you could do in the face of such evil.

She flexed her legs, doing a couple of squats and stretches. 'I feel quite strong, just need to eat. I've been on the drip for so long, I've lost a lot of weight.'

'OK, look then, we've got to get out of here and go after the murderous bastard or bastards behind all this death and destruction. We can't just sit around and hope for the best, hoping the LAPD will protect and serve us. We need to be proactive, otherwise one day, we'll be sitting having coffee and someone will shoot us dead, just like that, and I'm not going down without a fucking fight, let me tell you that.'

Police swarmed everywhere. Artie gave them his account of what happened, but it didn't take many words. The door opened, a tanned bare arm, wearing a black t-shirt, came around the door and fired twice directly at him, not knowing Jackie was sitting right in front of him. They couldn't have known.

It took what seemed like hours but as soon as the police were done with him, he and Kaz discharged themselves from hospital, each holding a bag of their belongings. It was nearly midnight.

'Shall we go back to Malibu?' said Kaz.

Artie winced at the very thought. 'I can't face that. Let's get a motel room. Then we'll buy a couple of guns. Then...'

'Guns? Are you sure?'

'Yeah. I'm done with this. I'm hunting these bastards down and I'm not stopping until they're dead because they won't stop until I'm dead and then they'll come for you.'

She gripped his arm as they left the hospital. 'I'm scared, and I hate being scared.'

'Don't be. I'll keep you safe. Or at least, I will when we've got some firepower. Have you ever fired a gun?'

'Of course not. Have you?'

'I once went to a shooting range with Ted Nugent and one of the other blokes in Damn Yankees. It's a piece of piss. You squeeze the trigger, rather than pull it.'

'You do know you've gone weird, don't you? I'm not complaining, I'm just saying.'

He did know. Even when you've lost your mind, there's a little part of you, a small quiet voice, telling you that you've gone off your rocker, but it's easily ignored; or, more precisely, you don't care what it's saying.

'Yeah, well, maybe being fucked up is the only way this gets sorted.'

She nodded. 'Jackie was dead nice to me.'

'Hmm, to me as well. Now she's just dead.'

'Why does someone want to kill us?'

'Because we know something.'

'I don't know anything.'

'You think you don't, but you do. I do. We don't know what it is, but they think we do and they're scared we'll tell someone.'

'Well, maybe we have told Mo Casson.'

'I don't think they know about Mo's investigation team, not yet. It's too early. They're working behind the scenes so far.'

'But you should tell Coll what we're doing.'

'You think?'

'She'll understand.'

'Will she?'

'Yeah, she's a cool woman, remember?'

He stood on the sidewalk and dialled the number. She answered. He explained the situation in as few words as possible, not even wanting to conjure the image of Jackie being killed.

Incredibly, she actually wasn't fazed. Her voice kept calm, perhaps picking up on his angst and realising the last thing the situation needed was another crazy person. 'That's just so terrible. But keep calm, Artie, OK? There's a diner across the street from the hospital. Go in there and wait for me. You need protection. I'll get you protection.'

'What? A bodyguard? Nah. Some guns would more useful. Meet fire with fire.'

'It was guns I had in mind. I'll be with you soon.'

They did as she suggested, sitting down at a booth and ordering fries, eggs and coffee.

Artie was totally wired, more than half expecting a gunman to walk into the restaurant and shoot them at any moment. He scoped out an exit route, noticing the kitchen door was at the far side. That was where they'd have to go. It was covered in a polished steel plate too, so the bullets would deflect off that, not go through it.

As the waitress brought the food, he was prepared for her to pull out a gun too, picking up his knife, ready to jam it into her arm to get her to drop the gun.

Kaz looked up at him out of the top of her eyes. 'Easy, man, she waits tables, she's not a paid assassin.' She began to shovel eggs into herself, feeling really hungry. Artie could hardly force anything down his gullet. It was as though the tension had closed up his throat. He picked at the fries, feeling like he needed a cigarette, but then he could hardly stand around on the sidewalk sucking down a Marlboro because anyone could take a potshot at him in the open.

'You know what I think? We survived the explosion but we weren't meant to. It was meant to kill us and it damn near did,' said Kaz, chugging down coffee and then taking a big fork of fries. 'So if that's the case, they must have wanted to kill us for something we'd seen or heard prior to that.'

'But how did they know we were going to go there? No-one knew, except me and you. You called me at Honest Joe's. They can't have blown up the store to get us, Kaz. That's not credible. That would have required someone hanging around on the off chance we'd turn up. No no no...'

She was a bit indignant. 'Alright, alright, I was just trying to work it out. Have you got a better idea?'

He drummed his fingers on the table and picked up a fry, gesturing towards her with it. 'Is it something to do with Ben Goldman? All of this started with him and that bloody soy jerky. Georgina said she thought she'd seen him running away from the explosion. She thought she saw him and although the CCTV doesn't prove that, it doesn't disprove it either. And he dated Carly.'

'And Fay did say he was a creep.'

'Exactly. She's a smart kid,' said Artie. 'But how does Goldman fit with the shooting of Jackie? It certainly wasn't him that shot her. It's the mercury poisoning that this all centres around. That's the crime at the centre of this.' He took out the sheet of paper the Paleo Patriots man had given him and tapped it with his index finger. 'The bloke who gave me this said I was in danger. He knew. So that means the people on this sheet - we need to check them out and see who could be behind the poisoning and why they've tried to kill me and you. There might be a disgruntled employee or something. We should go and put some pressure on these people, Pat Gunn and Keith Perez.'

She picked some food out of her teeth. 'What does "put pressure on them" mean?'

He folded his arms across his chest. 'I don't know, do I? Sticking guns in their faces and getting them to tell us what they know.'

She sneered at him. 'C'mon, that's shite. We'd be hauled off to jail right away. We need to be clever, not just go in bull-headed.' She looked at the waitress. 'Can I get a beer, please and some apple pie?' The waitress nodded and smiled at her. Kaz turned back to him. 'Look, you're right. We go in hard, but we go in hard *and* clever. Right? I'll bloody well blow someone's head off their shoulders, that's not a problem, but I want to know it's the right person. Get me? See...we're Leeds hard, but we're Leeds fair, as well. Keep your sodding feet on the ground, right?'

It was like she was some sort of rock 'n' roll, alternative headmistress. Artie looked in her eyes as she spoke and knew she was right. He was off on one, she was reeling him in.

'Yeah, yeah, OK. I just want to make this right.'

'Yeah, but that's yer typical male response, isn't it? Your revenge is like your lot's sex: all over in a couple of big bursts. We need to be smarter than that.'

She reached over and dragged his uneaten plate of food towards her 'No point in wasting this,' she said as she crammed another big forkful of fries into her face. 'I never ate anything for days. I'm thousands of calories down. These jeans are hanging off me. There's nothing like being in a coma for losing weight. They should offer it to celebrities...knock you out for four days and wake up thin. My belly hasn't felt this flat since I was 18. They weighed me and I was only 110 pounds. I lost nearly 30lbs.'

'I like you fleshy and gorgeous.'

She looked up at him, 'Saying words like that...'

'...like what?'

'Like *gorgeous*. That's really not helping, Artie.' She shook her head in exasperation. 'I don't want to hear any lovey dovey shit, right?'

He shrugged, not really understanding why she'd said it, but knowing from the scowl on her face that she was serious.

'OK. Sorry. I didn't mean anything by it.'

'Yes, you did. So shut it. This isn't the time for that shit.' She jabbed the fork at him and then looked down at the remains of the food and drank her beer. 'We've got to sort this out and stay alive. We've not time for anything else. Nothing.'

The diner door opened, Artie looked up, ready to move. It was Colleen. Dressed in a black leather jacket, her hair pushed up under a Dodgers baseball cap, she marched over to them, sitting down next to Kaz.

'Hey, you two. How are you both?'

'Better for having a belly full of food,' said Kaz.

Colleen smiled at her and put her hand to her cheek. 'Nice to have you back with us, missy. For someone who was recently in a drug-induced coma, you look very perky.'

'It's weird. I actually feel really good. I think it's the only bit of proper rest I've had since I was 15.'

Colleen turned to Artie. 'And poor you. Having to see something like that.' She lowered her voice. 'I've got you some protection in the car.'

'How do you have access to guns?' whispered Kaz.

'This is America, baby, we've all got access to guns.' She flashed her caramel eyes at her. 'But promise me you won't use them unless you have to.'

'Self-defence only,' said Kaz.

Artie nodded. He was going to kill whoever it was that had killed Jackie, if he got the chance. And he'd do the same to whoever was responsible for Carly and therefore for Robbie's death. Didn't it say to take an eye for eye and a tooth for a tooth, in the Bible? Admittedly, it also said to turn the other cheek, which did seem like hedging your bets, a bit.

She picked up the sheet of paper and looked at it. 'See this accountant, Patricia Gunn, it turns out she was a big mover and shaker in the Yippie movement in the early 70s. Worked out of Berkeley as part of a radical collective. Got major counterculture battle scars. I'm guessing she hooked up with Keith Perez - the dude who started Green on Green back in the late 60s - back in the day and they stayed tight. You should go and see her first. See if she's heard of this Paleo Patriots group, for all we know she's part of them. And talk to her about Green on Green's working practices. She must have handled the sale to Long Run. She might have some idea whose toes you've trodden on.'

'Has Mo Casson's team been up there yet?' said Artie.

Colleen shook her head. 'No. They're putting in all the legal ground-work down here first. When you're going after a company for corporate manslaughter, you've got to have it all sewn up tight if you want to be sure of winning and Mo is notorious for not losing. The way she works is to get all her ducks in a row, then she devises a strategy to take them down one by one. She's super methodical and doesn't just blunder into anything. I've had a quick word with her on the way over here. She says she'd rather you stayed out of things, but understands why you want to get involved given the threat on your life and that she'd appreciate any info you do acquire asap. Oh, and she said, and I quote, "don't break any fucking laws". So that's you guys told, right?' She pointed at each of them.

Artie looked at Kaz. She stared back at him, unblinking, thinking what he was thinking, that the chances of that happening were very small.

'So, what did this shooter look like?' said Colleen. 'Male or female?'

'Male. I only saw their arm and then them at a distance running away down the street to their car. I gave the cops my partial number plate guess.'

'Can't have been a professional hit. A proper gunman wouldn't have just stuck their arm around the door without looking. You'd do that if you didn't actually want to see the bullet hit home,' said Coll.

Kaz nodded. 'That's a great point, Coll. I never thought of that. It was a coward's shooting. They just assumed Artie was sitting there in bed, but he might not have been. He mightn't even have been in the room There's no window you can look through to see. And even if they knew he was in there, he could have been anywhere in the room.'

'Or I could have been lying down, in which case they'd have missed me,' said Artie. 'Is it possible that they didn't mean to kill me at all, but just scare me? If they thought I wasn't even in there, they might have intended to just put some bullets in the wall as a warning. But the fact is, they were total amateurs and screwed the whole thing up. I mean, there'll be CCTV of them. They didn't have a mask or balaclava on. That seems very amateur.'

'Yeah, that makes a lot of sense. Could it, in any universe, have been Ben Goldman?' Kaz asked Artie.

He shook his head. 'Deffo not. I wonder if we're not getting distracted by him. He's got his own agenda going on through this, but he seems an unlikely killer or terrorist.'

Colleen raised her hand a little. 'For what it's worth, Goldman has apparently retreated to his parents' Pacific Palisades mansion. I've put the address of it into a text for you, just in case you need it. Mo is trying to arrange an interview, but is getting nowhere, so far. That suggests he knows he's potentially in some sort of deep shit, even if he's not actually guilty of anything.'

'When he called me and wanted to meet up, he was very cagey. He claimed to be different from his parents and that he was on the side of keeping corporate life clean. But I didn't believe him, really. He was just unconvincing and when Fay arrived, he upped and left immediately.'

'Well, that at least I can appreciate,' said Colleen, wryly.

'Right, well, I think we need to be heading north to San Francisco,' said Artie. 'Are you coming with us, Coll?'

'Not yet, I've got still more meetings booked in the morning about sorting the legacy foundation.'

'Shit, yeah, that's such a big deal for you and it's getting totally overlooked,' said Artie. 'I'm sorry. How's it going?'

'It's been complicated but it'll be sorted soon. I've had to co-ordinate this with the accountants, and accountants are never available when you want them to be available. I don't know why that is. It seems to be an immutable law of the universe. The thing is, mom's estate is so widespread and covers 98 territories, so I need to get on top of all of those and make sure the funds are correctly channeled. Then I've got to get it all double-checked to make sure some unscrupulous accountant hasn't hived off a few million for themselves. It's nearly done, though. That's where we're at, right now. Make sure you stay in touch, though. OK? I want regular reports and don't hide anything from me. Even the crap stuff. I might be able to help.'

She reached into her inside jacket pocket and produced two black AMEX cards. 'You forgot these. You might need them in case you need to spend big on something...hire a helicopter or charter a plane or buy the Transamerica Building...actually, you might need to call me if you want to do that.' She grinned encouragingly at them both.

They followed her out to the Porsche. She handed Artie the keys. 'She's got a full tank. In the back is a case with two Smith & Wesson pistols and a ton of ammo. You know how to use a gun, don't you, Artie?'

He nodded. 'Thanks, Coll.'

'How are you getting home, if we're taking your car?' asked Kaz.

'I'll call a cab.'

CHAPTER 18

Artie accelerated away towards the 10, with the Porsche 911 Turbo S cutting through the warm night air like a hot knife through tofu. He then took the 110 through downtown and from there onto the 5 heading north.

'It always amazes me how you remember your way around LA. There are no landmarks on these roads. It's all so faceless. How the hell did you know it was the 10, then the 110 to get to the 5?'

'I dunno. It's just instinct, really. Once you've located the main arteries like the 10, 405, 1 and 5, it all falls into place. Compared to driving around London, it's a piece of piss.'

Kaz fiddled with the radio to find a rock station, finding one playing some early Blue Oyster Cult.

Artie looked in his rear-view mirror for traffic cops. There was nothing they'd like better than to pull over a high-performance car like this. 'Keep an eye out for police, Kaz, I'm going to put my foot down.'

'Right...' she looked all around. 'Nothing. Engage warp factor, Scotty.' She made a pointing gesture as Artie, a surge of electricity in his blood, put the pedal to the metal and took off into the night, eating up the empty road. The Porsche could do 0 to 60 in under four seconds. The surge of power when you really gunned it was almost overwhelming. It was a bloody rocket ship. As space opened up, he pressed down hard and fast. Kaz whooped as they sped away - 80, 90, 100, 120, 140, it didn't matter, the Porsche just purred like it was no effort. He took it up to 170, his hands sweating with the adrenaline as Motorhead's 'We Are the Road Crew' came on the radio.

'Cops oncoming!' she shouted, seeing a blue light coming into view. He came off the gas; 100 seemed slow, 65 was almost not moving at all. They'd covered 30 miles in just over 10 minutes. It was 380 miles to the Bay Area. It usually took about six hours. If he could keep it at 170mph he'd do it in just over two.

'Bloody hell. It might be a waste of money, but this is still one hell of a car,' said Kaz. 'I've gone a bit moist. I bloody love it. It's so smooth. It bloody purrs, it really does.'

'Yeah well, that's what $250,000 buys you.'

Kaz laughed. 'It is ludicrous, isn't it? Quarter of a mill on a car. Is she going to sell it?'

'Not said anything, but I reckon so. All part of the downsizing, isn't it?'

'I never thought she'd do that. I'm impressed, really. She's gone up in my estimation by a lot of points.'

Artie gave her a look. 'I know you don't really like her, you know...'

'...that's not fair, Artie. I do like her. She's just not my sort of person. That's not the same thing as disliking someone. She just doesn't sit right with me. Not least because she's always so bloody nice to me.'

'Well, she's a nice person.'

Kaz said something under her breath that he couldn't quite hear and sensed he probably didn't want to hear. They went quiet for a while. Artie chewed at his cheek, wondering how he was ever going to resolve being in love with two women, to both his and their mutual satisfaction. It wasn't possible, really. At some point one, two or all of them were going to have make a choice of some sort.

Concentrating hard, he kept his speed high on the long straight empty roads and they ate up the miles in no time at all. By just after 2am they were only 30 miles shy of San Francisco.

'I reckon we should get a room in before we cross Oakland Bridge into the city. Then get an early start and hit Pat Gunn's offices around 8.30am.'

'OK. Cool. I wonder if we could get a late snifter somewhere?'

'Yeah, deffo. We deserve it.' He turned to look at her again, illuminated only by the light from the dashboard panel. She glanced over at him and smiled. He smiled back as they drove through the blue-black Californian velvet darkness.

'Are you still feeling OK? Your head, I mean,' he said as they approached Pleasanton.

'Weirdly, yeah. Not even a headache, which is some going when you've got a fracture in the base of your skull.'

'Leeds heads are notoriously hard, though, aren't they? All those years of headbutting Manchester United fans has built up the thickness of skull.'

'True. That and the protective quality of chip fat. There's a thick coating of beef dripping around every Leeds head.'

They both laughed. Leeds seemed so far away when you were in a Porsche heading into northern California.

He took the Pleasanton turning and pointed to a Motel 6. 'This OK for you?'

'Our home from home, Artie.'

'Sure? We could go upmarket.'

'Why would we want to do that?

'I'm easy either way. None of it means anything to me.'

'Exactly. Motel 6 it is - and look, there's a bar just down the street. Let's hope it's still open.'

He parked the car and they walked into the reception. It smelled of coffee, cinnamon and pot pourri, as did almost everywhere in America.

It was just after 2.10am. 'Hey, there. Do you have any rooms?' said Artie.

A woman with a 1960s beehive hair-do worn, not as a retro-fashion statement, but because she was about 78 years old and hadn't altered her fashion choices since 1962, stood behind the desk.

'Sure we do. Whatcha need?' she said, chewing gum. This was the thing about America that Artie had noticed ever since his first trip, a lot of the locals appeared to be straight out of a movie at any time of the day or night. At times, you had to check over your shoulder to make sure you were not caught up in some Hollywood blockbuster. This old lady, with her lipstick badly applied in a wavy line around her mouth, was one of the stars in a movie she didn't know was being filmed.

'Have you got a twin?'

'Uh huh. Cost yer 40.'

He paid the money, took the key and they went in search of a drink. The bar Kaz had seen was part of a strip mall and was still serving booze to the six people in there - two guys playing pool, a couple canoodling in a booth and two at the bar watching sports replays on TV. It was dark and smelled of fried meat and onions. 'Mississippi Queen' by Mountain was playing on the jukebox. It felt like a home from home. This was the thing when you're a rock 'n' roll nomad on the road in the night. You set up a base camp, somewhere sympathetic, and you got your groove on, even if it's after 2am.

He ordered two Jack Daniels and Coke as they slid up onto two solid black oak bar stools.

'Here's to...to...to truth,' he said, clinking Kaz's glass.

He watched as she sank the whole glass and slammed it down on the bar and then did the same himself. The bar man, like all American bar staff, attuned to servicing those in need of booze, came over and merely flicked his eyebrows at Kaz. She pointed to the glasses and a refill was forthcoming.

'Well, this is another fine mess you've gotten me into,' she said, with a shrug.

'Yeah. I just keep trying to think what we must know, that means someone needs us dead.'

'Let's go through a few things that we know, then.' She pulled her thumb back. 'First, we know Ben Goldman is allergic to peanuts.'

'Everyone who saw him collapse could attest to that.'

'True, but only Georgina knew his name and they tried to blow her up as well. Next up, we knew both Carly and Robbie. Third, we had the mercury tests done.'

He tapped on the bar with his nail. 'Me and you, Georgina and Fay and Coll and HJH all knew about the mercury at the time the bomb went off. But by the time they tried to shoot me, Mo and her team all knew about it. So blowing us up or shooting me for that reason would have made no difference. The mercury cat was already out of the bag, so to speak.'

'OK, what else?' She paused. 'No. Hold on. What you said isn't right.' She took a drink. 'Danny Blind knew about the mercury as well. He was at the hospital with us, remember?'

'Oh, yeah. I forgot all about him. Just shows though, killing us wouldn't have stopped the mercury info from getting out.'

'Next, you'd viewed the CCTV footage before the shooting, so you might have seen something on that.'

'Again, true, but that had come via Coll who got it from Mo. So, again, nothing unique to me about that. Killing me for that reason wouldn't protect anyone. It changes nothing. Also no-one could have known I had those DVDs.'

'Maybe they're going to shoot them all too, or maybe they don't know they've seen it.'

'No. There's no way anyone is taking out a whole lawyer's office. And also, the recordings are known to exist. Eventually, whatever is trying to be hidden will be revealed.'

'I'm not so sure. One big bomb under their block in Laguna Beach and they'd all be toast along with the servers.'

'But all the evidence and records are all backed up and stored remotely on the cloud, so that'd do no good. Nah, that's not right.'

She teased out a few strands of her blonde hair, tugging on them in contemplation.

'So, me and you and Georgina don't seem to exclusively know anything. Nothing that needs us to be blown up'

'No. Maybe it's not about us, then.'

'Someone tried to shoot you. Of course it's about us, or about you, at the very least.'

He rubbed at stubble on his cheek. 'Yeah. Maybe. I still wonder if it wasn't just some prank that went wrong. And were just in the store at the wrong time. It was nothing to do with us being there. We were just unlucky.'

'That is some sodding bad luck, if that's the case.'

They had another two drinks and then went back to the motel.

'I've just realised, I've not got any clean clothes,' sad Kaz, as he unlocked their room door.

'Aye, we'll just have to buy some tomorrow at JC Penny or whatever.'

The room was basic in extremis. Two single beds, a chair and nothing else, except an old analogue TV.

Without even thinking, they defaulted to a routine. She went and got a shower first while he lay on the bed and put the TV on. Then, when she was done, he went and showered too, standing in the warm steam she'd left behind. This was their gig. The life they'd lived for 15 years from the arse end of nowhere to the big end of somewhere.

'Funny that we could stay in 5-star hotel if we wanted, but we don't want,' she said, getting into her bed in her t-shirt and underwear.

'Yeah, I'm not opposed to a bit of luxury occasionally, but ultimately, it makes no difference to a hotel room. As long as it's clean, you lie down and sleep, get up and leave. Why pay much money to do that?'

'Aye, that is good Yorkshire logic, Artie.' She yawned. 'I'm so knackered. So, do we keep the guns under our pillows?'

He looked at the pistol. 'Best not. Might somehow accidentally shoot ourselves in the head. Bedside table is fine.'

'You can see how so many people get shot in this country, though, can't you? Over here, if a drunk tries to get into your room by mistake, he gets his brains blown out. In the UK, he gets someone politely asking him to be on his way.'

'Yeah, it's a brutal country, in so many ways. That's what I used to like about it, actually - the feeling of independence and self-reliance. The cowboy spirit.'

'Aye, but you can't be independent when your thighs are so fat they rub together and give you blisters whenever you try to walk.'

Artie snorted air out of his nose and put out the light. 'Coll said something like that the other day. How she'd fallen out of love with America, in many ways. A once great country has turned on itself.'

'Aye, it is eating itself up, she's not wrong.' She paused for a bit. 'Artie? Will she know we're sharing a room?'

He stared at the TV. 'I don't know. Probably.'

'Doesn't it bother her?'

He turned to look at her. 'Why would it bother her?'

'Don't be thick. Most wives would think it was weird and wouldn't allow it.'

'Yeah, well, Coll isn't most wives.'

'Why isn't she jealous? Most women would be if their husband was staying a hotel room with another woman. You do know that isn't normal, don't you?'

'What is or isn't normal is beyond me, these days. But it's because she sees you as my mate. It's not like you're just some chick I'm banging. She gets that the way we've lived around each other has been weird and unusual. She likes that. And anyway, we're not a normal married couple, are we, me and Coll.'

'I suppose not...but even so. I'm not sure what you're saying is right. You know what? I think she thinks we're not just mates. In her mind, we're actually lovers. And, somehow, she accepts that.' She leaned on her elbow, looking at him.

'She's never said anything like that. Not since before the wedding, anyway. And we need to look after each other on a trip like this. I mean, some nutters are out to get us.'

But he knew that wasn't convincing. Not to him and not to Kaz. And it had occurred to him, even whilst they were on tour with Springsteen, before Coll joined them, that she was at heart a libertine and if he and Kaz were sleeping together sometimes, it didn't bother her, or she accepted it. And, of course, sometimes they were sleeping together, but never having sex. Just like this night. And it was weird. Normal for them, but still weird, all the same. Trouble was, both now and when they'd been on tour, he found himself thinking about it more and more, and enjoying thinking about it more and more, remembering the passionate sex they'd shared in Las Vegas. It was also much nicer staying with her, than in a room on his own. And, since she was always just as happy to share a room, be it a twin or a double, she obviously felt the same way. And why did they have to live like anyone else, anyway?

CHAPTER 19

Artie woke at 6.30am and went in search of coffee, which was, in itself, such a quintessentially American experience. In a society where most people did not expect to ever have to do anything for themselves, up to and including making coffee, it meant that even at 6.30am someone was trying to make a buck off your caffeine needs.

The strip mall had a coffee shop. He got coffees and two Danish pastries.

Kaz was up and dressed when he got back. 'Ah, the holy medicine. Thanks, man.'

She took the pastry and wolfed it down. 'I'm still dead hungry. I need bacon at some point before the day is too old. Aren't you hungry?'

'Nah. Not really. But I should be. You know what I'm like. Coffee is food to me.'

After checking out, they stood by the car in the pale gold of the early morning sun, the sound of traffic from the freeway in the distance. The air was soft and a little cool.

'I still love California, you know,' he said. 'Mornings like this, coming out of a motel, I don't know, man...it just feels great. Not just great, but, right. Do you know what I mean?'

She sucked in a deep breath through her nose. 'Yeah, it's bloody brilliant. Or at least it would be if some twat wasn't trying to kill us.'

They drove over Oakland Bridge into the city on a bright blue morning. San Francisco looked beautiful under the early summer sunshine.

'Sometimes I forget how great this place is,' said Kaz as they drove into the city, taking the 101 north in slow-moving traffic. 'It's just so funky. All the wooden buildings and hills - it just doesn't look like anywhere else. Oh, god, Artie. I love it. I love its rock tradition and its gay tradition. It's just...well, it's not Leeds.'

'Yeah, I've always liked it. Pity I have no idea where we're going. Any idea where Fillmore Street is from here?'

'Patricia Gunn's address is Pacific Heights, I know where that is. It's sort of over there.'

' "Sort of over there" is too vague. Look it up on your phone.'

'Oh, yeah, I always forget you can do that. Ha ha. I'm so analogue.' She pushed at the screen as they sat at a red light, looking up at the street signs. 'Got it. Take the next exit on Geary.'

He did as she said. 'Oh, I know where I am now. The original Fillmore West was at the junction with Fillmore, along here,' he said as he drove.

'The Fillmore being on Fillmore, yup, that makes sense. Is this address her home, or her office?'

Artie turned onto Fillmore and headed north again. 'I don't know. I assumed it was her office.'

Pacific Heights looked smart and upscale on a June morning, the sun casting sharp shadows across the pastel-coloured flat-board houses. It was one of the more expensive areas of the city to live in and it really showed, as they pulled through the commercial area. Kaz looked out for numbers. 'It must be on the next block.'

Artie parked the Porsche outside her address, leaned over and looked up at the impressive detached residence, with 15 wooden steps leading up to a rather gothic wooden porch. It was painted a lovely duck-egg blue and had slight Addams Family aspect to it. The ground floor was a garage, above it two more storeys and then an attic. 'Obviously, not an office. What I like about these places is they're grand in size, but humble in how they're made. They actually look handmade,' he said. They walked up the steps. 'This looks a bit like the famous Grateful Dead house at 710 Ashbury Street,' said Artie, looking at his watch. It was only 8.50am.

He pressed an illuminated doorbell. Somewhere down the hall, a chime played. It was familiar. Artie pointed in its direction. 'That's playing the "Dark Star" melody...'

'...the Grateful Dead? Bloody hell, this *is* a proper hippie house, Artie...look.' She pointed at a yin-yang symbol set into the front door in white and black coloured glass.' She sank a little at the knees. 'You know I've no patience for hippies. If she wants to do my star sign, I'm out of here.'

Pat Gunn opened the door. She was nearly six foot tall, about 70, tanned and with heavily etched lines on her brow and eyes, with loosely curled white hair to her shoulders. Around her neck was a silver chain with a small silver scorpion attached. She wore billowing MC Hammer-style pants made from a rough silk and a black t-shirt. Somehow, it was a specifically San Franciscan look for a woman of her generation; the well-off Baby Boomer hippie. A bangle on her wrists had small bells on it so she actually tinkled as she moved. She looked from Kaz to Artie with a beatific smile, that put Artie in mind of the greeter at Mother Earth.

'Hi, there. I'm Artie Taylor, this is Kaz Clarke. We've come from LA to talk to you about Green on Green.'

Pat gave them a quirky look. 'Oh, have you? Really? I have no involvement in the company anymore. I retired well over a year ago.'

'Oh, OK. Do you know what's happened?' said Artie.

She gave him a quizzical look. 'As regards what?'

'Have you heard of the Paleo Patriots?' asked Kaz.

'I'm sorry. Why are you asking me these things? Who are you?'

'We're two of the only three people who survived the bomb blast in the Mother Earth store in Topanga,' said Artie. 'Someone suggested we come and talk to you about Green on Green. We're trying to find out who was behind the explosion. It killed 15 people.'

She put her long-fingered hand to her mouth, her face creased in a frown. 'Seriously? You were in that explosion?' It wasn't surprising she might find it hard to believe.

'You can feel the bumps on the back of my head where one of the roofs beams hit me, if you like,' said Kaz, bouncing on her toes, a little, as she often did to make herself a bit taller.

'Look, can we go for coffee, if you've got a few minutes spare?' said Artie. 'We really need your help.'

Instead, she beckoned them into the house and said, 'Come in. I'll make some coffee for us.' A tabby cat emerged from the kitchen licking its lips, looking very pleased with itself. She scooped it up it her arms and kissed it on the head. 'This is Gracie.'

Artie liked cats. Always had. He gave her a stroke and tickled her ears, as Pat Gunn placed her on a kitchen chair. 'Hello, Gracie. Aren't you lovely?' he said. Animals can bring the best out of humans. Gracie, like all cats, knew she was very lovely indeed and broke into a low rumbling purr.

Glass jars of red, brown and green lentils, red, white and black beans, pasta, and brown rice were lined up on shelves. Rust-coloured earthenware tiles lined half of the wall, giving the place a rustic Mediterranean look. A large, oak farmhouse-style kitchen table sat centrally in the spacious bright kitchen. Artie looked at several framed pictures clustered on one wall. They were all from the late 60s to late 70s. He recognised some of the people in them.

'How did you come to know the Grateful Dead?' he said, tapping at photo of a woman who was still obviously Pat, all exploding hair and crocheted waistcoat, 45 years or more earlier, standing to one side of Jerry Garcia, Robert Hunter and Bob Weir outside of the Fillmore West.

'Oh, we mixed in the same circles. Green on Green had a concession stand at the Fillmore for a while, so everyone in the company would get free tickets for shows. A long time before I worked for them as an accountant, I did all sorts of other jobs for Keith, going back to day one.'

'And this is you with Quicksilver Messenger Service, Country Joe and Barry Melton; oh wow, and you're with Janis in this one.' He was genuinely thrilled to see these great old black-and-white pictures.

'Well, they were not stars to us, they were just local friends. There wasn't a separation in those days.' She busied herself making coffee as she talked. 'And of course green living and vegetarianism was a big part of the hippie culture, too. As you might know, that's how Green on Green got started.'

He peered closely at another black-and-white shot. 'Is this you with Arlo Guthrie at, is it Woodstock?'

'Yeah. He's a good friend. I was choppered in with him. Henry Diltz took that. The New York thruway was jammed up. We were freaked out, man, we were sooo high. Glory days...glory days.'

Artie had to tear himself away from the amazing pictures and get down to business.

'OK, Pat, I'll be straight with you. This might all sound incredible, but hear me out. Someone has been putting mercury in the Green on Green soy jerky that is sold in the Mother Earth stores. A friend of ours died because of it. It's also been contaminated with peanuts, when it's supposed to be nut free.'

She looked horrified. 'What? Are you sure?'

'We had tests done. The peanuts nearly killed someone called Ben Goldman, who is badly allergic.'

'We saved him with an adrenaline injection,' added Kaz.

The room began to fill with the rich smell of coffee as an expensive-looking Gaggia machine spat out the dark liquid from two nozzles.

'Ben Goldman? The music business people? The Goldman's boy?'

'You know him?'

'Yeah, sure I do. Well, I knew his parents, I've not seen Ben since he was about nine. They were part of the scene here for years. They got started here, in fact. I think they worked for Moby Grape or Mad River or one of those bands that everyone loved but no-one bought their records. And they worked for Bill Graham on and off for years. They did the legal stuff for the Us Festivals in 82 and 83 and really became very successful, at least if you measure success by wealth - which I don't. How do you like your coffee?'

'Black,' said Artie and Kaz together.

She gave each of them a mug with a star sign on. Artie's was Sagittarius; Kaz's, Leo. Both correct. He looked at Kaz, she looked back and twitched an eyebrow. Oh no, was she some sort of hippie visionary?

'Tell me what happened with Ben,' she said, sitting down at the head of the table.

Artie explained everything. Pat listened impassively. She was an impressive presence. Not your normal accountant type.

'Well, this is a strange coincidence. Who gave you my address?'

He explained that as well.

'That is veeery weird,' she said, when he'd finished.

'Have you heard of the Paleo Patriots?' said Kaz.

'Well, yes, I have...'

'...really? I couldn't find anything out about them online,' said Artie.

She raised her greying dark eyebrows. 'I don't know much. The Chief mentioned them.'

'The Chief?' said Artie.

'My old man...sorry...everyone calls him the Chief, on account of the fact he's a Lakota Indian.'

'Isn't that a bit un-PC to say?' said Kaz.

'Yes, Kaz, it is. But it's how he's always referred to himself so that makes it alright, apparently. Or...you know...whatever. I'm too old to keep up with the latest PC bullshit. Too much energy expended on that stuff, if you ask me. But he was talking about them. They're based somewhere in the city. They're a pressure group, against factory farming and pro grass-fed meat and organic. That's all very '69, in some ways, actually. And you're telling me that they gave you my name?'

'Yeah. It was on a list as someone who was sympathetic to being critical of Long Run.'

She sipped at her coffee. 'Well, I wasn't in favour of the buy-out. I knew how it'd work. G on G were the biggest producer of vegan foods on the west coast. As soon as they bought us out, I knew they'd make a move for a retailer. And I'd known Honest Joe for 45 years and it was obvious they'd swoop for him. They made him an offer only someone insane would refuse. They wanted his brand, his vibe, and to roll it out right across the state and eventually, I assume, across the country.

But...look, I hate - and I use that word advisedly - big business. I want nothing to do with it. Long Run are venal, amoral capitalists. They're all about money and not about people at all. Or not usually, anyway. But we struck a special deal with them.'

'So why did it happen?' said Artie. 'Why did Keith Perez sell out to them?'

'The old story. Same as HJH. Big money. Plain and simple. But, I'll be honest with you, I was disappointed in Keith, at first. But in the end, he did well by everyone. I have to say that. He kept the co-operative spirit of Green on Green intact.'

'What was your role in G on G?' asked Kaz.

'I ran the accounts department. I added up and I took away, but what you've got to understand is that G on G was much more than just a business. It was...' she waved her hand around in midair, grasping for the right word '...a lifestyle, a philosophy, a way to live. We were all vegans. We all believed. We thought we were making a better, less cruel world and not just for a year or two, but for decades. And it has washed down the generations. For example, soy milk and tofu is in every supermarket today. That's down to us and people like us.' She said it with pride, but Artie wondered how much of an achievement that really was.

That being said, Artie had really warmed to her. She seemed to be a good soul: a hippie who had just tried to make the world a better place. Whether you thought they'd gone about it the right way or not, it had all come from a good place and that was at least something to admire. So many people go through life just buying into the status quo, whatever that is, in any given era. Kicking back against prevailing wisdom, by how you live and not just by the what you say, is tougher gig than is often given credit for. A lot of the time it comes to nothing, but ultimately all change comes from those who do not accept the status quo and who fight it every day. There was much to annoy you about hippies, but much to like as well, however reluctant he was to sometimes acknowledge it.

Gracie hopped up onto his lap and began to settle down and to go to sleep. Having an animal sleep on you always feels like a privilege. They trust you so much that they're prepared to become unconscious on your lap. He stroked her a little as she curled up. This did not go unnoticed. Pat smiled at him.

'You must be giving off a good vibration for her to trust you like that. They pick up on that. Though they love to honour a cat-hater even more, like they're feline missionaries.' Kaz gave him a quick narrowing of the eyes to tell him it was all hippie bullshit, but Artie was inclined to go with Pat's version of the truth.

'OK, so given all you know about how Green on Green was bought out, who do you think might be interested in bringing the company down, by corrupting the integrity of their products, and then scaring everyone away from where they're being sold, by blowing a store up?' said Artie.

'Well, I'll be straight with you. When I heard what had happened...and it was all over the news here...my first thought was that it was an anarchist group.'

'Why would you think that?' said Kaz.

'There was a lot of bitterness towards Mother Earth and Green on Green because they'd been hand in hand for so long and then suddenly had both sold out to Long Run. A company named after the worst damn Eagles album!' At first Artie thought she was joking, but she wasn't. That fact upset her. 'It's been bubbling away for some time. You've got to understand that they were both, for so long, an example of how to run your business in a fair, humane, ecological and moral way. For that to be sold out to people who just wanted to exploit the vegan dollar for maximum profit, was deeply troubling for many people.'

It wasn't hard to see the passion behind her eyes. This was a fire that had not gone out. She was clearly still emotional about it all.

'So there's a chance it was an act of, what we might call, vegan terrorism?' said Kaz.

'Like I say, that was my first thought. Someone psychopathically angry at the sell-out.'

'But that's stupid. Vegans are supposed to be against killing things,' said Kaz.

'Against killing animals,' said Pat.

'Humans are animals,' said Kaz, curtly.

Pat sucked her lips in and then pouted a little. 'I don't agree with this, but it is not an uncommon viewpoint, at the radical end of the movement, that killing humans who hurt animals is justified. That the human animal is corrupt and other animals are innocent.'

'But that's anthropomorphic bollocks,' said Kaz, wearily. 'That cat will think nothing of half-killing a mouse and playing with its tortured body just for the hell of it, even when it's not hungry. Anyway, you can't apply human morals to animals. That's just childish.'

'I did say I didn't agree with it. But let me tell you, emotions on these matters run deep. However, to blow a store up and to poison food is a very radical, terrible thing to do - the work of someone who is unhinged and in a very dark place.'

'Where are the Green on Green products actually made?' said Artie, who finally felt like they were getting somewhere.

'Most are made here, in San Francisco just off Columbus.'

'Including the soy jerky?' said Kaz.

'All soy snack products like that, used to be made in the city at a big production unit in Russian Hill. If they were contaminated, that's where it must have happened, but I'm not sure how that's possible because when you sell something guaranteed as nut-free, the city's environmental health board regularly turn up unannounced to take samples. They'd shut it down in a heartbeat, if anything was out of line. In fact, Ben Goldman can't have reported it, because they'd probably already have shut it down. It's about as serious an issue as you can have. I very much doubt that any contamination took place there. It would have to be done after it had left the production unit...but mercury poisoning...that's...' she shook her head '...I just find that very difficult to believe. How do you even do that?'

'It was a slow poisoning, done over a long period of time,' said Artie, but even as he said it, a thought came to him. Carly had been ill for a year or more, and the post mortem said she had mercury in her body. And the soy jerky had tested positive for mercury, so naturally they'd connected those things together, but what if they were not connected? That would change everything.

Pat shook her head and folded her tanned arms across her chest. 'Unless things have changed a lot, that's just not possible. You simply can't systematically poison a foodstuff over a long period of time. It would get flagged up, sooner or later. Food production regs are tough at the best of times.'

Artie nodded and stroked the cat's ears. 'I'm puzzled as to why lots of people haven't got sick, the same way as Carly, the girl who died, did.'

'Poor girl. Could she have been targeted specifically?'

'For so long? That doesn't seem likely, does it?' said Kaz.

'No, it doesn't and anyway, it's not practical to do it. How could they know which soy jerky packets she was going to buy and when? They couldn't. The more I think about it the more I think we've been barking up the wrong tree,' said Artie.

The front door open and closed and heavy footsteps came toward the kitchen.

'Hey, Chief. This is Artie Taylor and Kaz Clarke,' said Pat as her husband entered.

Artie stood up and held out his hand. The Chief was well-named. He was about six foot four and built like an armoured car, despite obviously being in his late 60s. He wore a navy blue t-shirt with a print of a wolf on it and what looked like a pair of white karate pants, along with some sort of sandal. His long grey hair was fastened back in a ponytail.

'Good to meet you, Chief,' said Artie, shaking hands. The big man had an iron grip.

Kaz was a full foot shorter than him. 'Hey, big man,' she said, also shaking hands, looking up at him.

'You're English,' he said. 'I love an English accent.'

His wife briefly explained why they'd come, as she made the Chief coffee.

'So you guys are looking to find out who tried to kill you? That don't seem unreasonable. Pigs won't do it, especially the LA pigs. They're bad dudes.' Artie hadn't heard anyone refer to the police as 'pigs' for years. It was still apparently 1969 here, though. 'I said to Pat, when news of the explosion came through, that it wouldn't surprise me if Long Run had blown up their own store in some sort of financial scam.'

'He is one for a conspiracy theory,' his wife said, chiding him somewhat.

'Well, someone is damn well responsible, Pat. Who blows up a vegan store?' said the Chief.

'Crazy people do crazy things, man,' said Pat. 'A crazy person must be responsible for this.'

'Yeah, but Artie was shot at in the hospital. I mean, that's proof that there's a conspiracy of some sort going on. They must think you know something that only you can know. If you'd have died in the explosion along with those other folks, you'd have taken it to your grave. But you didn't,' said the Chief.

'So what do you know about the Paleo Patriots?' asked Artie.

The big man rubbed at his square jaw then stood up. 'Come with me to the diner.'

'The diner?' said Artie,

'I own a diner. It's only a block away. My chef was telling me about them. They're a new pressure group.'

168

Artie felt reluctant to have to wake up Gracie, putting her on down onto the floor. She stretched and jumped up onto the windowsill and began cleaning her fur.

'Nice to meet you, Pat. Thanks for your help and for being so trusting as to ask us into your home. I mean, you don't know us from Adam...' said Artie.

'...or Eve,' added Kaz.

'You both have good auras. Predominantly pink and orange,' she said.

'Auras? Oh, you don't see auras, do you?' said Kaz, a little wearily.

The Chief laughed and made a noise in his throat that sounded like a woodpecker on a drum. 'You got the two best colours there, baby.' He put a big hand on her shoulder.

'I'm sorry, I don't believe in all that New Age stuff,' said Kaz.

'That's cool. You don't have to believe in it. Like air, it's there, whether you believe in it or not.'

Artie waved his hand over his head. 'Not sure I suit pink and orange. My mother always said I suited green.'

They were about to leave the house when Artie turned back to Pat. 'Can I just ask one question? How did you know our star signs, in order to give us the right mugs?'

'Oh, she's good at that,' said the Chief. 'Never gets anyone wrong. It's one of her party tricks. Always blows my mind.'

'We are all children of the universe. We all physically manifested at a unique time. All star signs are is a way to interpret how that moment affects who you are. You are a classic Leo; Kaz, you're a classic Sagittarius. Artie, I could go into more detail, but I sense it'd be embarrassing for you.'

'How would it be embarrassing?' said Kaz.

'Because it would voice some things about you which you probably do not want to voice - not just yet, anyway.'

The Chief laughed again. 'She can be real cryptic when the mood takes her.'

She gave each of them a light hug and they walked down the steps.

'Don't worry so much. You're very compatible,' she said. Artie turned round.

'What?' he said.

Pat held her finger tips together into a pyramid in front of her and bowed a little at him, but didn't say anything else. They walked off down to the road. It was hard to keep up with the Chief because his stride was so long. Kaz was almost jogging.

'Do you believe in all that astrology and aura business, Chief?' said Artie.

'Sure. I've lived with Pat for 40 years. She's got the gift. Whatever you want to call it, she's got it. Sometimes she wishes she didn't. Don't worry though, she only uses her superpowers for good.' He flashed a big-toothed grin at him.

'So did you work at Green on Green as well?' asked Kaz, a little breathless.

'No. I've been in the restaurant trade. Still am.'

He pointed at a building with a painted sign which read 'Chief's'.

It was a classic old-school vegetarian restaurant with long wooden tables and the smell of tomatoes and herbs in the air. He acknowledged a couple of regulars and took them through to a small kitchen where a Mexican guy was standing at stove frying vegetarian sausages.

'Hey, Pancho, man, remember you were telling me about the Paleo Patriots?'

Pancho looked up at him and spoke in heavily accented English. 'Yeah? What 'bout them?'

'What do you know about them?' said Artie.

'They're new. Came here promoting their thing. I said, we're no meat, y'know? They say, that's who we want to change. I say, you're crazy. Vegetarian doesn't want to change. It's their thing, y'know. Gave me a lot of shit about soy...I say, yeah yeah, but I not listen really. Told him it's the Chief's place anyway, I'm just the cook. I told you Chief and me, I'm done with it.'

He served up the sausages onto a metal plate and pushed them across a counter to a waitress who was waiting, then pulled open a drawer. 'They left this. I haven't even read it.'

It was a small leaflet.

'Can I take this?' said Artie, glancing at it.

'Sure. Take it,' said Pancho.

'Would you folks like to have some breakfast?' said the Chief.

Kaz held her hands up. 'Thanks, big man, but no thanks. We're fans of products of slaughter to start the day.'

The Chief smiled. It made his face look like it was a wooden carving. You could imagine him riding through the Dakota badlands, 150 years ago, trying to drive out the white man. You didn't see a lot of men who looked like the classic Indians of the cowboy movies Artie had seen whilst growing up. Even though it was a hopelessly outdated cliché, if he'd referred to whisky as fire water, it wouldn't have been surprising to a kid brought up on Hollywood's version of American history.

'OK, well, I hope you find the people responsible for everything you have endured.' He handed Artie a card. 'Call me if you need help while you're in town.' He put his hands together and bowed a little to them in turn, just as Pat had done. It felt like a nice thing to do, so Artie responded likewise, while Kaz did a mock curtsey.

Artie read the leaflet as they walked back to the car.

'He was interesting. I liked him better than his wife. She was a bit of a witch, if you ask me,' said Kaz.

'Pat? I liked her.'

'You *liked* her?' She said it with an exaggerated mixture of surprise and disgust.

'Yeah. She had a nice vibe about her.'

'Artie, she was a hippie with a capital Hip. I mean, a proper one.' She made a mock shiver.

'She was, but I thought she was a good soul. She was nice and very trusting to two strangers. That's cool.'

'But she had a cat.'

'Gracie was a nice cat. She liked me.'

'Cats don't like me.'

'Only because you reject them because you don't want to be a stereotype lesbian.'

She hit him on the arm.

'Stop having insight, Artie, it's *not* a good look for you,' she said, crossly, but smiling nonetheless. 'And all that aura and horoscope shit, that curdles my blood, that does. There are no such things as auras. It makes no sense. You know that and I know that.'

'OK, maybe, but she believes it. The Chief does, too. And she got our star signs bang on. Is that just luck? I'm not sure. I think there's something in it. Not sure exactly what, but she had some sort of gift. And she knew about me and you, as well. You're not really that hard line, you know you're not. You're just being all Yorkshire for the hell of it.' He stopped and pointed to the leaflet. 'It says here the Paleo Patriots were formed to organise a response to the propaganda of the vegetarian and vegan food industry...'

'...I like the sound of them already. Bloody vegans, did you see all the lentils and brown rice in her kitchen? Bollocks to that.'

'They're also anti the big-meat businesses. They believe in natural food, nothing processed, everything organic, no industrial farming of animals, blah blah blah...err...this is a bit weird. It says that the way America produces food is un-American. "It is unpatriotic. It has led to the oppression and manipulation of the people by making them being fat and addicted to consumption"...'

'...well, that's what we were saying...'

He interrupted her. '...and what Coll was talking about, as well. The last bit here is interesting, too. It says, "vegetarians and vegans feel like they're more in harmony with nature, but this is a delusion fostered by Big Food - the same people who invented the five-a-day fallacy, the same people that pushed a low-fat agenda. They co-opted the vegans and vegetarians to work as shock troops for healthy eating, to keep people addicted to the old bad ways for the maximum profit of both the food processing and the pharmaceutical industry".'

'I agree with all of that. That's exactly right,' said Kaz. 'Bloody healthy eating is a tyranny. It makes people more ill with worry than the food they eat does. So what do they say we should be eating?'

'Err...all meats, offal, eggs, occasional dairy, green vegetables. No grains or sugary fruits. Grains are "alien to the human hunter-gatherer body". It says we've not evolved to digest them and we store their carbohydrate as fat. This is the biggest issue in America today.'

'Bloody hell. Maybe that's why I've always been 30 to 40 pounds overweight my whole adult life. I'm mad for bread and pasta.' She took the leaflet off him and read it quickly. 'I love this. I might start eating like they suggest. I'll end up a big fat old lady, the way I've been going. I love this. I'm all about steak, liver and eggs and no toast. Look, they say you should drink spirits 'cos they've got no carbs. See, I'm halfway there. I'm all about vodka and Jack these days. In fact, I'd like some now.'

'Yeah, me too, but let's save it for later. They've got an address on here.'

'Why does a pressure group have an address?'

'I don't know, but let's go there,' he said, as they reached the Porsche. He'd just got into the car and turned the ignition key when his phone vibrated. He took it out of his pocket. It was a message from Fay.

'Helen is severely anaemic (fucking vegan diet!!!), she doesn't have any mercury in her blood. She isn't ill like Carly was ill. Only Carly was poisoned. Where are you?'

He dialled her number.

'Hey, Artie.'

'Hey, Fay. So, Helen's going to be OK?'

'Yeah, apparently it's hard to get iron as a vegan. Damn crazy diet. I wish I'd never heard of it. What does it mean, Artie?'

'I'm not sure, but I think it must mean that Carly wasn't actually sick from what she'd eaten at Mother Earth, despite what we thought. There's no way only one person can consume mercury from food that sold to thousands of other people. She must have consumed it some other way.' He paused and a crazy thought came into his mind. 'How do we know she actually did have mercury in her blood?'

'Err...duh...because the hospital told us,' said Fay, in her rising-inflective, SoCal way.

'Yeah, but it was just one doctor...' he paused and chewed on his lip, half of an idea forming a shape in his brain. 'How do we even know the man who gave us the information was a real doctor? He came into the media room at the hospital with a white coat on, but anyone could do that. The white coat is the Access All Areas backstage pass in a hospital.'

'Brilliant. I like it. But why were they trying to fool us?' said Fay.

'To create a scandal against Green on Green and Mother Earth. To cause trouble for them. They heard we were coming in to get the results and fed us disinformation.'

'Err...OK...but why pick us, we're, like, nobody. And are you telling me the lab results are a con as well? They found mercury in the soy jerky, remember.'

Artie winced a little. 'Shit, yeah. That doesn't seem likely, but still not impossible. I need to think about it some more.'

He heard her take a breath and pause before speaking. 'OK. Call me anytime. Artie, I'm sorry I couldn't come and see you in the hospital. Cowardly of me. I was too upset and didn't know what to do when I heard...I was so scared for you. I'm very happy you're both OK. Though I'm worried you might, like, get shot or something.'

'Yeah, I am, too. It's OK, Fay, you didn't have to come to the hospital.'

'How's Kaz?'

'For a woman with a fracture in her skull, who was recently in a coma, she's pretty good.'

'That's good to hear. Tell her I asked after her.'

Her voice was stiff and awkward. These were words she wouldn't normally say. Maybe she thought they were likely to be dead soon, so wanted to make sure she said them.

'Sure, I will. She'll appreciate that.'

'Artie...?' She paused and cleared her throat a little, an odd thing for such a self-assured person like her to do.

'Yes, Fay?'

'Well, err, I'm just gonna come out and say this. You do know that you should've married Kaz and not mom, don't you?'

Her words made his heart leap painfully up into the base of his throat.

'And why do you say that?' he said, dry-mouthed.

Fay didn't say anything for fully nine seconds, and that's a long time on the phone.

'Whatever you are with mom, it's not what you are with Kaz. You two are like different sides of the same coin.' She paused again. 'If I've spoken out of turn, I apologise, but I think mom knows it too and you guys have been through so much together...I'm not trying to stir things, I'm just saying it to try and help you...that sounds very patronising, I'm sorry...I just mean...' she sighed '...I'm screwing this up because I'm dysfunctional. Sorry.' She paused again and came back with a different SoCal, light tone, like what she'd said was nothing. 'Jus', y'know, jus' sayin'!' And in doing so revealed clearly that the bratty SoCal kid thing was really all an act she could just put on in an instant, but that underneath was a perceptive, intelligent young woman.

'Yeah, well, to be honest, Fay, I don't know why you've chosen now to say it. We're under a lot of pressure. People are trying to kill us.'

That activated her defensive reflex. 'Why? That's exactly why. Because you two almost died, Artie. You were nearly shot in the fucking head. Don't be an asshole about this. Sooner or later, you've got to do the right thing. The right thing by Kaz and mom and by yourself.'

The line went dead, but he kept the phone to his ear all the same, while he considered what it all meant. He felt a little pathetic. How could a 53-year-old man end up being told this stuff by a kid like Fay? Of course he knew exactly what she was talking about, but doing something about it was much, much harder and there just wasn't time or space to even think about it, right now.

'What was that about? Was Little Miss Hoity-Toity getting her arse out?' said Kaz, who had been looking at a map of San Francisco on her phone.

'Oh, it was just Fay being Fay.' He told her about Helen's diagnosis. 'We need to check those post mortem results on Carly, you know. Make sure they were for real.'

She looked squarely at him. 'But if that was all bullshit and we've been conned, several people had to lie to you. First, you called the hospital to get the time for the results being announced. So whoever told you that time, had to be in on the con. And they couldn't just sit around waiting for you or anyone else to call, could they? So that's not possible. That had to be the time the results were due to be made available, even if the bloke in the white coat wasn't for real, in which case they risked getting walked in on by the actual doctor.'

'Maybe they locked him in cupboard or something?'

'Artie, this is the real world, not Laurel and Hardy. People don't get locked in cupboards.' She said it a little wearily. 'Let's go and check out this place where they make the soy jerky. It's not far away, it's just off Columbus Avenue, not far from North Beach. We could go into that bar we like there, remember? The one we went to after the Springsteen gig. The one run by the Greek fella with wild hair. Just up from City Lights bookshop. I could use a snifter. I might start every day with a bloody Mary with my breakfast like I did back in the day if this stressful lifestyle doesn't ease up.'

'Yeah, let's do that. Wanna drive?'

'Go on then.' He got out and walked around to the car as she jumped over into the driver's side. As he pulled open the passenger side door he looked back down the street, then got in. But as he was sitting down into the sporty, black, kid leather bucket seat of the Porsche, the image of what he'd seen with his subconscious mind flooded into his conscious mind. He turned to Kaz, who was clipping her seat belt in.

'What?' she said, looking at him with her pale blue eyes.

'I've just seen Danny Blind.'

'The journalist from the LA *Times*? Are you sure?'

'Positive.'

'Do you want to go and say hello?'

He stared at her as the cogs in his brain spun and tried to get a grip on reality. 'He was trying to hide from me.'

She shook her head. 'Sorry, you've lost me.'

175

'He saw me looking at him and ducked down behind a car, in a move that you'd only make when you were trying to avoid being seen.'

'Really?'

'Yeah, I looked down the street, saw him and he ducked down, like he'd been shot. He went behind an old orange Beetle. And it cannot be a coincidence that he's here. C'mon, it's a big state. He's been bloody well following us.'

CHAPTER 20

She pointed at him. 'He was there at the post mortem results - he's in on that con. He's the con's press man, publicising the so-called poisoning in order to bring down Green on Green.'

Artie wiped at the corners of his mouth with his left hand thumb and index finger. 'Should I go and confront him?'

She looked in the rear-view mirror. 'I can't see him. He's probably got away down a side street. You've got his number though, haven't you?'

'Good point. Should I call and have it out with him?'

She looked away and out of the windscreen, sucking her lips. 'He works for the LA *Times*, right?'

'Yeah, he does.'

'So he'll have a Twitter account.' She looked at her phone and began poking at the screen. 'Ah, here he is. Last tweet was 9.24am, promoting a link to his latest piece. Oh, yes! Trouble is, he forgot to turn off the location option. He posted it from San Francisco. Banged to rights, mate.' She captured the screen and saved it. 'Right, now, at least we've got proof he was here.'

'Proof for who?'

'Who knows? If they find us with bullets in our head, it might help them catch the killer.'

'Fucking hell, Kaz. Don't say that.'

'C'mon, be practical. You're from Yorkshire, don't forget. If we get twatted, I want the bastard who did it strung up.'

Artie blew out air. 'I guess so. Shit. What are we involved in here?'

Kaz started the car and moved out into traffic. 'I don't know, but it's going to need some serious ass-kicking before it's sorted, that much I do know. I'm just glad we've got those guns. Feels a bit weird having it stuck in your waistband all the time, but I sort of like it.'

Artie turned around and looked out of the rear window. 'Yeah, well, we might need to use them soon. If he's followed us up here, he'll be following us now.'

'OK. I tell you what, I'll go a mental route to the factory and see if anyone follows us.'

She began taking random lefts, then down two blocks, then random rights. San Francisco, being mostly just one massive grid, was ideal for this.

'Anyone following us?' she said looking in the rear-view mirror.

'Yeah, see the silver Toyota?...it's him.'

'Danny Blind?'

'Yup. He's been a few cars back since you pulled away. Given you've been going all over the place, he must suspect we've spotted him, but he's sticking with us.'

'You can't burn away from anyone in this city. It's all intersections and no freeways, but we've got to shake him off.'

'I know what to do. Double back onto the 101 and head for Golden Gate Bridge. There's a chance of using some speed to shake him off.'

She did exactly that, hitting the major artery and joining three lanes of slow-moving traffic which soon thinned out as they went through a short underpass. As soon as there was space, Kaz pushed hard on the gas and took the Porsche up to 95 in the blink of an eye, weaving through traffic and then accelerating away again, this time up to 120.

'At the risk of seeming shallow, if it was physically possible, I would fuck this car,' she said, one hand on the small steering wheel, as she carved through the traffic on the magnificent rust-red Golden Gate Bridge. 'I feel like a bloody movie star.'

Artie kept a lookout for cops and for the Toyota. Neither were in sight.

'Can't see the Toyota. I think you lost him.'

As they crossed the bridge, she took the Vista Point turn off, a tourist destination to stop and take pictures of the bridge and buy something grotesquely high carb from the cafe. It was jammed up. She went around the car park once, attracting a lot of admiring glances from car aficionados, then accelerated out and back onto the 101, taking the Alexander Avenue exit and then following the signs back into San Francisco. The silver Toyota was nowhere to be seen.

'You lost him, Kaz. Excellent work. Shall I call him and ask him why he was following us now that we know for sure he was?'

'Maybe later. Let's go to the Green on Green factory on Columbus first.' She turned and grinned at him. 'I could get used to being some sort of getaway driver.'

'It's a talent you didn't know you had.'

'Pity I had to discover it in these circumstances.'

They pulled up outside a large, unprepossessing, featureless concrete factory, set back from Columbus Avenue, one of San Francisco's main arteries, running through the city in the Russian Hill district. The entrance was adorned with the G on G logo of a leaf curled around a tree.

She parked the Porsche outside a door, which led into a reception and office area.

Artie pushed open the door and stepped out of the warm morning into the air-conditioned building. To the right was a large office with four people sitting at computers, ahead a set of double swing doors that presumably led into the production areas. The air had a strange flavour to it - both savoury and sweet.

An attractive, blue-eyed young woman stepped out of the office. With short, fair hair, she was dressed in brown regulation vegan non-sexist trousers, a baggy ecru linen sweater and tennis shoes that looked like they were made out of hemp. She oozed vegan and was exactly the sort of person you saw in the Mother Earth stores buying something made of tofu, sprouted buckwheat or goji berries.

'Hi, there. How are you today?' She had clearly been trained at the same place as the store greeters.

'I'm good, thanks. I'm Artie Taylor, this is my colleague Kaz Clarke. I'm here because we had some tests done on one of your soy jerky strips and it contained both peanuts and, weirdly, mercury, and I wanted to firstly make you aware of this and secondly to find out how that might have happened.'

The colour dropped from her already pale face. 'What? Are you sure? We haven't heard anything about this.'

'Yes. I can give you the details of the lab that did the tests.'

She looked around, clearly flustered. 'I'll have to...err...excuse me. Please wait in our visitor lounge across the hall.' She pointed to a room and then went into the office and picked up a phone.

The visitor lounge looked like a hippie flat, with basket chairs, antique tables and a big coffee table covered in a tie-dyed cloth. On one wall was a big picture, taken in the late 60s, of some hippies standing under the Haight-Ashbury signpost.

They didn't sit down. It got busy in the office. Footsteps came and went. People kept peering into the room at them and giving them reassuring smiles and nods.

'Have you noticed how *everyone* here is a hippie,' said Kaz. 'Or a 2014 version of a hippie, anyway. The baggy, natural clothes, the men are very much not alpha males, the women look like they all smell of organic soap and patchouli.'

'Yeah, totally. It's amazing how that's such a consistent thing from here to the stores. It's obviously a magnet for people of that persuasion.'

She ruffled her hair and squinted at him. 'I know I'm always taking the piss out of them, but these people are good people. Alright, we don't sympathise with the vegan thing, but all the same, they're gentle souls. The worst they are is annoying, but they're not bad people.'

'What are you saying?'

'I'm saying that an organisation like this is almost certainly incredibly moral and scrupulous. The hippie ethic goes from top to bottom. They believe in karma. What goes around comes around. And every big company reflects its management's attitude. It's a trickle-down culture. Here, by the look of it, they've preserved its west-coast freak ethic from the early days.'

'Yeah, I agree. So what does that mean for us?'

'That nothing snide is going on. That these people would think that if they did anything wrong, instant karma was gonna get them. Look at them, they're already shitting themselves.'

He nodded. That seemed about right.

An older woman came in and held out her hand, a smile on her lightly tanned, unmade-up face.

'Hi, there. I'm Michelle Foster. I'm chair of the Green on Green co-op committee. We can go into my office and talk there.' They walked down the corridor and took a left into a honeycomb of small office spaces that were divided from one another by glass walls, so the whole set-up was literally transparent. She showed them into one with her name on the door. 'Please take a seat. Can I get you anything?' she said, sitting down behind a small, slim desk.

'We're fine, thanks,' said Kaz.

'Well, thank you for coming in today. Can you just give me a brief outline of, y'know...everything?' She spread her hands out wide as if to represent the concept of 'everything'.

Artie went over the whole story. She made occasional notes on a sheet of paper as he did so. By the time he got to the part about being blown up, she had already put her hand over her mouth in shock.

'Oh, my goodness. That is so terrible.' She put the flat of her hand on her heart and then outwards towards each of them in a gesture of empathy. It was all very Green on Green, somehow.

'Well, as you might appreciate, we want to get the people who did this caught before they kill us both,' said Artie. 'We can't wait for the police to catch them. Have you had any threats, or is there anyone who wants to bring Green on Green down? A disgruntled employee, or someone like that?'

'Everything has been running normally. There's been no trouble of any sort and I have to say that it's impossible to believe that those tests on our soy jerky are accurate. A mistake has been made.'

'Why is it impossible?' said Kaz.

'Because our production regimens are so rigorous and hygiene is scrupulous, testing is routine to make sure things are peanut free, let alone mercury free. If that has happened, it has happened away from here. This whole place is peanut free. We're not even allowed to bring in peanuts to eat for lunch. It's strictly enforced. Nobody would do that.'

'But surely someone with a grudge could do it.'

'Well, we don't have anyone like that here. I'm not sure if you know, but we're a workers' co-operative; collectively, the workers own the company. We all get a dividend each year based on how profitable we are. In fact, I don't think we've had anyone leave the company for maybe three years. We pay well, we have great medical insurance, six weeks paid holiday per year. Being a G on G employee is a great job.'

On hearing this, Artie leaned forward. 'But you're owned by Long Run. You were bought out by them three years ago. They then bought Mother Earth in Topanga and used that as a springboard to launch a whole chain of vegan stores which you supply into. We've just spoken to Pat Gunn, who I'm sure you must know...' she nodded '...and she said a lot of vegan activists were furious that you sold out to Long Run.'

'You have done your research, haven't you? What you say is right. Long Run offered the G on G collective a lot of money for the company and we did sell to them. It has attracted some ire. But what those critics don't know is Long Run had to agree that the co-operative nature of the company remains intact. Everyone on the co-op committee helped write the sales document, in fact. The co-op is autonomous and isn't dictated to by Long Run in any way, other than in respect of what is in effect a royalty payment on every sale we make.'

'Really? That's amazing. So you all got an input into how the company would be run in the future?' said Kaz.

She nodded. 'The sale agreement was massively weighted in our favour. Keith Perez, our founder, was insistent that be the case and we all agreed, and it made sense to Long Run because it's how they do business. They buy an already successful asset, take a cut of the gross and leave it to be run by the people who made it successful in the first place. They don't trade companies on. They buy them, sit back and take a skim off the top. The deal secured the company's future and given their plans for a state-wide roll-out of vegan stores, would make us very successful, by expanding our market hugely and quickly. And so it has proven. The sale agreement stipulated we are a guaranteed supplier to any Long Run stores - such as Mother Earth - and that should Long Run ever wish to sell G on G, we have first option to purchase at a fee no greater than what it was sold for plus inflation, regardless of growth - which told us that they were in it for, as their name suggests, the long run. I mean, they really wanted a cut of the vegan market, seeing it as a long-term expanding market.'

'I see, so basically, they can't really make money by selling you and that proves they just want to keep you on the books long term,' said Artie.

She nodded again. 'And we are still a co-op and on a day-to-day basis, nothing has changed at all. In fact, since the buy-out, we've had just one meeting with the Long Run people. We are, to all intents and purposes, autonomous. It was a one-off deal that we struck. Everything we wanted, we got.'

Artie nodded. She spoke so eruditely and evenly paced, without pauses, explaining things simply.

'What if everyone decides soya is bad for you?' said Kaz. 'What if some science comes out and proves that it's harmful and everyone stops eating it? There are people who say it messes with your thyroid.'

She laughed a little. 'I don't think that'll happen, but if it did, we'd have to move on and develop other products.' She leaned on her desk and placed her fingertips together. 'Look, I will call in an independent testing company to make sure our production is clean. Obviously, I can't have our integrity impugned by contamination. From what you say, Mo Casson will be paying us a visit at some point, so I need to get my defence sorted for that.'

'She's not a venal lawyer. She just wants to get to the truth,' said Artie.

'Indeed. And so do I. This is of great concern. Our company motto is "Give Love, Get Love" and we take it seriously.'

One part of Artie's brain winced at such a hippie aphorism, but an older, wiser part knew it was no bad thing at all. It was a bloody harsh, cold world and, as Kaz had said earlier, these were people just trying to make things a bit better. We need more people who believe in the give love, get love principle, not less. Just as long as he didn't have to eat soy jerky to do so.

She went on. 'What I don't understand is if your friend Carly was slowly poisoned, that would mean what she was eating was always contaminated with mercury, batch after batch. How could that happen?'

'Well, we don't know.'

She stared for a few seconds at Artie and then at Kaz, in deep contemplation.

'Forgive me, but I don't think it's practically possible. Regular exposure to mercury in small doses is too hard to administer on an ad hoc basis.'

'What do you make of Ben Goldman's peanut allergy? That was clearly caused by eating the soy jerky.'

'I accept what you say. But I am certain that wasn't an issue that originated here. Actually, that is what concerns me most. If it had been a contamination issue here, we could address it. But if it's happening elsewhere, then it's not in our control and yet we will suffer the negativity. Being criticised and having no power to redeem the situation is the worst position to be in.'

'Ben Goldman was, by his own confession, very allergic to peanuts. So even a small trace on that soy jerky would set him off,' said Kaz. 'It wouldn't be hard to just open a few packets a little and put some peanut dust inside.'

Michelle Foster nodded and then held up a finger. 'That's true, but here's my question. The chances of doing that to a few packets and causing an allergic reaction are very small. OK, plenty of people have peanut allergies, but how many of them are buying soy jerky? Not many. It's one of the least popular things we make. Off the top of my head, it's probably the least popular soy product we make. So why choose that? It doesn't make any sense.'

'No, it doesn't,' said Artie. He paused for a moment. 'You know what I think? I think we've been wrong about every single thing.'

'I don't understand. Are you saying Goldman didn't have an allergic reaction?' said Kaz.

'He did, but it wasn't caused by the soy jerky. I think he did it to himself, somehow and for some reason. I think Carly had mercury in her for some other reason, or the tests were corrupt. Above all, I think we're getting four different things conflated; the jerky thing, Carly, the explosion and the shooting. Four different things which, because they happened close together, we've been thinking must be related. But maybe they're not.'

'I agree,' said Michelle Foster. 'From what you've told me, though, your lives are in danger. Why does someone want to kill you?'

'I don't know, but I will find out,' said Artie, standing up, knowing they were done here.

Outside in the hot early summer sun, they stood by the Porsche.

'Did you believe her?' said Artie. 'She wasn't spinning us a line, was she?'

'I totally believed her. Maybe she was just very good at pulling the wool over our eyes, but she seems 100 per cent sincere to me and everything she said just made sense.'

He nodded. 'Yeah, I think she was straight with us. Mo can check out the veracity of what she told us about the Long Run buy-out because it'll be a matter of legal record. I'd imagined this place would be some sort of manky factory knocking out industrial quantities of processed vegan foods. I never thought it'd be so clinical and so...'

'...moral?'

He pointed at her. 'Exactly, right down to their company motto. Right, well, let's go to the Paleo Patriots address and see what they've got to say for themselves,' he said, looking up the address on his phone. 'Shit, it's in the Tenderloin, near the Golden Gate Theatre.'

'Oh, yeah, we did the *Jersey Boys* cast shoot there, didn't we? The Tenderloin is alright during the day. It's only at night you're likely to get stabbed by a crazy person and we've worked at the Warfield loads of times and never had any trouble. That's on Market Street in the Tenderloin, isn't it?'

He started the car. 'Didn't we? I'm sure I remember a wild-haired man wearing a green shift dress and no underwear waving a large knife at us, some time.'

She laughed a little. 'He was alright. Just a bit overexcited. When you've been out on the piss in Leeds on a Friday night, a knife-wielding man in a dress is the least of your worries.'

Artie took Columbus Avenue, then Montgomery Street down to Market Street, which runs southwest right through the city and out into the Castro.

'Taylor Street exit,' said Kaz, pointing at the sign. He took a right and pulled up outside of a run-down block of apartments. Kaz looked up at it.

'So it's not an office. It's just someone's flat. I don't like the look of the place. It looks skanky and druggy.'

'Aye, but we've got guns. We'll be alright.'

They stood on the sidewalk. A warm breeze blew Artie's hair over his eyes. He pushed it behind his ears and looked around for Danny Blind's Toyota. Nothing.

'Artie. This isn't right,' said Kaz, coming back from looking at the list of bells with names alongside at the entrance to the apartment block. 'Why would someone running a pressure group give out their home address on a leaflet? What's to be gained by that? Are they hoping potential converts pop around for a chat?'

He frowned. 'Hmm, you're right. Could it be a front for something? Drugs or whatever.'

'Not unless Paleo is a new street word for heroin. Number 154 has the name Robson next to it. I just don't get it.' As she spoke, the lobby door to the block opened and an older Chinese man came out. Kaz spun round and trotted up to him. 'Hello, there,' she said, dropping into the smooth chat-up mode she used in her job. 'I'm looking for these people,' she took the leaflet from Artie, as he walked over, and pointed to the letter heading. 'Paleo Patriots. The address is in this building. Robson. Do you know them?'

The man squinted at the paper and shook his head. '154 not occupied for one, two years now.' He spoke with a heavy accent. 'Mail collected but that's it.'

'So it's just used as a mailing address?' said Artie.

The man nodded. 'Yeah, yeah. Just mail.'

'OK, thank you,' said Kaz, as the man walked off.

'We're getting nowhere with this,' said Artie, getting back into the car. 'Let's find that bar in North Beach and write down everything we know and I'll text Mo with all the latest info.'

He took went back the way they'd come, turning off Columbus and parking on Vallejo Street.

The NB was a typical hip little North Beach bar and grill. All funky lights, rotating roof fans, colourfully painted wooden tables, stained glass sunflowers and antique mirrors. They ordered two cheeseburgers and two beers and took a table outside, by the road.

Artie spotted a Chinese supermarket across the road, went over, bought 20 Marlboro and a box of matches.

He offered her one. She took it.

He lit hers and then his, sucking the smoke into his lungs, like a long lost friend. The burn and then the sweet release as the nicotine hit home was delicious.

Kaz tapped the ash off her cigarette. 'I feel like I should've just had sex, smoking one of these. Shit...' she looked at the glowing tip of the Marlboro '...sometimes I miss who I used to be.'

'Yeah, I totally know what you mean,' he said, drawing on the cigarette really deeply, in the way that only an ex-smoker can. 'OK, let's go over everything, then I'll email Mo and Coll.' He sucked down the cold Pabst.

'Right. First up, Ben Goldman. This all started with him.' She blew out smoke and took another deep hit.

'Yup. And I think everything we now know about the production of soy jerky suggests that the stock isn't poisoned en masse. So I think he peanutted himself. It's the only thing that makes sense. Maybe he was trying to drum up a lawsuit, just like his parents did, was taken by surprise by the ferocity of his reaction and so couldn't inject himself. That's when we stepped in.'

'Hold on though. He didn't even try to inject himself and then he paid Georgina to pretend she'd found the pen.'

Artie drew hard on the cigarette. 'Fuck, yeah. I forgot that.' He tapped off the ash. 'He wanted me to know he'd had a pen, when he either hadn't, or didn't try to use one.'

'Artie - if he had a pen and didn't try to use it, he was trying to kill himself. That means we stopped a suicide. Paying 50 grand to someone to pretend they'd found something tells us a lot about him. It tells us he's involved in some sort of deception and is happy to use the family money to fund it. It also speaks to the idea that he's tripping on some shit. He's unstable if you ask me. Was he involved in the bombing? Was he there?'

'We can't know. Georgina says she saw him. Maybe he was the shooter who took out the CCTV camera. But he's not randomly picked on Mother Earth for no reason to do his allergy act in, and we know he was sweet on Carly and that she dumped him and that she was a big Mother Earth fan.'

'So he blew up the store as revenge for being jilted? Nah. I'm not buying that,' said Kaz. 'That's just too mental.' She flicked the stub of the cigarette into the gutter. 'There's something wrong about him but not that.'

'But if it was him shouting "No!", it suggests that he's involved but that something went wrong. Maybe he had second thoughts. He struck me as a gauche kid.'

'Yeah, I agree with that.' She took another cigarette out of the pack and lit it with a match, narrowing her eyes as she did so. 'He's the sort of bloke that just doesn't get girls. Too nerdy and weird.' She laughed a small bitter chortle. 'I had a girlfriend once who used to call blokes like him "Not a Friday Fucky." By which she meant that you couldn't have a one-night-stand with him because he would just fall in love with you and go all puppy dog. Do you know what I mean? One of those blokes who can't tell the difference between a fuck and a relationship.'

He nodded. 'I totally agree.' He let the cigarette rest on his bottom lip while he tapped a text to Fay on his phone. *'How close was Ben Goldman to Carly? Did they go out for long?'*

Her reply came back right away. Kids had one eye on their phone every waking hour, and then some.

'He was crazy about her. He wrote her stupid love poems and that sort of crap. As soon as she realised he was like totally glommed on her, she dumped him. They had like four dates. They didn't even get to second base. Then, like I told you, he wouldn't leave her alone. Why are you asking? Where are you now?'

Artie replied. *'We're trying to work him out. We're still in San Francisco. We'll be back tomorrow.'*

'I told you he is like a total creep! Do not trust him.'

'Funny how when I read Fay's texts I can hear her voice so clearly. She writes like she talks,' said Artie, taking a last drag on the Marlboro and stubbing it out under his foot, but Kaz was staring into the middle distance, her lips moving a little as she talked to herself. He passed a hand in front of her eyes to distract her.

'I've just realised something important,' she said, shaking her head. 'We're so dumb.' She turned the silver ring that was over her right thumb around as she spoke. 'When we wanted to take the samples to the lab, what did we do?'

'We went to Mother Earth and bought a selection of vegan foods.'

She nodded and drummed her fingernail on the table. 'We did, but you added the soy jerky bar that you'd picked up when you'd visited the guitar shop. It was still in your top pocket, remember? And that was the only one to test positive for mercury.'

'I don't get you. They were all from Mother Earth,' he said, draining the bottle.

'They were, but only the soy jerky had spent time at Robbie's store or at their home. That's where it was contaminated. Yes! Yes! Get in.' She gripped her fist in the manner of a footballer who has scored a goal. 'Don't you see? We couldn't work out why only Carly got sick when, if Green on Green's stock was all contaminated, it would have affected a lot of people. Helen didn't have mercury in her either and she'd been eating it, too. This explains why. Carly's was being poisoned at home or in the shop, probably by Ben Goldman, as an act of revenge. Goldman is a nutter. He even poisoned himself to get back at the store Carly loved so much. I bet he blew the bloody place up as well. He planted the bomb. The curly-haired figure. I bet you anything. We've got to get him arrested, Artie.' She started talking faster and faster, excited by coming up with an answer. 'He's probably paid someone to try and shoot you, as well.'

'I get everything you say, except why does he want me dead?'

'You said it yourself, we saw something, or he thinks we did. For some reason, he thinks we saw him plant the bomb. He doesn't know we didn't.'

Artie took out another cigarette. 'Bloody hell, you might have cracked it, Clarkey. OK, clever clogs, tell me why Danny Blind is hiding from us, then? Why is he up here, when he works for the LA *Times*?'

'Are you sure he was hiding and that he was in the car following us?'

'Definitely.'

She sucked her cheeks in. 'He's doing a story on us; the explosion survivors.'

'Nah, that's no reason to hide or follow someone. He didn't want to be seen. And who the fuck are the Paleo Patriots? What are they to do with any of this?'

'Hmm, if you ask me, they're nothing to do with it at all. They're mad anti-vegans, so they're just trying to exploit the situation in some way. The man that came to the hospital was just busking it. Trying to make out he was a big man.'

'Yeah, I guess that visit could all have been bullshit. At the time, I found the bloke very unconvincing. He seemed phoney or just trying too hard to be secretive. All that quick code nonsense. It was all trying to be flash but it was crap. I thought so at the time. But I still think we should do some research on Danny Blind, though.'

They both looked him up on their phones and began looking for any information. There was a short biography on the LA *Times* website but didn't tell them very much apart from that he'd worked for the paper for four years and that his hobbies included hiking. Everyone said their hobbies included hiking because it sounds a very wholesome and generally blameless pursuit. No-one puts down lying on the sofa and eating crisps, even though they spend more time doing that than hiking.

'Ah, it says here that he has a degree in journalism from the University of California at Berkeley.'

Kaz looked at him and fiddled with the thick plain silver ring in her earlobe. 'Well, that's just over the Oakland Bridge. Maybe he's up here because he lives here.'

'Don't be daft, you don't work in LA and live 400 miles away.'

'Alright, pillock features, maybe he's got a place up here - a second home. How can we find that out?'

'How about the old-school phone directory? Can't be many Daniel Blinds in it.' He got up and walked into the bar. 'Hey, man,' he said the bar dude. 'Do you have a phone book, by any chance? Just want to look up a local number.'

The man looked under the bar and emerged holding a thick book covered in dust. 'Ain't never seen this thing for years.'

'Yeah, it is a bit of ancient relic,' said Artie, taking it off him. It dated from 2006.

'Is anyone in that, anymore? Surely everyone just has a mobile now. No-one has a landline,' said Kaz, seeing him return with the directory.

'It's eight years old. But actually, that's a good thing. More people were in it in 2006. Maybe he was living here back then.' He skimmed through the 'B' pages. 'Here we go. Blind, Daniel. No other Blinds, must be him.'

'What's the address?'

He stared at it.

She looked over at him. 'What?'

He fished in his pocket and pulled out the Paleo Patriots leaflet.

'It's the address we just went to in the Tenderloin.'

'You're kidding me.'

'Nope. Look.' He showed her the entry. 'At the risk of stating the obvious, that's not a coincidence, is it?'

'But surely he doesn't live there. It said Robson on the bell.'

'Probably an old tenant.' Artie paused to think. 'I reckon he still owns it and has rented it out for a while and now uses it as a mailing address for the Paleo Patriots group. Why didn't he tell us he was involved in that? It's not like it's an illegal political group.'

'It is if they blow someone's head off. He did say he was interested in food issues when we first met him.'

Artie rubbed his eyes, reached inside his jacket and pushed the gun further into his waistband. Bloody thing was digging into him.

'You know what?' He exhaled a long breath and let some tension ease from his body. 'I don't actually think either of us are in danger at all. I don't think anyone is out to get us.'

She looked at him, puzzled. 'At the risk of sounding like Fay, err...duh, Artie, you were shot at.'

'Yeah, I can't work out why that happened, I'm sure it wasn't meant to kill anyone. It was something that went wrong, or was badly thought through. I bet Danny Blind could tell us.'

'That's sodding ironic. We did a good job of shaking him off, when we really should be talking to him.'

'Well, I've got his card somewhere. Shall I call him?'

She instinctively touched her gun in her waistband under her sweat-shirt. 'Yeah, set up a meeting. We can always shoot the fucker if we have to. You're allowed to shoot people in America, aren't you?'

'I think they shoot you if you *don't* shoot people.'

'Make the call, then. Let's have it out with him.'

Artie found the card and dialled the number. It rang and rang and then went to automated voice mail.

'I'll try again later. He might call back if he put my number in his phone.'

Kaz puffed out her cheeks. 'So what now? I feel like we've been led on a wild goose chase up here by the Paleo arseholes. They've had us believing all sorts of shite. That document with names on it and the quick code to the website. That's all wank, isn't it? It's someone playing at being subversive. Someone getting off on being underground. It's a game to them.'

'Yeah, that bloke who came to the hospital was going on about how my life was in danger. He said people were out to get me, but that was all bollocks. Here's an idea. He gets a mate to come to the hospital and discharge a gun at me to "prove" I'm in danger, but accidentally murders someone that he had no idea was even there. He thought he'd send a bullet into the wall. But she's right in front of it and it takes off the top of her head. God rest Jackie Armstrong's soul. Food crazies, all of them. On all sides of this. Even Georgina, god bless her, she was so sure being vegan was the right thing to do.'

'Aye, well, I'm sure a nice lentil bake is helping her recover from being blind, silly cow.'

He kicked her on the shin. 'Hey, don't be a twat. She's not a bad person. She meant well. Her only crime was to want the world to be a nicer place. Don't have a go at her for that.'

Kaz scowled at him. 'Alright, don't go all sanctimonious on me. This whole pile of steaming shit revolves around that vegan store. The store that we nearly died in, lest you forget. I told you they give me the creeps, didn't I? Live and let live. Stop trying to impose your sodding lifestyle on the rest of us. Twats. They've got a moral certainty, like evangelical religious crazies, but everyone dies in the end. Sooner or later. Even vegans. Nobody gets out alive, so why can't they just accept that and get on with having a nice time?'

'Aye, well, in fairness, I think Georgina was doing that. She was hardly one for dishing out the anti-meat lecture, was she? She was really nice to us.'

She turned her mouth down. 'Alright, she was nice. And I do feel sorry for her.'

Artie's phone buzzed. He picked it up and squinted at the screen. 'Ah, Mr Blind.' He took the call. 'Hey, Danny.'

'Artie. Hi. I saw you called.' He was a little breathless, clearly walking somewhere.

'Yeah, I thought we should meet up.'

'Oh, right. Have you got something for me?'

Artie instinctively felt the gun in his waistband. 'Well, I think you might have something for us.'

'Really? What's that?'

'Well I was thinking you could tell me all about the Paleo Patriots, since they're based in your apartment in the Tenderloin.'

The line went quiet for a moment. 'How do you know that?'

'An old analogue thing called the phone directory. But thanks for confirming it.'

Blind breathed heavily into his phone, distorting the line.

'Where are you now?' he said.

'Well, you've been following us, Danny so you should know, shouldn't you? Why have you been following us?'

'You're crazy. Why would I do that?'

'OK, where are you, now, then?' said Artie, looking at his brown leather boot and then picking up Kaz's phone, skimming the screen to find Twitter and then typing in Danny Blind's name. He'd posted a link to his latest column an hour ago. Location: San Francisco.

'I'm in LA.'

'See, you're lying to me again. I don't like that.'

'I'm not lying.'

Artie groaned. 'I'm too old and ornery to argue with you like this Danny. I know you're in San Francisco. I saw you, remember? Yes, I did see you, you were not quick enough. And you just posted a link to a column on Twitter and left the location option on. It says you're in San Francisco. So quit the bullshit. We're at a bar in North Beach called the NB. It's on Vallejo. Come down and let's sort this out, eh?'

He can't have been far away because within 10 minutes the silver Toyota turned down the street and parked up nearby. Artie and Kaz had got more cold beer to keep the heat of the summer day at bay.

'Ah, here he is...' Artie stood up and held out his hand, instinctively '...don't give up the day job to become a private detective, Danny.'

He shook briefly and sat down across the table from them and made a bemused face.

'OK, Danny. You've got some explanations to give us,' said Artie, patting his gun, just to locate it.

'It's no big deal Artie. Really.'

'We'll be the judges of that,' said Kaz. 'How long have you been following us for?'

'I just saw you coming out of the restaurant and decided to see where you were going. That's all. I've been up here for a couple of days trying to get a story together for the paper about this mercury poisoning thing.'

'Hold on, wind it back. So you didn't follow us up here?'

'No, man, that'd be crazy. It's 400 miles. I just saw you and I wondered if you had a contact up here or knew someone who might be good for my story. Genuinely, I'm not shitting you. I'm trying to write a big exposé. I don't know much about you guys. You might be part of the story for all I know. I just thought I'd follow you to see what you were up to. Ok, I was crap at it. It's not my thing. But I'm trying to do something for the public good here.'

Artie felt cynical. 'Hmm. So tell me about your connection to the Paleo Patriots,' he said.

'Look, we're just a small local pressure group in the city. The health of this country is being screwed by the crap it puts in its face, but to challenge the status quo is to take on massively well-resourced parts of the food processing industry such as the soy, wheat and corn lobby. It's something I've believed in for years. And I won't lie to you, I'm looking at this story about mercury poisoning as a way to undermine the vegan and vegetarian processed food business. We should just eat natural, real food, not processed garbage, and I include bread and pasta in that. I won't bore you with the details...'

'...we saw your leaflet. I thought it made a lot of sense,' said Kaz.

He half-smiled and nodded. 'It's not a complicated idea, really. We've just got so dragged away from an innate understanding of what food really is, or should be. Anyway, after those results of the post mortem came through, I realised anything that could shake faith in that whole damn vegan soy thing could easily work to the advantage of the Paleo movement as a whole. So I came back up here to try and put together a story on exactly that - to ferment a sense of mistrust in the vegan wholefood movement. I lived here for years and kept my apartment on in case I hated it in LA. I just use it as a mailing address for the PP.'

'That's all very well, but why send someone to see me in hospital and tell me I was in grave danger?'

'What do you mean?'

'A Paleo Patriots guy came to see me and he gave me this...' he took the now-crumpled sheet of paper out of his pocket. 'He loaded a quick code on my phone to a website and said I was in serious danger. That people were out to kill me. Then someone tried to shoot me yesterday in the hospital, only they murdered a nurse instead.'

'What? I don't know anything about any of that. What shooting? I've been up here, I've not seen any LA news.'

Artie explained.

'That shooting was at you? I saw the story online, but your name wasn't in it and I didn't know you were even involved in that explosion, or were in the hospital. There were no names issued. You guys went through some bad shit. I'm sorry for you.'

'The nurse was sitting on my bed. They blew the top of her head off right in front of my eyes.'

The colour dropped from Blind's face, making it look like greyish, overworked putty.

'Jesus Christ. I swear we had nothing to do with that. Nothing at all. Have you told the police about us?'

'Of course I bloody have. They were all over the hospital. I told them about all my visitors. Haven't they been in touch?'

'No. Shit. LAPD are notoriously inefficient, though, and we're not exactly very public. Well, not public at all, really. There are only six of us. We're not fucking Greenpeace or someone. We've only been going for a few months. Oh, my god.' He rubbed at his forehead. 'Who the hell has given you this?' He looked at the sheet. 'I don't even know who any of these people are, except for Keith Perez because he's a Frisco counterculture legend.'

Danny Blind stared at the sheet and then shook his head. 'It doesn't make any sense. We, the Paleo Patriots, are just six internet nerds. Not killers. Or I've misread people really badly.'

'At the time, I thought he was unconvincing. Like it was a bit of a game to him, the way conspiracy theorists are.'

'I know that here in America, Big Money gets what Big Money wants. And if you want to call that a conspiracy, well, yes, there is one, but it's not hidden, really. Massive corporations shamelessly have one arm in Big Pharma and another in farming, and another in food processing. One side supports the other to their mutual benefit. The shocking thing is that it's not shocking. We've become immune to this sort of corruption to such an extent that we don't even see it as corruption. But it is corrupt.'

'I don't get you,' said Kaz. 'What have pharmaceuticals got to do with food?'

'Well, Kaz, look at it this way, say you're in the soy business and you want to expand your market. What do you do? You begin a long-term campaign to market all things soy as not just hip and cool, but also super healthy. To help this, the pharmaceutical side of the same corporation pays for science which "shows" that eating meat is bad for you and cholesterol will kill you. They invent a drug which will get rid of the cholesterol in your blood. Then they market this drug to the medical profession armed with science to "prove" they're right, science they've paid for, usually very covertly, as part of their marketing budget. Doctors suck this down and start advising people to cut back on meat and saturated fat and eat more healthy foods like soy, stop using animal fat and instead cook with soy oil, all the while prescribing statins to lower cholesterol. And there the circle is complete. Do you see? One side feeds the other in a perfect circle of profit. Whether any of it is true or not is irrelevant to them.'

Kaz pulled a face. 'Is that right? Is that actually what happened?'

'It's exactly what happened, yeah. Everyone got sick, trying to be healthy. Follow the money. It never fails to reveal the guilty parties.

There's a great book by a woman called Kaayla Daniel which shows how they took soy from being a byproduct of the motor oil industry to being the cool metropolitan hipster's lifestyle choice.'

Artie laughed. 'We've always taken the piss out of people who drink soya lattes, haven't we?' he said.

Kaz nodded. 'Always thought it was nonsense, just by instinct. I thought I was being arsey and ornery about that shit, but turns out I was right, all along.' She turned to Artie. 'It's like I was saying to you when you went to get that bloody chocolate for Coll, all the hippies and skinny health food-obsessed women are mad for the textured soya protein, like it's natural, when it's really the most contrived thing ever. It's an industrial product, whereas eating a cow that's been in a field is way more natural. How can the natural thing be bad for you, and the thing that's pumped out of a factory be good for you?'

Danny Blind laughed and pointed at Kaz. 'That is a great line. We should use that. And, yeah, you're dead on. That is exactly the deal. It's crazy.'

Artie could tell Kaz was totally getting into the whole Paleo idea and maybe Danny was right. But a grizzly side of him felt resistant to every and any idea about food and health. It was all a lottery. His old dad had smoked 60 fags a day for at least 70 years and only carked it aged 88. His mother, made almost entirely out of lard, Silk Cut tar and sponge cake, had made it to 87. But then, an old photographer friend, Tony Mattocks, had quit this mortal coil aged 59, despite being the fittest man he'd ever known, a non-smoker and all about the fruit and veg. Died of a heart attack. Food health advice was all bollocks and that was the only sensible route through it. Like with everything in life, you roll the dice and you take your chances. Anyone can throw a seven, and at any time. The human instinct to try and rationalise it all out into a followable plan for longevity was, to him, shite of the first water, but shite which a lot of industries exploited for huge money. Take your chances, don't be afraid of death. That was the only gig that made sense.

Almost as an act of rock 'n' roll defiance, Artie knocked a cigarette out of the packet of Marlboro and offered it to Danny; he, of course, refused. Kaz took it. He plucked one for himself and lit them, licking his fingers and nipping the end of the match to extinguish it. Sucking the smoke into his welcoming lungs, he squinted through the smoke at Danny.

'So if this bloke who came to see me wasn't one of your mob, who the hell was he?'

'I don't know. But he obviously knew about the PP. I don't know. What did he look like?'

'Shortish, quite solid looking. Tanned. Quite fit.'

Danny Blind pulled at his lips in contemplation. 'Christ, I might know who that is. I can assure you that whatever that person said to you is nothing to do with me and almost certainly untrue. The idea that you're in danger, I mean. That's bullshit. Surely.'

'Forgive me, Danny. Someone fired a gun at me in my hospital room, so we packed heat, just in case,' said Artie, pulling back his sweatshirt to reveal the gun.

Danny Blind held his hands up in surrender. 'I do not blame you in the slightest. You guys have been through serious shit.' He took his car keys from his pocket and messed with them. 'This is all so fucked up. The bomb and the shooting. I'm impressed that you're so stable.'

'Oh, we're not. We're just pretending,' said Kaz. 'Our lives and our psyches are fucked up beyond belief. You've done well to leave here alive.'

Danny Blind stood up. 'Well, good luck with it all. I don't mind telling you, I'm scared shitless by all of this. I'm going to wind down PP until all this has gone away. It makes you question how serious you even are about a cause when this shit happens. Stay safe, guys. I'll let you know if I find out who that person who shot at you is. Keep me in the loop.'

They watched him walk away.

'What do you make of him, Kaz?' said Artie, tossing the cigarette into the gutter.

'Danny? No guts, but a nice bloke and with no side to him.'

'So you believed him?'

'Yeah. Totally. He's just a geek, really. I dig his food shit. But he's totally out of his depth with this. He wasn't lying to us.'

'OK, so where does that leave us?'

She didn't say anything for a couple of minutes. She smoked and drank, drank and smoked, then flicked the dead cigarette away to the pavement. He watched it fall.

Existence is a weird thing. It's all we have, but we don't really know what it is. We live in a perpetual state of mystery, just busking our way through, without any understanding of what the seemingly random associations of chemical, hormones and minerals which make up being alive, really mean, if indeed they mean anything at all. Yet we're complacent about it, because how could you live otherwise? It isn't until the moment when your very existence is threatened with ending that you suddenly and profoundly feel alive, feel the nature of life, and you consciously grip tightly onto it.

And so it was as Artie watched the Marlboro fall to the ground, he looked up at a man walking towards them on the pavement, saw him, as though in slow motion, take out a handgun with his right hand from the left inside pocket of his blue jacket, and, as he drew level with Artie, saw him point it at his head, then pull the trigger once. The dull thudding noise of the silenced pistol was the only indication of what he'd done.

There was no time to move, no time to avoid being hit, not even any time turn to away. The man walked up, took out the gun and fired it. It was all over in what seemed like milliseconds. All Artie could do was flinch after the fact.

CHAPTER 21

But he didn't die.

The shooter fired but stumbled as he did so, stumbled because Kaz had clipped his heels, kicking out at him as he took out the gun. In the same way a defender nudges a striker a little to put him off balance and thus preventing him from shooting accurately, so Kaz's intervention did the same. The stumble sent the bullet ripping into the heavy wood table rather than into Artie. Kaz stood up, took the pistol from her waistband and with one eye closed aimed it at the man's legs as he sprinted away at top speed. She squeezed the trigger. He was probably only 20 feet away as she fired. There was a screeching of a car's tyres as it turned onto Vallejo at speed, revving its engine.

With a surprisingly undramatic cracking noise, the bullet flew from the gun and into the man's calf, ripping his flesh into a bloody pulp. She squeezed the trigger again, but missed as he fell to the ground. Artie's swimming brain came back into focus; leaping from his seat, he ran towards the man as he clutched his leg. The car zoomed up alongside the man; the passenger door opened and the injured man ~~leapt~~ clawed his way in. The car sped away with him half in, half out, his bloody leg trailing. Kaz fired a third time, hitting the car. There was no catching it, it was away and gone.

'What the hell's going on? Was that gunshots?' said someone, coming out of the bar.

'Are you alright?' said Kaz. Artie nodded.

'Your quick feet saved my life.'

'It was a classic bit of Norman Hunter-inspired Leeds-ing. If you get killed, I'll be out of work. Can't have that. Come on, I suggest we get out of here asap before we get buried under a hundred cops.'

They crossed the road and took off in the Porsche.

It felt safe in the car. Artie had no idea where he was going; his heart was beating fast and his brain was in a whirl.

'What do we do now?' he said, making a right, then a left, just driving for the sake of it. 'Who was that? Why does he want to kill me?'

'I don't know, do I?' said Kaz, temper in her voice. 'It was a red Ford Mustang that came to his rescue. I'd have nailed him in the other leg if it hadn't.' She looked around herself at the traffic on Columbus. 'I wish this bloody car wasn't so noticeable. Everyone looks at it. Makes me paranoid. Whoever is after us will know we're in a high-end Porsche.'

'Did you see the man's face?'

'Nope. He was about six foot, blue jeans and trainers, stocky, wearing a blue jacket. Baseball cap. Definitely a bloke, though.'

'I couldn't believe it when I saw that gun in his hand. I thought it was all over.'

'It was weird. It was like I knew what was going to happen, a split second before it did. Like, I saw it happen, and then it actually happened. The only thing I could do was trip him up.'

'That's what growing up watching Don Revie's teams does to you.'

'Aye, it's deep in your DNA to foul someone. Was pleased with my shot, though. Went right where I wanted it, pity the other two missed him. Maybe I should have killed him. My only thought though was if I kill him, he can't tell us why he's done this.'

'It's hard to shoot a moving target with your first ever shot. You did good.' He took California Street, heading towards Van Ness, the 101, which went south through the city. 'Let's go back to LA. I can't face hanging around here any longer. My nerves are shot to buggery. Will you text Mo and tell her what happened in as much detail as you can? What a fucking day, today has been.' He glanced at his watch. It was just after 4pm. It was a six- or seven-hour drive back unless he put his foot down but there was no chance of that at this time of day. He felt exhausted. So exhausted that he couldn't organise his thoughts. All he could do was flit from one thing to another. From Jackie to Georgina, to Carly...all of these people dead or hurt and over what? Because of what? He must know the answer, the answer must be in his head. That's why he had to be killed. But what the hell was it? What had he seen or heard?

Maybe nothing.

Maybe this was just a lunatic, fixated with an idea that wouldn't surrender to logic.

The 101 freeway south was bumper to bumper with rush hour traffic for miles and miles. It only began to thin out as they got into more open country, south of San Jose. It was a lovely golden sunny evening with olive green desert shrubbery, dirt, sun-bleached grass and azure blue skies, the landscape criss-crossed with stately electric pylons and wires.

Both still in shock, they sat in the insulated quiet of the expensive car as it effortlessly purred down the highway. He tried a forced smile at her. She returned the effort.

'I just can't understand what's happened to us, Artie. It feels like everything has gone totally bloody mad. Bombs and shooting - we are *so* in danger. I don't know who that bloke who gave you the sheet of names was - but he was right. Someone really is out to get us.'

'Out to get me, I think. Not you. You're just in danger because you're with me. That fella was trying to shoot me, not you. He came to you first, but he only wanted to shoot me.'

'Don't get shot, Artie. Please. I don't want to live without you.' She sighed and rubbed at her eyes.

He looked over at her in the low evening sun.

She was quietly crying. Kaz never cried. Never. In fact, Artie wasn't sure he'd ever seen her cry before. Even when she'd broken her arm, falling over a monitor backstage at the LA Forum at a Neil Young gig, and it hurt like hell, she'd screamed and sworn but she hadn't cried. She was tough. Hard, even. Leeds council estate hard. But it had all got too much for her.

He put his hand on her thigh and she gripped it with a hand wet from tears.

'I'm going nowhere. I'm not getting shot. We'll get through this, lass. C'mon, think about it, we've got the best lawyer in the whole of this sodding country batting for us. Mo Casson's team are more organised and ruthless than the LAPD, and without the inclination to dish out racist beatings. They'll find out who did what to whom and will get them banged up.' He patted her again firmly. She was nodding, still wiping at her eyes with a thumb. She snorted up some crying snot, swallowed it down and sighed again.

'I feel so messed up. I can't just go back to Malibu like this,' she said.

He drove on through the gloaming.

They'd just passed Santa Barbara, about 100 miles from home, when Kaz spoke again.

'Can we stop somewhere?'

'You need a piss?'

'No, I mean, let's get a room.'

'Well...it's not far now, only another 90 minutes.'

She turned and looked at him in the now almost dark.

'That doesn't matter. I'm not ready to go back to...all that.' She pointed down the road to Los Angeles. 'This is it, Artie. We can't ignore it any more.'

'OK. There's a Motel 6 somewhere near here. The best room $29.95 can buy you,' he said, trying to keep things light-hearted. But he was nervous. You don't get to 53 without knowing when big emotional shit is going down and this was definitely that.

'Great. Yeah, didn't we stay there after we did Jackson Browne in Santa Barbara, once?'

'Oh, yeah. Someone had given us a massive block of dope, remember? It was like a cricket ball of resin.'

She yelped a laugh. 'Yes! We shaved joints off that fucker for weeks.' He sighed and pushed at his straggling hair. 'God, I love Jackson.'

He gripped her hand.

'Don't confront me with my failures, I had not forgotten them.' They both sang the line from Browne's 'These Days' in unison. A favourite from back in the day. Then laughed. Oh, god.

'Oh, Artie...I've loved our times on the road. What a privilege it's been to spend my time around genius people like Jackson Browne and Bruce and...and everyone...god only knows, I was a dirty bitch from the arse end of Leeds. There was nothing down for me in life. No exams, no nothing. You believed in me and gave me access to all this...' she gestured at the west coast. 'I can't thank you enough. You made all my dreams of a better life than Leeds come true. And you did it all without ever wanting anything from me, other than for me to be who I was. That was so cool of you.'

She was crying again. And he couldn't help but follow suit. Big wet tears rolling down his cheeks as he took the exit, above which was a huge Motel 6 sign and an arrow. It felt like it was some sort of deathbed confession. Saying stuff that you might not get to say again. He pushed at the moisture with his fingers to try and remove it.

As he pulled into the motel's parking lot, he knew this was going to be a big moment in his life. Shit was coming to a head. He just knew it. You always know it.

They got out of the Porsche and walked round to the motel reception, the way they'd done several thousand times before in their 15 years together. As he normally did, he put his arm around her shoulder and she leaned into him, affectionately.

'Hey guys, how's it goin'?' said the Mexican dude on the desk as they walked in.

'Good, man,' said Kaz. 'You gotta double?'

'Uh huh. Best double in the house, comin' right atcha.'

Kaz leaned into Artie again, as he put 35 dollars down. He put his arm around her again.

It was a standard motel room, the like of which they'd slept in so often. A double bed against the left wall, a TV opposite it, a bathroom set back, to one side. It smelled clean and yet tired, old and beat down by life. Kind of suitable, then.

She threw her bag onto the bed, turned to him and said, 'You do know, we can't go on like this.'

'Like what?' he said, though he knew exactly what she meant.

'Like we're not massively in love with each other.'

He sat down on the bed and rubbed his face. 'Yeah, I know.'

'What I said when I thought I was going to die in the Mother Earth bombing, I meant every word. We're soulmates. We both know it and yet we won't admit it to each other. Well, given that both you and I have almost died several times recently, I'm not prepared to go on pretending anymore. Who knows how long we've got left alive? Whatever happens from now onwards, we have to have this out, Artie. I know we're Northern and emotionally repressed but the fact is this - I love you and I just want to be with you and to have you love me and I don't care that I'm a lesbian and that you're a skinny-arsed rock 'n' roll shagger. That's irrelevant. We are what we are. Only you understand me, only I understand you. That's a stone-cold fact. And I know you so well that I know you know that's true. You're just running from the confrontation with Coll. But we have to make it or we have to break it. It's fucking torture for me seeing you with Colleen. I push it all down, but it is. I'm sorry. I can't bear to go back to that. The danger we've been in, it's made me see how fragile our lives are. I'm not going to my grave, shot in the head by a vegan nutter without getting this off my chest. When you got married to Coll, I went along with it because you'd been so down and she'd cheered you up and made you get back out on the road. I thought I'd just see how it worked out. Then the Springsteen gig came up and that was like the old days again. Me and you on the road, doing what we do. Coll wasn't there for a couple of months, so it was all lovely. But I should never have gone along with it all really because, as I said at the time, the love cat was out of the bag and you can't put that puss back in, once she's out. So you've got to choose what to do. Split with Coll or split with me. I know it's all a bit bloody melodramatic but there's no other way to deal with it. Who knows how long we've got left? I was in a sodding coma a couple of days ago. I've got a crack in my head. It tends to make you focus on what's important in life. We can't go back to LA and pretend any more. I won't do it. It's time to choose.'

Artie blew out air, kicked off his shoes and sat on the bed. 'Well that was quite a bloody speech, lady.'

She pushed at her hair. 'Yeah, I don't think I've talked for so long since I last had to tell you I love you.'

He laughed a little. 'Well, you've passed the audition.' He stood up and pulled her into a hug. 'Thanks for saying all that. It needed saying.'

Holding her tight to him, feeling her body warmth and the softness of her skin, it wasn't as hard a choice as he thought it might be. When push came to shove, and push really had come to shove, there was an easy choice to make and he was going to make it.

'I choose you. Of course I do. I never loved anyone like I love you. We owe it to each other to be together and it's dumb that we're not already.'

'Well I should bloody hope so, and I am gorgeous.' She laughed a little and pulled away from him, standing with her hands on her hips. 'Right. Well, err, good. I'm proper pleased about that. What do we do now?'

'Just keep on as we are?'

She shrugged. 'Shouldn't we consummate our new relationship with some sort of sex session?'

'I'm not really in the mood. I'm totally knackered and I've got a big ball of scared worry in my gut, to be honest.'

'No, I'm not, either. Too stressed out. It'll be tight as a duck's arse down here.' She patted her crotch. 'And anyway, I'm going to need some lessons from you.'

'And we should probably have a long talk about that side of things over a few drinks, sometime soon.'

She nodded. 'No hurry. It's not about all that, not really.'

'No, it isn't. It's just all about having fun, isn't it? Whoever you're doing it with.'

'Yeah, I like having fun. It's much nicer than being shot at.'

They had showers and got into bed in t-shirts and underwear and cuddled up together. He kissed her damp hair and squeezed her tight, breathing in and out with her. What a bloody life.

They woke just before eight. He made coffee in the room. Outside the roar of traffic from the 101 rumbled without stopping.

'I didn't tell you but when Fay rang me when we were in the car in San Francisco she said, "You do know you married the wrong woman, don't you?"' said Artie, putting her coffee down on the beside table.

'Really? Ha. That's funny. Clever kid, Fay.'

'And she said she thought her mother knew this as well.'

'Of course she does. For what it's worth, I think she's known it from the start. She probably knew it before we did. She's just gone along for the ride because she likes you and because of where she is in her life, right now. I totally understand that. I think she'll be OK with it...or as OK as anyone is when they get dumped.'

'Well, we'll soon see. I'm not hanging around on this. It's not fair to her. I'll move out of the house, give her back the credit cards and we'll get an apartment in Santa Monica. Did you see anywhere suitable?'

She sipped at the coffee. 'Yeah, there was a place but it was above my budget. But if we're both pitching in, then it'll be affordable.' She found the website on her phone and the details of the apartment on Arizona Avenue. It was set in a white stucco block, behind two areas of date palms. It was basic but the sunshine and the trees made it look quite cool. 'It's one bedroom, decent size living room, separate kitchen and bathroom and it's furnished quite nicely. It's handy for 3rd Street and a lot of our usual hangouts.'

He skimmed at the screen to look at the photos. Like tens of thousands of apartments in LA it had almost no character to it and was all about what you could bring to the space. 'Yeah, that looks fine. Arizona is busy so it might be quite noisy, but I don't mind that. In fact, it's too quiet for me in Malibu.'

'I like traffic, as long as it's not too badly polluted. Busy means energy and things going on. That's what I like. I can reserve it online and then send in all the info they need about us.'

'Yeah, do that. We might need a bolt hole a bit sharpish. Might get nasty at the house, you never know.'

'Nah, it won't. So is this us setting up home together, then?'

'I suppose it must be. That's an odd thought, in part, because it doesn't feel any different to how we normally are.'

'Aye. It's not like I'm going to cook you dinner, wear make-up and play at housewife and be all lovey dovey.'

'God forbid. No lovey or dovey. Can we just be like we've always been?'

'I don't think we've got an option to be anything else. Not at our age. There will be a difference, though. No having sex with other people. We'll have to rely on each other for that pleasure.'

'Are you sure you'll be OK with that? I'm not being funny, Kaz, but if I was going from having it off with men to doing it with you, it'd be quite a change in my life. You really might not like it. It's not where your inclinations lie - you know that. You've hardly been inventing being gay for all these years. It wasn't act or a pose. It is who you are. The old meat and two veg are not your thing.'

She went for piss and a wash, returning drying her face with a white towel. 'I've been thinking about that for ages. Some of the more political of my gay friends will see it as some sort of sell-out or betrayal and I'm not saying I won't fancy women, in the same way I wouldn't expect you not to. But, the way I see it, most of us are, say, about 80 per cent one way or another. Some are 50-50, others 90-10, but we're all somewhere on the scale. It's not all or nothing, not usually anyway. And, though I'm probably 90 per cent gay, you are what the straight 10 per cent of me is into. Whatever our love is, it's about way more than our gender.'

He smiled. 'Yeah, I like that. It's true.'

'Rest assured if the sex makes me feel sick, I'll let you know and I'll ring a lass to come and do it properly.' She snorted a laugh. 'I'm not usually backwards in coming forwards, am I? But what about you?'

'What about me?'

'Well, you've got to go from a non-sexual relationship to a sexual one. You've not fancied me that way in the past.'

'That's not quite right. I never allowed myself to fancy you like that. When you first came for the job, I did.'

'Did you? You never said that before.'

'Well, I did. I've just blocked it off as out of bounds. Look, Kaz, it's easier for me. I'm a bloke. Give a bloke a naked woman, whatever she says her sexuality is, and we can pretty much always perform. Sex for men isn't nearly as intertwined with our emotional landscape. Rock 'n' roll should have taught you that. We can just do it for pleasure and nowt else. As long as you're happy with it, I'll be happy. But, y'know, we don't have to worry about all of that. It's about being together, I reckon. The details will take of themselves.' He kissed the top of her head and they held each other for a few seconds. 'I'm glad you forced me to make a choice. I've been wrestling with it for weeks now. I needed you to do that.'

'I know you did. I'm glad you made the right choice, for both of us. It'll be alright, Artie. Everything will be alright.'

'Even so, I'm not looking forward to telling Coll.' He groaned. He really wasn't. She was important to him and they were, after a fashion, quite close. He also worried what the split would mean for her. She was, for all her money, and possibly exactly because of it, quite an isolated person. Her butterfly life had had a lot of fellow travellers, but few who had stayed the course. She'd been leading a life of lies and intrigues before they'd hooked up. Their relationship had stabilised her; splitting up was likely to send her out of orbit and back into her old ways, ways which had made her very vulnerable to the attentions of bad people and to just doing the wrong thing. But then, she was 53, she should be able to keep her shit together by that age. And the long and the sort of it was, he was living a lie with her. He loved Kaz profoundly and he didn't love Coll in the same way at all. And that wasn't fair on all three of them. Maybe he didn't actually even love Coll, but he was very fond of her and felt a deep bond with her. This was going to be emotionally messy, he just knew it. And there was no good way to avoid it.

Once dressed, they put their guns into their waistbands again.

'Right. Let's get to LA,' he said.

She nodded firmly, then raised herself up on her toes and kissed him on the lips. It was something she never did; not a kiss on the lips. It was a small act, but, in their lives, a profound one, and emblematic of their overnight changed status. And in that second, he reflected on it and it felt so warm and so lovely...no...not just lovely, but loving, that he knew the decision he'd made, for all the shit it was going to create, was 100 per cent the right one.

But, as if the universe always wants to present you with extremes, in order to make you appreciate life, it was at that exact moment that there was a thud against the motel door. The thud of someone trying to kick it in. Bam, bam, bam!

Artie swung around. Motel doors, the world over, are light plywood. They're not built for violent assault and nobody good is trying to kick yours in. This one was about to give way. The violent burst of fear that leapt up into his chest drove him to grab the gun from his waistband, and arms outstretched, fire two rounds. The bullets ripped into the door with a sound that was both a dull thud and a wet tearing noise.

Whoever had been kicking the door, stopped.

Kaz ran around to the far side of the bed, using it as a defensive barrier, took out her gun, aiming at the door, in case someone came in.

But there was no more kicking.

He turned to her, they both had a wild dilated look in their eyes. 'Right, we're out of here. I'll open the door, you cover me,' he said.

'What the fuck does "cover me" mean?' she said.

'It means you shoot every fucker you can who looks like a bad guy.'

She blew out air and got up from behind the bed. 'This is going to take some sodding good Leeds-ing, Artie.'

'C'mon, this isn't Beeston, is it? American's are soft as shite. We all know that.'

She hi-fived him. 'Fuckin' right. Soft shites. Let's fuckin' 'ave them!' She yelled it out of ballsy fear, dropping into her thickest Leeds accent, the accent of her upbringing, of where she was from, as though to give herself resolution and power. She was from the toughest part of one of Britain's big cities. It was a good grounding for a situation like this.

'I'll make a run for the car. It's only across the lot, 60 paces at most. I'll drive.' He held up the keys. 'Shoot anyone who tries to shoot me. Then I'll cover you.'

He yanked the door open, expecting to see at least one body lying outside, but there was no-one. Worried that they were standing wide of the door, he stuck the gun out, to show some power. Nothing. He gestured for Kaz to join him.

She scurried over to him, gun grasped in both hands.

He turned to her. 'If I don't make it. I love you.'

She gripped his hand. 'You'll make it. We'll both make it.'

Artie wasn't so sure. 'They're somewhere, here. One, probably two.' As he said that he saw movement from behind the ice machine, along the way. 'Someone to the right. Hiding behind the ice machine. Right? Nail that fucker.'

He put his hand on her cheek, felt her warm love, then took off out of the door, both exhilarated and shit-your-pants scared all at the same time, hoping that if he was going to get shot, his murderer had a good aim, death being less frightening than pain. He ran in a zigzag pattern to try and make himself a harder target.

Fucking hell. Fucking hell. Shots rang out around him, hitting something, but not him. He looked to his left. A man in white t-shirt was aiming at him from the top-storey landing. Artie just fired the gun randomly at him, squeezing the trigger repeatedly, not even really looking, the weapon releasing its power in bursts of vibration. And he just kept going. It seemed to take forever to reach the car, but can only have been seven or eight seconds at the very most. More shots rang out behind him. Kaz was having a firefight with someone.

He reached the Porsche, breath short, heart in his throat, unlocking its doors at a distance. As he pulled open the door and got down behind it, to use it as cover, he looked back to the room door. Kaz was down on one knee, blowing the shit out of the ice machine, releasing round after round, stopping, quickly reloading, then going hard again. The man that had been behind it had moved back and was cowering behind a fire extinguisher, unable to move without getting shot. Artie looked to his right. White t-shirt was lying on the ground motionless. He must have hit him. He was dead. The man trying to avoid being hit by Kaz was bald and muscular in a short-sleeved checked shirt. He was well-protected from Kaz's bullets, but had left his right flank open to Artie.

It all happened in a split second. Artie took it all in, saw Baldy, turned to him, raised the gun and sent a bullet into his pink head, bursting it like a watermelon. He sank to the floor, dead. Wow. Killing people was so easy in America. No wonder the fucking place was going to the dogs.

'Kaz! It's clear!' he shouted.

She sprinted like he'd never seen her sprint before. Fast. Really fast. Her short, chunky legs vibrating with every size-four step she made, sprinting to the car.

He jumped into the driver's seat, started her up just as Kaz pulled open the other door and leapt in, whooping as she did so, full of the thrill of survival.

'Yes!! Yes!! Leeds fucking one, fucking America, fucking nil!!!!' she screamed.

But there was no time for celebration though, not least because the cops would be descending on the place like a plague of locusts.

He reversed the Porsche out, dropped the gears, hit the road and turned back onto the 101 southbound. It was rush-hour traffic with a lot of workers heading into Santa Barbara for the 9-to-5.

'You OK?' he said. She was wild-eyed, her mind racing.

'Aye. Turns out I love guns. I was pumping rounds into the ice machine. Felt bloody magnificent. Couldn't put a bullet in the twat, though.'

'Yeah, turns out I'm brill at killing people. I killed two. Yes! Don't fuckin' mess with Yorkshire. Boycott would have been proud. Yeah, they were for you, Geoffrey.'

She hi-fived him and yelped. 'Who the hell were they? Who sent them to kill us?'

'I have zero idea, but if someone is paying two people to shoot us, they'd have to be rich and also psychotic. I only know one rich and potentially psychotic person in this whole thing and that's Ben Goldman. He fits the bill. I don't understand it; maybe it's not understandable.'

'Yeah, he totally fits the bill. We've got to nail him, one way or another.'

'You do know that we're Butch and Sundance, don't you?' said Artie.

'I'd prefer we were Thelma and Louise. Then at least one of us would have had sex with Brad Pitt.'

'Beautiful, yeah. I could do that. As long as he didn't want cuddling afterwards.'

Kaz laughed. 'No hugging, just sex, Brad. OK?'

'Look, I tend to the view that shooting two people might be illegal and I might be on a one-way road to chokey here...if we survive it, that is, which is by no means guaranteed. Weirdly, I feel quite liberated, though. Must be the adrenaline.'

'Artie man, this is America, not the UK. They love a man who shoots someone who shoots at him first. The whole country is virtually built on that notion. You've never been nearer to being an American hero than you are now.'

'Yeah, but the cops will want to talk to me and you.'

'They will, but we've got Mo Casson in your corner, remember?'

'Have we? Not if I dump Colleen, we haven't. Five fucking grand a day, she costs.'

Kaz put her hand to her mouth and looked at him, fearfully. 'Shit. I forgot about that. We're really going to need her, but you can't say, "See you later, baby, oh, but can you pay your lawyer to keep me out of jail?" '

He wove through the traffic, found a gap and put the pedal to the metal.

'See, Colleen is our sugar mama, and we've become addicted to her sweetness,' he said.

'Fuck.' She said it again, louder and with more venom, hitting the expensive kid leather seat with her fist. 'Fuck!!'

'Look, take it easy. Right? This how we deal with this. Me and you, Artie loves Kaz, we put that on the backburner. We keep it to ourselves for now. We have to. Just while we deal with everything else first. Right? We have to. Self-preservation, right? No point in me being in jail and you making visits. We both know Mo Casson will make the self-defence case - which is right - and she will win. Right?'

'Yeah yeah yeah, totally. Agreed.' She sniffed at the cordite on her fingers. 'Artie. We're so fucked up here. We've broken a lot of laws.'

'I know. But we're the innocent parties.'

'I bloody hope we are. This country makes you feel like being a cow-girl is the natural order of things.'

The road cleared a little. Artie took a deep breath and relaxed a little. Inside the Porsche was still a brilliant place to be. That was when he noticed a sleek, fast, red Ford Mustang in his rear-view mirror.

'Kaz. Take a look at the red Mustang.'

She turned and looked at it.

'Is that the same one that picked up our shooter in Frisco? You don't see a lot of red Mustangs. Or am I just paranoid?'

She turned around in her seat and squinted at it. 'I can't tell. I hit the passenger-side door with a bullet. Get into the inside lane and then slow down so we can get a look at it.'

He did as she said, slowing down quickly to 40 so that the red sports car went past them on the outside. He glanced over. There was a hole in the base of the door with a chip of paint knocked out. It was the same car.

'Fucking hell.' He put pedal to the metal again, took off past the Mustang and accelerated away. 'This is a well-financed, well-coordinated hit on us, you know.'

'Well, it takes expensive silver bullets to kill people from Yorkshire, that's a well-known fact.'

She leaned over to the back seats, took out the box of ammunition and reloaded her gun. 'Give me your gun, I'll put more bullets in it,' she said.

He handed it over and she busied herself reloading it, then handed it back to him. He took it and jammed it back into his jeans waistband again. Like it or not, the guns had kept them alive.

They sped towards LA, but the Mustang always kept behind them.

'Shall I shoot their tyres out?' said Kaz. 'I think I could do it. It's what they do in the movies, so it must be the best thing to do. This life is more and more like a Steve McQueen film every hour that passes.'

'Nah, we need to keep self-defence as our modus operandi. If we go shooting cars off the road, we'll be even deeper in the clarts. And anyway, it might have been borrowed by someone's granny. We don't know it's a bad person in there.' He looked in his rear-view mirror. 'Any cops around?'

She looked backwards and forwards. 'Nope.'

'How fast can a Mustang go, do you reckon?'

'Doesn't look like a V8, so about 120, 130, I'd guess.'

He went from 60mph to 120 in seconds, the Porsche purring its revs like a nuclear cat. The speed of the acceleration was like no other car on PCH that day and at 120 it felt like it was going at 50, it was so smooth. The Mustang was caught off-guard by the move, but soon overtook traffic and resumed its position on their shoulder. The man driving had reflective shades on. Dark, slicked-back hair. Tanned.

'Would I be wrong to think he looks like a mafia hit man?' said Artie.

'He looks like a mafia hit man in a movie. And, like I said, we seem to be living in a bloody movie now, so yeah, he does. Could he be the man whose arm you saw come around the door and shoot Jackie?'

He glanced at him again.

'Could be. Impossible to tell. Still no cops around?'

She checked. 'Nope. Pedal to the metal, baby.'

He sank the accelerator and they surged off into an open stretch of road. The speedometer showed 202, he was gripping the wheel tight to keep it under control. Everything flew past in a blur. Kaz whooped.

'You left him for dead there. Bye bye, pal.'

Artie kept the pedal to the floor as the speed topped out at 215. Christ, it was as exhilarating as it was frightening. And you didn't half get to places quickly. They ate the miles up in no time, covering nearly 60 in 18 minutes and reaching the outskirts of LA. Traffic was heavy and there was simply no way to travel at that speed. He came down to 60 again. It felt like it was almost stationary. Everything passed by so slowly.

'When you've been going at such high speed, it now feels like I've got loads of time to do everything.'

'That was a hell of a ride. We did well not to get caught by the California Highway Patrol and I can't see any sign of the Mustang, we lost him almost immediately.'

'For now, anyway.' He handed her his phone. 'Look in my messages and get the Goldmans' address in Pacific Palisades, it's in a message from Coll, somewhere. Let's see if we can't have a word with him. He doesn't know that we know he paid Georgina 50,000 dollars to pretend she'd found his adrenaline pen. And, if you think about it, that's the only evidence we've got of any wrong-doing on his part. We know someone shot out the camera in the store, but the shadowy figure that did it, didn't look the right shape for him. We know someone with curly hair was running away from the explosion, but can't be sure that's him, either. We know that he had an allergy attack but also know that no peanuts were in the soy jerky packet I picked up, nor in any other nut-free G on G product. I'm sure he's involved but I just can't work out how.'

She flicked through the screens. 'Here you are. It's called Santa Ynez Villa on Arno Way. Take the next left, up Sunset. Arno Way is on the right after about half a mile.'

Artie swung the car up the intersection and began to weave around the famous, curving Sunset Boulevard, which runs 22 miles into the heart of LA. The first miles wind around some expensive real estate, some of it overlooking the ocean from what is, in effect, a rising hillside.

'Bloody hell, there's some big gaffs here,' said Kaz. 'This is the first place we've been where a car like this won't look out of place. It's probably entry level. Look, there's a Maserati next to an Aston Martin.'

Artie kept looking in the rear-view mirror, checking for the Mustang. But it was nowhere to be seen now. He turned right onto Arno Way.

Wealthy LA can deliver some jaw-dropping houses. As he turned down the small street, one house after another sprawled out in an interior design magazine-style exhibition of money and taste; all art deco shapes and Spanish Villa arches painted white or cream, with diamond-sparkling glass and blue pool water, all facing the ocean.

'It feels like this is a movie set,' said, Kaz, looking up at the houses. 'An 80s porno movie set, at that. Feels like there should be some Kenny G-style saxophone playing while an ugly well-hung man with a mullet penetrates a woman with badly permed hair on a white bed. I like 80s porn. The women still have pubic hair. That's how it should be.'

'Whoa, here we are.' He stopped outside a sign for Santa Ynez Villa and looked up at the house, on a wedge set into the hillside. It was a huge building, facing out towards the Pacific, with most of the oceanside of the house, glass. Palm and cypress trees added some shade and greenery. Places like this cost 15 or 20 million. Suing a lot of little people clearly made big money.

The house loomed up over them as they got out of the car, both sticking their guns into their waistbands as they did so. A tall, locked, wrought-iron gate with a buzzer, camera and intercom set into it blocked their progress up a steep row of concrete steps and into the property. Artie pressed the buzzer and stood looking around. It was a lovely summer day, the Pacific a stunning blue, a little breeze keeping the temperature into the mid 70s.

'You never see anyone around places like this, do you?' said Kaz. 'The more wealthy you are, the more invisible people seem to become. What are they doing all day?'

'Making porno movies, probably. Or silently weeping at the futility of materialism.'

There was no reply. He hit the buzzer again. Still nothing. Everything was quiet. No sign of any movement. No radio or TV noise. 'I wonder if Ben Goldman is in hiding?' said Artie.

Kaz walked around the width of the rock on which the house was built. 'There's a garage around here, up a slope.' He followed her around, up the steep ramp and towards a large double garage door. There was no way around it into the property.

'It's electronically locked,' said Artie, pointing to an infrared box.

Kaz walked up to it and pulled on a handle. It moved upwards in a smooth motion. 'But not actually locked...come on.'

CHAPTER 22

They got under the door and went into a large garage space. There were two cars, a high-end Lexus and a sporty BMW.

'This is an i8,' said Kaz. 'It's a super-fast hybrid sports car.'

'I have no idea what those words mean.'

'Basically, it's a fast car for people who like to think they're green.'

'Wankers, you mean?'

'Yeah. Louis Vuitton made luggage especially for it.'

'Really? Luggage? Christ. Looks like a very expensive car.'

'$130,000 dollars or more, I think. A lot less nice than Coll's Porsche. Then again, so is almost everything with wheels.'

Artie pointed to a door which led out of the garage, walked up two steps and tried it, thinking it would be locked, but it wasn't. This wasn't a house locked up while everyone was away. Someone must be at home. He leaned on the door and slowly opened it, feeling like a burglar.

Like Colleen's house in Malibu, the inner garage door opened out into the kitchen.

What he saw as he opened that door was not just shocking, it was barely believable. It wouldn't initially register on his eyes as possible.

The kitchen was no longer a kitchen.

The kitchen had become a killing floor; a charnel house.

He stared in disbelief.

Beside a washing machine was a bloody, severed head. An older man's head.

Across the kitchen, beside the cooker, was another bloody severed head. An older woman's head.

The bodies they'd once been attached to were a little further away, at the entrance to the kitchen, lying in a heap like slaughtered animals. Blood had oozed from them into a slick thick pool of dark red life force. A shaft of white California light shone through at an angle, picking out the contrast of dark red against the black and white tiled floor.

'Oh, god! Oh, my god!' exclaimed Artie, frozen in the doorway. He turned away from the horror and back to Kaz.

'What's wrong?' she said. Her face set in panic, she took out her gun.

He panted out the words in fear. 'There's two bodies and loads of blood. I think it might be the Goldmans.'

'Ben?'

'No. His parents. Don't look at it, it's fucking horrific.'

'Don't be daft, I grew up going to Elland Road in the 80s. I've seen real fucking horror.'

She squeezed past him, pushed open the door and immediately screamed, turned away, looked back and screamed again, holding her hands over her mouth. 'Oh, my good god...oh, god...fucking hell, Artie...oh, god, I'm going to puke.' She pushed past him and retched a thin stream of bile on the floor of the garage.

If it was the Goldmans and it seemed likely, as this was their house, and the severed heads looked about the right age, who had slaughtered them? His heart was pounding in his chest and he couldn't think straight. What was the best thing to do here? Call the cops? Run away? See if Ben Goldman was lying dead somewhere else? What? Was the killer the same one who had been after them? Maybe he was still in the house.

Come on, you've got to get your shit together, he thought. This is a matter of life and death.

'Are you OK?' he said.

She spat out some saliva. 'Yeah.' She panted a little and looked up at him, her face ashen. 'Oh, god. Those poor people. I wish I'd never seen that. Disgusting.'

'Kaz. Look. We have to keep our shit together. These murders, the shootings, it's got to be all part of the same thing, done by the same person or people.'

She nodded. 'Yeah. Right.'

'OK, so let's go through the house before we call the cops. We can nail them, whoever they are, if they're still here.'

'No way. We can't go in there. We'll be implicated in the murder. You know what the LAPD are like, they're not bothered about the truth, only about arresting someone. I don't care if we've got the best lawyer in the world on our side, I'm not getting arrested for murder. You should tell Coll and Mo about this. Text them.'

With shaking hands, he did as she suggested, telling them where they were and what they'd found.

'But if we're seen leaving here now, it'll look like we did it. If we stay and call the cops, then we've still got a lot of explaining to do because we broke in, or at least trespassed,' said Kaz.

There was a bang from inside the house. They froze and stared at each other. Artie's heart was pounding in his chest so hard, he wondered if he was actually having a heart attack. Sweat ran down his back, as he took the gun out of his waistband. Kaz did likewise. Visibly shaking, he opened the door a crack so he could see the full length of the kitchen. If anyone walked in, he'd see them.

Footsteps. A sliding noise, maybe a French door being pulled open and then closed. Someone had come in from the outdoor pool area at the back of the house. Footsteps. A man walked past the opening to the kitchen, walking right past the corpses and blood which were maybe 10 feet to his right. How hadn't he noticed them?

He had.

He reversed two steps and turned to look at the bloody devastation. The horror on his face told its own story. Clearly, whoever he was, he hadn't killed these people. He stood stock still, mouth agape, staring. Olive skin, swept-back dark hair, he had reflective sunglasses pushed up on his head. Artie suddenly recognised him. The Mustang driver. The one who looked like a Mafia hit man. What in shitting hell was going on here? Had he followed them? He began to try and make connections in his mind.

'Ben!!' The man almost screamed it. He turned and ran out of view, shouting the name over and over.

'It's Mustang man,' said Artie in a whisper.

'Has he followed us here?'

'Nah, we burned him off. He was coming back here. He knows that this is the Goldmans'. He must be working for Ben and that means Ben sent him to kill us.'

'Ben Goldman wants us dead. The twat. Psycho fuckup. It's all him. All of this is him, just like we said.' She quietly hissed the words with hate in her voice. 'It all started with him and it's all gonna end with him. Remember what Fay said? "A creepy fucked-up guy". She knew.' She began counting off reasons on her fingers. 'He killed Carly, poisoned himself, he planted the bomb, he's got money to pay people to shoot out a camera, and to kill us because he thinks we saw him plant the bomb and because we know how he killed her with mercury. He poisoned her food.' She slapped her hand over her mouth, took it away and mouthed 'Fay' at him. 'Text her, tell her to get out of town. Fuck, maybe he's got to her already. She was with us at the hospital. She knows about the mercury as well.'

Artie wasn't sure if she was right about all of that but texted Fay right away. '*Are you OK? Ben Goldman is VERY crazy. Leave town for a few days. Just in case.*'

He'd never been so relieved to get a text within 20 seconds.

'I'm fine. Leave town? Am I in danger?'

He replied. *'Yes. Do it.'*

Never one to be uncool, if she could help it, her final text simply said, *'Huh. Bummer. OK.'*

'She's fine...' said Artie, but raised voices made him stop speaking.

Two voices now. Mustang and another arguing. No. Not arguing, that was too polite a word. It was a screaming match.

Then Mustang dragged someone into view, outside of the kitchen. Artie squinted through the door crack at them. Mustang was holding the other man by his hair. His curly brown hair. It was Ben Goldman.

'Look at them! Look at what you've done, you crazy muthafucking asshole!! Oh, my God! You cut their fucking heads off. What sort of evil bastard are you?!!'

'Let go of me, Mikey. Let go and I'll tell you. There's a perfectly reasonable explanation to all of this.'

'You're shitting me, man. I'm calling the cops. This is just fucking wrong. I'm tellin' ya, it's wrong. You've lost your shit, man. No excuses. Nothing justifies this. Jesus! I'm so screwed, what the fuck did I get involved with you for? You're fucking fucked up, you fucker!!!!'

He held onto Ben Goldman tightly, gripping a big clump of his hair. Goldman was thinner and much less well-developed than the muscular Mustang driver and couldn't fight him. Mustang took out his phone. As he did so, Ben Goldman, though bent over in a stoop due to being held by his hair, reached into the waistband of his chinos. Hidden by his grey sweatshirt was a steel meat cleaver. In one smooth move he took it out and slashed into Mustang's arm, cutting a wedge of flesh out of him. It must have been incredibly sharp as it sliced through skin and flesh like it was butter, sending a cross section of his forearm flying through the air like a small cut of steak.

Mustang man let go of him as the pain of the wound surged through him and he let out a scream.

This couldn't be allowed to stand.

'Cover me,' said Artie, for the second unbelievable time that day, and kicked open the door, walking into the kitchen, arms outstretched, the gun held in his eyesight and focused on Ben Goldman, who now stood square on to them with the meat cleaver in his hand. He had clearly been ready to decapitate Mustang, who was now on his knees holding his bleeding arm, letting out screams of pain. Luckily, the blade had missed an artery, but even so, he was in a lot of distress and bleeding heavily.

Goldman looked at Artie with a shocked face, his jaw hanging heavy, gaping in surprise.

Kaz ran around Artie, jumped over the pool of blood, holding her gun at Goldman all the while, grabbing at a towel hanging on a hook by the cooker and running to Mustang man. She kneeled in front of him, put her right hand onto his cheek, and spoke into his face. 'You're going to be fine. Relax. I'm going to tie off this wound to cut down on the bleeding.' She yanked his arm up and tied the towel around as tightly as possible, then reached inside her pocket and took out a small packet of pills, gave him two. 'Swallow these. They're powerful but they'll help take the pain away.'

As she was tending to Mustang, Artie advanced on Ben Goldman, who wore a strange expression, staring at him in the way he had stared at him when he was suffering the allergy attack. A sort of blank anger in his eyes.

'Why don't you drop the cleaver, Ben?' said Artie, his mouth dry with fear, but his inner rock 'n' roll twat well to the fore. 'Or I can shoot you in the head, if you like. The choice is yours.'

'Artie Taylor, Kaz Clarke.' Goldman looked at him and then her. 'You're clever people. I admire that. I knew you were clever when I first met you.'

'You mean when you dosed yourself with peanuts to induce an allergic attack, in order to damage the reputation of the store that Carly loved so much. But when that didn't happen, you thought you'd blow it up instead.'

'Some of that is correct. Some incorrect. If you must know, I wanted to kill myself. I thought Mother Earth was a good place to do it. I saw a chance to inflict some bad publicity on that fucking place that as you rightly say, Carly loved so much.' He spoke precisely, a little robotically, almost. 'Only you two stopped me, didn't you? I hated you for stopping me. Couldn't you tell how much I hated you? A couple of do-gooders.' He spat at Artie but missed him, the gob landing at his feet.

'I wish we had let you die,' said Artie. 'So the bomb was just more revenge? Revenge for us saving you and for Carly liking the store?'

'Indeed. So you see, it's really all *your* fault.'

'How the hell did you know when we were going to return there?'

'I paid the manager to call you.'

'Yeah, I know that. But you didn't know when we'd return after that.'

'The plan was to explode the bombs when you first went back, when she'd called you, but the device in the doorway didn't go off. I got the wiring wrong. So I had to get it back and make another. But I knew you'd go back there soon enough. So Mikey here had you followed for a couple of days. You were too dumb to spot the fact. All I had to do was plant the first bomb again - it was in a paper bag in a recycling bin - then wait until you returned. Mikey gave me the call and I came a few minutes after you. This time it worked perfectly. The first one drove all the fucking vegans to the back. Mikey shot out the camera, I walked in and put the bomb down at the back. Someone saw me do it and shouted something. But it was too late. That evil fucking store goes boom and kills you two in the process. Perfect.'

'Yeah, not quite perfect. We're from Yorkshire, so we're pretty indestructible,' said Artie. 'How did you get out? It could have killed you.'

'That's what he wanted,' said Mikey. 'But somehow the muthafucker just walked out of the place as it fell around him. He's living a charmed life. He just got lucky.'

'I got clever, Mikey, not lucky. And he's right, I didn't care if it did kill me. Though I'm glad I got to see the utter fucking destruction of all those holier-than-though pricks.' He spat the words out.

Kaz dialled 911 and demanded an ambulance for Mustang, and the cops. 'There are two headless people here,' she said, adding '...of course they're dead. They're headless!' Doing such a thing whilst they stood around the decapitated corpses wasn't just very surreal, it was almost unbearable. Artie jammed his gun into Goldman's temple. 'Why did you kill Carly?'

'What?'

'You heard me. You poisoned Carly. Why? Just because she didn't want to go out with you? She was a lovely girl.'

Goldman laughed and just stared back at him. 'I did *not* kill her. She was ill. That damn store made her sick. And I withdraw my comment about you being clever.' He looked down at the cleaver.

'Drop that or I'll blow your hand off,' said Kaz pointing her gun at him, as she rang off the phone. 'Do it. Or I'll kill you, if that's what you want. I don't fucking care. I'll fucking kill you. Yeah? Make a choice, son, and do it quick.' She commanded more authority than Artie. It was her flat, aggressive and unwavering Yorkshire accent that did it. Artie's wasn't quite so blunt after being softened by over 25 years of transatlantic exposure, but Kaz, when in extremis, sounded like everyone's hard-faced

Yorkshire matriarch scolding their kids for misbehaving. When you wanted to boss someone around, a Leeds accent is a great weapon to have in your armory. 'Bloody do it. I'll not tell you again.'

Goldman weighed up whether to obey her or not. And, like many a man when faced with an angry Yorkshire woman, he did what she wanted, tossing the cleaver aside.

'The cops will be here soon enough, so you might as well tell us why you sent someone to shoot me in the hospital...' said Artie, but Goldman interrupted him.

'What? Nope, I didn't do that, and I didn't kill Carly.' He was dismissive and curt.

'But you paid this bloke to follow us out of San Francisco.' He pointed at Mustang, who was lying on the floor with his arm up in the air; despite his olive skin, he looked ashen.

'He paid me to kill you,' said Mustang, almost quietly. 'I'm sorry. I'm in a bad way financially. I said I'd do it but I couldn't face it, so I paid another guy to do it, but he missed you, obviously. Then you fucked over another two I paid off at the motel. You're a regular Bonnie and fuckin' Clyde, you two.'

'Butch and Sundance, I think you'll find,' said Artie.

'Thelma and Louise, actually,' said Kaz.

'I tried to follow you, but you were too fast. I can't believe you came here.'

'Why do you want to kill us so badly, Ben? We didn't see you plant the bomb at the store, you know. We had nothing on you.'

Goldman stared at the floor and began speaking calmly. 'Oh, I don't care who or what you saw. I just hate you. I hate people like you. You think you're so damn cool in your rock music business and with your glamorous wife and sexy girlfriend. The sort of people my parents spent all their time around and I fucking hated them for what they did to me. So I hate you, too. Perfectly reasonable.' He gestured at Kaz then at the bodies of his parents.

'I'm not his sexy girlfriend, you prick. And you must be proper sodding crazy if you think I am.'

Goldman sneered at her and spat in her direction. He'd lost his mind. There was no getting reason or logic out of him.

'Why have you done this to your parents?' said Artie, still not able to rest his eyes on their corpses for anything more than a few seconds.

'They were evil. They abused me my whole life. And you know what their reputation was. I told you, didn't I? I'm not like them. I have principles.'

'You're fucked up, man,' spat out Kaz. 'You're batshit mental.'

Goldman looked at Artie. 'Are you going to shoot me?'

'Not unless you do something stupid.'

'You wouldn't shoot me. She would. But you won't.'

'Don't be so sure.'

'Nah. You won't. I can tell.' And with that he turned to Kaz, who was retying the now blood-soaked towel on Mustang Mikey's arm. She had tucked the gun under her right armpit to free her hands.

That was a mistake.

Goldman lashed out at her with his foot, kicking the gun loose, sending it skidding across the tiled floor and into the now-congealing puddle of blood.

He stepped across the room and fished it out. As he picked it up, it dripped with blood. Artie should have shot him in the head, but instead he paused, then aimed for Goldman's leg instead, letting off two shots.

Somehow he missed. His hands were shaking so badly, he couldn't aim. Goldman moved quickly to Kaz, grabbing her around the neck with bloody hands and dragging her backwards, holding the gun to her head.

'Fuck off!' yelled Kaz, as he wrestled her to a standing position.

'Stop fighting or I'll blow your head off,' said Goldman, pointing the gun at the crown of her head.

'He'll do it,' said Mustang. 'Look at what he's already done.'

'You think I don't already fucking know that?' said Kaz, scared and furious in equal measure.

'Ben, the cops will be here soon,' said Artie, pointing the gun at him. 'Let her go.'

Goldman shouted. 'Give me the Mustang keys, Mikey.'

'I can't. You fucking cut my fucking arm! They're in my right pocket.'

Keeping the gun aimed at Kaz, Goldman kneeled down and took them from the still-prone man.

'Right Kaz, you're coming with me.' He pulled at her arm, gun to the back of her head, and dragged her out towards the poolside door. The Mustang must have been parked up at the back of the property. Artie followed him, gun at the ready. There had to be a chance to shoot him when he got into the car. He'd have to push Kaz into the car and then walk around to the driver's side. Hopefully Kaz would realise that, too, and get down as far as possible so she wouldn't get hit by a stray bullet. Artie wasn't going to miss this time. He was cursing his shaking hands and his reluctance to murder Goldman. Next time, he'd keep shooting until he took him out. No second chances.

The bright sun cast sharp shadows as he took her around the pool and towards a wrought-iron gate at the back of the property, the red Mustang visible beyond it.

'Come on, Ben. You can't get away in that car, it's too distinctive,' said Artie, as Goldman pulled open the gate and walked backwards through it, staring at him, gun still to Kaz's head.

The moment was coming. How was he going to play this? Outside the property was shrubbery and tall palm trees. A narrow dirt track ran in a long curve and headed out towards Sunset, but avoiding the street. A rat run, a shortcut, in effect. Coll had mentioned that when she'd been to parties here, they'd used it to avoid the paparazzi.

A cloud of dust rolled down the track on the back of a gust of sea breeze. Goldman turned to look. A black Ford pickup was approaching and effectively blocking his escape route.

It was slung around by 45 degrees, on a hand-brake turn, blocking the track with its width. There was no way past. Colleen jumped out and looked around. 'You guys alright?' she said.

'I've been better, Coll, to be honest,' said Kaz, sarcastically.

'Move the car,' said Goldman, 'Or Kaz loses her brains.'

'I don't think so, honey.' She reached into her back pocket and took out a pistol, the same sort as she'd given Artie and Kaz. 'And I'm a crack shot. So I think this is over. Two guns beats one. Huh, you used to be such a polite young boy, Ben Goldman. What went wrong with you?'

'What went wrong with me? My parents whored me out to paedophiles, that's what went wrong with me. Now, shut up.' He pushed Kaz in front of him towards the passenger side of the car, pulled open the door, wound down the window, pushed her inside and slammed it shut, still holding the gun to her head, now through the open window. 'I'm going to walk around the car and drive it away. If you don't move the Ford, I'll kill her. Now move it.'

'You kill her and you're dead,' said Artie.

'Twice,' added Colleen.

It was a Mexican standoff.

You'd be crazy to make the first move in a situation like this. They all knew that.

But Ben Goldman was crazy, 100 per cent, certifiably insane and he probably had been for some time. Certainly ever since he'd decided to commit suicide in Mother Earth.

So that's why he did what he did, in the full knowledge of what would happen when he did it.

In that moment he decided to give up on life. He knew he was a dead man and that's what he wanted more than anything else. But even so, his ego was still intact and that drove him to want to go out in as dramatic a fashion as possible.

So he relaxed his arm a little, raising the gun away from Kaz's head, as though he was giving in.

But he wasn't.

He just shifted its aim and fired. Three shots. Two of them buried themselves into Colleen's body, the third went skyward as he fell to the ground, dead from Artie's retaliatory bullet to his brain. It ripped a hole in his head. Colleen had fired once too, hitting Goldman in the neck.

Artie stood fixed to the spot in horror. His body had locked up with shock. Kaz got out of the car and ran over to Colleen. She was lying on her back, eyes closed, dark hair spilled out across the dirt track.

'Coll! Coll! Come on, lady.' She tapped her lightly on her face, holding her pulse. Then she straddled her and began pumping on her chest with the palms of her hand. 'Come on, come back to me, Coll! Come back! Come back!' She pumped more and more desperately. But there was no indication it was having any effect.

Artie had known as soon as the bullets had struck her. The dead fall through the air in a different, more still way than an alive person, and more than that, you can feel a life cease to be. Something just goes. Death alters the molecules, somehow.

He walked to Kaz, leaned over and put his hand on her back, glancing at Coll's expressionless face.

'It's no use, Kaz. She's gone.'

'No, she hasn't. I won't let her!' She pumped on Coll's chest again. Blood had soaked through the black t-shirt she was wearing and now stained Kaz's hands. She had taken both bullets around her heart. It was an instant kill. No time to even feel any pain. Artie put his arm around Kaz.

'Come on. Those sirens in the distance will be the paramedics and the police. We need to keep our shit together, here. And we'll need Mo Casson.' He took out his phone, wrote a quick text; '*Coll has been shot dead,*

I've shot three men dead in self-defence. Need your help.' He entered the address and sent it.

Kaz gave up pumping on Coll's chest and slumped forward and hugged her. 'I'm sorry Coll. I'm so sorry for all of this. Bless you. You were so good to me.' She kissed her on the cheek. 'Thank you, lady. Thank you for everything.' Her tears dripped onto the dead woman's face.

Artie couldn't let himself feel it, couldn't give room to his emotions. He knew there'd be a time when he'd have to, but not now. She'd gone. Nothing could change it. Now he had to be calm and functional. He lifted Kaz up and hugged her to him and kissed her on the head, as she kept crying. 'Come on. We've got a lot of questions to answer. I've killed three men, even the LAPD won't let that slide.'

'I want her to be alive. I want her to sit up and smile at me. I can't believe she's gone. I *can't* believe it. How can that happen, just like that? This fucking murderous country. And think of Fay, the poor lass. She's lost her mother. She's only young.'

'Fay will deal with it. She's very independent.'

'And you've lost your wife, Artie. You loved her. She loved you.'

'I know. But I can't think about it now. I can't let my brain touch it. We've got to be practical. There'll be time to grieve. But not now.' She put her hand to her face and wiped tears from her pink cheeks as cop cars and paramedics screeched down Arlo Way. 'Come on, let's do this. Right? You OK?'

She sighed and nodded.

'Good lass. I'll tell you something, this is going to need some serious Leeds-ing.'

CHAPTER 23

The week that followed was, to say the least, intense. Most of it was spent in interviews with police and with Mo Casson and her team. Colleen's death became a fact that was discussed, the way you might discuss a car or the weather.

Fay, being Fay, took the news of her mother's death in her stride. Her lack of empathy for her mother was real. She was sad about her death, but it didn't affect her profoundly, or not obviously, anyway. Whether it would have a wash out in the future was hard to say.

A week after the shooting, Artie and Kaz drove down to Laguna Beach in the Ford pickup, for a meeting at Mo Casson's offices. It was a beautiful blue Southern California day, with intense summer white light turning the ocean into a hypnotic sea of diamonds.

Things had been difficult.

The one thing neither of them could acknowledge or voice was that Colleen's death had released Artie to be with Kaz and for Kaz to be with Artie, exactly as they had planned and wanted. It seemed vulgar to even say it. But all the same, they'd stayed all week in a motel in Venice Beach, unable to face going to the Malibu house, which was so quintessentially Colleen Holmes. Artie had spent so long talking to the police about what had happened that it all felt, not like reality, but like a story, the plot of which only he knew.

They parked outside the three-storey glass and concrete building that was the hub of Mo Casson's empire. It was right on the beach with almost every room having panoramic views of Laguna Beach sand and ocean. It couldn't have been more quintessentialy Southern California millionaire hipster if it had been a backstage pass for Fleetwood Mac's Rumours tour in 1977.

'I love Laguna Beach,' said Kaz, as they got out. 'I could live here, you know.'

'Yeah, me too. Rents are expensive for us, though.'

'Aye, well, it's very gay and very gay places are always expensive.'

He leaned into her and put his arm around her shoulder and she her arm around his waist.

'I'm really not looking forward to this,' said Kaz, in a quiet voice.

'No. Me neither.'

Mo was sitting in her air-conditioned office, wearing silver-rimmed glasses, an ecru linen suit and a silk collarless white shirt, her left wrist covered in silver and turquoise jewellery. She looked up from her computer as they walked in, got to her feet and embraced each of them in turn, a grim look of sorrow on her face.

A woman dressed in a loose white shirt, loose white trousers and white trainers came in and poured them all sparkling water, then bowed and gave them the Buddhist namasté sign.

'Thanks for coming down. As I said on the phone, there are some very interesting developments that I need to make you aware of.'

Although Mo had been a long-time friend of Colleen's - friends in the LA way, anyway - she had huge emotional detachment and dealt with it all as though it was someone she'd never known. That was her intense professionalism, of course. But sometimes, it was disconcerting.

She let out a small sigh. 'Firstly, the funeral has been scheduled for next Saturday. The police have confirmed they don't...err...need her any longer. I shall make all the arrangements.'

'Thanks,' said Artie, holding Kaz's hand.

'Next thing to tell you is that, as you know, Colleen had restructured her financial affairs.' Her fine light brown eyebrows were knitted together in a frown. 'But we hadn't completed things. Did she talk to you about this?'

Artie shook his head. 'No, except to say it was happening. We were...busy.'

'Uh huh. Well, I won't bore you with the details and I'll cut to the chase, instead. The Holmes empire, by which I mean the income from books, TV syndications and the like, has been, or will be, funneled into an investment trust fund and a number of charitable causes earmarked to benefit from what looks likely to be $20-35 million a year for at least the next five years, declining thereafter at maybe 15 per cent per year. Then again, it'd only take one Hollywood movie of one of her mother's books to kick the whole thing up a gear. She selected these organisations to be the beneficiaries and signed off on the deal.'

She passed Artie a sheet of paper with a list of 15 organisations on it. Kaz leaned in and took a look. They covered everything from environmental causes to women's charities, providing musical instruments to poor kids and animal care organisations. A lot of people were set to benefit from Colleen Holmes's death.

Artie sighed. Bless her. His eyes washed with tears, he tilted his head to the heavens and sent his love to her, wherever she now was. Kaz squeezed his hand.

'I do realise this is tough stuff for you to deal with,' said Mo Casson. 'But I need to tell you something. Coll had intended to rewrite her will to divide all her material possessions and investments between you both and Fay, with some other beneficiaries specified for specific items.'

'Hold on, you said me,' said Kaz. 'Are you sure that's right? She had no reason to leave me anything.'

Mo pushed a sheet of paper to her with handwriting on. Colleen's handwriting. It said, simply. "All money in banks and possessions on my death to be split equally between Artie, Kaz and Fay. Fay gets the Malibu house. Kaz gets the New York apartment, Artie the London flat." It was dated just two weeks previously.

Kaz looked at Artie, astonished. 'Where...where is this New York apartment, Mo?' she said, taking a sip of water.

'It's on the Upper West Side, overlooking Central Park. Nice three-bedroom place. Worth about three million, I reckon.'

'Fucking hell. Why had she left me that? I'm nobody to her...'

Mo Casson held up her hand to halt Kaz's words. 'Not true, but let me finish. We have a big problem.'

'Not as big a problem as Coll,' said Artie.

Mo grimaced at him. 'True. But the thing is, these notes were her intention. But she died before they'd been drawn up and signed off. So, you know, they're not law and her previous will, which in essence gave everything to Fay, still stands.' She took a sip of green tea. 'How do you guys feel about that?'

'Speaking for myself, I'm cool with it. I don't want anything. I don't deserve it. I only knew Coll for little more than a year of her life. For me, Fay should have everything.'

Kaz nodded. 'Me, too. She was a generous person, but the idea I'd own her posh flat in New York is daft. It's not me. I'd not know what to do with it. And I don't deserve it, either. I'd see her ghost everywhere, too.'

Mo looked at them in turn. 'My my, you two...' She turned away and bit her bottom lip, tears obviously in her eyes. 'She chose her friends well, is all I can say.'

'Look, Mo, Fay should inherit. We'll go our own way. We'd been sort of planning this anyway,' said Artie.

'Planning? Planning what?'

He looked at Kaz and then back to Mo. 'The fact is, we were going to...I was going to tell her that I want to be with Kaz. Get a divorce, I

mean. Me and Kaz...well...it's complicated but...relationships are, sometimes. Now, it feels just vulgar to even say this but it was our intention to
tell her right away. Fay agrees with this; I think she sort of knew me and
Kaz loved each other. It wouldn't have been a shock.'

Kaz interrupted him. 'Mo. This sounds stupid, I know, but until Artie
got involved with Colleen, we didn't know we were in love with each
other - not like that, anyway. It's...it's complicated. We're only just trying
to understand our own feelings.'

'Yeah, so the long and short of it is, it wouldn't be right for me to take
anything at all of Colleen's, for that reason alone.'

'Not me, either. I couldn't.'

For all the floaty, hippyness Mo Casson was a very worldly wise
woman who had pretty much seen it all over her long career. Her expression didn't change much, she just nodded slowly. 'I see. That's all understandable and actually makes our lives a little more simple. We can go
with the existing will. I'll inform Fay. Should I mention your new relationship to her?'

'She already knows, Mo,' said Artie. 'In some ways, she's wise beyond
her years, that girl.'

Mo nodded again, and took another sip of tea. 'OK, leave it with me.
Now, onto other matters. Something quite shocking has become appar-
ent.' She took out a sheet of paper from a folder. 'Forensic investigators
at the Saunders house found syringes of mercury in what had been a
locked room, to which only Robbie had the key, a key which was among
the possessions recovered from his body. Mercury was also in the soy
jerky strips in the guitar store. A box of them was analysed and all had
mercury in them.'

'What? I don't understand. Was Carly doing it to herself?' said Kaz.

'No. I'm afraid not. The tragic and inescapable conclusion we have to
draw is that Robbie was responsible for slowly poisoning his own daughter.'

'Oh, come on, that can't be right. He loved Carly. After his wife died,
she was all he had. Well, that and the store,' said Artie.

'There are other documents in the house which itemize purchases of
mercury that he paid for online. I've just this morning received medical
records which suggest he had been treated for depression and anxiety
since his wife died, the last of which flagged him up as a suicide risk.'
She shook her head in sadness. 'My speculation is that he hated Carly's

lifestyle choice, and, as his mind got more disturbed, his aim was to make her sick, so that she'd quit being vegan.'

'That's horrible. I can't believe that of him,' said Artie. 'I don't want to believe that.'

'You said he was very uptight that day,' sad Kaz.

'Yeah, he had these bursts of anger. But I thought it was just stress.'

'I'm afraid a disturbed person often looks very like a stressed person,' said Mo. 'It's an inescapable conclusion, I'm afraid. He tried to make her ill to change her lifestyle choices. For what it's worth, I'm sure he didn't mean to kill her. He wanted to scare her and maybe it would've worked if Carly had lived long enough to see Coll's diet doctor friend.' She took off her glasses and rubbed her eyes with thumb and forefinger. 'We'll get this wrapped up in the coming weeks, it needn't trouble you.' She sipped tea again and composed herself. 'So what will you guys do now?'

'We're moving into a one-bedroom apartment on Arizona, we pick up the keys later today,' said Kaz. 'Looking forward to living somewhere of our own again. Neither of us felt at home in Malibu. The lifestyles of the rich and famous are something we like to photograph, rather than live.'

'Well, I hope you'll be very happy together. Love is a beautiful thing in a painful world.'

'To be honest, we've been together for 15 years already. So it won't be much of a change for us.'

'Are you sure you don't want anything from Coll's estate? I'm sure it could be arranged.'

'No. Well, we'd like the car, but we couldn't afford to even insure it, let alone run it. Also, having a 250,000 dollar car seems a bit obscene,' said Artie,

'But it is a brilliant car, all the same,' added Kaz, sighing. 'But Artie's right, there's no way we could even afford to put gas in it. It only does about 12 miles to the gallon.'

Mo nodded. 'Well, that's everything I needed to tell you; oh, except for the fact that Danny Blind has led the police to a member of the Paleo Patriots, who has subsequently been arrested for murder. Security cameras got a good shot of him. Blind knew who it was right away. That was a terrible, terrible business. What he was thinking of, I just can't imagine. Playing at being a undercover spy or something. Pathetic. Treating life as if it's all a TV show.' Her bitterness was undisguised.

Artie curled a lip. 'That was just disgusting. He murdered a lovely woman.'

'I imagine defence will go for manslaughter. I'm sure his intention was to try and stir things up against the vegan and soy business and thought he'd exploit your situation to do that. It was naïve and ridiculous and evil. This whole thing has been evil.' Her voice tailed off and she ran her hand through her hair. 'It's going to take us all some time to get over it.'

Artie stood up and went to the floor-to-ceiling window and stared out at the relentless ocean.

'I'm not sure we ever will,' he said.

* * *

A month later, Artie was pulling clean t-shirts out of the dryer in their small utility room.

'Have you got enough clean knickers for this trip or do you want me to wash some?' he said.

Kaz yawned, leaning on their small kitchen table, and sipped at a mug of tea. 'Yes, mother. Well, I've got my usual baggy-arsed seven pairs.'

'Yeah, you do have very ragged underwear, it's true, that. The elastic is going on half of them.'

'You can talk. You don't want me to wear sexy underwear, do you? I'd look bloody ridiculous.'

He laughed and kissed her on the top of the head. 'Nah, you're alright. I can't see you in a thong, somehow.'

'I don't think they come in my size. It'd be like a cheese wire on a massive truckle of cheddar.'

Artie howled in laughter. 'That's a striking image.'

She looked at her laptop. 'I'm looking forward to working on a tour with Tom Petty again. Nice fella. And after all that's happened in the last month, I'm also looking forward to getting out of town for a while and just grafting. We've really been through the wringer, with the funeral, the lawyers and the cops. Moving in here and...you know...me and you and everything.'

'Yeah. It's been emotional, to say the least,' he said, folding up the t-shirts into rough squares, then reaching into the fridge and taking out two bottles of Miller, handing one to her.

She took the bottle and then held his hand. 'Are you feeling OK now?'

With a watery smile, he squeezed it, then twisted the cap off the bottle. 'Yeah, when it hit me, it was a tsunami of feelings.'

A couple of days previously, the dam of emotion that he'd swallowed down for weeks, finally broke.

'Crying for a whole day isn't something I plan on doing again. I think it got a lot of...I don't know...a lot of the poison out of me. I feel better for it, though I feel guilty for feeling better, when Coll's in her grave.'

'It had to happen sometime. You'd been bottling it up for weeks.'

'Well, before all of this, I'd hardly ever seen you cry.'

'I don't mind saying it's deeply affected me. Not just Coll dying, but everything else we went through. The bomb, the shooting, having to fight for our lives, the beheaded bodies, the blood. It was all so weird and not normal. We were lucky to survive at all, Artie. I'm not sure we'll ever really get over it.'

'No. I don't think we will. We got lucky, but we were also very tough. We fought for our bloody lives in that motel. Seeing you blasting the shit out of that ice machine is a sight I won't easily forget. Jesus, it feels like nightmare I had, now. I keep wishing that I'd shot Goldman in the head when I had the chance and not aimed at his leg and missed. I don't know why I did that. I was shaking so much and I was worried about being prosecuted for being a murderer. It was all over so quickly.'

'Don't blame yourself, lad. I was papping my pants, as well. I mean, being in a room with two severed heads and decapitated bodies is just...mind blowing. How can you ever deal with that?'

'At least we both went through it, so we both understand it. But I'm not sure we'll ever get a grip on it. It's too...out there.'

'Fay has been brilliant, though.' She sat back and swigged from the bottle. 'She's a real star.'

'Aye, she's got balls of steel, if you ask me. She seems to have matured and become a grown woman in the last few weeks. The way she's risen to dealing with the legal stuff has been amazing. To see her at Mo's in a suit, hair tied up, was as shocking as anything. Well...almost.'

'And she's a multi-millionaire now,' said Kaz.

'Yeah, not sure she's especially impressed by that fact. I don't see her living in Malibu, do you?'

'God, no. That'd be, what she'd once have called, "severely barfo". Ha ha. I hope she doesn't lose all that attitude and become too vanilla.'

'No way. She's got all of mother's attitude, but none of her flakiness. She'll be alright. If she doesn't end up being important, in one way or another, I'll be amazed. The kid has got star quality. We both see that. She's just finding herself.' A surge of tears welled up in his eyes, again. Kaz patted him on the arm. This shit was so hard to deal with.

The door buzzer went.

'That'll be the mail guy,' said Kaz.

'I'll go,' said Artie, walking to the intercom and hitting the buzzer to let him in, then taking the door off the latch and leaving it ajar, returning to the kitchen and picking up his beer, sucking it down. Kaz patted him on his belly.

'This is a cool place to live, though, isn't it?' she said. 'I love living in Santa Monica. Feels...' it was her turn to suffer a swell of emotion, suddenly. It kept happening to both of them. 'Feels like our sort of place.'

He hugged her into him. 'I know, luv. It is.'

There was a tap at the door. Artie walked back to open it fully. A long-haired 30-something dude was standing there. He looked like Kid Rock, only cool.

'Hey, man. Are you Artie Taylor?' he said.

'Yeah, you got him.'

'Cool. Miss Fay Holmes has sent you a gift.'

'Fay? Really?'

'Yeah, man.'

He held up a familiar set of keys and handed them to him along with a card. 'You're a lucky man.' The delivery guy turned and walked out of the building and down the street.

Artie opened up the card. A plastic Shell fuel card was inside, with a note. He read Fay's neat handwriting.

Mom would have wanted you to have this. I love you both, so please enjoy it. And as you sad old dudes would inevitably say, "rock on." Oh, and there's 50 grand on the fuel card, so you can actually afford to drive it. And it's insured for as long as you want it. Think of it as one last gift from our Sugar Mama.

Artie looked at the Porsche parked up outside the apartment block and turned his eyes up to the sky.

Yeah. Rock on, Coll. Rock on.

THE END

Books in the Archie Taylor Series
Published by HEAD PUBLISHING

1. The Girl Can't Help It (2014)
2. Sugar Mama (2016)

Kindle/Paperback

http://www.johnnicholsonwriter.co.uk

Books in the Nick Guymer Series
Published by HEAD PUBLISHING

Kindle/Paperback

http://www.johnnicholsonwriter.co.uk

About John Nicholson

John is a well-known football writer whose work is read by tens of thousands of people every week. He's a columnist for Football365.com and has worked for the Daily Record, The Mirror, Sky and many other publications over the last 14 years.

Other John Nicholson Books
published by Biteback Publishing

We Ate All The Pies -
How Football Swallowed Britain Whole (2010)

The Meat Fix -
How 26 Years of Healthy Eating Nearly Killed Me (2012)